Jeff Noon & Steve Beard

GOGMAGOG

A FIRST CHRONICLE OF LUDWICH

ANGRY ROBOT
An imprint of Watkins Media Ltd

Unit 11, Shepperton House
89-93 Shepperton Road
London N1 3DF
UK

angryrobotbooks.com
twitter.com/angryrobotbooks
A bit of rot makes things more beautiful

An Angry Robot paperback original, 2024

ISBN 978 1 91520 282 6
Ebook ISBN 978 1 91520 283 3

Printed and bound in the United Kingdom by TJ Books Limited

9 8 7 6 5 4 3 2 1

In memory of
Jack Baker

1982–2022

PART ONE

The Winding Way

I speak of the city of Ludwyche, and of the river Nysis which flows through it down to the sea, and of the ghostly Faynr who haunts the river a full sixty miles from head to tail. I speak also of the dragon Haakenur, who died that Ludwyche might be born, and from whose body the ghost Faynr did arise. I speak of these things and of subsequent happenings by which Kethra ebbed and flowed in fortune, from the Year of First Arrival onwards.

Mistress Pynne – A Chronicle of the Kethran Isles, Their Varied Peoples, and Their Rulers.

The Never-Nevers

Cady woke up at six o'clock, from old habit, groaned and sat up in bed. Her eyes were glued shut and her throat coated in sand. But all she had to do was grope out a hand to find her breakfast, set on the bedside table: a glass of malt vinegar in which a raw egg had been cracked. She drank it down with glee. Then she got up, belched, and managed to get to the toilet just in time to have a piss and a shit. The day was set fair: distant shores beckoned.

She wasn't going anywhere.

Cady was seventy-eight years old. She lived in a home for dried-up sailors not far from the waterfront in Anglestume. She needed to smell the salt air and hear the drumming of the wind in the masts and wires of the boats at their moorings. Without such, she would have likely stayed in bed until noon, drinking rum and singing the old songs. But sunlight called her out, and this day was no different. She washed her face and armpits and drew on her tattered smock and bell-bottoms and punched out the dents in her bowler hat. Her hair was short on top, long in the back, braided in a complex knot that only needed to be unwrapped once a month to be washed.

She was puffing on her third roll-up of the day by the time she reached the harbour. People laughed at her, or nodded, or made some snide comment. One or two had a smile for her, but she scowled at them all the same. She drew in clean air, mixed it with the smoke in her lungs, and coughed and brought up a great glob of phlegm. It hit the water with a splash: something nice for the fish to nibble on. Then she made her way to a building in a side street. The offices of the Amalgamated Union of Bargemen, Waterwomen, River Pilots and Apprentices was a crumbling edifice, eaten by salt. The door was locked. She banged on it and started to shout and swear. A panel slid open and a man's face peeped out. At first all she could see was the dark grey triangle on his brow, but then his eyes came into view, and then his mouth.

"It's pension day," she told him.

"No, it isn't."

"I believe it is. Every Wednesday…"

"It's not Wednesday."

"Are you sure? You little pizzlecrack. You're pulling one over on me."

"Cady?"

"Yes?"

"It's Tuesday."

"Is it? Right. I see. But the thing is, I'm a bit bloody skint, Meesha, truth be known."

"You always are."

"In which case, how about a handout, a little payment on account."

"On account of what?"

Cady's anger spilled over. "On account of all my years of service on the goddamn stinking river, that's what!" She could have added: on account of the mottled skin and the scarred hands, and the frostbitten fingers, the deep lines on her brow, the salt spray in her eyes, and the black mist in her lungs, her pockmarked tongue, the stench on her breath, and never mind the dawn-lit departures, and the all-night journeys. And the untold people she'd delivered safely to their ports of call, and most of all those lost on the way, the drowned, the damaged ones, the dying…

The emotions took hold of her, and her body shook head to toe, and she wiped back the tears.

But she kept her silence.

Meesha, the clerk on duty that morning, looked at her with no little sympathy. But rules were rules, as he now pointed out to her: page nineteen, paragraph two of the union handbook.

"I'm sorry, Cady. You know how it is."

"Do I?"

"Come back tomorrow, and we'll have a nice little chat."

The panel slid shut.

Harrumphing like an old tugboat pulling a liner, Cady trudged off back along the waterfront. Her friend Yanish had set up his rod and line with the other fishermen on the south quay. The light glinted on his binoculars as he looked out to sea. She made a careful search of her purse and found a few bits of brass and silver, and a couple more in the lining. And a fur-covered cough drop. She licked at this. Hmm, tasty. A bit of rot made things more beautiful. There were many secrets to a good life, and this was one of them.

The tin bell over the door rang as she entered Fable's Corner Shop on Pebble Street.

"An ounce of Bosun's, please."

"And how are you, this morning, Cady dear?"

"As to be expected."

Fable poured the rolling tobacco into the basin of a weighing scale. Cady watched the needle carefully. "A little more, I think. And a little more… That's it, spot on!"

"It's over the mark, actually."

"Only by a few flakes."

Fable tutted. She tilted the tobacco directly into Cady's pouch, and then started to count the pile of coins given in exchange, saying, "Some of these aren't legal tender."

"Are they not?"

"Blimey. This one's got Queen Hilda's face on it. That's centuries old."

"Let me see that." Cady took the coin back. "Coo, yes. I might get it valued. It must be worth a fortune!"

The shopkeeper laughed gleefully. "Even if you had a fortune, would anyone ever see it? No, they would not!"

Fable Duncliffe was one of the few who gave Cady as good as they got. They were both old Wodwo stock, going way back, although Cady had more or less given up on her tribe. But Fable was proud, upstanding, well-rooted, and a bit witchlike, even if she did overdo it with the cackle. Her skin had that greenish undertone the older members of the tribe developed. She wore a floral apron and a hairnet. Her blue-tinted locks poked out through the mesh. Her eyes were red where they used to be white, and grey where they used to be brown. It might have been the aftermath of disease, or evidence of having seen too much, but Fable never said which, not to anyone.

Cady nodded at the bottles of boiled sweets on the shelf. "I've got a taste for those cough drops. How about a tuppeny bag? I can pay you tomorrow."

"I can let you have half a dozen, on account."

There was that blasted word again! Sometimes, Cady had to admit, these days her whole life was on account, always waiting for something that never quite arrived.

"Aye, that will do me."

The shopkeeper counted the lozenges from the bottle. "One, two, three… Oh and by the way, some people were asking about you. Four, five…"

"About me?"

"And six. That's right. Wanted to know where you lived. Strange looking, they were, the both of them."

"I don't like the sound of that."

"No, I was the same. I never told them anything. Because why, one of them being a creature of unusual nature."

"How's that?"

"You know, one of those artificial men."

"A Thrawl?"

"The same, the very same. A terrible sight to look upon." Cady was lost in thought, mumbling to herself as she rolled a cigarette. "A Thrawl…"

"That's right."

"You don't see many of those, these days."

"No you do not, thank the Lord of all Flowers in his glory."

"They were banned, weren't they?" Cady dug in her pockets and brought up some specks of grass and seeds, which she sprinkled on the baccy.

"That they were. From all corners of Great Kethra, north, south, east and west. Banned, and then dismantled."

"Not dismantled, put into storage, I think."

The shopkeeper grimaced at this. She stretched her back, groaning, and then said, "Anyway, so the other one…"

"The other what?"

"The other person, looking for you. There were two of them, I said that."

"Did you?" Cady lit the roll-up and drew on it. "Ah, that's nice! Go on, go on."

"The other one was a lass, a youngster, like. An Alkhym girl."

"An Alkhym? In Anglestume?"

"My thoughts exactly. It can't be right."

Cady frowned. "How young was she, did you say?"

"I didn't. But under ten years, most definitely. Because why, she didn't have the whatsits, you know, at the temples, like. The antennae. The *hesti*, that's the word."

"I see." Cady pondered for a moment. "And what did they want, these two?"

"I couldn't say, we never got that far."

"But they were looking for me?"

"Oh yes. Asked by name." Fable ran a yellow duster over the counter. "Your full-spoken name, mind. Arcadia Meade, like they knew you, good and proper."

Cady was exasperated. "Luddin' heck. Fable! You didn't tell them where to find me, I hope?"

"I did not. Because why, I'm thinking you might not want to be found. Not by a Thrawl, at the least. Gives me the shivers, just thinking about it."

Cady left the shop. Her knees were playing up something rotten as she walked back to the promenade. There was a little more activity now, as people went about their morning business. There were even a few holidaymakers, something the town hadn't seen since before the war. One lad was running up and down the prom, screaming at the skirls, making them take off in a flurry of wings. He was going to get his eyes pecked out if he wasn't careful. Bloody jumped-up little shit! Kids. More trouble than they're worth, and they ain't worth a freckle on a loblolly's arse.

She cadged a lift on the back of the rag-and-bone man's cart, taking the road that edged the salt flats, along the south coast of the island. She jumped off at Omega Point. It was here that the sea turned into the river, or the river turned into the sea, depending on your direction of travel. Cady had sailed up and down the River Nysis, from Anglestume to the city of Ludwich and back again, for many years, too many years, and knew all the calling points along the way. She watched the marker buoys turn restlessly on the tide, letting her mind drift over the steely grey expanse of the waters. The air stank: rotten seaweed, fish, the tang of salt. It got on the tongue, in her hair, her clothes, and she loved it to glory and back.

It was good to get away from the village. She usually came out this way, every two days or so, stopping here next to the jetty. The remains of a concrete gun casement had been invaded by lichen and bird shit. Behind her, the flats stretched away into the distance until they reached the wired enclosures of the prisoner of war camp, now empty.

The river was six miles wide here, the opposite bank a dark smudge of mist. Cady could just about make out the steeple of St Aethel the Martyr. Yet the estuary was quiet. Only a few boats passed by, one of them a cargo steamer, no doubt heading for the trading post at Maddenholt, the furthest people travelled upriver these days. It got her thinking of the years gone by, when the Nysis was filled with noise and life, with smoke from the funnels, the foghorns blaring, the waters jam-packed with barges, yachts, tugs, warships and dredgers, and her own river taxi chugging along, always with a full passenger load. The *Juniper* had been a small boat, a steam launch carrying a dozen passengers and a crew of two, herself and whatever young guttersnipe she could take on as deckhand. Aye, good days, bloody good days when they weren't bad.

Damn, she was getting sentimental!

She wetted a palm and held her hand up above her head to feel the wind. South by south-east, seventeen maybe eighteen knots, holding steady. The tide coming in, easy like. The mathematics of flow and contraflow, the secret channels and sudden depths, the rocks that lay hidden, a quickening current. Cady knew it all by heart; she had spent too many years on the water – it never left you. In the end, only one thing mattered: the course of the river in her veins.

They called it the Winding Way, and by Lud they were right to do so, with so many twists and turns along its length from source to sea, freshwater to salt. But you could never get lost; the Nysis always carried you onwards.

And then Cady frowned. And froze, stock-still.

For she had heard a sound, a single breath, in and out. Her optic gland tingled. *Well fuck me.* Someone had crept up on her.

Out here, in the flatlands.

She turned her head slightly and saw a flickering shape at the edge of her vision, the shape of a woman. But when Cady turned fully the land was empty all around, only the salt marshes and the dance of a skirl on the wing. A crab scuttled away from her step. Silence settled into every dip and rise; even the river flowed on without a sound. She was tempted to scarper back home and kip down with a bottle of rum for company, a nice tune on the crystal set, and a racy book.

But the sound came again, a sudden exhalation.

Pfft.

The air flickered darkly and folded upon itself, some few yards away, in a different position from the first apparition. It took on a fleeting form, this time of a man's shape, before it too drifted apart, and away, scattered on the wind.

Cady felt herself shudder, for she knew what this meant.

Pfft, pfft.

Her eyes darted this way and that as a third and fourth cloud of dust erupted from the ground, each forming themselves into the shape of a body. This time Cady went over to one spot, and caught sight of the seeds as they floated away. At her feet was the open funnel of a never-never, a flowering plant that usually dispersed its seeds in a random pattern – but every so often the seed clouds took on momentary human form. As now. *Pfft, pfft, pfft.* All across the salt flats the figures appeared, and disappeared. The skirls were going mad, scrawing loudly, swooping down to catch the seeds. It looked like the birds were attacking the figures. Cady looked on in both dread and excitement: it was that time again. And she sang out loud to a tune of her own invention, "Change is in the air, change is in the air!" She snatched a handful of the seeds from the nearest figure as it appeared, and held them in her palm, tiny blue ovoids – before popping them into a buttoned pocket in her purse. She would need them later, for the special pictures they could bring her.

The image of the seed people stayed with her as she tramped back into town.

She was knackered and her corns were throbbing by the time she reached the quay. Yanish was still there, fishing away, his keep net flapping with a couple of haddock. He speared a tagworm on a hook, working deftly.

"Very nice," she said, "that egg and vinegar you set out for me."

He shrugged.

"The egg had gone off, just how I like it."

Cady tutted to herself. How in Lud's name do I tell him? Where to begin? Matter-of-factly she said, "The never-nevers were clouding, just before."

"So?" He cast the line out over the waters with a nimble flick of the wrist.

"I mean really clouding."

And the life came into his eyes, hearing this. "In human shape?"

"Exactly so."

"Whereabouts?"

"Omega Point. But they only last a day or so."

Yanish placed his fishing rod in the rest, leaned on the seat of his propped-up motorcycle, and lit a cigarette. "I'll ride out there, this afternoon. I can get an hour off."

But Cady's voice lowered. "It's a sign, a definite sign."

"What are you babbling on about?"

Cady shook her head, clearing the thoughts away. "Yanish, some people might be asking after me."

"Oh yes?" His attention was back on his fishing float as it bobbed on the water.

"I'm going to be busy. So I don't need anyone bothering me, not just now."

"Too late, old chiv," he said.

Yanish Khalan was eighteen years old. He was born of the Azeel tribe and, like Meesha at the Union office, had a triangle of hard flesh at the centre of his brow – the *aphelon*, the sign of his faith. He had angular features, perfectly symmetrical, reaching a point at his chin. His hair was short at the back and sides, long on top and slicked back with oil, but teased into a long drooping curl at the front. He was always combing the style into place, trying to make himself look like one of those stars of stage and crystal. His work jeans and leather jacket were well-worn, but clean. Until last year, he'd always worn a tie, and Cady had bought him a pin for it on his birthday. She was pleased to see he had the pin clipped to his lapel, like a badge. They'd known each other since Yanish was thirteen, when she'd pulled him out of the river, a bedraggled wreck of a boy. Both his parents had died in the war. Like many such orphans, he'd run wild, wild and free and fast enough to not see the brick wall that waited for him. Crack! He'd toppled over into the dark clutches of the Nysis.

"What do you mean, too late?" she asked.

"I talked to them already."

"You did?"

He looked at her properly. "Sure, a girl, and a Thrawl."

"That's them."

"They nearly caused a riot."

"We don't have riots in Anglestume."

Yanish put on his "wireless news" voice. "Today in Sleepy Town, a commotion broke out on the waterfront, involving the townsfolk and walking talking machine man. Apparently, one old biddy threw a tray of cockles at him."

Cady couldn't help grinning. "Yes well... don't let them know where I live."

"I already told them."

"Why? Why, why?" She fumed and spat and gibbered. "Why would you do that? Why?!"

"They've got a job for you."

This gave her a start. Nobody had asked such a thing of her, not in a good long time.

"I don't want a job."

"You're living off rum and cigarette smoke."

"Diet of the Gods."

Yanish pulled on his ciggie with a deft overhand grip, jutting it to one corner of his mouth. To Cady's eye he looked like Claude Lumero in that crystal show, oh, what was it called now... She'd seen it last month... that war story... he'd kissed that woman who turned out to be an Enakor spy... *Rendezvous at Midnight*... something like that...

But her mind drifted along...

"Damn it!"

Yanish's curse startled her. He had grabbed the fishing rod and was now jerking it backwards and to the side, trying to land a fish. But the line went slack.

"That's your fault." He flicked his cigarette into the water.

"It's your smell, it's putting them off."

Cady grunted. "Those two look nice enough." She nodded at the keep net. "Perhaps tonight we can fry them up... um... what do you say? Oh, I know! I have to visit the outer fields later on, so I'll gather some of my special herbs, I know you like those."

He stared at her without speaking.

"The thing is, Yan, I need to talk to you. About the never-nevers."

"What about them?"

Her lips moved in a curious motion, as though tasting the words before she said them. She longed to tell him the truth, but she knew that Yanish, for all his poise and aplomb, would be upset. And so instead, with a forced grin that showed off her missing teeth, she said, "Remember, the last time we partook, eh? The visions you had! You were squealing with delight, you were, talking of Queen

Luda and how you'd like to climb inside the dragon's womb with her."

The triangle on Yanish's brow brightened, showing his pleasure: he couldn't hide it. "You and your outer fields! One day, I swear, I'll follow you and find out where they are. Dig up my own supply. I'll be sitting pretty!"

Cady snorted at such a notion. "You could follow me all the day long and you would never see where I was going."

Yanish gathered in his line and placed his angling gear back in his pannier. With a swift blow he killed the two fishes and wrapped them in newspaper. When he stood up, his face caught the sunlight just so, and was tinted with lilac. Cady admired his looks, and she was awful proud of him, especially since he'd taken the job looking after the old folks at the hostel: all that mopping up of piss and vomit, ugh!

She said, "Tell me, at least, these people looking for me, what was the nature of the job on offer?"

"They wouldn't say. But there was something wrong with the girl."

"How do you mean?"

"She had the shakes. And her eyes were tuned out." He kickstarted the motorcycle's engine: it took him five or six thrusts of his boot before a gust of black smoke belched out of the exhaust. He had to shout over the noise: "Tonight, old chiv, we shall dine!" Then he set off along the quay, the sound of the engine backfiring heard long after he'd turned onto the prom road.

Cady sat down on an upturned lobster pot and prepared another roll-up, adding a dash of knill weed plucked from a gap in the stones. It crackled when lit, and gave off a lovely scent. Her nostrils tingled. And after a series of racking coughs and splutters, and a few choice expletives, she felt a lot better, a whole lot better. She decided once and for all that tonight she would tell Yanish everything, all about what the sight of the seed people meant, and her own true and secret nature. That would knock him for six, arse over tit, yes indeed!

She set off for Guillemot Lane, and the sailor's hostel. Guillemot was an especially narrow gloom-laden street. The buildings leaned over almost to embrace each other.

"Oh buggeration! Bugger me backwards!"

There they were, waiting outside the door to her lodgings – a man and a girl. Cady ducked into a ginnel, peeking out from behind the wall. The Thrawl was chattering away, while the girl was just sitting there, staring into space. A tiny ball of twinkling violet light was circling her head, around and around; Cady had no idea what it was. They had a couple of suitcases with them, resting on the pavement, one brown and tattered, the other smaller with a flowery pattern. Cady wished she had her eyeglass with her, then she could have a good look at them, from a safer distance.

And then Mr Tattersall came out of his ironmonger's shop and started shouting at the Thrawl, demanding that he remove himself from the vicinity. The Thrawl stood up and placed himself in front of the girl. He was very tall and very thin, unnaturally so. But the girl remained calm; she reached up to play with the little ball of light, batting it this way and that.

Tattersall – who was a cantankerous soul; much abused in life, and wanting to visit the same on anyone he didn't take a fancy to – made a rude gesture, the kind that only an Ephreme of a certain age would understand. Maybe the Thrawl had such things lodged in his brain, which acted, or so Cady had heard, rather like an encyclopaedia with endless pages – in which case he would understand just how rude Tattersall was being. But the Thrawl made no response. He just stood there, feet apart, arms at his side ready for action. Cady wondered

Tattersall bent down to the pavement. Cady wondered what he was up to, until she spotted the piece of chalk in his hand. He was drawing a sigil on the slabs, right in front of the Thrawl. The ironmonger was always boasting of his knowledge of the symbols of magic, and the casting of the runes. The Thrawl couldn't resist this so easily; his eyes were drawn to the symbol, and a strange whining sound came from his lips. The girl looked worried. And then she too saw the sign written on the ground, and it had a far more drastic effect on her, given the fact that she was fully alive, rather than a man-made creature like the Thrawl. She spun around in a circle, and kept on spinning and spinning and would surely fall over, dizzy, or worse.

By now Cady was miffed, somewhat mightily. All she wanted to do was get back to her rooms and start the process of the never-never ritual. She left the safety of the ginnel and marched across the street, where she confronted Tattersall head on: "What in the pit of heaven's arsehole are you doing, disturbing my friends?"

To which Tattersall replied, "Your friends? Specimens like this?"

It took all of Cady's willpower not to peek at the magic symbol. She stretched herself as lofty as she could, announcing, "My very good friends, sir! So sling your hook! Go on, bollock off, that's it."

This was enough to cause Tattersall to mumble and fret: "You're as bad as each other," and then to retire to his shop across the lane. As he retreated, the tiny wings that poked through the shoulder vents of his jacket wafted about ineffectually.

"Well, that's sent him packing."

Quickly she scuffed over the chalk drawing with the heel of her boot. The Thrawl looked at her. She did the same to him. The girl was peeping out from the Thrawl's side. All that Cady could see for sure was a mass of flaxen hair, matted with dust and salt.

"What do you want?"

The Thrawl answered in a rasping tone; it was grating to the ear. "I'm waiting here to speak with Arcadia Meade. Otherwise known as Cady."

"Why?"

"On private business."

"You tell me what it is, and I'll tell her."

"Who are you?"

"Cady Meade, her own true self."

"You're Cady Meade?"

"I just said as such, didn't you hear?"

The Thrawl closed his eyes. Cady had to admit, she didn't like the look of him. Not that she had anything against the concept, in theory, no, but then again, they had called trouble in the past. And the covering on his face did him no favours, the rubber skin stretched loosely over the skull, a very pale orange in colour. There was a scar down one side of his face, the covering torn and then stitched back together with twine. And the more she looked, the more scars and fissures she saw. And his suit of purple cloth was scuffed and well-patched: she'd seen mudlarks and night-soil men in smarter attire.

Cady was about to make her excuses, when the Thrawl brought himself back to attention, like a motor winding up, and his eyes sparkled blue and gold as though someone had switched on a couple of tiny lightbulbs. "I heard you were a river pilot," he said. "A captain?"

"Aye. Both of those in my time. In addition to which: helmswoman, deckhand, gunner, third mate, second mate, navigator, bosun, bosun's mate, loblolly and powder monkey." She counted them off until she ran out of fingers.

"But I haven't set foot on the river since the war ended."

"I wasn't told that." And then: "How do you set *foot* on a river?"

"Now look here, Mr Wind-Up, I am currently engaged on business of national importance. So what is it you want of me?"

The Thrawl blinked. It was too rapid a movement for any human eye to make. But then he actually made a little bow, and said, "My name is Lek. May we talk inside?"

"No."

"People are watching."

"They can fuck a monkey upside-down for all I care."

Cady could see Thrawl Lek was taken aback by this simple-enough statement. And she heard the girl sniggering.

"Come on, out with it. My bladder's fit to burst."

Lek's mouth set in a line. "We are seeking a journey along the River Nysis."

"How far along?"

"The city of Ludwich."

Cady had to laugh, she couldn't help it. "Ludwich? By river?"

"That's right, at the earliest opportunity."

"Well, see, how it is…" She couldn't stop laughing.

"We can pay you," Lek said.

"But still…"

"Whatever you require."

"That is tempting, I must say."

"Up to a certain amount."

Cady thought of all the rum and baccy and filthy books and cough drops she could buy. But then she thought of the little blue seeds in her purse and she took a deep breath.

"Now here's the thing. Nobody goes by boat to Ludwich, not anymore, not from here."

"I know that, but—"

"My last such voyage was a nightmare. Let's see now. I had a podsnapper, a rogue of the court, a couple of manky-men, three dollymops with their rich gentlemen clients, a widow in mourning, and a priest. All of them hoping to escape the bombing of the city."

"What happened to them?"

"What happened? One over the side, drowned. Two screaming for their mothers. Another two fighting each other. A stabbing. One dollymop leapt overboard and ran off into the misty fields, Lud knows where. The priest was hiding in the bilge, gibbering like a madman. Need I go on?" Cady answered her own question by continuing: "Meanwhile, the saucy rouge was praying to both Lud and Luda for forgiveness, hoping to ease the pain of life. But it won't be eased!" Her lungs were wheezing and specks of black dust erupted from her mouth. "Now see, you've set me going!"

She coughed and retched. Her face was even greener than it usually was. Every part of her where flesh rubbed against flesh was damp and sticky.

"I'm very sorry, madam."

Thrawl Lek was downcast. Cady would never have

thought a goddamn machine could display such emotions – yet it wasn't quite real enough, more a learned set of facial movements, which he clicked through one after the next.

"It's not for me," he told her. "It's for the girl. The journey, I mean."

"Is that so?"

"It's for Brin."

Cady considered this, knowing a story was hiding itself away. But she spoke firmly: "A boat set off last month, Ludwich bound. The *Speckled Dove*. They vanished into the ghost waters, and were never seen again. I don't intend to follow the same course—"

"You used to do it."

"*Used* to. Used to! I swear by all that is holy…"

Cady restrained herself, for the girl had stepped out the Thrawl's shadow, presenting herself for all to see – and quite a sight it was.

Nine or ten. Delightful snub nose, round eyes. Sturdy for her age. A bit posh. Smarmy, even. Surly with it. But then again, that was the Alkhym way. Mind, she wasn't dressed as she ought to be, given her station in life. Her flowery dress and her yellow cardigan had no doubt been fancy to begin with, but were now torn and tatty, bearing the strains of a long journey, decorated with specks of oil. But her eyes were the worst, possessed of a far-away gaze – perhaps the furthest Cady had ever seen anyone look, without actually seeing anything. It was unnerving to view such a thing on one so young. And the girl's hands trembled continuously. She remembered Yanish saying the girl was poorly. And like Fable had said: not even the first speck of antenna at the temples. But it must be close to that time for her, yes, perhaps very close.

Cady thought for a moment. "This is for the Hesting festival, I presume?"

"That's correct," Lek answered. "Miss Brin was ten in March, and I made a promise: that I'd get her to the city on time, by this Friday preferably. Isn't that right?"

He directed this last question to the girl herself, who merely nodded in answer. The tiny globe of violet light flew around and around her head at speed, and then came to a sudden stop to hover in front of her face. She opened her mouth and the spark popped inside.

"Is she swallowing that thing?"

Lek smiled. "It's only a sprite. She's keeping it safe."

Cady nodded. The sight of the girl had flummoxed her a little. But she had to be strong. "Look, Mr... Mr Lek... You should take the bus. There's one every other day, leaves at half past two or thereabouts, from the high street."

"No! No, that can't happen."

"Righty-ho, the bus does get hijacked now and then. There's always a lorry—"

"I've told you, no!"

The Thrawl's face clicked into fierce anger: *Angry Face No. 4*, something like that.

"Brin needs to sail upriver, through the ghost waters. She *has* to do this." His voice had taken on a piercing tone. "Nothing else matters..."

His mouth was poised halfway through a phrase. Something was happening. Or rather... *not* happening. He had suddenly become very still, his entire body held rigid in place, his arms frozen in an awkward gesture, his face set in one expression, which could only be described as *Pained*.

"What's wrong with him?"

Brin didn't answer. But her hands were shaking even

more than usual. Despite this, the girl took action; she grabbed hold of Lek's sleeve and gently led him over to the low wall. He shuffled along like a giant-sized doll. They sat together on the wall. Cady looked up at her second-floor window, pondering a quick escape. But she couldn't help joining the strange pair, sitting on the other side of the Thrawl. The moments passed. Lek remained in his frozen state, his head straight, his hands folded in his lap. His eyes were closed.

"Does he get like this very often?"

The girl leaned forward. She nodded her head.

Cady bent forward as well, so they could see each other.

"How long does it last?"

A shrug in answer.

Cady explored a hole in a tooth with her tongue. "Brin, is that what he called you?"

It seemed like another shrug was in order, but the girl changed her mind. "Yes." A twitch of the head. "It's short for Sabrina." Her hands were quivering madly, almost a blur.

"Very swish, I'm sure."

"I won't tell you my full Alkhym name, it's too long to remember."

"Right you are."

They fell back into silence. The girl was sneaking crafty looks at Cady's leathery arms, at the tattoos of anchors, mermaids, and sea serpents. The old lady rolled the sleeve higher and stretched out her arm fully, flexing her wiry muscles to give the viewer a nice little show.

"You should see my back, girlie. I have the dragon Haakenur inked on there, head to tail. And a tiny little King Lud fighting her with his sword."

Brin's eyes widened.

"I had that done, ooh, more than forty years before you were born, I'll bet. In a tattoo parlour in Tolly Hoo. It was a Thrawl who did it for me, now I come to think on it."

"Really?"

"Oh, they were more accepted back then, the Thrawl, before the Frenzy took place."

The girl nodded. There was a sadness on her young face. She said, "I'd really like to journey down the Nysis. It means so much to me."

Cady frowned. "Look, Brin, how it is, I can't go back on the river, I just can't. People get hurt on the ghost waters. They go cuckoo, or worse, they jump overboard. I can't lose anyone else to the Nysis, I just can't. Terrible, terrible. These last few years… Oh my."

She took a breather. Grit rattled in her throat.

Brin stared ahead, her eyes back on that far-away invisible object. Her mouth opened, and the little ball of light popped out and went into orbit. Was that a good thing? Cady had no way of knowing. But then the girl stood up. She nudged a section of the Thrawl's rubber mask to the side, right where it had been stitched over the temple. Cady leaned in to get a good look.

There was a bullet lodged in the clear plastic skull.

Brin explained, "This is why he goes to sleep every so often."

"When did this happen?"

"About a year ago. We're always getting into trouble."

"I see."

A wave of vexation come over Cady. This posh girl, and the Thrawl, they were nothing but fuss and bother. Nothing but! And yet, against her own best wishes, she made to touch the bullet. But her fingers jerked away as the Thrawl stirred and moaned. He was coming awake, his eyes opening, his chest shuddering into life.

This was a sign. Cady stood up and jammed her bowler back on her head. "I have to take my leave of you. Goodbye." And she was gone, back inside the sailor's hostel, taking the stairs as fast as she could, up to her rooms. That's it, old girl, batten the hatches, hold tight, no entry, private property, senior officers only, trespassers will be prosecuted!

Her heart was racing.

She had a much delayed wee: a nice yellow flow, then green, then flecks of orange. Lovely. Once the kettle was on and nicely boiling, she searched her cupboard for leftovers: a hunk of bread and some cheese covered in green mould. Oh, that was good! Of all the moulds, blue was her favourite. But green was her second favourite. So that was nice, and the tea, with a dash of Jim Brimstone's Navy Rum in it, even nicer. But she was only doing one thing: steeling herself.

Right then. Time for work. First of all, a visit to the outer fields. Cady stared unblinking at the wall for the duration of the journey. There and back, it took three minutes, ample time to pluck the necessary herbs – hagbane, pennywort, crone's poppy.

Not the once did she leave her armchair.

She placed the bounty in her mortar, its bowl already stained a hundred colours. She took the seeds of the never-never plant from her purse, nine of them altogether. Yes, that would do it. These were added to the mixture and the pestle brought to bear, grinding all to a fine powder, the colour of a summer's sky streaked with sunlight. This she poured into the finger of rum in her glass.

Cady thought of all the places she had visited in her long life, the bustling ports, the harbours, the wharves and the half-hidden tributaries. But there were always more destinations. Other rivers, those not yet mapped. She downed the contents of the glass in one gulp, not even thinking about it. There was a burn in her throat, that was all, as though a red lamp had been lit, deep down, deep down, deep down...

She lay on her little bed and closed her eyes. A figure moved in the dark of her skull. One figure, and a second. One more. The seed people. They called to her.

Maps and Shadows

The old lady twisted her body sideways to squeeze through a narrow underwater channel, breathing easily, her arms and legs working with remarkable strength. The tidal currents pushed her along. It was a glorious feeling, to be swimming fathoms deep in and out of the weeds and rocks. Omega Point was behind her; now she was moving upriver. Every so often the water turned black as though with squid ink and then she would be at some other part of the Nysis, suddenly, without memory of travel. It happened enough times for Cady to lose all sense of her whereabouts, but for now at least the waters were clear and she could find her way around upcoming obstacles, using the tidal path as her guidance. The optic gland at the centre of her brow glowed, further aiding her navigation of the depths.

She didn't question at all that she could breathe underwater, but a vague thought came to her, that she might be journeying through a dream world. Her hands were dark with mud as she pulled herself along the riverbed, dodging under the prow of a sunken barque. In this way, she rounded a meander that she guessed was Archer's Bow, its distinctive horseshoe shape on the charts fixed in her mind. If this was true, her last blackout had pushed her miles ahead. Yes, here the river widened into what could only be Tivertara Pool, a basin famed for its easy-going current – all the watermen loved this passage as they sailed upriver towards Maddenholt. But a surprise greeted her. She came to a stone structure, the remains of a temple, reduced over time to a circle of crumbling pillars and the cracked patterns of a mosaicked floor. At the centre was a large stone altar covered in markings, pictograms she recognised as early Alkhym writing. The temple must have been part of the settler village at Tivertara, from the time of the first separation of the tribes. Ages old. Ages! Cady swam in and out of the pillars like a silvery slippery lady eel, only to have the ink flood over her, blinding her to the river's delights.

When her vision cleared once more, she had moved beyond Maddenholt trading post, perhaps towards the embedded rocks of Catlin Creek, a hazard for any boat with a deep draft. The river was still very wide at this point, clouded with silt. And then she came upon an object she recognised: the old church bell of St Kellina's, which had fallen from the steeple and plunged into the Nysis during the year of... oh, Lud knows when! All that mattered was the touch and feel of the bronze under her fingers, the crumbling patina, the crusted shells of countless clags and tallycastles. She could see a half sentence of engraved lettering on the bell and couldn't help but think of the craftsman who had carved it: the clang of the hammer on the chisel, the blade digging into the curved metal.

The bell glowed with a sudden light, rather like a flashbulb exploding underwater: it left an image in Cady's mind, burnt in red.

Mark this. Remember it!

Here then was the first object of her quest. The never-nevers had spoken.

Church bell.

The dream tide gathered speed, rushing towards Hingle Bowl. Soon she would reach the ghost waters, where the phantom presence known as the Faynr takes possession of the River Nysis, and Cady had a sudden fear of being asleep when that happened, that she might never wake up again. But the flow carried her. A large tombstone lay half-hidden in the mud and rubble of the riverbed, lying flat, inscription uppermost – but the name of the deceased had long since been worn away.

As she approached, the stone glowed with the same red light as the church bell.

First object, second object.

Bell, gravestone.

Quite deliberately Cady placed the two items in her memory.

She swam into the Tamlin area of the Nysis. The water here was suffused with a green mist. A large metal object lay part-buried in the riverbed, its upper portion visible with a set of fins and a name written down the side: *Gogmagog*. It was a rocket. An unexploded X2 flying bomb, no doubt sent over from Enakor in the last years of the war. The shell was covered in rust and stained with algae and moss. Again she saw the glow of the red light, illuminating the half-buried missile. This then was the third element to be collected.

Bell, Stone, Bomb.

The green mist was issuing from a fissure in the rocket's casing; it could only mean one thing – poisonous gas. Cady's arms and legs jerked about helplessly. She tried to swim backwards, hardly knowing how to work her body properly; she was a puppet to her own fear. And then, with an icy-cold shiver, she realised that she wasn't alone. The poisonous mist was forming into a shape, a writhing serpentine body blackened and charred, its yellow eyes glittering. The creature clutched at Cady and she felt the scratching of its claws in her flesh. It spoke to her in a voice both old and young, deepening on every word. *Keep still. Stop struggling.* The claws pierced the skin of her face, drawing blood. She was growing weak. Precious bubbles of air escaped her lips.

Wake up!

The waters flowed over her. The creature grinned madly. If only she could push and kick herself away, but her limbs were too heavy.

Cady, Cady, can you hear me?

The creature knew her name. She screamed out loud but without words, only a senseless wail. The water entered her throat and her vision blurred.

"Cady, keep still, stop it!"

That was enough, a signal. A known voice. The river loosened its grip.

It was Yanish. He was holding her down, to stop her from thrashing about on the bed. He had to half shout, "That's it, nice and easy."

"Get off me!" Cady's voice was muffled.

"Wakey wakey."

"I'm bloody well awake, thank you."

"You've wet the bed."

That shut her up, at least for a moment or two. And then:

"Oh fuck. Oh fuck."

"I should get danger money for this job."

Cady struggled to get off the bed. "It's not piss, actually. If you must know."

"It's smells like piss."

"It's the river."

"So now you're pissing out the waters of the Nysis?"

"I told you, it's not piss!" At last she was on her feet.

"Take those trousers off. They're wet through."

She did so. She padded over to the wash basin. "Get me some clothes, will you."

Yanish was happy to avert his eyes. He went over to the wardrobe. There was a pair of tartan bell-bottoms slung over the pole. He took these, and a pair of bloomers from a shelf. Cady grabbed the items of clothing off him and struggled to pull them on.

Yanish dragged the damp sheets off the bed. "I'll take these down to the laundry later." He opened the door of the room, throwing the sheets into the corridor.

"Don't leave them out there, for anyone to see! For Lud's sake. Put them in the wardrobe, we can sort them out after supper." She rubbed sand from her eyes and looked to the window. It was getting dark outside. "What time is it anyway?"

"Gone seven."

"Oh heavens. I've been out cold for hours. Where did the day go?"

Yanish spotted the pestle and mortar on the table. Both items were caked with a blue and yellow residue.

"You've been having fun without me, chiv."

"Well, you know. Needs must."

"I was looking forward to that. I need a way out of this town." Yanish cast his shadow away from his body on a long strand of silky smokiness. It was an Azeelian trait, but Cady had never seen him do it before with such zeal. The shadow skittered to and fro on the wall, dancing madly, clinging to the ceiling. He called out after it: "I need to escape. I need to smash something! I need to leap free!" It was the kind of things they said in those crystal shows he liked: all those frustrated young scuttlers and roustabouts who never got to fight in the war.

Cady licked her lips. She was suddenly starving. "Where's those haddock you promised me?"

His shadow came back to his side. "I fried them in butter and parsley. This afternoon."

"Why would you do that?"

"I shared them with Frank Hebble. You know, the trawlerman."

"It's me you should be sharing it with. Me! Bloody Frank Hebble, indeed! He's got fish coming out of his lugholes!" Cady fumed. "I mean to say, what am I supposed to eat now?"

Yanish handed her a tin. "I brought you this instead."

"Sergeant Bully's Finest Corned Beef? Blimey heck, I thought the war was over!"

"It's good stuff, that. Tasty."

"Aye, but it's hardly the same as a nice piece of haddock." But Cady pulled the key from the tin, using it to peel back the lid. She was digging her fingers into the meat and slathering her lips with it, before Yanish managed to grab the tin off her.

"I'll cook up a few spuds, and an onion," he said. "That will do us."

His shadow longed to dance on the walls again. Something was troubling him; Cady saw it in his face. She had a quick look around the room and spotted a long cardboard tube propped against the wall in a corner. At first, she couldn't think what it might contain: a flag, a roll of canvas – Yanish was a keen artist – or even a finished painting. But then she understood, and her heart went cold a little. But she didn't say anything, not yet: when he was ready to speak, he would do.

Ten minutes later the stew pot was boiling on the little stove. Cady stood by the open window, peeking out at the lane below. The gas lamp outside the ironmongers was lit, giving the scene a pale glow, like a crystal screen just before the show begins.

Yanish tested the potatoes with a fork. He glanced at Cady. "What are you looking for?"

"That kid, and the Thrawl."

"Did you talk to them?"

"I did. And you'll never guess what they wanted. Passage to Ludwich."

He stirred the onion and the corned beef in the frying pan. "You set them straight, did you?"

"I said *no*, if that's what you mean."

"You don't even have a boat."

"There's that, certainly."

Yanish poured the spuds into the frying pan, mixing everything together with a dollop of Hunnock's brown sauce. The room was filling up with steam and tasty aromas. But Cady's stomach yearned for stranger foods. Idly, her fingernails scratched at the damp wallpaper, tearing off a thin strip. She sucked on this, and revelled in the taste of the glue and the dye.

She said, "This trawlerman?"

"Frank Hebble."

"That's the one." She glanced again to the cardboard

tube. "He brought you something, did he, a gift from his seafaring?"

"Uh-huh." Yanish was doing his best to concentrate on the cooking.

"That's why you ate the fish with him, and broke bread, no doubt? And maybe paid him a bit of moolah, for his trouble?"

Yanish shrugged. "I really didn't want to. I wanted Frank to take it away, back to where it belongs. In a dump somewhere. Aye, maybe I'll do that later on. Or else tear it into shreds." He piled food onto two enamel plates. "There you go. Tastier than wallpaper."

They ate at the table. Cady sucked the gravy off each chunk of meat, before putting her good remaining teeth to work.

Yanish broke the silence. "I went out to see the never-nevers."

"Oh aye?"

"Too many tourists and reporters. Everyone taking snapshots of the seeds as they drifted through the air. It was amazing, though. One old codger had set up an easel and was trying to capture them in watercolours."

Cady laughed. "Sweet Luda, but he'd have to be quick!"

"Yes." But the light went from Yanish's eyes, quite suddenly.

She tried to urge him on. "You came back home then, did you? You saw Hebble's trawler coming in?"

"He was waiting for me."

But he still wasn't ready. Instead, he nodded over to the pestle and mortar. "So how were the outer fields?"

"Ripe and lush, as always. I gathered a little pennywort." She spat out a piece of gristle. "And then, let's see… yes,

I added some hagbane, and a sprinkle of crone's poppy."

"That's some witch's brew."

She spoke quickly, outwitting her own reticence: "I added some never-never seeds."

He was surprised at this. "They're poisonous, aren't they?"

"Not if you treat them right."

"I remember that song they taught us in school."

Never never ever ever
Eat a never-never
Never eat a never-never
Never ever ever.

He had a lovely singing voice, even on such a ditty.

Cady wiped up the last of her meal with a piece of bread. "Well, see, taking the seeds in this way, mixed with bane and wort and poppy, it brings on a special kind of vision. I went dreaming in the Nysis." Her voice softened and her eyes grew wistful. "Yanish, you should've seen me! I was seven fathoms deep, gliding my way along. The things that I saw!" Her face lit up. "Where are my charts? Fetch them for me. Go on! On top of the wardrobe."

Cady quickly shoved everything off the table onto the bed, dirty plates and cups and all. The charts, when they landed on the tabletop, raised up a cloud of dust that set Cady coughing.

"The silverfish have been at them," she said. "Bloody pests."

"They're getting a bit tatty, aren't they?"

"These are the best charts ever made, as you well know. Maguire & Hill, cartographers to His Royal Majesty King Osbert IV. Drawn up fifty years ago, that's all."

"But the river's changed a fair bit since then. Two wars, erosion, floods, drought, the sickness of the ghost waters—"

"Just help me find the right one, that's all I ask."

"What are we looking for?"

"I'm trying to remember. Let me remember!"

Yanish was amused. "Let me get this straight, old chiv: you've had a dream about swimming in the river, and now you're checking your charts to see where you travelled?"

"That's right."

He shook his head in wonder. "You're ready for Dottyville, you do know that?"

She dismissed the idea with a grunt. "Now let's see... yes, I passed St Kellina's in the Marsh. Of course!"

"The old church? It's just a ruin, these days."

"The tower was struck by lightning, oh, and then it was sacked, and then set afire, until the whole thing collapsed and the bell ended up underwater. Which is where I found it. I swam past it, this close, Yanish. This close! I could read the inscription in the metal, after all this time, or at least part of it – it was a prayer, written in the Old Wodwo tongue."

"What happened then?" Yanish was fascinated by now.

The old lady's brow furrowed in concentration as she searched through the charts, each one depicting a different stretch of the Nysis river, from the trickling source high up on Chigley Tor, down to Pinchbeck estuary and the sea, every section annotated with Cady's handwritten notes. The rejected sheets slid to the floor with a *shushing* sound. "They're not in the right order," she said. "Wait, wait! Ah, here it is! Chart number six. Yes, yes!" They spread the chart out, holding it flat with sauce bottle and salt cellar. Cady peered over it, her finger tracing the course upriver, past

St Kellina's church and onwards. "It's all coming back to me now." Her finger continued around the bend of Archer's Bow before it reached the edge of the map. "Quickly, I need the next chart along, number seven, where is it?" She was leafing through the sheets of paper, causing them all to fall off the table's edge. She bent down. Yanish joined her and helped in the search and eventually they found the needed map. "Leave it on the floor, that's right." But then she stopped suddenly in her journey.

"Cady?" Yanish asked. "Where did you go next?"

She looked up from the river's course. "I'm worried about that girl. About Brin."

"That's her name, is it?"

"Yes."

"I did hear something, about the strangers."

"Tell me."

"From Mr Sunnylove… you know, on the top floor?"

"Oh, that old curmudgeon."

"He was down the Westward Ho this teatime, drinking his fill. And he got chatting with the skipper of the boat they came in on. They sailed from Stranach Isle."

"By heavens, that's a fair bit away."

"And neutral in the war."

"They must have been on the run. The poor little blighter."

Yanish studied her. "Why are you so interested? You give kids a wide berth, usually."

Cady waved his remarks away, and went back to tracing the curves of the Nysis on the charts. Her eyes were as deep as the river, as blue-green as the sea, as her finger reached the widening pool at Tivertara. "Right there," she said. "There's a temple, under the water."

Yanish nodded. "There was an Alkhym settlement. People

are always finding bits of pottery, coins, arrowheads in the mud banks."

Cady followed the river a little further and then came to a halt. Her finger pressed against the yellowing paper at the point marked *Hingle Bowl*.

Yanish leaned over, trying to see anything of interest.

"What is it you're pointing to?"

"First of all, a gravestone."

"Underwater? But there's no church at Hingle. No cemetery, nothing like that."

She ignored this. "And a little further on, here, at Tamlin." Her voice lowered to a whisper. "An Enakor flying bomb, half-sunk in the riverbed. Unexploded."

"Really?"

"It was marked with the word *Gogmagog*."

Yanish shook his head. "I've no idea what that means."

"Me neither. The rocket was lit up in a red light. The same as the bell was, and the gravestone. They were being pointed out to me."

"I wish I had dreams like this."

Cady mused on the three elements. "Church bell, gravestone, flying bomb." And then, quieter still: "This is the vision. The never-nevers are trying to tell me something."

"I'm sorry, what?"

"The people of the seeds. As released from the never-nevers. They're the ones who give me the vision."

"But they're only present for a few seconds—"

"Pah! They have a hidden life! They tell me what I have to do next. My task. But see, they haven't got mouths, or hands to write with. So all they can do is show me things, objects… And then I have to…" She shook her head. "It's like a riddle. It begins with a bell. And it ends with the Gogmagog rocket. And in between: a gravestone. They work… oh, I don't know… like three cards from a madwoman's Tarot deck – the task ahead. All I have to do now is work it out."

Yanish went to make a joke about this, but then stopped himself.

Cady's eyes had taken on the spirit of the seeds, tiny figures seen in her pupils. They were there for a moment only, enough to put a scare on him.

"Please tell me what's going on."

This time she hesitated before speaking. "I might have to leave," she said. "Tomorrow, or the day after. Depending."

A blunt expression settled on Yanish's face. He got to his feet. Cady tried to follow him, but had to haul herself up by the table's edge. She was out of breath.

"Where are you going?" he asked.

"I'm not sure. I never know, not until I get there."

Yanish laughed. It was an automatic response. "Friggin' hell, old chiv. I swear you're more crumbs than biscuit, these days."

"I know, I know. But look, let me explain…"

He waited. Cady made to speak. But the memory of her dream trip along the Nysis came back to her, all its details roused by the map-reading. And she knew for sure that whatever the next few days or weeks might bring, it would likely be a dangerous time, even deadly. And suddenly, she wasn't sure if she wanted to involve her friend at all. And so she turned away from him.

There was a framed oil painting above the fireplace. Yanish had painted it, to celebrate Cady's retirement from sailing. It showed the Ludwich parliament – the Great House of Witan – with the River Nysis in the foreground and a collection of boats on the water. But the focus of the image was the towering shape of a dragon that rose up in the skies to the west of the city, its writhing body rendered in bright yellow and red pigment. The painting's title was *The Night of the Dragon*. Yanish and Cady had been on the river that evening, aboard the *Juniper*, and had seen the apparition in the sky, a creature made out of projected light, at least that was the theory proposed by the press and the crystal reels. The phenomenon had lasted a few minutes only. It was a propaganda exercise, almost certainly, but for that short period of time, Great Haakenur had once again ruled over the land, a protective spirit in that terrible fifth year of the war.

Yanish said now, "I'll come with you. When you go away."

"No." She went to the window. "No, I have to do this on my own."

From far away came the sound of music: Harry Micklethwaite's Parlour Dance Band playing at the Lido Hotel. It sounded like a waltz played by a phantom orchestra. Then Cady peered forward, hardly believing her eyes. A small bright ball of violet light appeared outside the window, dancing madly in the air. It was there for a moment before flickering away, but she recognised it: Brin's toy sprite. Strangely, it acted upon the old sailor as a semaphore lamp out at sea in the fog, a distant stuttering hope.

Turning to face Yanish, she spoke gently. "Shall we look at the shroud now?"

The lad started to speak, but then faltered.

"Come on," Cady said gently. "We'll do it together. I know you want that."

Without speaking, he fetched the cardboard tube from the corner of the room. It was marked with various dates and wax seals and official stamps, most of them naming towns and cities in the country of Saliscana. There was a dent in one end. And an animal's teeth-marks in the middle.

"It's been on its travels," Cady said.

He nodded at this, still unsure.

"Where was it found?"

"In the cellar of a village hall," he answered. "A whole load of them had been stored in there, just piled up in the dark. After the battle at Jorgens Pass." A pause. "All of them belonging to deserters, apparently. That's why they were dumped there." Under his breath, he added, "Best place for them."

"You can't know what happened, not really."

Yanish's fingers moved over the indentations in the cardboard. "Looks like the rats have had a go at it." There was a choking sound in his throat.

"Come on," Cady said. "I've never seen one before, not up close."

"I don't know what I'm supposed to feel." He turned to Cady. "Help me. What am I supposed to feel?" His otherwise smooth young face was creased up at the brow, and his aphelon flickered from dark to light grey: two states of mind, superimposed. His shadow trembled at the edge of his skin, longing to escape.

"You'll know, when you see it... believe me."

Cady made the move for him. She tore off the seal at the end of the tube and pulled out the contents, a roll of cloth, which she spread out across the tabletop. It was an Azeelian shroud, six feet in length, three feet wide, a light brown in colour, made of a coarsely woven hessian material.

"I can't see anything," Cady said. "Do you have to be part of the tribe, to..."

"They're usually on silk," Yanish explained. "Mum and Dad used to take me to the shroud garden, every Sunday, when I was a kid. They prayed to the great god, Naphet, that he might look upon our souls with love. But I just liked to look at the silk shrouds. It was amazing to see them dancing in the breeze, like flags, a celebration of colour, of life, even in death. But this... this sackcloth." He gestured to the shroud. "This just disgusts me."

Cady held her true feelings in check. She said carefully, "Who knows what they could find, eh, on the battlefield? Perhaps this was all they had to hand?"

"No, they do this for criminals. And the unblessed."

Yanish pulled the lamp closer. They both tilted their heads at the correct angle, just so... and then the aura was seen. It was the shadow of a dying man's body, burnt into the cloth. The shadow was marked by several channels and pathways in a lighter shade, the broadest of which stretched from the feet to the top of the head, a curving channel that looked very like the river on the charts, but without colour or markings.

Cady shivered, she couldn't help herself. She saw Yanish's hands gripping the table edge, and when she looked up at his face, she saw that his aphelion had turned almost white: she'd never seen it take on such a brightness before. It scared her a little. In truth, she could not decode it: anger, grief, sadness, or even courage: courage against despair?

Now Yanish held his hand flat over the cloth, a couple of inches above the heart of the figure.

He spoke the official litany, his voice quite cold.

"Here rests the shadow of the Most Honourable Zehmet, of the House of Khalan. Chartered accountant. Corporal in the First Swandown Fusiliers. Son of Yarbaros. Wife to

Helina, late of this world." A pause in the speech. Then: "And father to Yanish, his only child."

He went back to the very first phrase, changing a single word.

"The most *dishonourable* Zehmet." And then another word, spat out: "Coward!"

Cady knew that Yanish was making every effort not to cry. But she didn't look at him. Instead she focussed on the shroud, and what it held. It was a hazy portrait, the features blurred, with many tiny rips in the cloth, and a ragged hole to mark the left eye. The place on the forehead where the aphelon would have been was now burned pitch-black, evidence of the body's final process: the projection of the Azeel's shadow to the cloth.

Cady repeated the comforts she had used before: "You can't know what really happened, how can you? Perhaps your father..."

But it was hopeless. Yanish was rolling up the shroud, slotting it back inside its container.

"Yanish?"

He said the strangest thing in reply, something unexpected: "It should be on silk."

This seemed to contradict his feelings about his father. Cady wanted to ask him about this but he was already at the door. He hesitated and looked at her.

"Goodbye," he said. "Goodbye, Cady."

The door closed softly.

The room was suddenly very small, and very quiet. Cady picked up the charts from the floor and collected them together on the table, trying to keep them neat and square. She looked at the bed, stripped of its sheets, the bare mattress. It was badly stained. The supper plates were still piled up there with the dirty cutlery. She took a clean set of linen from a drawer and started to make the bed, but gave up after a minute. She ended up sitting on a corner of the mattress, mumbling to herself. Her eyes darted about her room, taking stock of her few possessions: brass ornaments, various souvenirs from far-off lands, scrimshaw carvings. Not much for several lifetimes of seafaring and riverwandering. Her gaze settled on one photograph on the wall, of her and Yanish aboard the *Juniper*, him as cabin boy, Captain Cady resplendent in her cap and peacoat, brass buttons all polished. They were smiling, the old lady and the young man. Smiling during warfare. That's the way! The words inscribed on the submerged church bell came to her. She knew the prayer by heart, having learned it from the pages of the Book of Dark Eden, the Wodwo bible.

Pray for us, now and in our days of need.

At the time of planting, and in the Autumn months when the flowers fade and fall.

So the first of the Gardener Priests had written. To truly face the threat foretold by the never-nevers, it was best to be young, strong in limb and leaf. But Cady was too old for such shenanigans. She would have to regrow herself.

Tomorrow she would begin again on the task of her life, her secret life.

Wickerwork

The pig stared at Cady and Cady stared back, neither willing to give way. The animal shifted its bulk and blew air out of its nostrils. The two other passengers – a farmer and a schoolboy – would feel nothing, of course, but Cady sensed the boat listing to starboard, and then the same to port as the pig shifted about on the wooden deck. She could still perceive the *Juniper's* intimate moods like this, after so long a parting, and it excited her tremendously. The vibrations of the engine rose up through her feet, into her legs, her stomach, her chest. *Lovely old Junie, beautiful old girl, still going strong.* Cady felt the breeze on her face. Damn good sailing weather. Pity she was wasting it on a ferry ride, crossing the estuary towards the south bank; but still, it had to be done.

She was sitting in the open afterdeck of the ferry, beneath a blue-and-white striped awning. This was far preferable to the passenger cabin, amidships, where the schoolboy sat with his face pressed against the glass. She liked the salt tang of the air and the spray of water on her skin. But she did have to share it with the pig. Great fat wallowing beastie!

The morning sun was low over the waters. The skirls waited patiently on their favourite posts. Cady knew that the birds would eat potatoes, if nothing tastier was around: the farmer with the pig had also hauled five sacks of spuds aboard. At least the pig had taken its eyes off her, that was a blessing. The farmer himself sat diagonal from Cady, face impassive, as he chewed on a wad of tobacco. Behind him the dragon ensign fluttered on the stern mast. The cabin girl scampered here and there. Once or twice she almost fell in the water but always caught hold of a stanchion or cleat in time. Cady turned to view the schoolboy. He had a haughty look in his eye. It was true, she wasn't looking her best, if she had a *best*, but she had made a little effort, for instance brushing the stains of last night's tater hash from her smock. After all, this was an important day.

They were halfway across the estuary. Another ferry passed them in the opposite direction, heading for Anglestume. This was the *Juniper's* sister ship, the *Ibraxus*. The two vessels swapped a blast of their whistles. Cady smiled. Lord of all the Flowers, that was a good sound to hear! The pig oinked in return, and overly roused, promptly had a shit on the afterdeck, a great steaming lump of it. The cabin girl swooped into action with pan and brush. With a practised hand she threw the offending matter overboard. That was enough: Cady stood up and entered the cabin, walking through to reach the opposite door that led to the wheelhouse. The captain nodded at her, his hands nudging the wheel this way and that, keeping the boat steady.

"Arcadia."

"Jed."

A moment passed. Cady eyed the boat: thirty feet long, prow to rudder, six and a half feet at the beam. Built by GW Dockerell & Sons of Ludwich, fifty-four years ago. Launched the year after. Cady Meade stepped aboard as a deckhand at the age of twenty-four, when the vessel was a decade old. Within three years she was the sole owner, with a deckhand of her own, an Ephreme kid named Amos. Dead now, he was. Taken by the river in his sixteenth year on the planet.

"New engine, I see. Diesel."

The captain shrugged. "Had to."

"The old one served her well."

"Broke down, last December. Near fell apart."

Neither of them allowed a single expression on their faces. But Cady studied the captain with keen interest. Jed Pennebrygge was a man more recognisable in profile than portrait. This was on account of his nose, broken in his youth and badly mended by a ship's doctor in a force nine gale. A large bump at the top, squished in at the bottom, it really was an ugly thing. Still, the rest of his face was nicely proportioned, and his hair was still thick, made grey and wiry by the years of sea air. His robust beer belly pressed against the wheel. Cady liked that. Once, in another time, he and she had shared a bed. A hammock, actually. She remembered the night with affection, as no doubt did he. Nevertheless, neither of them spoke of it. Not ever.

"Plenty of empty seats," Cady observed. She rubbed it in: "Nine of them."

"I charge one and a half for the pig, on account of the weight. And a quarter each for the sacks of produce."

"I was always full capacity, spring, summer, autumn."

"Well, those days have gone, for sure."

She studied the engine and the funnel, loving the sight of the pistons moving up and down and the gleam of the oil. "You've kept her spick and span. I'll give you that."

"Aye."

"How's the bilge?"

"Tared her myself, not three months back."

"What about Mr Carmichael? He's still living down there, I hope."

"Oh yes."

"You feeding him?"

"Shrimp, mussels, bloodworms. As per your instructions."

"Um." Cady was eager to find something wrong. "Shame about the pig shit."

"You know how it is: pigs shit on the outside, men and women... on the inside."

"That's philosophical."

"Oh aye." A slight pause. "I have time to think."

He made an adjustment of the wheel as a sudden wave thrust itself against the port beam. The wind was picking up, blowing in from the sea. The south-side jetty was now in sight. Cady's fingers twitched. She longed to take over, but not because he was doing badly – no, Jed Pennebrygge was a fine sailor – but just because the *Juniper* was calling to her: every vibration, every clunk of the crankshaft, every lurch of the deck.

"I'm wishing now," she said: "that I'd never sold her to you." She laughed, to make it seem like a joke.

"I wish you hadn't. Surely."

"That so?"

He groaned. "Terrible arthritis, I have. And not to mention the lumbago."

"You should take a day off now and then."

"I do, Arcadia. I do. Weekends. That pal of yours takes over."

"Pal of mine?"

"Yanish."

Cady spat and hissed. "That sniffling thimbleful of dragon

snot! How dare he! Oh, my flabber is well and truly gasted!" She kicked at the binnacle, setting the compass needle atremble. "He never told me any of this."

"Good lad. Knows the boat."

"Of course he bloody well knows the boat! I taught him everything."

"I've passed a few things his way myself—"

She kicked out again. "I'll tan his stringy pockmarked Azeelian hide for him!"

Pennebrygge gave her a sideways smile. "What's wrong, Arcadia? You're not jealous, are you?" There was a flash of mischief in his eye. It caused her to snarl at him.

"Keep your eye on the jetty, for Lud's sake!"

Without thinking, Cady took over at the helm, pushing Pennebrygge's hands off the wheel. The *Juniper* made a smooth swing to starboard, bumping nicely against the fenders, allowing the cabin girl to cast a mooring line over a bollard. The schoolboy leapt the gap between boat and jetty with ease and started off at a run towards a bus stop where some other kids in uniform were waiting. A gangplank clattered down, and there was a commotion as the pig, the farmer and the five sacks of spuds made their way to dry land, one heavy object at a time. Cady was the last to disembark, reluctant in her bones. She said to Pennebrygge, "Did you see me there, Jed? I've still got the knack, haven't I?"

To which the reply came, "My love, you were always the best of us. Always." And her insides gave a little flutter, like a flower opening or a butterfly taking flight, or some such rot! Curse that man!

Ten minutes later she was walking along the bankside lane, moving upriver. The way ahead narrowed to an overgrown pathway, an enclosed tunnel through the trees.

Speckles of sunlight made their way through the branches. The river could not be seen, only heard. A bird sang in the thicket. On a leaf was a globule of cuckoo spit. Cady pushed gently at the bubbly mass until she saw the yellow spittle bug inside its little nest. This gladdened her so much that she couldn't help but lick the spit off her fingertips. To any curious predator it tasted horrible, but Cady quite liked it. It stirred the spirit. Her heart beat proudly, her green heart, which resembled in shape the bulb of a plant, its network of tubers and fibres feeding every part of her body.

Voices came through the trees: the sound of prayer. The destination was close at hand. Cady steeled herself. A few yards of struggle brought her out into the open. Before her stood the church of St Aethel the Martyr. The steeple clock told her it was five past nine. A gathering stood around a grave, the prayer silent now, as heads were bowed. This was a Wodwo churchyard, so the graves were marked not by stone or cross, rather by wickerwork figures, male or female in outline, with a few smaller in size, representing children. Many of the figures were decorated with garlands and lace handkerchiefs and glass jewels, their leafage shaped into topiaric representations of the person buried beneath, while other effigies lay in disrepair. As she walked to the older part of the graveyard at the rear of the church, Cady felt she was entering the womb of the green world.

A stone wall enclosed the churchyard. The lychgate was locked, as it always was, but Cady had brought the key with her, the brass key she kept hidden in her room, taped to the bottom of a drawer. Very few people came this way. She closed the gate after her and took a path through Rothermuse Woods. The oldest tree in the woods was a bruised, bent and leafless yew. She stopped before it.

There was a mirror hanging on a nail knocked into the bark. The vicar of St Aethel's cleaned the glass with a damp cloth once a week. Cady took off her bowler hat and hung it on the nail, hiding the mirror's face. This done, she hurried on, suddenly impatient. It didn't take long to reach the clearing. A lone effigy stood there, its metal and wickerwork body covered in the vines and tiny pink and white petals of the haegra flower, the plant's ancient roots fed by an underground tributary of the Nysis. The figure's head was woven from bindroot stalks. This was Cady's very own effigy, fashioned by herself in her own image. A somewhat cruddy amateurish mishmash of an image it had to be said, looking more like her drunken lopsided down-in-the-gutter self than her sober self. One of the metal struts was decorated with a series of notches, each older than the last, and each one carved by Cady on her previous visits here. They marked out her true age. It was useful, because she always forgot; she was so used to telling people that she was seventy-six, seventy-seven, seventy-eight. And my, how the years blurred together! But now she made the calculation, feeling the weight of the numbers as they climbed higher. For she was born in the Year of Separation, when Kethra was ruled by King Yarrow, and the land was locked in endless wars; when the Alkhym first rose to power, and the clang of sparks flew from sword and pike against shield, and blood flowed freely in the River Nysis.

Arcadia Meade was one thousand, four hundred, and eighty-six years old.

Her heart raced. When she stepped out of the effigy, she would take her penknife and make another notch. For as the scriptures tell it: day by day, the roots return to the seeds.

Right then. She unhooked the loop of wire that acted as a latch and pulled at the door of the effigy. The whole front half swung open. She turned around and stepped backwards into the figure, pulling the door to against her bosoms, belly and thighs. It was a snug fit. She felt the onset of claustrophobia, and the fear, of course. The usual fears. No, she'd never gotten used to it, no matter how many times she underwent the process. But within an hour, Lud willing, she would feel herself renewed, younger in both body and spirit. She would turn up for the return trip on the ferry and give Jed Pennebrygge a nice little shock, yes indeed! In such manner, she prepared herself.

Clusters of haegra thorns were positioned on each side of the effigy, halfway down, that her wrists might press against them. Her inner wrists, that tender flesh where the blood pulsed. It was a little awkward, twisting her arms around. Her knees ached. Sweat sprung out on her skin. But now all was ready. She took a deep breath.

A small bird, a winnet, landed on the effigy's shoulder, close to Cady's face. She tried to shoo it away with a blowing noise, but the bird was singing merrily. So then she let out a great shout, which startled the creature, causing it to flutter off into the trees. At the same time as the cry came from her lips, Cady's hands jabbed violently sideways, left and right.

Her wrists thrust hard against the thorns.

The hooks dug into her flesh.

Her blood was thick, almost syrupy, and coloured a dark sickly green – turning crimson as the air mixed with it. The big red droplets fell onto the white petals, onto the vines, the wicker, into the soil. Cady's body arched backwards, constrained by the cage. Then she jerked forward. Her eyes popped wide open, the pupils almost disappearing into the upper lids. Her teeth were gritted, where she had teeth to grit: the rest was blackness in her mouth.

The tendrils of the plant tightened further, seeking their way through the wicker support. She felt their innumerable thorns pricking at her flesh, on her arms, her neck; her face, creeping inside her clothing, down her spine, around her legs. Now her eyes were closed and her mouth had settled into a fixed narrow line. Finally, her body was at rest. Her last thoughts were of the elements she had discovered in her dream. What was the task that bound those three items together? Hopefully, when she emerged, and when she was young again, and bright, and strong, then it would all make sense. Her voice ebbed away.

Church bell… gravestone… bomb…

Church bell… gravestone…

Church bell…

And then silence inside and out.

The leaves shivered as a breeze blew into the clearing. Other than that, nothing moved. The animals and birds kept away, perhaps aware that something untoward was streaming along the veins of the world, between flesh and flower. Everything would now be made anew.

A light rain fell, lasting a few minutes only. It dampened the dirt and got the worms crawling. The sun rose higher in the sky. One side of the clearing was shadowed.

A spell was underway. From the dank soil, from the memories of the witches of Dark Eden, from the gardener priests of the Wodwo clan as they huddled around their camp fire in the days of snow and iron. From the flow of sap, from the river's tides. From the Deep Root. Aye, and from the dreams of the Old Ones, as they fell to earth in Year of First Arrival.

Cady received it all. Such was the Code of the Haegra, as laid down in the ancient texts.

Around the half-hour mark she gave a great heave, pressing herself against the wicker. Her mouth opened as though to scream, but no sound came forth. Her eyes remained closed, but were screwed up tight into fierce ridges of flesh. Her hands spasmed, almost pulling free of the thorn's grip. It was soon over, this convulsion, and then she fell back into sleep.

All was quiet, all still.

One by one the birds and insects returned to the clearing. Unattended, a thin trickle of brackish blood ran down from Cady's left nostril.

Nine minutes later the vines slithered loose from Cady's body. Now she stirred, her chest rising and falling with sudden breaths.

Her eyes opened, peeking out through the leaves.

Blink, blink.

Testing her fingers. One, two, three…

Spitting out saliva the colour of amber resin.

She put her first thoughts together.

Who am I? What is my name?

The answer came quickly, which pleased her.

Cady.

Arcadia Meade.

That was enough for now, an adequate amount of knowledge. Anything else would be painful. Not until she had loosened herself from the wicker enclosure. She pulled her hands away from the thorns and felt their final sting as the flesh clung on.

Memories, memories…

Yes. She was still herself. All good. A little hazy at the edges, that was all.

Suddenly, the horrors kicked in and she started to panic and to push against the cage of twigs. Something was wrong. The structure was tightening again, surely, yes, all around her, against her neck and skull especially. If she could only get one good clean breath, she might be alright, but it was hopeless, and her throat closed up. The effigy rattled from side to side. One hand was trapped, the other fumbled at the wire loop, the way out. No escape. It was like being buried alive but in the full light of day, with no one around to help her, to save her! But then her fingers caught at the loop and she tumbled out of the effigy, breathing at last, pulling every last gasp of air into her lungs. Stupid, stupid! Why had she panicked so!

For a good while Cady remained as she was, bent over, her hands on her thighs. Her hands, trembling; they didn't look right somehow. Liver spots, crinkled skin, brown patches. The old cuts and long-ago scars. Broken fingernails. All still there, the skin map of the years.

Warts and all.

A line of thin creamy vomit dribbled from her chin.

She raised her hands to her face, feeling the deep lines and wrinkles at brow and cheek. She knew them all so well, every last pockmark and blemish, the mole on her neck, the three wiry hairs growing from it. The runnel where the fisherman's knife had struck her, that time, that time…

Long ago.

She made her stumbling way along the path, to the yew tree where the mirror was hanging. There was a semaphore beetle sitting on her bowler hat, its dazzling multicoloured body making a mockery of her own greyness. It flew away as Cady knocked the bowler to the soil. Then she held the mirror with both hands, one on each side, and gazed deeply of what she saw: herself, her old self. Nothing had changed. If anything, she was even more haggard than usual. Yes, clapped out, knackered, past her prime, the old nag, hag, harridan, crone, chiv, harpy, fishwife, termagant – all the things people liked to call her. There it was, the same goddamn visage. Herself! *Oh bloody hell.* She'd been hoping for twenty years old, younger even, or twenty-five at the most. Last time she'd come back as a seventeen year-old, for Lud's sake! Instead, here she stood: Cady Watchwoman Meade, seventy-eight years old.

This had never happened before. Not once. Not once in all her regrowths.

She started to scratch at her arm, her left forearm, it was itching like crazy. She really needed to get her nails dug in, so painful it was and no matter what she did, it never went away, and that was that. She did a little stamping dance, one step, two steps. All her bodily irritation had gathered in one spot alone. She pushed up her sleeve and saw the bump on her arm, right in the middle of her tattoo of a sea monster. The pustule was halfpenny-size, discoloured, almost purple. The skin stretched tight. She'd never seen the like before. Not there this morning, that was a fact. So then, maybe some weird effect of the failed regrowth? Or some other ailment, typical of her age, her hellish sodding age! Her fingers pressed at the hard lump. Some intrusion had made itself at home beneath her skin. She was being invaded, infiltrated.

She stood there, her legs aching and her face slick with sweat. Her spine was one long spasm of pain, arse to neck. *I am alone. I am alone in this work.*

Cady sank to the ground.

Gods in the earth and the roots, I don't have the strength for this, whatever you have planned for me, how can I carry on? I am too old. My body is weak.

Her fingers clawed at the damp soil.

Dance of the Sprite

All around, the lights flickered and danced in their many colours, but Cady saw them only as a blur at the edges of her vision. Likewise, the fizzes, pops, whizzes and clicks and shouts and cries of delight and anguish: heard as a wash of sound, far-off. Only the three tumblers meant anything to her, with their ever-changing symbols.

Cherry, crown, cloverleaf.

She fed in another penny and pulled the handle of the one-armed bandit.

Bell, horseshoe, plum.

And again:

Plum, cherry, crown.

Again:

Bell, stone, cloverleaf...

Over and over:

Crown, cherry, plum.

Bell, cherry, cloverleaf.

Bell, stone, bomb.

Cherry, cherry... crown.

Damn it to hell and back! So close!

That was the last of her coins. With a curse she stumbled

away from the machine, walking at a slant as though aboard a ship, prowling the aisles of the amusement arcade, bumping into people, staring at their faces, grabbing them, hoping only to locate the young lady in the change booth: she needed more pennies, more pennies! But the booth seemed to have vanished down some long glittering corridor of lights and noise. Her hand dug in her pocket for her purse, suddenly worried about her pension. She had collected it this morning, hadn't she? It was all a bit fuzzy. Yes, phew, there it was, what little was left of it! She waved a ten-bob note around, asking that someone give her pennies in exchange, and lots of them, just to continue on her quest for a big win. But there was nobody. Men shouted at her, women snarled, horrible little brats pointed and prattled.

She was sad and drunk by now. A couple of pints in the *Westward Ho* had helped with that, and then the half bottle of rum she'd purchased, now drained. Too old, too damn old, that was the trouble. Some petrified specimen, crinkled, ready for the grave. Oh death come embrace me, that I might kick you in the balls. That damn Captain Pennebrygge! She had waited at the south-side jetty for the *Juniper* to return, but the bloody thing hadn't turned up, not at all, and then more waiting, cursing, the other passengers at the quay backing away from her, until finally the Ibraxus had pulled into the jetty. All aboard, all aboard! That pug-faced old coot of a captain blowing the whistle, but it just wasn't the same, nothing like the *Juniper*, not ever.

She took off along a different aisle, her body leaning away from the direction of travel. Her voice was high and off-pitch in a sea shanty.

I once knew a lass, her hair was red
She worked her passage in the captain's bed.

But that caused even more offence, for some reason. All these faces in a haze. The lights and the flashes of colour and the raucous music and the slot machines pinging and zinging and whirring and purring... *Jackpot!* Some lucky geezer had spun up three crowns on the very machine she'd just vacated and the coins tumbled into the little metal dish and then overspilled onto the floor. But that was hers, most surely, that was Cady's money! She had nursed those tumblers with great tenderness. A scuffle ensued, but the man was wiry and wired and he wanted his winnings, and so Cady spun on her way from one machine to the next, the lights flashing on and off all around, whichever way she looked. Now she stood swaying before a pinball machine, suddenly fascinated. The display panel showed a stylised cartoon version of the death of the great dragon Haakenur and the rising of the ghost Faynr from the dragon's body. Faynr lay along the course of the River Nysis, whose waters flowed onto the playing area of the machine. A young kid was playing the game. *Ding. Ding, ding!* But it was one particular light that held Cady's attention, amid the greens, golds and reds. A small violet globe of sparks that hovered by itself in the air above the machine.

It was the girl's toy; Cady saw that now. The sprite.

Lovely Brin's lovely little light of love.

It came close to Cady's face. She might almost reach up and pluck it from the air!

But the sprite took off on its own path.

Cady pried off her bowler, wiped her brow, put her hat back in place. Then she followed the sprite outside. The frontage of the Palace of Fun dazzled the eyes with its sleek façade and candy-coloured lettering. But Cady had her own light to follow, along the pier, along the prom. She was huffing and puffing as she tried to keep up, but soon enough they reached the docks. The sprite slipped through a knothole in a wooden fence. Cady followed, pushing open a gate onto a boatyard. For a moment she only stared ahead.

The *Juniper* was sitting on a pair of large trestles, the keel of the hull a foot or so above the concrete floor of the yard. A ladder rested against the stern gunwale. Pulleys and chains hung down from overhead beams, connected to the heavy-duty winch that sat in a corner. A workbench was piled high with a jumble of tools and half-dismantled boat parts. The air was rich with the smells of engine oil and tar and seaweed. Jed Pennebrygge was standing near the exposed rudder, talking to another man: this was Yanish.

So it was true, her friend had been helping out on the ferry.

They were inspecting the propeller. There was a loud clanking sound from inside the boat: someone was working on the engine.

"What the effin' bloody cockin' hell is going on?"

The two men turned to see Cady standing by the gate. They both recoiled from her dark green looks and her wild eyes. "Captain Pennebrygge," she snarled, "I was waiting for you at the quayside for my return trip, as promised, as paid for."

"It was a free trip, no cost—"

Cady spluttered. "I was most incon… incon…" With a mighty effort she put the syllables of the word together: "Inconvenienced! Incon-fuckin'-venienced!" And then, after a breath to recuperate: "Well, sir? Will you speak?"

GOGMAGOG

64

He tried. But failed after a stuttering start.

She turned her attention to Yanish, who was busily combing his hair into place, a sure sign of nervousness. "And you, you tuppeny shit, shagging my wife behind my back! How dare you!"

"What? What are you saying?"

"She's referring to the *Juniper*, I think," Pennebrygge said.

"Is that right, Arcadia—"

"Don't you *Arcadia* me!"

Pennebrygge informed Yanish, "I told her about you working for me, like, on weekends, and whatnot."

"That's right, he did." Cady came forward, her hands bunched into fists. "And it disgusts me. I feel sullied, all over."

Yanish stood close to her. He spoke in a gentle way. "I wanted to let you know, I really did, but I knew you'd go all dolly mixtures on me."

"Dolly mixtures?"

"Yeah, you know, crazy like—"

She pushed him aside. Her eyes had now locked onto the darling spark of violet light. The sprite was circling around the boat's funnel, before travelling on towards the stern. Here, it hovered about the top of a person's head. This head raised up a little until the eyes were seen peeping over the gunwale rail. It was the Alkhym girl, Brin.

"Now see, now I'm bewildered. What in the bollockin' blazes is going on?"

Nobody answered. The clanging sound was still coming from inside the *Juniper*'s hull. Cady looked from one face to another: Yanish, Pennebrygge, the girl.

Eventually, it was Pennebrygge who spoke: "The thing is, Arcadia, darling: good Yanish here, he made me an offer, only this morning, I could hardly refuse it, now could I, after what I said about my lumbago and my other complaints, as I told you?"

"An offer?"

"That's right."

"To do what, exactly?"

"Why, uh... to buy the boat off me."

For once, Cady was silent. Her mouth opened, and closed. Pennebrygge went on. "That's why, see, I never sailed back for you." He waited for a sign that this might placate her in any way. It didn't. "But the Ibraxus turned up on time, I'm sure. It wasn't too long a wait—

He suddenly ran out of words, for Cady had raised up a hand, palm outwards, almost touching his face. Her gaze turned from Pennebrygge to Yanish. And then to Brin, who was now climbing down the ladder. The banging sound had come to an end. Another figure appeared on the deck, the thin rubber skin clinging to his face marred with oil and dirt. The Thrawl. Lek. He waved to Cady, a large spanner in his hand. There was a strangely crooked smile on his face, something he had not practised enough, or more likely did not possess the correct instructions for, within that plastic skull of his.

Pennebrygge tried again: "All of which means, I am no longer captain of the *Juniper*."

Cady grunted.

Yanish girded himself. "Cady, it's like this—

"I know what it's like," she said, cutting him off. "Oh, I know what's it like. Brin and Lek here have put up the money, no doubt."

"It was a good offer," Pennebrygge said. "A more than generous amount."

The Thrawl slid down the ladder deftly. Cady looked at him. "And you Thrawl Lek, you'll be the new deckhand, is that it?" She laughed fiercely.

Lek responded in a flat tone: "I'm the chief engineer."

"Even worse, far worse."

Now her gaze settled on Yanish. "And you'll be wanting me to be the new skipper. As if I would do such a thing!"

"Actually..." His face hardened. "I'm the captain."

Cady spat on the concrete. Her phlegm glowed bright green amid the oil stains.

Yanish kept his cool. "But we are looking for a pilot, someone experienced."

"Oh yes?"

"To guide us safely through the ghost waters."

"And when the voices of the dead come calling? Or a great beastie rises up from the depths? What then?"

"The *Juniper* will prevail."

"Oh aye, she will, damn right. Lud bless and keep her. Junie will steam into Ludwich, flag flying, whistle blowing. But you lot..." She took in all present. "You lazy landlubbers, lollyheads, muckle-drinkers, pricks of the devil, quarterwits, musterfucks, buggerknaps, and general all-round spittle-arsed tolly-floppers!"

Brin gasped aloud. Lek covered the girl's ears.

Cady carried straight on: "You'll be writhing on the deck, screaming for mercy."

Everyone fell silent.

Cady licked froth on her lips. Her fingers snuck up her sleeve and scratched at the bump on her forearm. The heavily-spiced rum gurgled around her innards. It took all she had, not to throw up. And when next she spoke, her voice was a whisper.

"Man, machine, and child – crazy, crazy, every last one of you."

Only Yanish properly heard this last statement. He drew her to one side and spoke quietly, to herself alone. "Cady, I need to do this—"

"Don't touch me!" Cady pushed his hand away. "Oh, you're the big man all of a sudden, eh? The big tough-nut." She turned to the others. "Nothing but a bit of driftwood, he was, when I found him. Rank and damp and covered in bird shit. I've given him everything, I have, everything!" She fixed her attention back onto Yanish. "You think I'm not up for skippering, is that it?"

"Old chiv, your blade's getting rusty."

"My blade is keen! I'll scupper you with it, watch me!"

The young man stood his ground. "I'm the captain. And that's that."

They stared at each other, daggers in their eyes, glistening. But then Yanish drew her close again. And he said, "Here's the thing. Mr Lek here, well he's of the opinion... that he can scan the shroud for me."

This caught Cady by surprise. "Your father's shroud?"

"That's right. Get the shadow read, nice and proper. All hunky dory, like."

"You need an Azeel priest to do that, surely?"

"Yeah, but you know they embellish, they weave a tale, they sweeten the poison with sugar. And what I need, is the full picture, the zig-zag-zig."

Cady looked over to the Thrawl, who stared back at her, his face in neutral.

Yanish carried on: "And then... Then I'll know for sure, won't I? Just what happened to my father, at the end, in those last moments of his life."

"And that what?"

"And then, if the story's a good one…"

"What do you think, your old man turns out to be a hero?" She laughed. "This isn't one of your crystal shows, you know? There's no happy ever after."

Yanish's eyes narrowed against the remark. He pushed on regardless: "And then, if the story's good, I'll have a priest transfer the shadow to silk. I'm going to rescue my father's honour."

Cady looked at him. She shook her head in disbelief.

"You little fluffwit. He's having you on. Look at him! This lump of tin and plastic and rubber? He can't read a shroud! Oh, there's a name for this, and it's not a nice one. *Scam.*"

The Thrawl reacted, sounding for all the world like a butler. "I can assure, you, madam—"

"Shut up."

"I have the very best of intentions."

"You must eat cake with your shithole, because all I'm hearing from your cakehole… is shit!"

They all looked at her, not knowing what to say.

The girl spoke first. "Mrs Meade, please don't talk to my butler like that."

Cady guffawed. "Oh, your *butler*. Oh my. Now there's the thing."

Brin gave her an imploring look. It was too much to bear and the old lady's feelings bubbled over. She let out a harsh cry from deep down in the roots of her being, causing a spray of black mist to speckle the air. Anger turned into fever. She scratched at the new growth on her arm, feeling sap or pus leaking from it. Her fingertips burned from the contact, and she felt faint. Everything seemed to be very far away, all except for Yanish's hands, reaching out for her. She cried out in horror. Somehow or other she backed away, to reach the *Juniper*. The curve of the hull matched the curve of her spine. The sprite was flying around Cady's head. She waved at it irritably.

"You sent that thing after me, eh, is that right?"

Brin nodded eagerly. "I did. I had to—"

"You bloody little spy!"

"But... But... But I want you to come along with us, on the voyage."

"Voyage? This isn't some Sunday outing up the river, you know?"

"Please, Mrs Meade."

But Cady snarled at her. "Go on, piss off!"

A look of shock came to the girl's face. She wiped at the droplets of spittle Cady had sent her way. Tears glistened in her eyes. Oh, for Lud's sake! And yet for a moment Cady felt like joining in, and she didn't have a clue why.

"Are you alright?" Lek asked of Brin.

The girl didn't answer. Her fingers had risen to the hesting points on her temples, left and right. Of course, she had not yet developed the full antennae, but the two spots were red raw and she rubbed at them fiercely. The shakes took charge of her. She could not stop shivering. Cady grabbed at the girl's shoulders, trying to hold her steady. "Stop it, stop it!" The command had no effect; in fact, it only made the quivering twitching trembling even worse. Which in turn made Cady's grip tighten. The two of them, old lady and young girl, were locked in a spasm dance.

Thrawl Lek stepped up to them both. He was wielding the heavy spanner as a cudgel. "Get away from her!" His facial expression was set to *Furious*, full measure.

Cady pressed herself against the *Juniper's* hull for comfort.

The Thrawl's eyes were red and red only, bright as fire. Cady had time to speak one sentence – "The girl needs to know the truth." – before Lek took a swing at her. He missed by one quarter of an inch. The head of the spanner dug into the *Juniper's* hull. A sliver of wood flashed past Cady's face. Brin screamed.

The Visitor

Moonlight patterned the floor. The window was open and a cool breeze fluttered the ghost of the lace curtain. From the roof opposite a night bird called for a mate, receiving no answer. Cady woke up and automatically groped for her glass of vinegar. But the bedside table was empty. Her eyelids would scarcely part. It took a minute or so to realise it was still nighttime. Something had roused her, a noise perhaps, and she sat up in bed. The corners of the room were softly shadowed. Was that a figure sitting there in her armchair?

She called out, "Yanish? What are you doing here? Yanish?"

There was no answer.

But now the visitor stood up and took two paces across the floor. Cady's entire body was rigid with fear. A scream filled her throat to bursting, but her jaw would not work to let it out. She knew in that moment how death must feel, the real death, the one she had cheated for so long, so very long. Was it catching up with her now? Oh Lud, yes. Her body was seizing up! Her eyes were filled with sleep dirt and salt crystals, and would not close to keep the darkness at bay.

All she could do was stare ahead.

The visitor walked to the wall and stood before Yanish's painting of the Night of the Dragon. The colours of the image seemed to glow with their own light, even though the moonlight did not reach that far. The dragon Haakenur rose up beyond the House of Witan, and the yellow clock-face of the tower seemed the eye of a Cyclopean demon, angry, staring, accusing.

Now the figure, still draped in darkness, turned to face Cady. The shadows crept away from the face, revealing the Alkhym child Brin. She held in her grasp a handbell, which she rang, raising and lowering her arm in a slow steady rhythm. But there was no sound, not in the room, only a muffled *jang, jang, jang,* inside the old lady's head. The first element of the riddle, repeated to her. It was either a call to arms, or a warning.

Cady could now move. Carefully, slowly, she drew herself from the sheets and placed her feet on the floor. Her shadow was a quivering tree-like shape on the wall. The river charts lay on the table. Her skin was loose and mottled and formed in dark ridges, a map itself. The tattoos on her skin were a portrait of her life, in different episodes.

She went over to the figure.

The girl's face was perfectly formed, and yet it trembled, not quite made of flesh. It crumbled and reformed, or tried to. Cady watched in fascination. Brin was actually made from the seeds of the never-never flower, many thousands of them, gathered into this one space to sculpt this figure in the air. The bell continued to chime, that constant calling.

Jang, jang, jang. Join us, join us. Jang, jang.

At the next stroke the figure drifted away, skin, clothes, handbell and all, escaping through the open window. Cady stood alone. She saw the funnel of a never-never plant poking up from a gap in the floorboards. It was a stunted version, looking more like a fungus from outer space. Was she still asleep, still dreaming? Her hand went to the pustule on her forearm, scratching at it. The fingers moved on, finding another bump a little further up her arm. One, two. How many more would there be?

The river on the charts flowed in blue ink across the paper.

The tide pulled at her.

A True and Full Name

Cady sat in the *Juniper's* cabin. Through the window she could see Yanish at the helm, working the wheel. His back was to her. She placed her hands flat on the table, picking up the vibrations of the boat's engine. She saw them clearly in her mind, these lines of force, rather like the patterns a magnet reveals in iron filings. The cardboard tube with the shroud inside it was lying beside her on the seat. She stood up, lifted up the bench and placed the shroud in the storage locker, alongside the charts and the boat's papers and various other odds and ends. Then she went out onto the afterdeck. The awning flapped gently above her head. The last of the morning mist was blowing away as sunlight slowly heated the Nysis. They were moving upriver at a steady pace, helped along by the early morning tide. She lifted her hands high and grabbed on to whatever years months weeks days of life she might have left. She looked like a madwoman trying to catch an invisible balloon. A cry of defiance came from her lips.

Something hit the hull with a hard crack. And then again, the same sound.

There were two pipsqueak scuttlers on the bank, throwing stones at the *Juniper*. They stood on a waterside tip amid a detritus of industrial parts, and broken hulls and masts.

"Bugger off, you little sods!"

Cady raised her fist at them, and then had to duck as a stone almost hit her on the head. Her pipe fell from her pocket. She bent down to retrieve it and felt a sudden crick in her back.

"Oh Mother of Lud!"

The lads' rude chants sounded in her ears. Cady rallied, and fired off her own volley. "Go and get stuffed, you arse-wiping, shit-eating, tallow-sniffing, chiffer-chaffing, sons-of-whores! I'll feed you to the five-legged mare!" In reply to which a fusillade of stones hit the decking with increased force, some of them landing on the awning above with dull thuds. Cady beat a retreat to the cabin, cursing childkind for its inerrant nastiness.

Presently, Omega Point hove into view on the north bank.

Two figures – one tall and thin, the other half that height – were standing on the jetty, their suitcases in hand. Cady threw the mooring line to them, and Lek and Brin working together dropped it over the bollard. They came aboard and settled their belongings into the cabin. The girl was dressed in a new outfit, a little cleaner than yesterday's: baggy trousers and a white blouse with a bit of frill to it under a navy-blue jacket, and a bobble hat squeezed over her hair. It was a nice outfit, even if everything was a bit tatty. Brin smiled broadly with surprise when she saw Cady. Lek gave out a more punishing look and then bent down to inspect the engine and to chat with Yanish. Cady stood near the cabin door, not knowing quite what to do. The girl blurted out, "Mrs Meade! I didn't know you'd be here."

"As I stand, here I am."

"But you ran away yesterday."

"I did not."

"You ran away screaming."

"I was not screaming. You were screaming. Blue murder, it was."

"We were both screaming. And that's that."

Cady harrumphed loudly. She couldn't keep a scowl from her face, no matter how she tried. Bloody little tyke! Her stomach churned. She had an urge to scratch at the two pustules on her arm, but managed to resist. And the kid was still looking at her, still giving her that stupid grin.

"What have you got there, Mrs Meade?"

"Eh? Oh, this..." Cady was holding a triangle of rag, which she unfolded with some care and attention. "It's my old flag," she said. "The dragon ensign. Every vessel has to fly it, by law."

The flag hung from her hands – moth-eaten, bullet-riddled, bloodstained, burnt at one outside corner, and ripped at another. It was a plain blue in colour except for the left top quarter, which displayed the Kethran national emblem: Great Haakenur the Dragon in full flight.

"Do we tie it to the pole?"

"We run it up the mast, if that's what you mean."

Brin nodded. "Can I help?"

Cady struggled mightily to stop herself from frowning. "Aye, come on, then." Every word was an effort. But she led the girl to the stern and showed her how to lower the existing flag and replace it with this new one. Of course, *new* wasn't quite the word for it. "It doesn't look like it's going to last very long," Brin observed. "It might wither away."

"Aye, it's seen some action. You see that nasty rip in it, a cutlass did that. At the Battle of Mystique."

Brin rolled her eyes. "The Battle of Mystique! Don't be silly. That was centuries ago. In the Year of the Whirlpool."

"That's right. I was standing next to Admiral Baxter when the Enakor marines boarded us, their cutlasses unsheathed."

Brin looked up at her puzzled, but Cady was far away, in her eyes, in her mind.

"Oh look!" The girl's attention suddenly shifted. She was pointing across the flats, where a vehicle could be seen rattling along the road at speed.

"Who the hell's that?" Cady took out her eyeglass and sighted down it. "I can't get my eyes in focus. You have a look, girl, tell me what you see."

Brin took the eyeglass and peered through it. "It's the shopkeeper. Mrs Duncliffe." She read aloud the wording on the delivery van's side. "*Duncliffe's. Purveyors of finest quality groceries and household goods.* I ordered some things from her. For the journey."

The blue van pulled up just beyond the jetty. Lek jumped down from the boat and ran along the jetty to help Fable tip a tea-chest over the lip of the van. This done, she waved at Cady, and shouted, "Alright, my dear? Grand day for it."

Lek balanced the chest on his shoulder easily, and carried it aboard.

Cady leaned over the gunwale to chat. "You've changed your tune, haven't you? The other day you were saying you wanted nothing to do with Thrawls."

"I have put my distaste aside, momentarily," Fable replied in a haughty manner. She quickly reverted to her usual Wodwodian drawl: "Because why, the kid's got money."

"I know that. She's bought the blooming boat!"

"Mr Lek keeps it in a…" Fable's voice lowered to a whisper. "…in a secret *compartment*, somewhere on his body."

"What do you mean, up his arse?"

The shopkeeper preferred to change the subject. "Cady, I hear it's worse than ever on the river, especially past Woodwane Spar. I'm worried for you."

"I wasn't going to come along, it's true."

"What changed your mind?"

"I had a visitor in the night."

"Ooh, I haven't had a night visitor, not since Fred Haycastle passed away, Lud bless him."

"Not that kind of visitor."

"What kind then?"

"The… the *seedy* kind."

This only increased Fable's curiosity, but Cady would not answer further. She looked out over the salt marshes, empty now of all figurations. The never-nevers had gone back to sleep in the heart of the Deep Root, having done their job and roused her to strife and puzzlement. Even last night, sending a messenger, a reminder.

Fable leaned against the door of her van, waving as the *Juniper* chugged away from the jetty. Cady stood in the stern, watching the shopkeeper and the van and Omega Point dwindle into the distance. Anglestume – her home of the last two years – was already lost in a haze. Soon they would leave the Isle of Pinchbeck behind as well. She had a sudden wonder, about when she might see it again. If ever. And so, as they must, yesterday's events came back in earnest, one painful memory at a time, and she felt the weight of human flesh decaying upon her bones. The regrowth ritual had failed. Why? It just didn't make sense.

"What doesn't?"

She turned and saw the girl standing at the cabin door. "Uh?"

"You were talking to yourself, Mrs Meade. You said it doesn't make sense."

"It doesn't matter," Cady said. "Nothing. It doesn't matter." And then, in a harsher voice: "Go on, scarper, you little brat."

The kid retreated back into the cabin. Cady's head bowed down, and she stared at the decking. One hand reached into her sleeve to scratch at the two strange growths. A wave of cold fear ran through her. Her stomach cramped as tight as Fable Dundliffe's purse, and droplets of black sweat seeped from her pores.

Oh Lud, the years, the years… and all the things forgotten…

Cady stood up straight, pulling herself together. The roll and rhythm of the *Juniper* did its best to mollify her. The journey was underway. It was a Thursday, the twenty-ninth of May, in the Year of Speculation.

They made good time and within half an hour the *Juniper* was steaming past Shorneholdings. An empty gasometer cut a skeletal silhouette against the pink-and-blue streaked sky. Lek had joined Cady on the afterdeck. He was leaning over the rail, gazing at the water, entranced by the tiniest eddy, whirl and ripple. She asked him what he was doing.

"Analysing the river."

She guffawed. "The Nysis speaks to me, direct line."

Lek kept to his studies. "I'm looking for patterns beyond the wind and the pull of the moon."

"What on earth for?"

"I'm working out our expected time of arrival."

Cady smiled at this. "There's no way you can even know what's around the next bend. They don't call it the Winding

Way for nothing. And once we hit the ghost waters, all bets are off."

The Thrawl replied in a flat tone, "By my estimation, we should arrive at Ludwich by nine o'clock tonight."

"Nine o'clock! You'll be lucky. If at all."

A flustered look settled on Lek's face. It was strange to see it appear, arriving from within like a face at a foggy window. "I'm happy to adjust my calculations, as new information turns up."

Cady spat into the water. "What's your heart made of, cogs and gears?"

"Why do you say that?"

"You might have got Vanish on your side, but listen good; I'm made of hardier stuff."

Lek stared at her intently. He said, "You paint yourself as a true-born Wodwo, but I'm not so sure." His eyes emitted twin beams of light – sharp and tightly focused, a penetrating shade of blue – which started to scan down Cady's face and upper chest in a zigzag motion.

It worried her. "What are you up to?"

"Your skin is very tough, I must say. Like old leather. Or is it bark?"

"What are you doing, you pervert!"

"Seeing what you really are."

"Never you mind what I am—"

"Hm, lots of plant elements mixed with human. Interesting. And quite old, as well—"

"That's enough!"

"I'd like to do further analysis."

Cady raised her fists in a pugilistic stance. She glared at him. "I imagine you're too heavy to swim?"

"Why would you ask—"

"I'm about to tip you over the side."

Lek's face twitched, reminding Cady of a machine that was breaking down. He shifted rapidly through his full set of facial expressions, seeking the correct one. It couldn't be found. And this upset him even more. His voice squeaked. "Just get Brin and me to Ludwich in time for the Hesting festival, tomorrow at noon. That's the deal we've struck with Yanish, the *captain*."

The emphasis on the last word rankled her. She said, "Do you know how maddening the ghost waters can be, these days?"

"Of course. I lived in Ludwich for many years."

"There's a reason the Government closed that section of the River Nysis down. Poor Faynr is very, very sick." She shook her head. "And it's even worse than you remember."

"So?"

"How could you even think of letting a child undertake such a thing?"

Now a shiver of doubt passed over Lek's face, or at least the programmed version of doubt. Cady was learning to pick up the signals he gave off.

His eyes glowed fiercely. "It's my job to look after Brin. I will do so. I made a promise."

"Is that what you were doing the other day, when you shut down?"

"I didn't... I didn't shut... down."

"You were out for ten minutes. The kid showed me the bullet in your head."

By now the Thrawl was opening and closing his mouth repeatedly, as though he'd lost control of the mechanism. Cady came close to him. She said, "There's something going on here, isn't there? Something untoward. Eh, wiseacre? What have you done, kidnapped her?"

"I don't know what you mean—"

"You're lying to me."

"I'm incapable of lying."

For a moment, a look came to his face that was entirely cruel, and cold. His voice was drained of all human pretence:

Cady planted her feet firmly on the deck. "Bollocks of Lud! You Thrawl are just as bad as the rest of us. I mean to say, Lek, why the fuck haven't you been dismantled, or put in storage, eh? Like the rest of your brothers and sisters?"

"Not all of us—"

"Most of you, most of you!"

"My family…"

"Yes? Spit it out."

"The family I worked for… Brin's family… they have some influence…"

"Oh I see, fancy, are they? Above the law?"

He made to reply but then glanced aside as Brin came through from the cabin. She was looking at them both, perhaps sensing the tension between them. "What are you two talking about?" she asked.

"Oh, you know," Lek replied, "the wind and the tide and suchlike."

Proof enough, Cady thought: he can lie, even to the girl. Brin moved to the stern and climbed up onto the transom, where she clung to the flagpole as she gazed out at the boat's wake.

Cady leaned in close to the Thrawl, her voice a whisper: "This isn't over, Mister Machine. I'm going to undo your screws. I'm going to cut you open with a saw and dismantle your heart. Maybe I'll grind you down into metal shavings and let you blow away into the river. How would you like that?"

Lek stared at her. Cady pressed her lips right against his cold ear and said with a hushed snarl, "One thing's for damn certain. I'm going to find out what the fuck you're up to."

It seemed that Brin was listening, because she snapped round and said, "Are you two going to be squabbling like this for the whole trip?"

Cady made a mocking laugh. She jammed her bowler further down on her head. And just to prove some kind of ridiculous point, she climbed up onto the narrow ledge at the cabin's side, holding onto the grab rail that ran above the windows, moving along hand over hand. Wild heavens, she hadn't done this in a good long while! She hung out over the water and almost slipped, and by the time she clambered into the wheelhouse she was badly out of breath, and her hands were curled up into claws. Vexation took charge. Even the sight of Yanish at the wheel set her teeth on edge. How dare a deckhand usurp her like this? Oh, she would prove them all wrong before this journey was out. She would be Captain Cady once more, queen of the river!

"Archer's Bow coming up, old chiv," he said to her. "Didn't you point that out on your charts, the other evening? This is where you started your dream."

Cady wanted to wrench the wheel from his grip. But she took control of herself when she saw a vessel approaching on the port side, a pleasure craft converted into a sturdy little cargo boat with the use of corrugated metal sheets, and netting. Its decks were piled high with crates. The captain gestured to the *Juniper* as it passed and Yanish gave him a blast on the whistle. This was only the third boat they had seen, since Omega.

Cady said coldly, "Let me know when we reach Tivertara."

"Will do."

Brin had returned to the cabin. Cady went to join her, sitting down on the opposite bench. The kid was dipping into the tea-chest, laying out the tins of peaches, pineapple chunks, luncheon meat, corned beef, condensed milk, alongside bottles of pop, packets of ship's crackers, and a paper bag of sherbet lemons, Cady's second favourite boiled sweet. She said to the girl, "You've got a sharp eye for the swag, haven't you? We'll make a whip-jack of you yet."

"Mrs Duncliffe said she would need all this."

"Fable would say that. Her purse is always hungry. Any beer in there?"

"I can't see any."

"Gin, whiskey, anything like that? A nice drop of Jim Brimstone?"

"Nothing."

"Now that's a bastard. Ah well, I'll pick something up at Maddenholt."

Brin smiled. "Mummy always said it was rude to swear."

"Oh, you have a mummy, do you?"

There was the slightest tremor to the girl's face. "I think this is for you." She handed over a packet from the chest.

"Ah yes! Bosun's Choice Ready Rubbed Navy Cut. Good old Fable, she knows I would swap over to a pipe, once onboard." She took out an antique nose-warmer and started to stuff the bowl with baccy, working with neat precision. "Often I sit and smoke at my leisure and muse upon the vicissitudes of life, which are many and various."

Brin took all this in with interest. She asked, "So why do you swap over to a pipe, onboard?"

"Easier to load up. Under fire. Or in a storm."

"Are we expecting a storm?"

"Let's check the wireless."

She pointed over to the metal box in the corner of the cabin, its surface dented and a bit rusted here and there, with one of the knobs missing. Some of the stations marked on the dial had long since vanished from the ether. "Go on then, switch it on." Brin did so. The blue crystal mounted on the top lit up and started to pulse, as it attempted to pick up waves from the air. "One of my old buffs built this for me," Cady explained, with a little smile on her lips. "Way back when. A randy Ephreme bootlegger he was, whose name... oh dear... I can't remember it! What a dreadful tart I am! Anyway, this little machine's saved my bacon more than a few times." She picked up the microphone and spoke a mock alert into it: "Mayday, mayday! This is Cady Meade, Captain of the *Juniper*, Ludwich bound. I am a good-for nothing layabout, drunk and disorderly. I am puking my guts out, I am black with smoke, I am twirling in a whirlpool, and out of my mind on crone's poppy. Save me! Save me!"

Brin giggled. Her eyes took in Cady's lined and pockmarked face. She was rapt with attention for everything the old lady did. But Cady reacted badly. "For all the blood in Lud's wounds, stop looking at me!"

The kid jerked back from the words and their sudden viciousness. "But I was only..."

"I really don't need this, by the way. All this bother! All this fluff and bother! No, no! I should be at home right down, feet up, getting blotto."

Brin's head bowed down.

Cady looked around the cabin, taking in the row of brass ornaments she'd brought from her room for company, and the Night of the Dragon painting that now hung on a nail, and the two pairs of bloomers draped over a line of string. Yes, taking everything in, except for the girl.

"I don't understand, Mrs Meade? One minute you're nice to me, all smiles, and the next..."

"The next what? Don't leave a sentence hanging, it'll likely break its neck."

"The next horrible. Why are you like this?"

Cady grimaced at her own anger. "It's because, well... Oh, shut up, will you!"

Everything was painful: either liking the girl, or not liking her. "I don't get on with nippers, see? That's it. That's all."

"How old are you, Mrs Meade?"

"As old as my tongue, and a little bit older than my teeth."

"Well then, you must have children, or grandchildren, somewhere—"

"No, I bloody don't! And I'm too old now, to start being a mollycoddler."

"Well, I'm not a molly, and I don't need to be coddled."

Oh Lud, now the girl had put on a brave face and a brave voice. But her eyes were glistening, despite the effort. She reached out to the wireless and twisted the dial, seeking a clear broadcast. There was none. Only crackle. Brin looked disappointed. "I think it needs a new crystal."

There was a silence. Cady groped forward. She pointed to her own neck, saying. "Here, how do you like this for a lovely picture, eh?" She showed off the revealed tattoo. "Do you know what that is?"

"It looks like a rune, an old Wodwo rune?"

"You know the ancient languages, do you?"

"Lek is teaching me lots of things, two or three hours every day. It's so boring!"

"Well, this is the one known as *Kaah.*"

"Ha! There's no such rune with that name. You're making it up."

Cady's lowered her voice. "You know about infra-red, and ultraviolet, do you?"

"Special magical colours, beyond those the naked eye can see."

"This is the same idea. There are extra runes, before the first runes of the alphabet, and just beyond the last runes. Secret runes. But don't go telling Mr Tinplate any of this. Do you promise?"

The girl nodded, all agog.

"Now then, take the name of the dragon Haakenur, and spell it backwards. What do you get?"

Brin worked it out, and her eyes widened with delight. "Oh my, that's so special. It's so... it's so *secret*. It's like a secret code!"

"Exactly. The runekaah, as we call it. The symbol of the dragon's power. All of life, you see, is contained within the battle between Haakenur and King Lud. And sometimes I'm on Lud's side, and other times I side with the dragon, and that's it. That's my philosophy."

"What about Queen Luda? She's my favourite."

"Oh aye, she laid the very first stone of Ludwich city. Without her, we'd still be living in mud huts along the river."

Brin was very excited. "We used to do a lot of riddles, myself and Lek, in the big house. Working out special codes and puzzles and such."

"What is this *big house?*"

"It was called Blinnings. But I can't say too much about it. It's all very *hush hush.*"

The old lady watched the girl closely; one by one, she knew, all the secrets would come out.

"Come on, squirt, clear those tins away. I need to check my maps."

Cady lifted her charts from underneath the bench and set them out on the table, and spent a very pleasant ten minutes pointing out sunken wrecks, hidden sandbanks, and whirlpools. Brin's little sprite danced over the river's winding course.

"Where does Faynr start?" she asked.

"That will be chart number eight. Find it for me, will you."

Brin did so, and together they poured over that section of the Nysis. Cady's finger moved across the icon for St Kellina's church, and then a short distance past Hingle Bowl, until she landed on the symbol for a jutting spit of land at a place named Islinghurst Marsh.

"This is Woodwane Spar. And just beyond, see?" A wavery line marked the edge of the ghost waters, Faynr's territory.

"How long is the river, from there, to Ludwich?"

"Thirty-four miles."

Brin smiled broadly. "Faynr is so special. She's the only dragon's ghost in the whole world!" She washed down a cracker with a swig of Duncliffe's Finest Sarsaparilla.

Cady explained, "These charts were drawn up by two gentlemen, one called Maguire, and the other called Hill. Have you heard of them?"

"No."

"It's a sorry old tale. Mr Henry Maguire ended up as crazy as a bat in a biscuit tin."

"Why? What happened to him?"

"The two of them started out with one aim: to map the city and the river, to help travellers and sailors find their way. But Maguire was taken over by a different obsession. He became fascinated with trying to measure the true extent and nature of Faynr's body. But of course, being the ghost of a dragon, Faynr cannot be measured, not accurately. The task drove Maguire cuckoo."

"Did they lock him away?"

"Oh yes, they had to. They put him in Medlock Asylum. Dottyville. From what I know, he's still there, the poor thing, scrawling on the walls and floor, trying to complete his map of the city and the river, Faynr, and everything!"

They both fell into silence, contemplating in their old and young ways this impossible task. After a moment, Cady asked, "Are you looking forward to the Hesting festival?"

"Oh yes. I can't wait."

"It starts tomorrow, does it?"

Brin nodded. "At midday. Will you get us there in time, Mrs Meade?"

Cady answered truthfully. "We'll probably end up stuck in a mire, or swallowed by a fog beast, or stranded on Ludforsakenland."

The girl's eyes never left hers. "But still, you'll do your best? There's a chance?"

Cady's heart lightened, a feeling she hadn't had in a long time. "Oh, we'll battle on. And then, after the Hesting, well, you'll be a proper Alkhym young lady then, won't you? Your temples will be all aglow."

The girl nodded. But her eyes had taken on a cloudy look. Her hand was trembling over chart number eight.

Cady spoke carefully: "Brin. Is your mother alive?"

"Lek says I mustn't talk about that."

"You always do what he says?"

"I don't like it… Mrs Meade… it hurts."

"What does?"

The girl didn't answer. Her hands were shaking badly, her legs the same. Before Cady could even react, the girl was shuddering head to foot. She gripped the table's edge, desperately trying to hold her body still. It was no good, and her fingers lost their hold. She started to thrash around. Tins of food fell off the bench to the deck. The charts went flying. By now Cady had managed to move, and was reaching across the table. The merest touch froze Brin to the spot. Not a single movement. She was barely breathing. Cady felt helpless. Now the girl was murmuring to herself. Cady leaned in to listen, and was shocked by what she heard.

Just one word, a single word, spoken in a whisper, and then cut off.

Brin was soon shivering and shaking, even worse so than before. The word came again, over and over. Cady demanded, "What are you saying? Brin! What does it mean? Tell me." But there was no answer beyond the word itself. Cady thought to shout at her, to startle her into alertness; but then Thrawl Lek came in from the afterdeck. Immediately he took charge, pushing Cady out of the way. He took hold of Brin by the shoulders.

Cady asked of him, "What's wrong? What's happening to her?"

Lek didn't answer. He clasped Brin fiercely to him, but the shaking wouldn't stop. He spoke in a firm manner: "Sabrina? Sabrina Clementine? Can you hear me? Your full name is Sabrina Clementine Far-Sight Abigail... Can you hear me?"

"What are you doing to her?"

Lek hissed at Cady, making her back away. He went on

with his spell, or anti-spell, his voice gritty and cold and straining at the very edges of artificial life.

"Your true and full name is Sabrina Clementine Far-Sight Abigail Maid-Of-The-Vale Xiomara Delphine Poppy-Moth Mina-Moth Marion Hollenbeck Halsegger the Third."

By the end he was shouting, practically shrieking. But it was enough to silence the girl, and to calm her. Her breathing slowed, her eyes refocused. She looked around in a daze. "Did I go away, did I go away… where did I go?" The girl's voice was strange, otherworldly. She fell back against the seat, smiling to herself, almost at some inner joke.

The effects of the attack had soon passed.

But Lek made an angry noise, something no flesh and blood creature could ever make. He leaned in close to Cady's face. "What did you do to her?"

"It just started. I didn't touch—"

"Leave her alone."

Lek's cogs were spinning madly: they made a whirring sound in his chest. Gaining some half measure of control, he said, "Brin needs to hest. That's the only way you can help her."

Cady nodded. "I see that now."

"Otherwise, this will only get worse."

Yanish appeared at the door. For a moment he seemed confused by the scene in the cabin. But then he said, matter-of-factly, "Tivertara's coming up."

Cady was glad to get out of the enclosed space. "Good." She followed him out and looked over the side of the boat. Nothing could be seen, only the dark water flowing by and the spume of the wake. Brin joined her at the gunwale. She was still a little woozy, but she could speak well enough.

"What are you looking for?"

Cady didn't answer. But Yanish explained, "Cady reckons there's an underwater temple here. She saw it in a dream."

"Really? Let me see!" The kid stood on tippy-toes to lean over as far as she could. "What kind of temple?"

"An old one," Cady said. "It belonged to an Alkhym settlement, from the early days, when your people first left Ludwich city, going into exile."

Lek appeared at the wheelhouse door. "What's going on?" Nobody answered. They were all too busy, Yanish at the helm, Brin and Cady both looking down over the rail.

Yanish asked of Cady, "See anything?"

"Not yet. The river's too dirty."

But Brin shouted out, "No, I can see something! Look! Under the water."

Cady followed the girl's gesture. It took a moment for her eyes to focus, and then she too saw it. But it wasn't the temple she'd visited in the dream, with its pillars and central altar. No, this was a dark shape in the dark water. And it was moving! It looked like a long patch of waterweed, the length and the vague shape of a person, waving back and forth as it rose from the depths into view. No, not waterweed, for it appeared to be alive. It swam along beside the boat, still half-hidden.

"It's a voor!" Brin cried.

Lek said to her, "Now you know that's not possible, not here."

"I saw it in a picture book."

"Yes, but they don't live in this part of the river—"

"There! Look!"

The creature had risen fully to the water's surface. Brin jumped up onto the cabin's ledge, holding onto the grab rail and leaning far out over the water. Lek shouted after her: "Brin, get down, this minute!" He made to grab her but she scampered further along the ledge. Cady couldn't help but admire the girl's agility. But Lek wasn't having any of it. "Come back here!" Brin ignored him.

Cady called out to Yanish, "Dead slow ahead!"

The boat slowed almost to a halt.

But the thing had vanished from the water. Cady's eyes darted this way and that. "Where is it? I can't see it anymore."

"There, there!" Brin shouted.

Yes, there it was, clinging to the *Juniper's* hull. It certainly looked like a voor, but how could that be, so far from the ghost waters?

Brin cried out, "It looked at me!" And she leaned even further out over the water, disregarding Lek's orders. "Its eyes were sparkling. It was looking at me!"

The voor had the appearance of a long slimy body of fronds and river muck and effluent and twigs, with dead sparrows and fish caught in its mass. A swarm of midges flew above the shape, adding to its horrible nature. It moved in a sinuous manner, twisting and writhing. In colour it was dark green, and almost black in places with flashes of crimson and sickly yellow patches. It looked rotten and putrid, oozing a thick oily substance along its surface. But Cady could not yet see the eyes that Brin had mentioned. And then the fronds parted to reveal the creature's face, its green skin and whiskers, and a mouth with long spindly teeth and a black tongue. And eyes as black as the tongue, shining with speckles of white.

Lek had pulled the boathook from where it was lodged on the bulwark and was leaning over the side, trying to push the voor away from the *Juniper*, but the long pole was having little or no effect: the weeds of the creature's body simply parted around the hook, and then reformed.

And then Brin cried out, "Look, it's following me."

The girl moved her outstretched hand over the water. The voor did seem to be aware of her, swimming this way and that, mirroring the movements. Tiny sparkles of violet light flickered around Brin's fingertips. Cady could not understand what she was seeing.

Lek thrust more forcibly with the boathook, still with little result. Brin shouted out, "Don't hurt it!" But then suddenly the creature vanished from sight. "Where is it?"

For a moment nothing could be seen. And then the creature appeared again, keeping up with the boat for a short while, but then dropping away to stern. And then it submerged into the depths, slowly, fading from sight as an idea or a dream might fade in the dawn, leaving only flickers of light on the river. And then the waters were clear once more and the *Juniper* moved on, gathering speed as it sailed away from Tivertara, towards the still distant city of Ludwich.

Cady moved to the afterdeck, wanting to be alone.

The voors were an offspring of Faynr, one of her many children. They were both real, and unreal, as only a phantom creature could be. For some reason, this specimen had broken away from the body of its mother, swimming downstream. Cady thought back to her vision of the river, and the temple she had seen under the Nysis. Had her dream in some way disturbed the voor's new home? Was that even possible? In these new strange days, all the old certainties were drifting away.

In light of this, her thoughts turned to her own predicament.

Perhaps the regrowth process in the effigy had failed on purpose? She was being prepared for some great, as yet obscure, undertaking, but what could it be?

Only one thing was certain: in this task she was joined to the young passenger, Brin. Cady knew this now, as a truth. A single word bound them together, the one spoken over and over in the cabin, in the midst of the girl's convulsions.

Gogmagog.

The Reading

Lek's hand moved slowly over the shroud, palm downwards, only a few inches above the cloth. It moved from one side to the other and then across at a sharp diagonal to start again, a little lower down, with the second row. The pattern continued in this way, one line at a time. The hand glowed with a deep blue light, the same hue Cady had seen coming from Lek's eyes when he'd read her own body for its secrets. A soft clicking sound was heard as a kind of valve opened and closed in the Thrawl's palm.

"Have you ever done this before?" she asked in a whisper.

Lek didn't reply. He was concentrating on the task. But Brin answered for him: "Don't worry. Mr Lek has the best-ever blue crystal. It can receive and transmit signals at one hundred thousand miles per second. That's a fact."

The hand moved on. The shadow vibrated on the shroud as the information embedded within was drawn up via a web of circuitry into the Thrawl's skull-pan, into the crystal embedded there, at the centre of his being.

The *Juniper* was moored at a quay, near a long-abandoned cottage. They would soon sail on to the outpost at Maddenholt, where an old friend of Cady's lived, a bloodlark. But for now they had more important work to do. Brin was sitting on the starboard bench. Lek stood at the foot of the cabin table, leaning over to do his reading. Yanish stood at the head, staring intently at the length of hessian. He was combing his hair, one needless stroke of the comb after another. His aphelon glowed in shiny anguish, the usual grey almost turned to silver: would this process truly reveal his father's dying moments?

Brin suddenly said, "I wish I had a picture of my Daddy."

Hearing this, Lek's hand faltered. Yanish slipped his comb into a pocket on his leather jacket. He said to the girl, "Kiddo, this is more than a penny-store crystal snap. This is the real deal, the smoke of fancy, the Black Tornado himself, come a-calling." In demonstration, his own shadow did a jitterbug jive one step away from his body. Brin clapped along with glee. And the Thrawl's glowing blue light went on its way: one row, across, the next row, across.

Cady knew the basic idea: for half an hour or so after they die, the shadow of an Azeel clings to the body. This shadow can be captured in the weave of silk, or some other cloth. Lek claimed he could scan and analyse these final traces of Zehmet Khalan. Cady still wasn't sure. More than anything she was anxious; she desperately wanted Yanish to be at peace, beyond the dancing and the slang and the scuttler bravado. And if this is what it took, well then, let it be.

Lek's hand came to a halt. His fingers trembled and the blue light flickered on and off. There were only a few lines to go.

Yanish asked, "What is it? Why have you stopped?"

"I don't know," the Thrawl answered. "There's something wrong, inside my head. I don't... I don't think I can do this."

Yanish reached out to grab Lek's hand, holding it firmly above the shroud. "Oh you're doing it, old pal. Don't go spinning my wheels now."

Lek's face looked like a glazed mask. He spoke in a soft monotone. "The lights are flashing behind my eyes."

Yanish tightened his grip on the metal wrist: "You're a low-down grifter, you are. Where's your full-speed-ahead button?"

Brin cried out, "Stop it, please Yanish. Let him go!"

Lek stopped struggling. Cady was the first to notice. His eyes were not blank or closed; they were open wide and fully cognisant, staring down at the shroud. Yet his right arm was frozen in this one position. And then the hand shuddered, once, twice. The blue light clicked off.

There was no warning.

Lek suddenly exploded into movement. He shot backwards, hitting the door with tremendous force, his elbows jerking like a spinning jenny gone haywire, knocking against the window with a hard crack. Brass ornaments tumbled to the floor. Lek's body stayed rigid against the closed door. His muscles had locked.

Brin got to her feet, her face in shock. Cady ducked. Yanish half turned from the violence, his shadow darting away half a second quicker than he did. For a moment all four of them were caught in their different positions. Five, including the shadow.

And then the light returned to Lek's eyes. Whatever was inside his skull, was now projected out into the world along twin beams of flickering blue. Cady could see images dancing madly on the walls and ceiling and tabletop. It was like some kind of crazy crystal show! Lek could not control his movements, that was the trouble: his head juddered back and forth and up and down, and because of this the images would not settle. But Cady saw enough.

A battlefield, smoke, two soldiers running away from the point of vision.

There was no sound. Only these few seconds of action, blurred, sepia-tinged.

By now Yanish had realised what was being shown. At first, absurdly, he touched at the wall with his hand, trying to hold onto the pictures. The final moments of his father's life played over his face. Then he rushed over to Lek, grabbing him by the shoulders and then the neck, trying to hold him steady, to focus the image. "Let me see!" he snarled. "Let me see!" He sounded like a man suddenly made blind, crying out to his God Naphet for light. But it was no good. Even as Cady managed to take hold of Yanish and to pull him away from Lek; even as Brin crouched in the corner, mewling in madcap astonishment; even as Lek opened his eyes wider to project further, stronger, even then...

The pictures died on the walls.

A Visit to the Bloodlark

Cady dodged the first three blows, swerving this way and that on feet suddenly made nimble, but the fourth jab grazed her as she spun away, breaking open her lip. The taste of her own blood made her reel and stumble, and she went down flat on the ground, dust rising up around her in a cloud. Oof! She was dizzy for a moment, terribly aware of her aches and pains. That was a close one! But she struggled to her knees and then to her feet before her opponent could make another move. With sweat-filled eyes she scanned the square, and the crowd of people who had quickly gathered once the fight had started.

Where the hell was he? Where the hell was Lek?

Everything was blurry.

She heard a tumult of voices, most of all the brazen calls of one enterprising chap, who had quickly started a book on the fight's outcome: he was shouting out the odds. Money changed hands. Other spectators were jeering, cheering, guffawing, or howling with vicious delight. And then a man with a loudhailer appointed himself the official commentator of the match.

"Ladies and Gentlemen! Good citizens of Maddenholt! Ephreme, Alkhym, Wodwo, Azeel. All are welcome! Thieves, bounders, scoundrels, smugglers, scuttlers, dollymops… One and all gather around for the Brawl of the Century!"

There was laughter at this, which infuriated Cady further.

"I am not some joke for you to banter on! Fuckwit!"

The commentator ignored her insult. He doffed his trilby. "Our gladiators, for this bout… On the side of flesh and blood, a little old lady… name of… name of…"

"Cady! Arcadia Meade. And shove all that *little old lady* palaver! I am a swashbuckler!"

She put up her fists in a stance more appropriate to a heavyweight prizefighter. This brought more laughter and cheers.

"And on the side of metal, crystal and rubber… The one… The only… The Mighty Thrawl!"

The crowd booed loudly.

"Where is he?" Cady spun around. "I'll flatten him. I'll take him to the scrapyard!"

In answer to her boasts, Lek rushed towards her from the other side of the square, his right arm raised, hand clenched into a fist. *Not this time, Metal Man!* She moved with surprising agility, perching up on her toes and then swinging round like a dancer, to slip beneath the Thrawl's outstretched arm, and then away. She goaded him as she settled back on her heels: "Come on then, Fog-Face. Tinpot. Rust Bucket. Mister Fuck-Fuck!" This last one made no sense at all, but by then her lip was gooey and puffed. No matter. She bawled out her finest insult: "You fight like a butler serving a cream tea!"

The fight continued, with the Thrawl giving it his best. But mostly his haymakers and right hooks and jabs were clumsy and badly aimed. Meanwhile, Cady skipped and balanced, and tottered, and ducked and dived and pirouetted. The Way of the Willow, she called it, an ancient fighting art learned two centuries ago from the master-at-arms of a pirate ship off the Meldina Islands. Also, she was happy to play dirty, scooping up a handful of gravel which she threw in Lek's face, followed by a swift if somewhat feeble kick to his tinplate testicles. Or whatever he had down there. Probably nothing! And this brought forth another string of tasty insults, all calling the Thrawl's thrawlhood into question. In truth, her foot was giving her torment, from where it had made contact. But she wasn't going to let her opponent or the crowd know that.

Lek spluttered, wiping the gravel from his eye sockets. The grit must have been getting in his circuits, for he reeled on his feet. His eyes flickered on and off. Taking advantage of this, Cady skipped away from his line of sight. Lek swung this way and that, squinting. The crowd called out all the names flesh can call metal.

There was a clanging sound as a heavy pint-pot smashed into Lek's skull.

He spun round, only to find Cady waiting for him, another pint-pot in hand. She let it fly.

Lek caught it in mid-flight. By the handle.

The crowd oohed and aahed.

Cady did her best stamping dance. She snarled: "You Thrawls! All you've ever brought us is trouble. Ever since that day when you all went mad, all of you, all at the same time! The Frenzy! The Frenzy!"

The crowd cheered this, and roared in anger at their memories.

Lek's rubber mask crinkled into one all-over frown. "That wasn't my fault," he cried.

"No? You just like smashing things up, do you? All in a day's routine. Eh?"

The spectators were all on Cady's side by now, as she goaded them, even the ones who had bet against her. She was playing to the crowd, walking the wide circle, making little bowing gestures to her admirers.

Lek attacked her from behind, without warning, moving at incredible speed.

But Cady had danced herself into a tingle. The *ultimate* tingle.

She had stepped into that zone of infinite knowledge – the Deep Root – where all the world's plants intermingle. She felt Lek's approach in the breaking of grass stalks in the dirt, the shiver of seeds in the ground, the whirl of a dandelion clock through the air disturbed by the Thrawl's motion. She saw his approach in the widened eyes of the spectators nearest to her. But most of all, she felt it in the pustules on her arms. They pulsed and throbbed and threatened to burst. So her body relaxed, every last muscle turning to fronds in the wind – the Way of the Willow. Lek hit her at force and she was propelled forward by his weight, but only as a bunch of leaves might be blown through the air by an autumn wind.

The circle of the crowd parted to let them through. The fighters barrelled onwards, the tangled pair of them. Cady's willowy motion was stopped only by the wooden post of a pub's sign against her belly. She slipped aside. *Easy, easy. Easy now, swing to port, handsomely does it.* The Thrawl hit the post at speed, almost knocking it over. He fell to the ground, Cady atop him. The crowd rushed in to take up its new position. The Thrawl and the old lady rolled over and over in the dirt, both of them covered in gravel, dust and dog shit. Now Cady was trapped beneath his bulk and she could feel the life's breath being squeezed out of her. His metal hands felt like pincers on her neck.

But she wasn't quite ready to die yet.

Her fingers reached up to claw at Lek's skull. And they found what they were looking for – the bullet that was lodged there. Cady pressed, and pressed hard! Really, she made very little impact on the bullet, but it was enough. Lek froze in mid-action on top of her. Cady called for help and only managed to breathe properly when two beefy onlookers had dislodged her opponent from her. She needed aid herself, to get to her feet. She gazed down at the Thrawl. He was just lying there, out cold. She called to her helpers, "Help me get the lump up, will you? Come on, let's get him inside. I need a sit-down. Oh!" She felt her back ping and crackle painfully as she bent over, and so she left the task to the men.

Five minutes later the two combatants were sitting at a table in the snug room of the pub, an establishment called the *Beck and Call*. Cady's desire to see her old friend the bloodlark had been delayed by the fight, but she was more than happy to just rest here awhile. The landlady placed two bottles of Crowley's Best Stout on the table. "One for you, and one for the tin man. On the house, dearie. I haven't had such custom, not in a long week." Indeed, the public bar was crammed to capacity with the fight's spectators, and a raucous ding-dong of a sing-song had started up accompanied by a lung-diseased accordion. Cady nodded her thanks to the landlady and took both bottles for herself, prising the cap off the first with her two best teeth – happily aligned for such purpose – and set upon the beer without delay. Her lips were soon covered in froth. Lek sat there, his head bowed, his eyes devoid of all light. Cady enjoyed the sight of the dent she'd made in his skull with the pint pot. Bloody good shot, that was! Oh yes. She breathed a sigh of relief as the alcohol warmed her. She would be bruised and aching in a couple of hours, but for now she was good. She made a belch and lit up her pipe.

The curtains of the snug were pulled shut even in the daytime. A cloud of pipe smoke soon hung in the air. Nailed up above the fireplace was the head and torso of a Thrawl, displayed like a hunting trophy. Modelled on the features of Queen Hilde, it bore the sorry remains of a horsehair wig coloured with green vegetable dye. Very little of the rubber mask clung to the transparent face, and the inner workings were on view. The space in the skull where the blue crystal would normally be housed was empty; all thoughts lost, all calculations. The torso ended in a ragged line of wires, tubes, and jagged shards of metal. Cady wouldn't have given it tuppence-worth of thought usually, but now, with Lek aboard the *Juniper*, she pondered it for a moment.

He still hadn't moved.

Cady wiped some beer off the end of her nose. "I wonder how Yan and Brin are getting on? Back on the boat? Probably sunk the old Junie by now. Eh, what do you say?"

Lek had nothing to say. He remained as he was, a sealed machine.

Cady puffed out her cheeks. "Well, this is a lively chat, I must say." She stared at the Thrawl. "I hope I haven't caused you permanent damage."

His eyes were blank, his mouth closed.

Cady had to talk, it was in her nature. "I want to explain…

why I called you what I did. Why I called you a traitor, Lek. Well then, to be precise, a good-for-nothing, cock-chaffing, Enakor-loving, shit-swallowing traitor!" Puff, puff, puff on her pipe. A swig of beer. "Because that's why you took a swing at me, isn't it?"

He just sat there: no reaction.

"It all started when you said Brin's full name, do you remember? When she was having her bout of fits on the boat, what was it now? Sabrina Brinky-Bottom Godalming Botherington Wessex-Smythe Horse-Bracket Apple-Blossom Tully-Quip. Oh, all that family-tree palaver the Alkhym toffs go in for! But when you said the last name of the list – *Halsegger* – that one I recognised, right, because who wouldn't, I mean, who wouldn't in all of Kethra recognise that shitty name, eh?"

She took a gulp from the bottle and smacked her lips. It was quiet in the snug, just a couple of biddies at the next table who insisted on giving the Thrawl a nasty look now and then.

Cady continued with her story, happy to not have Lek answering her back, for once.

"Which is why I called you a traitor. Because the Halseggers were traitors in the war, were they not? Famously so. And if that once great family turned their coats, then why on earth wouldn't their butler, eh? Because that's what you were, am I right? Mr Lek? Can you hear me?"

Lek stared at the table, unseeing.

"Really, I didn't think it would upset you so much." Her mood turned cold. "*Halsegger*. That stinking family. They used to run the country, and now look at them, living the high life in Enakor, I shouldn't wonder. And they left their kid behind. Or what? You stole Brin away from them, is that it? Eh, me laddio?"

She rapped loudly on the pewter tabletop. The two biddies gazed over, roused by the noise. They frowned at her. Cady frowned back. She was the better frowner; she was the Grand Mistress of Frowning, ten years running, and the ladies quickly returned to their port and lemons.

Cady shifted her attention back to Lek. "Lud's blood! No wonder you wanted to keep that girl's true name a secret. People will tear her limb from limb, and no matter her age."

The answering voice was so quiet, it might have been travelled here from the moon. But Cady knew it for what it was: Lek had spoken.

"What was that? Speak up."

He did so, a little louder. "I can't let that happen. I mustn't let Brin come to harm." His hand went to the exposed bullet in his skull, feeling at it tenderly. He winced, and stood up. "I have to go back to the *Juniper*. I need to make sure she's safe."

"Oh, she's safe. She'll be bossing Yanish around, making him scrub the deck. Come on, plonk yourself down, let's have a natter."

He looked at the door for an eager moment and then sat back down.

Cady put her thoughts together. "Somebody is looking for Brin. Is that right?"

Lek didn't answer right away. His eyes were dark, and his rubber mask looked like something out of a horror show. And when at last he spoke, it wasn't to answer her question. One croaky word at a time, painfully, with searching patience, he said, "Brin is a very special child."

"Oh aye, the world revolves around her."

Lek stared at Cady. It was the first proper look since his defeat in battle, and a pure-white light flickered behind his eyes. He was coming back into full operation, one mechanism at a time.

"I have served the Halsegger family for eighty... eighty... eighty-six years."

That fact remembered, his crystal brain took further charge of itself.

"I was second footman, first footman, butler. Then personal valet to Sir James Halsegger."

A look of absurd pride came over his damaged mask of a face.

"So you've known Brin since she was born?" Cady asked. He nodded. "My position in the household forbade me from seeing her often. But it was soon known below stairs, that the child was unusual."

"In what way?"

He paused before answering. Something hidden away was being retrieved and brought into the light. "You may know, that once in a long while, every hundred years or more..."

"Yes?"

"A human child is born who belongs to Faynr. Someone who has within her a strain of Queen Luda's blood, passed on down the centuries."

Cady had to smile at this. "I've seen a few Alkhym families in my time, making such a claim for one or other of their brats. It's always been wishful thinking. Or, at worst, a con."

"Not in this case."

Now she eyed him suspiciously. "What are you saying? That Brin..."

"Brin is such a child." Lek erased every last sign of emotion from his face. "Luda's blood sings in the girl's body, and Faynr listens, and desires to envelop her."

"I knew there was something!" Cady whistled. "Her fingers were sparkling, when she made the voor dance in the water. And I thought to myself then, those sparks look very like the gleams of a Xillith."

"Exactly so. The Xillith are beings of pure energy. They are the most successful of all the creatures to take up residence inside Faynr, and Brin has some power over them."

His voice was back to full strength. But every so often his face would find its most painful expression as he told the story.

"Sir James Halsegger noticed his daughter's gift when he took her on her first river jaunt, aboard the family's yacht. She was two years old, but her little hands reached out eagerly towards the Xillith as they frolicked over the water, always up to mischief, as they like. A number of them attached themselves to Brin's fingers, and to her face. They seeped into her skin. I was in attendance that day, and I saw it all with my own two eyes, although I found it hard to believe."

"I can imagine."

Lek nodded. "The stories soon spread among the servants, about the dancing sparks, and the strange little creatures seen in Brin's bedroom, and the planets and stars that circled above her bed, without any wire or string to hold them up."

"She made these things herself?"

"Yes. The family encouraged her. They made sure she had her own supply of Faynr in a little vase beside the bed. Using the Xilliths as a kind of binding material, she would form the mists and strands and bubbles of Faynr into so many different shapes." Lek smiled broadly. "Little Brin was a marvellous conjuror!"

Cady was surprised at this display of feeling; perhaps the

first evidence of pure joy she had seen on the Thrawl's face. It didn't last long, however. His voice took on a sombre tone.

"When the war began, people expected the Halseggers to support the country's efforts, like the other great Alkhym families. With money, resources, expertise. And that the young men of the household would do their bit, by signing up."

Cady started on the second bottle of stout. "Aye, and then the press revealed the truth. Shame, that. The family's treason came to light."

"It wasn't treason."

"Conspiring with the enemy? I call that—"

"Sir James was acting in the best interests of the country."

"Piffle!"

"He... and many like him... They feared the worst. That the country would be lost, in war, in devastation—"

"Bollocks!" Cady's spittle sprayed out in a fan.

But Lek insisted: "The deal he struck with the Enakor government would have saved so many lives."

Cady roared, "He wanted us to surrender. Kethrans never surrender!" The ashtray rattled on the table as her fist banged down on the tabletop.

The little old ladies on the other table made a quick retreat out of the snug.

The Thrawl's face was blank. He carried on with a flat-toned voice. "The time of exile came. Banishment. I could not believe it. We were all packed up and ready to go, suitcases and shipping cases on the steps of the mansion, and the motor vehicles waiting on the drive. But a man came to see Sir James, just before we set off, a friend of the family, and one of James's closest business partners. His name was Olan Pettifer."

"I've heard of that name, I think."

"He's a lord, in the House of Witan. A Wodwo, actually. But one of the better such families."

"Aye, we can't all be slobs and slatterns."

Lek chose to ignore this remark. "Pettifer was involved in the defence of the realm, and he recognised that Brin's particular talents would be very useful in the war effort." He sighed. "Lord Pettifer took her away from the family. He became the child's legal guardian."

"How old was she?"

"Six."

Three or more years ago, Cady worked out. The war in full spate, so many people already dead. "And Brin's mother agreed to all this?" she asked.

"The family had no choice, according to the deal they struck with the authorities. It was exile, and hand over the child. Or the hangman's rope for the whole lot of them." Lek reflected on this sorry fact, and then continued, "Brin was given a goodly portion of funds, by her father. I kept the money safe for her."

"Enough to buy a boat, eh?"

"Yes. It seemed an appropriate purchase. There is some little left, in my possession."

Cady grunted. "So you went along with all this, eh? Dutiful, as ever?"

"I made a promise to Lady Halsegger that day, that I would look after her daughter, no matter what ill might prevail. And by the Thrawl's Oath of Fealty, I am duty bound to fulfil that promise." His hand reached up to the bullet once more, as though to ease some inner pain. "I was given a new job, to be Brin's companion. We were taken to a manor house in the west of Ludwich, called Blinnings."

"Brin mentioned that name to me. What did you do there?"

"There were so many rooms, so many floors. Researchers, clerks, medical staff, scientists. And Olan Pettifer in charge of it all. And, of course, the subjects. Almost all of them young, and each with a magical talent of some kind. There were experiments..." His head shook with the effort of remembering. "Long-distance spying, codebreaking, camouflage, mind reading, mind control." His mouth found a tiny smile, projected from within. "Brin was the best of them, quite easily! Lord Pettifer confided this to me."

Another slight adjustment of the bullet.

"Blinnings was built on the ruins of an Azeel monastery, on the banks of the Nysis. Brin worked in the cellar mainly, with a rivulet of the Nysis creeping across the floor and the mists of Faynr clinging to the walls. She learned to master and project her Xillithic abilities to ever greater degrees, bringing magical objects to life, right before our eyes. She could transform Faynr into anything she desired, or so it seemed. Magical swords, faery kings, imaginary friends, even good Queen Luda herself folded up inside the womb of Haakenur. How they sparkled and gleamed and danced freely in the dark." Another pause. "Of course, they didn't last very long, these creations. No. They were the dreams of a young child, and so they fluttered away."

Cady was troubled by the idea. "The kid was forced to do this?"

"I believe she was happy in the task, and she enjoyed leaning new tricks. Pettifer is rather a flash character, very knowledgeable, full of stories. Brin was taken with him. He taught her how to form the toy sprite, the one she has with her, by packing many Xilliths into a tiny space. It was a way of focusing her powers of manipulation. He took infinite care and patience with Brin. But in this easy manner, yes… Pettifer kept pushing her, and pushing her. He had control."

"And you went along with it?"

"Many of the new inventions and devices that came out of Blinnings were saving lives, both here and on the battlefields of Saliscana and Enakor. Soldiers, sailors, civilians."

"But the child. Six years old!"

Lek rubbed at his mask, crinkling the rubber into even deeper furrows. Cady gave him a moment to settle. Then she asked, "What were Pettifer's plans for Brin?"

"I don't know. But something… something important, and powerful."

"A weapon?"

"Perhaps. But I don't think this was just about winning the war anymore. It was personal for him, the expression of a hidden desire. Something to do with Dr Dee."

The name startled Cady. Her throat was suddenly dry and she had to take an extra glug of booze. "I'm sorry… who?" Now she was choking; the beer went down the wrong way.

"Are you alright, madam? Would you like me to—"

She knocked his helping hands away. A mixture of beer and bile came back up, which she spat out onto the floor; luckily it was covered in sawdust. Then she managed to ask: "Who did you say? Dr Dee?" Her voice was a growl.

"That is correct. The scientist and magical explorer of Queen Hilde's era."

A tumble of thoughts took over Cady's mind. She had met with John Dee a few times during his lifetime. How long ago now? Three and a half centuries, something like that. A man of many talents: oracle, crystallographer, mazeologist, occult engineer. He had helped Cady during a difficult period in her career as a Ludwich watchwoman, when the Blight had plagued the city.

"That long-dead coot," she snorted. "What has he got to do with Lord Pettifer?"

Lek thought for a moment. "I cannot say, for sure. But Pettifer was obsessed with the scientist and his work. He collected rare editions of his books and diagrams, as well as some of the doctor's home-made instruments and devices. I believe he was following one of Dr Dee's prophecies. And that Brin was part of that grand project."

The pub had quietened a little. They had the snug to themselves.

"And then came our final night at Blinnings. Two and a half years ago." Lek spoke in an earnest voice. "I slept in the attic, in what used to be a footman's room. One night I was woken by some… some feeling… I don't know what it was…"

"A bad dream?"

"No, no… I never dream. But some inkling that Brin was in danger. I got up and looked out of the window. Down below in the grounds, I saw two figures walking, one tall, the other smaller, a child."

"Did you go down, to see?"

"I tried to. But the door was locked. They had locked me in. Luckily…"

Lek extended his right hand, fingers pointing forward. From the tip of the index finger a sliver of metal protruded. Cady was intrigued as the metal shaped itself into a changing array of patterns, all of them key-like.

"That's a nice bit of fancy, isn't it now?"

Lek nodded. "I followed them at some distance. I could see Pettifer and Brin walking towards the old observatory at the far end of the monastery's herb garden. There was a series of runnels in the ground, leading away from the Nysis, taking the Faynr towards the domed building."

"And what on earth were they doing in there? Looking at the stars?"

Now Lek stared at Cady intently, his eyes at their most impossibly human. His rubber mask stretched in wonder.

"A great light shot upwards from the aperture of the observatory."

"You mean from the telescope?"

"No, no that had been taken away, long ago. Pettifer was using the place as way of focussing Brin's mind: here was a building that had once gathered information from the sky, and would now send information into the skies."

Cady understood at last. "So this was… this was the Night of the Dragon?"

"Yes!" Lek's eyes shone brightly. "Let me show you, if I may."

"How do you mean?"

The Thrawl's eyes blinked. Blue, red, blue, red, blue. Cady didn't like the look of it. He made a high-pitched buzzing sound. Two thin beams of sapphire light emerged from his pupils, pinprick spotlights finding Cady's face, her mouth, moving across the bridge of her nose.

"Hey, what are you up to?"

"I am transmitting myself to you. My thoughts, my memories—"

"Bloody cheek. Keep those filthy beams away from me!"

"Don't worry." His eye beams moved directly into her eyes, where they locked on. *Click.* Cady could not move, no matter how she tried. Lek had her in a spell. Her body shivered along every green fibre of her being as an image slowly formed in her mind.

She was standing outside an observatory, an old building, whose dome was cracked, its walls riddled with weeds. A cloud of Faynr mist swirled above the building, and many Xilliths flashed and sparked within this mist, moulding it into a new shape. Cady could not believe her eyes.

It was the dragon Haakenur, conjured as though alive.

Cady realised that she was actually inside Lek's head at this moment. Her vision was hazy at the edges with shards of jagged coloured light, as a diamond might give off, but at the centre all was crystal-clear. Through the years and across the miles, she looked out through the eyeholes in the Thrawl's mask. The public house at Maddenholt had vanished clean away. Only the scene in front of her mattered, to be experienced fully from the man-machine's point of view. Oh Lud! It was amazing. She was a human plant-lady growing inside a crystal brain, a new amalgam, never before experienced.

Cady looked on in awe as the animated dragon, small as yet, writhed above the dome of the observatory. It grew in size and rose up, and up, stretching to some impossible height, until its head disappeared in a cloud, and then it swooped down again and commenced to fly about here and there, but always tethered by its long thin tail to the observatory.

Cady gasped. To be there, on that night! And so close!

Now she was moving. Or rather, Lek was moving towards the observatory. Together, one contained within the other, they rushed through the door. Both were shocked and delighted by what they saw: the Thrawl back then, in memory; and Cady now, reliving that moment through him.

The aperture in the dome was wide open, showing most of the night sky. Little Brin, eight or so years old, was standing at the centre of the room, her eyes closed, her arms raised in front of her. The entire building was filled with Faynr mist, which came in through various ducts in the floor. Her hands moved in expert patterns to manipulate the Xilliths, which in turn wove the Faynr into this fantastic new shape. The dragon! It was, Cady realised, a version of Haakenur that Brin must have seen in the picture books she read, when younger. A Fairy Tale dragon. Not some grotesque overgrown lizard. And it flew up high, even though it had no *wings*. It soared under the girl's power, turning and twisting in a complex aerial ballet. Then it swooped down towards the observatory, at great speed, as though to dive-bomb into it…

Cady came back to herself, crying out in alarm. *Oh!*

With a violent spasm she swiped across the table and sent both beer bottles flying, as well as the ashtray and its contents. She half stood, almost knocking the entire table over in her need to get away from whatever it was that was following her, into this world. But there was nothing, nothing, only the little back room in the pub. She slumped down into her seat like a sack of heavy seed, and pressed a hand over her heart, to try and steady the insistent throb.

Lek was looking at her. The light in his eyes had stilled itself to a softer blue. Cady was no longer connected to his memories. She wanted to knock him for six, but she had already damaged him enough this day. She got her breath back. The Night of the Dragon was still playing in her eyes, or at least the aftermath of it, in little sparkles and dots of colours. She tried to speak, and then stopped. No words seemed adequate.

"Did you enjoy that, Cady?"

"Did I what?"

"I have other memories you could visit."

"Thank you, no, I'll stick to my own, thank you. Fuck! My brain is leaking. I need a drink. Get me a drink. Something stronger this time."

The landlady was happy to supply this, this time for a payment from Lek's pocket. Cady was soon settled, as a tot of rum did its work. "Chuffin' heck. So it was Brin who conjured up the Night of the Dragon? One little girl on her own?"

Lek nodded. "Yes. Under Lord Pettifer's tutelage, or command, or whatever hold he had upon her."

"Let me get this straight." Cady took another sip. "She created the image of the dragon from the very body of the dragon's own ghost. I mean, it hardly seems possible."

"Do you not believe me now, that she has Queen Luda's blood within her? How else to explain such power? How else?"

Cady's reply was succinct: "Well bugger me sideways!" Then she asked, "But where was Lord Pettifer in all this?"

"He was sitting out of sight in an alcove, watching, taking notes. Then he stepped forward."

"Did he see you?"

"No. His attentions were elsewhere. He was fascinated by the other dragon."

"What in Lud's name does that mean? I didn't see any other dragon?"

"It arrived in the final moments of Brin's performance. It was a much smaller creature, quite stunted in nature. It could not soar into the skies, but could only fly around inside the dome of the observatory. It was trapped, and it was screaming, and just… just howling in pain and anger."

"Who was it? Another monster from one of her story books?"

"No, something new, never before seen."

"What did it look like?"

The Thrawl's eyes focused. "A beast. Something terrible. But it was partially formed only, blurred in body, made of smoke, with two eyes of yellow light, and it seemed to… to scratch at the air with ill-made claws, trying to hold on to life, to… to *drag* itself into the world!"

Cady breathed out slowly, aware of her green heart beating. "Brin never talked about this creature, later on?"

"No. But Pettifer gave it a name. He called to it, as though to draw the creature to him." Lek looked directly at Cady.

"*Gogmagog.* That was the name he used."

A cold shiver ran through the old lady. Instantly the three elements of the never-nevers' riddle played in her mind. Oh, the river of her life, would it never stop twisting and coursing!

"What happened next," she asked, finishing her rum. "After the performance?"

"The bombs fell."

She had not heard Lek properly. But now she looked at him. "The bombs?"

"Yes. I reached out for Brin, and broke the spell with my touch. Lord Pettifer scowled at me, and called me the worst name possible. But I was already pulling Brin from the observatory. I heard planes flying above and looked up and saw the black silhouettes painted against the cloud layer. The most amazing thing happened."

"And what was that?"

"The projection of Haakenur was still in the sky, or at least the last traces of her, and… to my eyes she appeared to be fighting the enemy planes! But she was a creature of very little substance at that point, so her attack had no effect.

Still, it was remarkable. And then she vanished completely. And presumably, Gogmagog with her."

Lek took a moment to gather rest of the story.

"The Enakor knew of Blinnings, or at least of a house where strange practices were carried out; they had lost many battles because of the inventions produced there. And so, they were keen to pinpoint the location." His fingernails scratched at the tabletop. "And that night they found it. The bombs fell in waves, at least three of them making direct hits on the house. I thank Lud and Luda themselves combined that Brin was not in residence!"

"What did Pettifer do?"

"He ran for the house. The flames had already caught and people were streaming out through the door, staff and pupils alike. But I had only one instruction in my mind, the promise I had made to Lady Halsegger. I picked Brin up in my arms and carried her to the garage. I put her in one of the vans there and drove away as fast as I could."

Cady shook her head in wonder at all this. "And you've been on the run ever since?"

"For more than two years now. Different places, always moving on."

Some other people tumbled from the public bar, into the snug, lorry drivers, from the look of them. Others among them, florid-faced women, assorted hangers-on, one of them a loud-mouthed youth with a passion for bawdy jokes. One of the women laughed heartily.

Cady drew nearer to Lek across the table. "Does Pettifer still have an interest in Brin?"

"We have been tracked down a number of times, by people I can only believe are Pettifer's agents."

"But you shook them off?"

"Up to now, yes." His hand fluttered around his wounded skull. "I think Lord Pettifer wants to kidnap Brin."

"But why?" Cady's mind was on her task. "Does this have something to do with Gogmagog, that second dragon? It must do, right?"

"I'm not sure—"

"Oh, I know it! Using the girl's powers, his Lordship will once again find Gogmagog. Ah! It is all coming together. But why? What's Pettifer's purpose? If I can just work that out…"

"You're very interested in all this, Cady."

"Eh? Oh yes, you know. I have a spiky mind. Things get stuck on it." She steered the talk onto safer ground: "Despite the danger, Lek, you're willing to head back into Ludwich?"

"Brin's hesting is very important."

"I think there's more than that going on." Her stomach made a deep gurgling sound. "See, all the time I was asking myself, why the river? Why does Lek need to travel via the Nysis? And now I think I have the answer. The kid's obviously messed up, perhaps ill in some way. Palpitations, shivering and shaking, convulsions."

The Thrawl's head bowed a little.

She went straight on: "Here's my notion: that by reconnecting with Faynr, you think this will cure Brin in some way?"

"It has to." There was a desperate tone in his voice. "It *has* to work!"

"Lud in paradise! You don't know, any more than I do. You poor fuckin' sod."

Lek's face settled into a blank. A mask of light covering a bullet-holed skull, covering a globe of ghost fog, covering a shining blue crystal. But then he suddenly stood up, completely refocussed. Without a word he turned from the table and strode over to the bar.

Cady called after him, "Lek. Wait, where are you going?" He had no time for listening; he was too busy grabbing a loud-mouthed youth by the lapels and lifting him bodily off the floor. The Thrawl's rubber face was pressed up against the fleshy face. The man's friends scattered away, glasses and bottles fell to the floor.

"Who are you working for?" Lek demanded. "Answer me!" Cady hurried over, trying to pull Lek away. It was a hopeless task, his body had taken on extra strength. Lud knows what was fuelling it: a gear-shift into extreme anger.

"Come on. I saw you following us before."

The youth was squeaking in terror. His friends had found their courage; one made an effort to stop the Thrawl, only to be met with the sudden force of a weighted arm punching at his chest. The poor bloke staggered back, almost falling over.

Cady bashed her fists against Lek's back. "Stop, stop it! Let him go."

After one more squeeze, threatening to snap the man's brittle neck, the Thrawl responded to Cady's voice, and he lowered the youth, but still kept a hold of him.

"You've been following us, don't try to deny it."

The young man was nothing much to look at, a dirt-poor Azeel, his body all height, no width, no weight, his hair long and straggly, falling over the aphelon on his brow – or at least what was left of it; Cady saw to her dismay that the aphelon had been prised loose, leaving an empty triangular scar in its place. Aphelons brought a pretty price on the black market, but it meant the Azeel would be forever cut off from the true knowledge of his clan's ancestors. Only the most desperate would do such a thing.

Lek kept on at him: "You're working for Pettifer, isn't that true?"

"Who? Who? I've never heard of…"

The Azeel's eyes were screwed up tight and his teeth chittered, top against bottom.

Cady was screaming at Lek to stop. But a very distinctive sound did the job for her: a shotgun being pumped, ready for action. The landlady of the *Beck and Call* was holding the weapon, the stock nudged up against her elbow, a finger of the other hand on the trigger guard.

"I'll kindly ask you to leave my establishment, gentlemen, lady." She gave Cady an extra curl of the lip, just for good measure.

Lek stepped back, allowing the youth all the time and space needed – he fell gratefully into the company of his friends. But Lek wasn't quite finished: with a grunt he pulled the Thrawl trophy from the wall and clasped it to him like a half-born twin. "I will not be exhibited!" he cried to all and sundry, a statement that made little sense outside of the Thrawl mindset.

Cady was laughing by the time they got outside.

Lek's eyes blinked rapidly. "I have to go back to the *Juniper*, to make sure Brin is safe." He still held onto the model of Queen Hilde.

"Yes, you do that. But listen, don't tell them we had a fight, OK? Tell Brin we were set upon by band of roughneck stevedores. Yes, that will do nicely. But we fought back hard against them. And that between us, we gave them a plateful of knuckle sandwiches. Do you have that? And make out that I was the toughest fuck in the box."

Lek set off at a loping pace, disappearing round a corner.

Cady still had her errand to run, the reason they had

come to the trading post in the first place. As she trudged on alone, her thoughts could not help but return to the news that little Brin and Gogmagog were connected in some way. Oh, those never-nevers and their roundabout riddles! But what did it mean, why did a flying bomb have the name of a newly conjured dragon on the side?

Bell, gravestone, bomb.

Bell, stone, Gogmagog?

Was Gogmagog linked to some kind of explosion? It sounded terrible. Well, she would have to find out, somehow or other. One item at a time. Only then could her duties as a watchwoman be fulfilled. If she lasted long enough, that is. She had never gone about her obligations at this age before, always young, refreshed, and full of life.

Her feet slowed to a trundle as though a great burden pressed down on her.

Maddenholt was the last populated village before the ghost of Haakenur took over the river. It was built around a large man-made harbour, crammed with houseboats of all kinds: junks, scows, barges. The boats were so close together they merged into one giant vessel connected by a network of gangways, with hulls and masts lashed together with lines, and tarpaulin sheets covering one, two, three or even four boats, making a common roof. Infants bawled, a penny whistle played a reel, hens clucked in wire pens. One boat acted as a floating classroom. The teacher was writing a list of words on a blackboard: ALKHYM, AZEEL, EPHREME, NEBULIM, THRAWL, WODWO. The six known tribes who together made up the Kindred People.

Cady reached a landlocked cargo boat flying the flag of the Sacred Guild of Bloodlarks. The interior of the hold was darkly lit, lined with fish tanks and cages. Things moved in the shadows of these enclosures: the flash of sharp teeth, whiskered faces. Scales, claws, a tentacle that ended in a glowing bulb. Half a dozen of these illuminated creatures were dotted about the place, giving the only light: scarlet, gold, azure blue. The various creatures made their various noises.

The bloodlark's name was Lisbert. A good few tribes had gone into her makeup, the most prominent strand being Ephreme, which gave her the darkling skin and the gold-flecked eyes. Two diamond-shaped vents at the back of her dress allowed the vestigial wings their freedom. Her face was always in half shadow, no matter where she moved.

They exchanged pleasantries, talking of love and loss, and the price of fish, and the absurdity of travelling towards Ludwich in these times such as they are; and then they got down to business. Lisbert slid three slippery slimy creatures into a rubber pouch. "There you go. A trio of syqod, for the use of."

"Thank you." Money exchanged hands.

"You sure you don't need an extra, Cady, just in case? I can do a special offer."

"This will do." But the old lady didn't make a move.

Lisbert looked at her for a while. "Something bothering you, is it?"

It didn't take long for Cady to make her decision. She took off her peacoat and rolled back her sleeve, saying, "Lisbert, as a bloodlark, you've seen most examples of how life might be lived, haven't you?"

"Most, if not all. And the weirder, the better."

"Have you seen anything like this?"

Cady showed her the two bumps on her left arm, and the third that had recently emerged on her right forearm.

The pustules were an inch in diameter, domed, purplish, but with no sign of coming to a head. Lisbert pulled the tentacle of the nearest lamp into position. She hummed and hawed as she examined the growths, prodding one with the tip of a pencil. Then she took a dusty volume from a shelf and flipped through the pages. Cady saw glimpses of anatomical and botanical plates, with monstrous looking plants and animals on view. She had to feel worried. But finally Lisbert settled on one page and studied a diagram: it looked like the combination of a root system, the map of a temple floor, and a grotesque sex organ.

"How old are you now, Cady?"

"As far as most people know, seventy-eight."

"And in truth?"

"One thousand years old, if you must know."

"And? Keep going?"

"Oh you, you're such a bither-bother! One thousand, four hundred and eight-six years old. There, happy now?"

"And this has never happened to you before?"

"Never."

"Interesting. Yes, very."

"Whatever it is, just let me know, will you?"

Lisbert looked up. The lamp creature moved itself instinctively to cast her face into the perfect pattern of light and shade.

"Cady, my dear. It's time for you to breed."

Mr Carmichael's Palladium

Cady stood in the cabin, gazing at Yanish's painting of the Night of the Dragon. The image took on a whole new perspective now, after Lek's story. An approximation in oils was one thing, but to see it and feel it and hear it up close was a very different experience, even if it was through a Thrawl's memories. She went out onto the foredeck, where Brin and Yanish were playing a game together. Their hands moved into different shapes, one against the other, as they tried to outwit and second guess the next shape made. The game was Crickle Crack, a sailor's pastime from way back. Cady had taught it to Yan when he had joined the *Juniper* as a boy, and now the young man was teaching it to Brin. At the same time he was spinning yarns from the crystal shows, thrilling tales of the Electric Witch, and Professor Sinister, and not forgetting his number one favourite character: "The villain dashes about, his evil plans in disarray under the mighty power of the... Black Tornado! And so ends the Whiplash's reign of terror." His shadow played along in mock heroics.

Brin laughed and then shouted out, "Crackle crack! Ah, you lose, you lose!"

Cady couldn't help feeling a bit miffed: Yan got on so easily with the girl, whereas she was still struggling along, wondering what to say for the best. Then she realised: two orphans, after a kind. So what did that make her, the rotten old grandma? Yikes. Lud save me!

"I'm going to hit the head."

Neither of them responded, so Cady climbed down through the forward hatch, and closed it above her. The hold was the only private place on the boat. She squatted on the bucket in the aft of the bilge and did the business, wiping her arse on a clump of pages torn from old copies of *The Crystal Times: Deedee Monroe Serenades the Troops. That's the spirit, Deedee! Pah!* The only serenade Cady needed was the sound of the propeller shaft turning in its casing: nice and smooth, it was, and she had to admit that Lek had made some lovely adjustments to the engine. She shuffled over to the large glass tank that sat in the middle of the hold. The water within the tank was murky and filled with sediment. Sitting down on a creaky three-legged stool, she tapped on the glass.

"Mr Carmichael? Are you there? Yoo-hoo! Mr Carmichael?"

Cady dropped a few dried shrimp into the water, but even that brought no response. Next she tried using a hand torch; she pumped the handle around and around to get the bulb flickering. The resulting beam was weak as it moved across the glass, but at least it got the occupant of the tank stirring. The water glowed with a soft grey light. And within this light, a dimly-lit monochrome picture emerged. It looked like a tall building. Or was it a child's toy? No, more like one of those giant newfangled sculptures all the hoity-toities gawked at in Ludwich Art Gallery.

The display faded away after a few seconds.

"Oh sodding hell, Mr Carmichael! I was hoping for a nice little picture show!"

She contemplated making a pipe, but something put her off. No matter how she tried to avoid it, her mind would always circle back to Lisbert, and her diagnosis. The bloodlark freely admitted she had no clear knowledge of the process, but despite this she had rambled on merrily about ovules, ichors, pistils, eager wet stamen, quivering antherpods, pollination, secretion of sap, sticky burrs. The pustules on Cady's body were, Lisbert insisted, buds, soon to blossom into flowers.

Queen Luda help me now!

Cady's dugs were sore, her hair was greasy. Her breath stank of the sewage pits. Her armpits squelched. Her eyes were gritty and overcast with the blurs. Her throat held more bile than breath. Her flesh crawled. Her feet itched madly. She felt queasy. And angry. And joyous. And nervous. And excited. All at the same time! More than anything she wanted to leap off the boat onto dry land and run naked into the nearest field and just dig herself deep into the soil, her proper home.

But it all made sense, in a way. Even the failure of the regrowth ritual. She would die once and for all in this life, her last life, as this strange and decrepit creature. She had finally become mortal, after so many centuries. Yet, before such a thing came to pass, such a terrible thing… something would be born from her. Cady trembled with nerves. What would it be? What form would it take? A new flower, perhaps? What colour would it be? How many petals?

"It smells funny down here."

It was Brin, of course. She had dropped down from the now-open hatch.

"Aye, it would do. I've just had a shit."

The girl wrinkled her nose and rolled her eyes; she could do both at the same time. "What's inside there?" She was nodding towards the glass tank.

"Mr Carmichael. But he's asleep. He sleeps a lot, for days on end, sometimes."

Brin's nose was pressed flat against the glass. "I can't see anything. What is he, a fish?"

"I'm not quite sure, to be honest. More like an eel. He's a crystalback."

"Really? Oh, that's very rare!"

Cady started to clean the bowl of her pipe with her penknife. Brin sat down on the floor cross-legged, her back against the tank.

"I've never seen a lady smoke a pipe before."

"That's because I'm a sailor first, and a lady second, and various other species, third, fourth and fifth."

"Yanish says we'll be passing Woodwane Spar soon. And then we reach Faynr."

"Aye, the ghost is closing in. I can feel it in my bones."

Cady hesitated. "I've been meaning to talk to you, child."

Brin cranked the handle of the torch to get the dynamo whirring. She pointed the beam up towards her own face, making a scary horror-show expression. Then she giggled.

Cady looked at her. That faraway stare she'd had back in Anglestume had vanished, and that was a glad sight to see. But the resulting innocence in Brin's eyes almost broke Cady's heart.

She said, "There are some things I have to tell you, before

we reach the ghost waters. Watch closely." Cady held out her hand, palm upwards.

"What are you doing, Mrs Meade?"

Cady didn't reply. Her eyes were closed, and her frown lines had multiplied twentyfold. The held-out hand was trembling. Brin's eyes were fixed upon it. She turned the beam of the torch onto the old lady's palm, illuminating the wrinkles and liver spots. The skin was parting at the centre of the palm. Something was pushing its way up from the flesh beneath. There was no blood, only a trickle of green sap around the stalk that had emerged. A pair of tiny leaves sprouted from the stalk.

Brin's mouth fell open.

A tiny plant was growing from the hand.

"I call these the *outer fields*," Cady explained. "My hands, both left and right. Lovely things grow there." The stalk reached its greatest height, just one inch above the skin. "This is pennywort, a herb. I use it in various preparations." Her voice lowered. "You mustn't tell Yanish about this, about the outer fields. Will you promise?"

Brin nodded. She was still too shocked to speak.

"Only, he's been dying to know where they are, for ages now." A gentle laugh. "He thinks the fields are somewhere on Pinchbeck Island, outside of Anglestume." The girl reached out. "That's right, you can pluck it loose. Only don't eat it. It'll turn your head into a merry-go-round."

Brin held the tiny herb in her fingers, gazing at it, and smiling.

Cady spoke next with some difficulty, for she had rarely told of her secrets, her true secrets. "Tell me, what do you know about the Haegra?"

"It's a flower," Brin replied.

"A very special bloom. And long ago, in the days after Haakenur the great dragon had fallen to earth, and a few years after Faynr had taken to haunting the river, the Wodwo tribe found a way of coaxing the haegra flower into a very different kind of life."

"I know, I know! Lek told me about it once."

"Mistress Pynne tells it best. Do you know the work of Mistress Pynne?"

Brin shook her head.

"She was the first great historian of the Wodwo people. In her Chronicle of the Kethran Isles, she writes, *"From the seeds of the haegra a goodly potion was made, which added to human flesh created a new matter, one to the other woven about. This matter is planted in soil for a year and six moons, after which time a child crawls forth, of flower and flesh both made."*

She now had Brin's full attention.

"Did you hear that? *Of flower and flesh both made.*"

"Yes." Brin's voice was very quiet.

"And from that flower, over time, a people were born. The Haegra. The Seventh Tribe. Now this happened in the Year of Separation, when your people split away from the Wodwo, thanks to the power of the newly created myridi-flies. The Haegra were formed as a protection against future clashes between the tribes. And from there we grew, and developed."

"But... but... but... but..."

"Yes, what is it, child?"

"But the Haegra people all died out, years ago, a long time ago!"

"Yes, yes. The Great Wilting, they called it. But a tiny few of us live on, dotted here and there in the land. Alas, I hardly see them, not these days. No, I'm alone now."

Brin jumped to her feet. "You're making it up, all of it!" She was hopping from foot to foot. "I just don't know what... I don't think I can... I really think you're... Oh, Mrs Meade, is it really true?"

And so on and so forth, until Cady grabbed hold of her. "Hush now, girlie. Don't let the boys hear, otherwise they'll be telling me what to do, and how to do it for the best, and drawing up timetables and diagrams, and what not. Bless them."

"You mean not even Yanish knows?"

"Oh, he might have his suspicions, but I have never confirmed them."

"It's our secret, Mrs Meade?" Her eyes twinkled.

"That it is." And Cady felt better, to have spoken of these things.

"So you're very old?"

"Ancient."

"But you don't look *old*. I mean, you *do* look old, but not centuries old."

"I grow myself anew, every so often. I might begin again at eighteen or twenty years, each time. But I've only been your age once, a mere stripling, when first I rose up from the soil and my roots were severed."

Brin grimaced at this idea. "Who looked after you, that first time?"

"The family who made me, who gave me their blood, who planted me, and tended me. The Meades of Witherhithe." Cady nodded. "So I have always thought of myself as a Meade, and in each cycle I have been readopted into the family. I usually live with them, in houses of mud, and wattle, and stone, and brick, through the ages as they pass. And then, after a short while, I become all wanderlusty and have to set off on my travels again. Aye, I've led a nomadic life." She sighed deeply. "I'm a restless spirit."

Brin's mood shifted from excitement to puzzlement, one after the other. "So, will you soon regrow yourself?"

"I tried to, yesterday. But this time it didn't work."

"Oh. Why ever not?"

Cady frowned. "I don't know. It's worrying."

As always, at times of worry or confusion she took strength from the *Juniper*, the vibrations of the hull, the sound of the engine, the stench of oil. She tried to explain: "In exchange for this long, long life, I have certain tasks to undertake, as the old gardener priests ordained, to set things in balance, as they need to be, every so often, as I am called to do so." She spat out speckles of black mist. "In other words, I'm a watchwoman. Do you know what that means?"

Brin shook her head.

"There are these people, the seed people. Well they're not *people* as such, more plant spirits, anyway, they live inside the never-nevers, now that's a kind of flower, and every so often the seed people appear in public, and then... well this represents some kind of disturbance in the city of Ludwich or nearabouts, because the seed people pick up signals from the Deep Root." She took a breath. "Now then, are you following me?"

Brin alternated between nodding and shaking her head.

"Good, good, so the seed people give me a message, a warning of danger ahead, like a 'battle stations' klaxon on a ship. And I have to respond, as best I can. And of course it's better if I'm young, or youngish, when that happens. So if I'm old at the time, well then I regrow myself. Like a plant in the spring."

"How do you do that?"

"I climb inside an effigy, and… Oh, never mind all that. What's important is that this time, something went wrong, and here I am, old and slow and weary in my bones, but ready, oh yes more than ready." She made a left-right punching routine. "Fighting fit!" And she let out a warrior's roar, which just made her cough mightily.

Brin's face lit up. "It sounds dangerous. Is it dangerous?"

"Oh my Lud, yes. One time I had to track down and kill a murderer, a very evil man. The Tolly Hoo Strangler, they called him. At other times… Well, there's too many to tell. I have aided monarchs and paupers, and all in-between. I helped out in the Year of the Blight, fighting against the plague. Once I had to stop the tower clock in the Great House of Witan."

"Why?"

"Because with the ten o'clock chimes of the Old Bell of Bleary, a man would be hanged from the gallows, an innocent man. Such are the many trials of watchwomanship." She took the girl's hands in hers. "And this time… this time, you're a part of it, Brin, you!"

The girl looked at her, her eyes wide in wonder.

"But I don't know what to do, Mrs Meade."

"What does the word *Gogmagog* mean to you?"

"Nothing. I've never heard—"

"Now listen to me. You said *Gogmagog*. You said it over and over again. This morning. And Lek told me the story of the observatory, and of Lord Pettifer. Speak! You have to remember!"

"I can't! I can't! You're hurting me!"

Brin pulled away violently and clattered against Mr Carmichael's tank. It rocked on its base. And when it settled again the murkiness within took on a milky hue that seemed to vibrate. The glow of the tank filled the entire bilge with its eerie light.

"What's happening?" Brin's voice was hushed. "What did I do?"

Instantly, the mood had changed. "You've woken him up," Cady whispered. "Look at that!"

Mr Carmichael was now clearly seen, swimming about in his home. He did resemble an eel in many ways, with his long slimy body, his pointed snout, his mouth showing two sets of tiny sharp teeth. But there were other aspects to him: he had stunted legs, fore and aft, which helped him to swim; and, most wondrous of all, his skin was encrusted with many tiny fragments of blue crystal, both light and dark in shade. It looked as though someone had dusted him with sapphires.

Brin was mesmerised. Sparks of Xillithic energy leapt from her fingertips, onto the glass.

Cady explained, "His kind used to swim the Nysis. They were farmed by the Nebulim. But those days are gone now. I do believe, he might be the last of his species."

"No, there's another," Brin said with delight. "There is! They keep her in a pool, in a private garden in Old Hallows. Daddy took me to see her, once. I was very young." She turned to Cady. "Where did you get him from?"

"I have a friend who specialises in unusual creatures, a bloodlark. We have helped each other out over the years, and this little beauty was a gift."

Now the tank flickered into a colourful display of moving pictures, an ever-changing array: Ludwich Zoo, the waterside fair at the Shrivings, the delights on offer in Tolly Hoo. And many more such places from Ludwich and beyond.

"Mr Carmichael's doing this, isn't he!" Brin didn't wait for Cady's answer. "His crystals are picking up waves from the air, from all the different broadcasts."

Cady nodded. "He's usually at his best once we enter the Faynr. But you, girl, I think you've intensified his powers, or perhaps made the signals stronger, so he can pick them up more easily. Your little sparks have set him off. Lud in paradise. This is better than Sunday Night at the Ludwich Palladium!"

Brin's fingertips crackled with violet-blue fire. She pressed her hands against the tank. In response, the glass flickered from one image to another as the eel-picked up signals from wireless sets and telephone boxes, from television screens and telegraphs, from aerial to aerial – wherever a crystal pulsed and communicated one to another. Here was the chaotic babble and play of Ludwich in all its glory.

"Brin! What are you doing down here?"

It was Lek speaking. He had dropped down from the hatch with a heavy thump. He bent down to fit his height under the deck beams.

"Mr Lek! Guess what? We're watching a picture show!"

The Thrawl came to a halt almost immediately. Several expressions crossed his face, each one clicking away as the next replaced it: doubt, confusion, worry, pain. He fell to his knees.

Brin scrambled over to him. "Lek! Lek, what's wrong?"

The Thrawl's skull was glowing, the entire globe shining powerfully behind the rubber mask. A high-pitched sound came from his lips. Brin was clinging to him, trying to help him, trying to get him to talk, to tell her what was wrong. But he couldn't answer. The whistling sound continued.

His hands came up to press at his skull. Beams of blue light streamed from his eyes, hitting the glass of the tank. Mr Carmichael was thrashing about, curling into knots and then unslithering himself, over and over. The crystals along his body glittered brightly. A new picture show was forming on the screen. It played out for half a minute and then repeated itself, over and over. Cady knew that Yanish would want to see this, no matter how painful it might be for him.

She called to Brin. "Go up top, fetch Yanish. Now!"

It broke her heart to do so.

Five minutes later, the *Juniper* was moored up just this side of Woodwane Spar. The crew was gathered in the hold. The Thrawl had calmed down a little. His skull was still aglow with its blue light, and Mr Carmichael's tank had taken on the same hue – they were matched, and connected, across the vast intricate webs and weaves of the crystal world. Lek took a pace forward, which activated the transferral process. He actually looked relieved now, that the whole thing was finally being released from his interior.

They all watched intently as the images drawn from Lek's skull, the images he had taken from the Azeelian shroud, now came to life and flowed across the tank's screen. Here were the final moments in the life of Zehmet Khalan, Yanish's father.

Brin hid herself away from the sight.

Cady watched Yanish throughout. The young man's eyes were fixed on the revealed footage. His face was bathed in the colours of the battlefield. His brow furrowed as the machine-gun blasts stuttered out. His aphelon darkened, and darkened further, and then flashed with a burst of silver. His shadow, untethered, crept one inch away from his skin, and trembled there.

The images played out for a second time, a third time.

They would never end.

Yanish could not look away.

The Battle of
Red Moon Hill

As soon as the *Juniper* passed the spar, a strange haunted mood fell over the vessel. The silence was intense. Even the birds in the riverside trees were quiet. Cady took up the pilot's position in the bow. Lek had fastened the Queen Hilde Thrawl to the prow, making a crude figurehead. It was as good a symbol as any, to represent this crazy endeavour.

A quarter of a mile away, hanging like a shroud over the Nysis, the first dark shimmer of the ghost waters awaited them. From this point on, the river would be taken over by Faynr, the spirit of a long-dead dragon. Taken over, possessed, transformed. A series of large buoys marked the limits of safe travel, each one fitted with signs warning of the perils ahead. *Unsafe For Passage*. The House of Witan had voted on this measure last year, to keep people away from the river's more perilous stretches. There had been too many shipwrecks, too many deaths, because of Faynr's sickness. The *Juniper* ignored the warning, taking a course between two of the buoys. The wind whipped up suddenly and the boat veered towards one of the obstructions. Cady felt the skill of centuries past rising up in her, as she called out to Yanish, "Steady now, steady, slow to starboard, handsomely does it." She looked back, to see him at the helm, following her instructions to the letter. His face gave nothing away, set rigid, his aphelon a flat grey, showing no sign of the shroud's vision. But Lud knows what he was thinking and feeling inside.

Cady continued her instructions: "Nice and easy, nudge to port... slow... easy..."

The boat made its way into clear water.

"Ah Junie, you lovely old tub. Ha ha!"

Soon the threshold of Faynr was seen clearly, a billowing jet-black cloud of fog that hovered across the three-mile width of the river from bank to bank, drifting neither forward nor back with the tides, only its front face showing any movement as the features of a dragon formed and faded, formed and faded, formed and faded, never quite settling. Cady was held by the sight. And then, for one heart-stopping moment, the fog took on vivid form. It was shaped like a giant lizard's head, combined with the jaws of a lion or a tiger. Twin horns emerged from the temples. Colours swirled in the fog, so that the creature's teeth flashed with jewels of golden light, and a blue stripe ran down the long snout. Cady gasped. She imagined the great and noble beast roaring in anger, ready for battle; but then the fog roiled and churned in chaotic splendour, and the illusion was lost. A mirage, that was all.

It was time for work. She pulled at a rope tied to a cleat and raised a rubber pouch from the water, the one she had purchased at the bloodlark's store. She reached inside and pulled out a syqod. The slimy worm-like creature squirmed in her hands. She gave this one to Yanish, and a second syqod to Brin, keeping the third for herself. The Thrawl would have no need of such devices.

They were only a few yards away from the curtain of fog, its thick darkness dotted with little specks of yellow light. Cady checked to see that Brin had attached the syqod to her face correctly. Yes, the creature had slithered around her head, covering the girl's eyes. A quick peek to the helm showed that Yanish had taken the same measure: his eyes were seen through the transparent body of the syqod. But Cady decided to wait until she was actually inside of Faynr's body: she wanted to experience the transition completely, at least to begin with.

Only a short stretch of water remained, a few feet only. Brin stepped forward in anticipation. She was shaking badly. But Cady ignored this. Her whole attention was on the dragon's skin.

So close now, so very close.

Hold yourself, old girl, stay alert!

Cady had the sensation that a cluster of fireworks had been set off just under her nose: the smell was very distinct. It was the ghost of a dragon's flame. She could not believe how strange it felt, no doubt due to the years away, and the oddness of the current quest, and the womanly plant-like changes in her body – so many reasons all bound together. But the smell of burning faded in an instant. Now the prow of the *Juniper* pushed against the fog. For a moment it seemed that Faynr would not allow them passage, and Cady felt a backwards tug in the boat's hull. This was a new experience, so different from earlier voyages: like an old friend pushing her away. But the threshold parted at last, and the boat inched forward. The Queen Hilde figurehead was taken first, cloaked in black, and then the bow, amidships, aft, stern, to the last flutter of the ensign flying on the pole. The fog closed around them completely.

Now all was silent, and dark.

A silence made of darkness, and darkness made of silence. Yanish had turned on the *Juniper's* navigation lights, red on the port beam, green on starboard, white at stern and bow. But the colour of the lights died almost immediately in the thick air. He didn't even bother with the spotlight on the cabin's roof, knowing it would be useless, just a waste of battery power. The winds of the outside world had died away completely. The boat seemed to be at a standstill, but Cady could feel the vibrations of the engine in her fibres: the only sign that forward movement was being made. The *Juniper* sailed on.

Brin was standing next to Cady. The girl was calm now, her body at rest. She breathed greatly of the ghost-fumed air, and laughed. It was a good sound to hear. Cady remembered her own trips through this region, before the sickness had taken over. How wonderful it all seemed back then, so full of mystery and delight.

Faynr was the ghost of the dragon Haakenur, haunting the river Nysis with her memories and terrors, her spectral realms, her dreams and her enduring thoughts, whispered in the dark of sailor's heads through the centuries. From head to tail the ghost measured more than sixty miles in length, every inch of it clinging to the river as it snaked towards Ludwich and beyond into the west, to the Tangle Wood where the ghost rose from the ground, from the hidden burial place of Haakenur.

This first section was known as the Glaw.

The breath of the ghost. It touched at Cady like the fingers of many hands, tugging, prodding, pulling at flesh and cloth.

She shivered and turned to look at Brin. The young girl had disappeared from sight except for the yellow glow of the syqod creature that clung to her eyes, and whose body had now taken on a luminous quality in reaction to Faynr. Even Lek was affected by the Glaw; his eyes emitted a burnt-orange glow. But for these few dots of colour, all was eaten by black gloom.

"Cady! A little help, please, Pilot!"

It was Yanish, calling to her. His aphelon was a whitish triangle floating in the fog. Cady came out of the trance the Glaw cast upon her. She took the last of the syqods from the net and fitted it over her eyes. It was cold and wet and clammy, as befits a distant relative of the squid, and it clung to her with ease, wrapping its long thin tubular form around her temples and brow. Cady could now see through its translucent body, into the Glaw. The syqod was eating the fog particles, breaking them down, and emitting rays of photons. Light! Cady could see for only a few yards ahead, but that was enough to catch sight of a green marker buoy bobbing in the river. Yes, good; they were on the right course. Cady shouted out her directions. "Easy, to port, to port, easy. Half ahead. Steady." In this manner the *Juniper* made its way between the bright clusters and arcs of electrical discharge, the spectral remains of the dragon's long-dead apparatus of fire. The Glaw had always been a difficult stretch to navigate, even in the best of days – hot, humid, the air sticky to the touch. A jungle atmosphere. A vast swarm of midges flew in the midst of the fog. Other insects made strange ticking noises.

The further they travelled, the more Cady found her old skills returning, rising easily from the depths of memory. The years fell away, and she recalled the many times she had sailed the varied regions of Faynr: in a coracle past a row of carved totems on the bank; as first mate on a wherry carrying Queen Hilde to the grand palace at Old Hallows; or aloft in the rigging of a galleon bound for distant shores; or down in the filthy engine room of a cargo boat; or riding the tide in a sleek-hulled sailing barge, its bowsprit piercing the dawn light. So many journeys.

For a few seconds she lost all sense of the present day, and that was all it took. The *Juniper's* starboard bow banged into an old lookout tower, long crumbled into the Nysis. The hull scraped across the stonework, and a terrible shrieking noise rent the silence clean in two. To Cady's ears it sounded as though Haakenur herself was crying out from the slopes of Red Moon Hill, when the warriors' swords and lances had slashed at her sides and neck.

Yanish shouted in alarm, as he wrestled the wheel around, to clear the boat of the obstacle.

Lek stood firm, but Brin lurched on her feet and almost fell to the deck.

"I have it," Cady called. "Port seven!"

The boat moved away from the half-submerged structure. They were now heading at speed towards the south bank of the river. There would be risks that way as well, beyond the syqod's vision – the conning tower of a wreck, a hidden sandbank, jagged rocks… or… what the hell was that? It looked like a corpse floating in the water. "Starboard five. Easy now. Easy!" The *Juniper* followed these orders as though sailing under Cady's hands alone. It was an illusion she relished, as she felt herself fusing with the vessel, the green flourishing matter of her body linking to the timbers of the hull, the bulkheads, the decking. In her mind the river charts unfolded, each feature as marked out by Messrs

Maguire & Hill imprinted brightly on the bulb-like optic gland that sat beneath the skin between her eyes. "Ease to ten. Steady. Steady as she goes." And the channel blossomed open once more and the boat ploughed on, gathering speed under Cady's call of "Full ahead."

But the near accident had disturbed Lek. He glared at Cady and shouted at her, "I thought you were the best, the best pilot!" Cady ignored him, concentrating her full attention on the way ahead. Her vision was darkening. The syqod was reaching its limit of ingestion and the details of the world were already slipping back into the thick black haze of the Glaw. But she didn't panic; she kept the boat on its steady course, knowing well that the fairway buoy would soon be visible.

Her breath caught in her throat and her body froze.

A buzzing, hissing noise was heard.

Cady tried her best to track it through the darkness, but it could not be pinpointed. The sound flitted about, left to right, and overhead, or else circling madly at speed. The air trembled in places, like a ghost of electricity. It flew near to Cady's head and more by instinct than thought, she ducked down. But there was nothing there, no physical presence – only the noise, and the shivering air.

Lek called to her, "That noise. Cady? What is it?"

But there was silence now.

Had the thing landed on the foremast? Or the deck? She held her hand up, ready to give a signal to Yanish, if needed.

No sight, no sound.

Her hand remained in place, waiting...

The boat nudged ahead, parting the fog in slow waves. Silence.

Silence.

Silence.

And then a great sweep of noise, high-pitched and shrill, that made people's eardrums pop and crackle. Brin screamed almost to the same pitch. Yanish cried out to the god Naphet for guidance. Lek recited irrational number sequences at speed, up to the one hundredth number.

And Cady?

Nobody saw it happen. Not the helmsman, not the girl, not even the Thrawl. One second the noise was circling the deck at speed, whistling like a miniature banshee in the dark, the next it was quivering on the foremast, pierced through its body by the blade of a penknife.

As the noise faded, an insect was now visible in its place. It looked like an overlarge glowbug, with a lighted milky belly, and huge overlapping wings. Cady gave the blade of her penknife a twist and the insect squeaked its last ever sound. The bulb of its body went out. She pulled the knife loose and wiped gunk off the blade onto the sleeve of her coat. By now, everyone was calling out to her. She spoke calmly in reply: "A kreel beetle. Highly poisonous." Then she returned to the prow to do her job, viewing the river ahead and guiding the boat along a chosen course with hand gestures and simple directions.

"Steady, steady to port, five, half ahead."

The darkness parted at last.

And yes, there it was, the white fairway buoy: a welcome sign.

Five minutes later, the *Juniper* left the fogbound water. With great relief Cady tore the syqod from her sweating face. Its body was pitch black, full to capacity. She flung it over the side and watched as it swam away. She did the same with the other two creatures from Brin and Yanish. She took a moment to watch the girl, wondering if Lek's insistence on entering Faynr's territory would work; would the little tyke be cured of her ills? But for the now Brin seemed happy to stand in the bow next to the Thrawl figurehead, both of them gazing upriver.

Thirty-five miles of sailing lay ahead, before they reached Ludwich, with many an obstacle along the way. Cady knew that time would stretch out and run away from itself, as Faynr took charge of the vessel, but she kept to a hope of reaching the city before midnight.

The *Juniper* had now entered a wide stretch of the River Nysis known as the Haax. What a contrast it made to the Glaw. The air was clearer and brighter than any summer's day, and was always so, no matter the season. The water was transparent, allowing fish and river mammals to be viewed flitting about in the depths; it was easy to imagine that only an inch more of vision would reveal the riverbed, many fathoms down. In this region the skin of Faynr was more like a carapace of blue mist, paper-thin, set high above, replacing the sky, and touching the distance of each bank in a gossamer arch stretched over the river. The two eyes of the dragon's ghost floated in mid-air like a pair of small low-lying suns, one red, the other yellow. They looked out over faraway vistas. Every so often a lighting flash of electromagnetic energy arced across from one orb to the other. Cady was reminded of the phrase that various Granny Meades had told her down the years: *Never let your left eye see what your right eye is blind to.* It sounded like great wisdom, and was treated as such, but in truth Cady had never quite worked out what it meant.

Before the current troubles, the Haax had been the most

popular section of the Faynr. Cady made herself a tidy profit, carrying pleasure seekers downriver from Ludwich to this pool of water. She remembered how the voices of the commentators on the big river cruisers used to crackle from the tannoy speakers, and the cries of delight from her own passengers, and the sudden gasps of wonder as the Grand Illumination took place. Not an echo of that remained. The pleasure trips were over. Far ahead, Cady could glimpse the stone-built amphitheatre on the north side of the river, and the rows of cheaper wooden seats on the southern bank. The *Juniper* sailed on easily, with Lek at the helm, working the wheel. The Thrawl was a quick learner.

Yanish joined her at the starboard beam. He lit a cigarette and smoked it, staring at the fish in the water. His face was drawn, the skin stretched tight, the aphelion the same sickly white it had turned in the fog. The despair that had taken over after viewing his father's shroud had been kept at bay by the need to concentrate on steering the boat through the various obstacles: but it came back now, magnified. His shadow crept halfway across his face like a veil.

The rusted ruin of an abandoned motorbus hove into view, the rear end of the vehicle lodged on the slope of the bank, the front half sunk in the river up to the top of the bonnet. The windows were broken. The destination plate above the cracked windscreen read *Grand Illumination*. A skirl sat atop the driver's cabin, one of those hardy specimens, mutated for life inside the realm of Faynr. The bus's sides were decorated with images of King Lud and the dragon Haakenur locked in mortal combat, flames sizzling from the tip of Lud's sword, the mystical blade known in legend as Ibraxus. A crudely painted meteor flashed across the blue sky depicted above the bus's windows.

Yanish spoke quietly. "He worked all the hours Naphet gave him."

At first, Cady did not understand who he was talking about. But then she realised.

She had learned only a little of Yanish's family. She knew for instance that the Khalan family had arrived in Kethra more than sixty years ago, and that Zehmet had been a lowly accountant in the North Templeton district, before the outbreak of war. But other than that, nothing.

"It was all about improving your lot in life," Yanish continued.

"Oh yes?"

"That whole Azeelian thing: do your best, work hard, make something of yourself. Long hours, dismal wages, but he never stopped trying!"

Cady knew better than to interrupt. Best to let the lad carry on; let it be said, whatever had to be said.

"He railed against the invasion of Saliscana. The Year of the Lightning Bolt. But he welcomed the war, and the chance to fight, and all that. To be a good and useful man. He was one of the first in the queue at the recruitment office." A smile found its slow way to his lips. "My whole view of him brightened at that point. He was a hero."

"How old were you then? Ten?"

"Eleven, just gone. I used to listen to the wireless, every teatime, and watch all the news reels at the local crystal show, hoping to see my dad in the flickering images from the battlefront. But I never did, not one glimpse. I didn't understand it." He paused, contemplating his childhood, as the dragon's ghost unfurled around the boat. "I liked to read the penny comics and imagine myself fighting in the war, just like Captain Valiant in *The Weekly Lion*. That's how I saw my dad. Pathetic, isn't it? I've never told anyone that. I used to make up stories, where he took on an enemy machine-gun post single-handedly." Yanish's eyes dimmed a little. He flicked his ciggie into the Nysis. "But on leave, he never talked of such exploits. Not ever. It was very strange."

Cady watched her friend closely, still wary of interrupting.

His voice quietened again. "My mum died in a bomb blast."

"I know."

"It destroyed three of the houses on our street. I was out at the time, down the canal, fishing for perch. The poison gas hung around for days afterwards. I had to wear my mask all the time. By then, I'd moved in with Mr and Mrs Healey at number 27. They were very kind to me, but I could never feel at ease."

"And what about your dad? Did he come home to see you?"

"He came back to Ludwich for the funeral, of course, and went off again. After that, no, I never saw him much. The occasional letter. He came home on leave one more time. He was quiet, awkward with me. But we did go fishing. I liked that. That was the last time I ever saw him."

He paused. "I was thirteen by then. I liked to hang around the docks, watching the warships and gunboats come and go. And well, you know what happened next, Cady."

"Aye, some old crock asked you to help her get the passengers aboard her launch."

"That's right."

"And we've been together ever since, haven't we, eh lad?"

They both smiled gently at the memory.

Cady continued, "You know, I've never been able to have kids."

"Sure. I guessed that."

"I'm just saying, like, well, you're special to me, Yan, and you always will be."

Yanish didn't answer. Instead, he made a simple statement.

"I'm going to buy a silk shroud at Ponperreth."

Cady was surprised to hear this.

The lad kept his eyes on the waters ahead. "The Nebulim make the finest in all the land."

"I know that, but..." She didn't know what to say.

Yanish's face was fixed, determined. And yet she saw also the crazed defiance of youth. What on earth was he thinking?

"Yan, your father... He ran away, you saw that! The Thrawl and Mr Carmichael showed it to you. He was a deserter." It was cruel to say it, but what else could she do?

"He was shot in the back—"

"No!" His voice rang out over the Nysis. "My father died in action. That's all I need to know." A hard breath. "His image belongs on silk, in the shroud garden. I will put it there myself."

A sudden cry from Brin shook them both out of the mood. The girl had climbed onto the roof of the cabin and was dancing about gleefully, pointing with her outstretched arm towards the large oval of clouds – grey and white, pink at the edges – that hung over the river ahead. The cloud bank was massive, easily half a mile wide and half that in height. At its lowest point it hovered fifty feet above the water. Crackles of energy flashed within the airy structure, sparking in different colours. By common consent, the cloud was thought of as the once-living brain of Haakenur, now turned into pure *thought* alone. A realm of ghostly dreams.

Slowly, the boat entered the waters of the amphitheatre. Cady looked to both banks, north and south, mindful of former glories, seeing only patches of moss and bird shit covering the rows of seats and the crumbling notice boards and the broken roof of the covered pavilion where the posh people used to sit. But then she caught a movement in the stalls. It was a man, but with a strangely trembling shape, more haze than body, as though he were standing at the centre of a mirage. And the more Cady looked at him, the more he faded away; she had to always shift her line of sight to catch a renewed glimpse. He looked to be a ghost himself, a spiritual resident of Faynr. One more turn of Cady's head, and the lone spectator vanished completely from view.

The cloud bank flickered into life, spilling over with light and colour. The Grand Illumination had begun. In the days before Faynr's sickness, this phenomenon had drawn people from all over the world. The ultimate picture show, even if it always projected the same story every time.

Yanish went to join Lek at the helm, taking over at the wheel, letting the boat drift along at its slowest pace. Cady was fascinated by the vision on the clouds, even though she had seen it many times before. The first images were damaged, fragmentary and indistinct. Faynr's dream of her own creation had been corrupted by the sickness. The memories were dying.

Yanish told it true: "I can't see it properly."

Cady replied to him, "I knew it would like be this. Poor Faynr."

She looked to the cabin roof, seeing the disappointment on Brin's face. But then the girl's expression changed, becoming determined. She stood firm, her legs spread for balance. She raised her hands and called out in as loud a voice as she could muster, "Oh Mighty Faynr! We are gathered here to tell your story!" It was the kind of language, Cady realised, that she would have heard in an Alkhym chapel on a Sunday morning. Now Brin gestured to her audience on the foredeck as she continued in the same tone, "In the early days of this land, the Great Beasts ruled with their jagged teeth and their iron-stone claws." The words *beasts* and *teeth* and *claws* were spat out. Brin stamped her feet on the roof, to further emphasise her words.

"Fiercest among them was Haakenur! The Lizard Queen of the Marshlands and of the roaring tumbling Nysis river." Cady said, "I don't think it's ever roared and tumbled."

But Lek admonished her: "No interruptions from the audience, please. Let the performance continue!" He was glad to see Brin enjoying herself.

The tale went on. "Haakenur often slept beside the river in the moon's warm glow, her jaws red with the blood of her prey." Brin made a mighty roar, or as mighty a roar as a ten year-old Alkhym girl could make. Yanish helped her out by pulling on the *Juniper's* whistle.

The boat was still some way away from the clouds, but the giant images were easily seen. As the story played out, Cady looked up at the clouds and saw the fragments of the dragon's memory, the details lost or marred with darkness, but all brought to life by Brin's extraordinary narration. This passionate young girl was now the conduit through which the legend would manifest itself.

The story had to live!

Brin continued briskly, "And so they ruled, these mighty Beasts, until the Sky Fire came. It was the Year of

First Arrival. The star chariots fell across the land in great number, like a shower of meteors. Haakenur was wounded badly by one of these meteors, which plunged into her side. The great lizard howled in pain."

Yanish pulled on the whistle again, stretching the sound out, making it flutter and wail.

"But Haakenur was strong and fierce, and was not yet ready to die."

Cady saw the injured dragon on the clouds, this image momentarily stark and clear, the flow of blood gleaming in the daylight, and the wound flickering with flames.

Brin's voice changed, lowering in tone. "As they cooled, the star chariots cracked open like seeds and the first of the Kindred stepped out, the Wodwo, with their swords in hand and their faces painted with blue streaks. They were a fierce people. Right, Cady!"

"Damn right, the fiercest!"

"And they banished the Great Beasts from Kethra. Until only Haakenur remained, licking her wound, coiled five times around in the dark of a cave under Red Moon Hill. The meteor glowed within her body." Brin jumped down nimbly onto the foredeck and looked at each member of the crew in turn, drawing them into the story. "Among the Wodwo the most powerful of them all was Lud, who became their King." She pointed to the Thrawl. "Lek, you'll be playing King Lud."

"Me, no, no... not me... I don't know how to... I can't pretend..."

Brin waved his protests away. She pulled the boathook from its fittings below the gunwale, and hefted it aloft as high as she could. But it was too heavy for her, and Lek had to take it from her hands. And she said to him,

"I present to you, Ibraxus, the legendary sword of magical power!"

Lek swung the boathook to and fro; he had no choice.

"But King Lud was sad, so very sad," Brin explained.

"Lek... *sad* expression. Quickly!"

The Thrawl clicked through his collection of emotions until he found the *Face of Standard Human Sadness*.

Brin continued, "He was sad because his good sister, Luda, had not emerged from her star vessel. King Lud set off with his mightiest warriors, in order to find his sister, alive or dead. He searched for fifty whole years, and he was an old man when at last he found the cave of Haakenur." The girl's voice rose in volume. "And so began the battle of Red Moon Hill, man against dragon! The river flowed red with the blood of the slain, until only King Lud remained of the warriors, Ibraxus in hand."

Cady could see the story on the clouds, which had now turned a deep crimson. Blood seemed to drip down towards the *Juniper*'s deck, as the boat sailed directly beneath the Grand Illumination. The drops of blood vanished from sight just a few inches above their heads.

By now, Lek had fallen under the spell of the tale, and was brandishing the boathook as King Lud might his sword, thrusting it at the clouds above, at the hissing, roaring dragon. The Thrawl's face was painted a stark red, the colour reflected from the images of falling blood.

Brin used her every tone and gesture to play-act the battle: "Haakenur and Lud fought for many hours, until the full red moon rose, at which time Ibraxus found the weakest spot, in the neck of the dragon. In her last desperate moments, her long tail flailed this way and that, and the barbed hook at its end managed to find King Lud's chest, and to stab him!"

The venom of Haakenur flowed into the king's body. And then the brave dragon died at last, her body falling along the river's bank. King Lud was badly injured, in great pain, but he raised Ibraxus one last time and plunged it deep, deep into the dragon's side, where the meteor's glow was seen."

Lek mimicked the story's actions, driving the point of the boathook into the deck. The clouds above darkened, as though with their own sadness.

Brin went on: "The star chariots had fallen in the belly of Haakenur."

"She means the womb," Yanish said. But Cady shushed him. She was working on a length of rope, quickly knotting it into a loop.

Brin's voice slowed. "The dragon's innards were curled around the meteor, and in places had made their way inside. King Lud tore the star vessel open. His sister Luda lay within, tangled in the dragon's veins and arteries. Many of the veins had entered her body and the blood flowed back and forth. Luda was sleeping... or dead..."

Brin paused. Cady, Yanish and Lek were all looking at her, waiting eagerly.

The girl moved her hands in a circular motion. "With a gentle touch the king roused his sister and she stepped out into the moonlight. The belly of Haakenur had preserved her, and she was just sixteen years old, as she was on the day of the Sky Fire. Seeing this, old King Lud fell to the earth, sorely weakened by his wounds, and by the poison that seeped through him."

On cue, Lek staggered and fell to the deck, the magical sword Ibraxus slipping from his grasp. His face clicked to extreme agony, then to lasting pain, then to acceptance, and finally to bliss, as King Lud died.

"It was the Year of Lud's Death."

This statement from Brin brought silence to the *Juniper*.

Slowly, slowly, the boat was emerging from the far side of the cloud bank.

The girl stood over Lek's fallen body. "Young Luda was crowned as the Queen."

Cady placed the loop of rope on the girl's head.

"Queen Luda decreed a great city to be built, which she named Ludwich, in her brother's honour."

These same drops of blood were now dripping from the clouds, in ghostly form. As before, they vanished just above Cady's head. And yet one of them travelled a little further and splashed on Brin's upturned face. It made a crimson stain. In some way, the blood had become real.

The performance faltered. "But Queen Luda reigned in sorrow, not for her brother Lud, but for Haakenur, and the time she had spent inside the warmth of the dragon's belly. She thought of Haakenur as her mother, her true mother."

Sadness came over the girl's bloodied face as she said these words. Cady thought back on the story Lek had told in the public house at Maddenholt. And she wondered how much Brin must be missing her family.

Brin tried to carry on with the end of the story, but she turned her head away. Cady stepped in to take up the tale, saying, "The years of Luda's reign came and went. Lamentation would not leave her. One day, she called for the Wodwo high priest and a ritual was performed, to conjure up the ghost of Haakenur, which the queen named Faynr, after the *Mother* rune in the tribe's word hoard. And so began the Year of Conjuring."

Cady spread her arms out wide, taking in the whole width of the river.

"Faynr settled over the waters of the Nysis, which she made her home. Her body was formed of mist and moonlight, and stretched for two thirds of the river's length. Two thirds! Faynr vowed to always protect Luda, and Luda's children down the years. Ludwich's history would forever be coiled with that of the dragon's ghost. One could not survive without the other."

Cady looked back at the billowing clouds where the final moments of the legend were being played out, still fragmented, still damaged, but the spectral form of Faynr was clearly seen as she emerged from dead Haakenur's skull, to settle over the river.

"So it was, in the first years of our landing on this planet." A lovely feeling of communion came upon Cady, and she continued in a quieter voice, "Let us pray for the spirit of the Kindred, from whose star seeds we have all descended in our subtle varieties."

The Grand Illumination came to an end.

Lek had risen to his feet and was replacing the boathook in its fittings. Yanish worked the throttle, bringing the boat up to half ahead. Brin was standing in the bow, alone. Cady went to her. The girl was staring into the distance. Neither of them spoke. The clouds of Haax were already fading from view.

They came to the final curve of the auditorium. The trembling man was there, Cady could see him once more. He seemed to be looking in the boat's direction, but was soon out of sight. Probably some connoisseur of dragons, that's all, peeking into the heart of the ghost.

She turned to look at Brin. The girl's brow was still discoloured by the blood of Haakenur, as it had fallen from the grand display. It should not be capable of interacting with human flesh; Cady had never heard of such a thing, not in all her long years, and she thought again of Lek's conviction that Brin was a descendent of Luda, and therefore also a child of the dragon, for two species had mixed in that alchemical bowl, the fiery womb: the legend told it so.

Wilfully returning the old lady's stare, Brin touched at her brow, to smear the blood across her skin and down her face, to mark her cheekbones left and right, the bridge of her nose, and her chin. Mere decoration? War paint? Or some binding connection to Faynr?

The young girl smiled.

A Spell of Drowsy

It was half past eleven in the morning. Outside of Faynr's skin, the sun shone down brightly across the farmlands and estates. Yet within the ghost's body, only darkness reigned. It was always night in the Myhr region. Always. The *Juniper* moved on a sluggish tide, her spotlight showing the way ahead. The lanterns of Ponperreth blinked and fluttered in the distance. Cady looked down to the riverbank, where a number of bulbous grey shapes could be made out, lying flat on the dried mud – lifeless forms, hard clay shells in roughly human shape. These were the stillborn Nebulim. They should have been carried into the village church by now, and consecrated; but here they lay rotting, unattended. Cady felt sick to her stomach. She couldn't help thinking of what lay within them, the trapped spirits of the dead, waiting for a sacred flame to spring them into life. However, because of Faynr's sickness, the creation of Nebulim had more or less come to a halt. And so these clay bodies lay in the shallows, hopeful perhaps of a fresh tide, when the dragon's ghost might be cleansed.

Myridi flies darted over the river's surface, their bodies golden, glowing. The cocoon farms were close by, occupying the marshlands on the north side of the Nysis. Only a few Nebulim workers were seen, dark shapes amid the reeds. It was unsettling. With the Ludwich Hesting festival starting soon, this should be the village's busiest time of the year; the Alkhym coming-of-age ritual depended on a good supply of myridi cocoons.

Cady's breathing slowed to the same beat as the tide. She guided Yanish with hand signals only – *gently, handsomely* – her gestures indicating the degrees needed. They were moving towards the first of the raised platforms at Ponperreth. Flames danced inside colourful paper lanterns; red, green and blue. The houses were built on stilts that rose out of the waters, each dwelling connected to the others by a web of rope bridges. A number of the villagers looked down on the *Juniper's* arrival, their jagged outlines silhouetted in the lantern glow, their faces a set of trembling masks.

Something didn't feel right, yet Cady could not articulate it. She would have wished to sail on upriver, bypassing the village entirely, but Yanish insisted on making a stop here, to purchase a length of silk for his father's new shroud. She had to let him have his way. To reinforce her fears, the boat's spotlight picked out a wooden sign at the water's edge.

STAY AWAY
NOT WELCOME

The boat's crystal wireless had surrendered itself to the ghost, offering nothing more than a voice of static and interference. This noise was multiplied by sudden loud crackling sounds from the river, as a series of explosions of light illuminated the darkness around the *Juniper*. These were the Xillith. They danced above the waters in mischievous abandon, casting out sparks in great cascades of violet and turquoise, arcs of fire passing from one to the next. They darted hither and fro in bursts of super effervescence, their tiny heads branching into seven, nine or eleven long thin arms, while a longer thinner tail acted as a propulsion device, allowing them to swim through the air. Cady thought of the creatures as a kind of adopted nervous system, living in symbiotic relationship with Faynr, travelling her body from head to tail and acting as network of thoughts and feelings: in this way, the ghost must surely be aware of the *Juniper*, of the passengers, and of her chosen favourite, Brin Halsegger – if Lek's fanciful tale were true, that is. Cady was still in two or three or four minds about it. She turned now to look at the girl: Brin was staring in utter enchantment at the Xilliths, her hands reaching up, hoping to coax them nearer with the few sparks of the same nature that danced around her fingertips. The creatures were indeed tempted, for they hovered over the girl's head, searching, examining, analysing. And then they moved away upriver, perhaps carrying Brin's information with them. Yes, Faynr would know: the long-lost distant child had returned.

Lek's face struggled with its toolkit of emotions.

Cady brought her attention to the landing stage. The Nebulim had not moved on the platform. It didn't bode well. They would usually welcome visitors gladly. At the very least, they would be keen to trade goods. But there were no salutations as the *Juniper* bumped against the fenders. Before anyone could stop her, Brin leapt over the gunwale and from there down to the jetty. She was away, clambering at speed up the rope ladder that led to the platform above. Lek followed quickly enough, but still too slow to catch up with the girl before she vanished over the platform's rim. Cady went along at her own pace, huffing for breath as she climbed up onto the walkway. Lek was alone there. He was shouting Brin's name, demanding she come back to him, right this minute. But there was no response from the areas of shadow, nor from the glow of the lanterns, nor from the trio of Nebulim who stood there, slowly turning their heavy bodies towards the newcomers. Only their faces moved in any active way, their features flickering with a soft fire behind the glass visage set in the hard clay of their heads. One of the glass plates was cracked, another smeared with dirt. Their voices, when they tried to speak, were nothing more than grumbles, grunts, mutters. Faynr's decline had cast a spell of drowsy upon the village, the people.

Cady was alerted by Lek's cry. Brin had scrambled across to the next platform, nearer the riverbank, and was now standing under one of the paper lanterns. She was staring at a Nebulim's face, in rapt attention. Lek and Cady made their way across, Cady taking careful steps over the bridge, wary of the dark waters six feet beneath the rope netting.

"Isn't it marvellous!" Brin said, when Cady had finally made it to the wooden boards. "Their faces are made of fire!"

Cady stood behind the girl, looking at the Nebulim. The clay figure was five feet tall. Her face was a little more lively than those on the first platform. Her body was wrapped in lengths of wire and string and twine, through which the hard reddish flesh was glimpsed. The helmet-like head was bound with wires. The transparent plate of the face had been wiped clean recently, leaving a fan of clear glass through which a spectator could peer inside.

It was a teenage girl's face within, only a few years older than Brin.

The wraith-like occupants of the Nebulim had one thing in common: they were the drowned ones. The men, women and children who had fallen into the Nysis and been dragged under; or those poor souls who had willingly stepped into the current, their bodies weighed down with stones. Or, in earlier times, the ritual sacrifices given to the river, in hope of a good year to come, or an end to suffering. In every case, the dragon's ghost kept their spirits safe, until such a time as they might be raised up, conjured into being once more by an Ephreme priest. First, oils secreted from certain glands in Faynr's body were collected, and then set aflame: this flame was life-giving, with the power of resurrecting the drowned, whose spirits were then placed within the clay receptacles. And so their second life would begin. Cady had grown to love the Nebulim over the years, from visiting settlements such as this one; grown to love their faces of blue and red flames, their flickering eyes, the glow of their lips. She likened it to glimpsing a face in an open fire, an illusion only, but that illusion remade every second, again and again, the same face every time, fragile in its permanence.

The Nebulim teenager moved slowly, twisting at the waist with a creak. The wires and strings, usually tended to with pride, looked filthy and bedraggled, without any of the usual quirks of decoration that each Nebulim deemed so important. Her eyes brightened with orange flickers, a colour viewed as profane by the tribe's rulings. She tried to speak, but her words were barely heard. Was she warning them to stay away, as the painted sign on the bank had done?

Yanish joined them on the platform. Cady knew of an expert silk weaver, an old friend, and she told Yanish that she would take him to the woman's premises. Lek took charge of Brin and led her back to the boat, telling her off gently as they walked along the rope bridge.

Cady and Yanish set off, reaching the end of the raised platforms, climbing down onto solid ground. They walked the darkened alleyways of Ponperreth, with only an occasional lamp to give them direction. Any villagers met on the way were as benumbed as those on the platforms: they stood in shadowed doorways or stared at the visitors from the windows of dwelling houses and weaving sheds. A few went about their work – unravelling the myriad cocoons into strands of silk, or packing the still-intact cocoons into boxes for delivery to the hesting pools in Ludwich – but they did so at a caterpillar's pace, without passion, their eyes blank. None spoke. In some, the sacred flames of their faces gutted pitifully on the wicks, or else had died completely, and only darkness stirred behind the glass plates. The spirit vapours had seeped away. These empty shells leaned against walls, or sat on benches, propped in their final positions. To her horror, Cady saw one poor Nebulim disintegrate right in front of her eyes: the light flickering out, the clay cracking and fissuring, and then crumbling to dust, revealing the workings within, the little canisters of fuel, the wick, the various levers and mechanisms. For a moment only the wire skeleton remained, taking a step forward, until this too crumpled and bent, and the poor creature remained where he was, angled over, propped up against a lantern post.

Yanish looked on aghast. "What's happening here, Cady?"

"I don't know."

"Is this to do with Faynr, and her sickness?"

"Yes, maybe. But I didn't think it would be this bad."

"I just want to buy a new shroud. And then get back to the *Juniper*. This place gives me the shivers."

A few streets on they heard the sound of stamping feet, chanting, and rattles and whistles. Was it a celebration of some kind? Cady pulled Yanish to a halt beside her and they peered out from the shadows. The village square was filled with Nebulim, lively specimens, or at least livelier than the others they had seen. They moved at a steady half-pace, circling around a roaring bonfire of profane colours, throwing their possessions to the orange flames: chairs, suitcases, curtains, walking sticks, tyres, framed paintings, as well as many icons of Queen Luda, broken into pieces and cast into the fire. It was funeral pyre for everything they had once owned, believed in, loved or coveted.

Cady recognised the archmage of the village, Una Goodperson. She was an old Ephreme. She stood on a raised dais, leading the crowd in their devotion, her body shuddering in ecstasy, her hair long and wild around her shoulders, wings fluttering madly. Perhaps these villagers had suffered less from the illness that affected Ponperreth, or had been better protected?

The ceremony went on, the people chanting out words that sounded horrible to Cady's ears. She was reminded that the old plague pits existed beneath Ponperreth, when the city of Ludwich had shipped out its dead, the barges piled high with malformed corpses. She herself had worked one such vessel, as a deckhand. Lud, that was heart-rending work! And now, looking at the savage raucous scene before her, she could easily believe that in some way those victims of the Blight had risen up, goaded on by the archmage, to take over the villager's souls.

The palls of smoke parted, revealing the object of the crowd's veneration. It was a huge statue of a dragon, crudely sculpted from clay and timber and bound together with fishing nets and thick hawsers and barbed wire. It stood upright on its back legs, almost as high as the nearby church spire. Lud knows how long it had taken the Nebulim to build. At first sight, Cady thought it a badly executed representation of Haakenur. But no, it bore no true resemblance to the usual iconic figures and images: this was an entirely different beast, its long snout leading to a bared mouth filled with jagged metal teeth, its eyes shining yellow with clusters of headlamps. A pair of twisted horns ending in caps of silvered steel sprouted from its head. A penis fashioned from a ship's mast rose from between its hind legs.

The creature was monstrous.

A halo of myridi flies, millions of them, flew around the dragon's head, their glowing bodies lending its features a sheen of gold. The eyes of the dragon blinked and opened again, wider this time, perhaps worked by some hidden lever. And the people stamped and clapped and roared their approval, and bowed down before the icon, and rose up again, their hands held high, their voices sounding as one voice, one chant, one unutterable howl of madness.

Cady stood entranced.

Those eyes of yellow light, how they stared at her!

With an angry gesture, Yanish drew her away from the sight. They made their way through a warren of ginnels and back alleys, before stopping outside a squat sturdy-looking dwelling made of wattle and daub. It was a weaver's house. Cady rapped on the door. The lace curtains twitched, and then the door was quickly opened by a Nebulim woman. To her immense relief, Cady saw that Numi Tan was still her old self, or at least partway so: she was a little slow in her movements, and her speech was drawled, but clear. Her clay body creaked and cracked, and she groaned under its duress: but most of all, she was glad to see Cady. They embraced. It was good to feel the wires and strings of Numi's body, and to share the warmth of her flame close up.

"Oh, Numi, it's so good to see you!"

The Nebulim's eyes flickered with a fine cerise light behind the glass visor. Numi had been a Wodwo woman in her first life, and her features still retained the tribal bone structure, even though now made of flame.

Yanish asked to see the weaver's best rolls of shroud silk. Numi was pleased to show him her wares, but was also ashamed of the quality. "It hasn't been a good harvest." She looked embarrassed when Yanish frowned at the threadbare material on offer. "Many of the flies hatched early," she explained. "And the cocoons we could gather were weak, with loose strands."

"Faynr's the cause of this, is she?"

Numi's face fluttered. Cady knew the Nebulim flames for *worry*, and also those for a *lie* – and Numi's features were caught somewhere between the two.

"Numi, what's really going on in Ponperreth? We saw a ceremony before, a bonfire."

"Faynr's sickness affected us badly," Cady's friend answered. "Some worse than others. We fell ill, the entire village."

Yanish looked up from his inspection of the silks. "People seem to be moving very slowly, frozen, even."

"And worse than that," Cady added. "Some of them were breaking apart. Dying."

Numi turned away. She whispered, "I don't know what to do." The weaver was sickening, if not yet as bad as some of the others.

"We can get you help," Cady said.

Numi shook her head. "There is none, I'm afraid."

Cady despaired, seeing her friend in this state. "At least tell us about Ponperreth. It seems very badly changed." Numi's hands pulled repeatedly at one of the strands of wire around her waist, rather like a nun worrying at a string of beads. Then she looked up and composed herself as best she could.

"We are the Nebuli."

The use of the archaic plural form surprised Cady, but she let Numi carry on.

"As you know, the dragon's ghost, in her bounty, gives us a second chance at life. Because of this, we are bound to Faynr's many moods and seasons; and so we fall ill as she falls ill. But there is more, a further symptom."

"Be strong, dearest," Cady said. "Tell it true."

"A demonic creature might be taking advantage of Faynr's sickness."

"The thing they were worshipping in the square?" Numi's flames darkened into grey flickers. "So many of us believe that by paying homage and making sacrifice, this new beast will protect us, and make us powerful."

"It sounds like folly, Numi. Of the worst kind."

"Maybe, yes maybe."

Her voice trailed off. But Cady felt her anger rising. "What is this creature?"

"Another ghost of the dragon, born when Faynr was born. According to the new gospel, when Queen Luda and her priests made their initial conjuring, both of Haakenur's spirits were released at the same time. Two ghosts."

"You mean... Faynr has a twin?"

Numi's body creaked as she lowered herself into a chair.

"Yes, that's one explanation. A twin brother, cast into exile. A shadow self." She rubbed at her visor. "You know of Una Goodperson, I think?"

Cady nodded. "The Ponperreth archmage."

"Una started to preach about this new ghost a few weeks ago. She calls him the Night Serpent. In her Sunday sermons, she told of his origin, his birth from the poison sac in Haakenur's tail."

"You mean the poison that killed King Lud, in the legend?" Cady asked.

"The very same."

"Oh my. I don't like the sound of that, not at all."

Numi nodded in agreement. "Goodperson told us of the Night Serpent's purpose in the world, only now revealed. She claims that Queen Luda quickly suppressed this second spirit, out of fear, and cast him for all of time away from Ludwich, and from Kethra, even."

"Where did he go?"

"A place of darkness. Its name is unknown. There he lies in bondage. But now, roused once more, he seeks readmittance to our world."

"Villagers were throwing statues of Luda to the flames," Yanish observed.

"Yes. A terrible thing. According to Una Goodperson a new glorious age is upon us. But the Night Serpent is a fierce master. We must all give in to his demands. Thus the archmage proclaims, in full and fiery voice, and the people bow down in their prayers."

Yanish asked for the dragon's name.

Numi paused again. And then said: "They call him Gogmagog."

Cady drew in a sharp breath. Her mind tumbled with

images, feelings, fragments, with church bells under the water and unexploded bombs, and gravestones, and above all... questions, so many damned questions! But before she had time to ask even one of them, there was a commotion from outside. The sound of running feet, chanting, drums beating, glass breaking nearby.

"It's been like this, these last few days," Numi explained. "People are so scared, their fear tips over into anger, and violence—" She cut off her own speech, not wanting to carry the thoughts any further.

Yanish went to the door and peeped out. "They've gone now," he said. "Just kids, from the look of it. Teenagers."

Numi nodded. "The young have fallen under Goodperson's influence. They truly believe that Gogmagog will save them. And they do not take kindly to unbelievers."

Cady cursed to herself, before saying, "You mentioned that Gogmagog is taking advantage of Faynr's illness, to find a doorway. Can that be true?"

Numi considered: "I believe it to be so. And by these means he will become the new ruler of the River Nysis, and of the towns and cities along its course. So the archmage claims."

Yanish asked a question: "Why Ponperreth? Did something draw Gogmagog here?"

"Some believe he feeds on everything that is rotten and decayed, and that the restless dead of the Blight pits bring him succour. Others think he cannot move beyond the village's range, for now, at least, that he needs our worship to keep his grip on the world. But he grows in power, day by day."

Yanish's shadow trembled across the wall in agitation. "This is some crazy crystal show. Because no one's actually seen this Gogmagog guy, have they? It's a tale told by a mad mage."

But Numi was serious. "I feel that he draws closer every day, every night, and will soon be present entirely, in body and spirit."

Cady wished to dismiss all that she was hearing, and yet the riddle of the never-nevers still called to her, for an answer. She drew up close to her Nebulim friend. "Numi, you cannot stay here. Come with us, to Ludwich."

"This is my home."

"I know, I know. I understand. But the place has changed so much. It no longer nurtures your flame."

Numi Tan's fiery face twisted into tangled skeins of silver and black. It was the sign of dread. But Cady had to fight against such considerations.

"You have family there, don't you, Numi? In Ludwich?"

"Yes, in Timmusk village."

"Well then, come with us. You have to!"

Yanish chose a length of silk. "I'll take this one," he said. "For my father's shadow, a place of rest."

Numi would not accept payment, but Yanish insisted and he placed the coins, far too many of them, in her clay-lined palm. Her face fluttered with a bright fire of gladness.

Cady turned to the door. She felt her optic gland tingling. Something was wrong, something not yet seen. The answer came immediately, as the window of the room smashed inwards, shocking them all. A large stone landed on the floorboards. Shards of glass flew everywhere, and Numi's pet cat – hidden until now behind a loom – dashed out of the room with a mewling shriek. The air glittered with silvery dust. Cady instinctively ducked down in panic, covering her head with her hands. Yanish stood calm. His aphelon pulsed from dark grey to white and his shadow danced madly before he managed to drag it back to its home in the flesh. Numi Tan remained seated, quite still. The flames of her face guttered out and the visage was dark, inky black. It was a momentary effect, luckily: the wick sputtered back into life, flickering and at last catching fire. A few more seconds of darkness would have killed the spirit in its mask of clay and she would have keeled over, in a faint. But no. Numi stood up, her face setting into angry ripples of fire and she hurried to the front door, stepping outside to confront the mob.

Yanish moved to follow her, Cady soon after. "Where is she?" Yanish didn't answer. He was looking up and down the narrow alleyway, now deserted. There was no sign of Numi. But the far end of the alleyway was dark, and within that darkness a small lick of blue flame was glimpsed. It flickered a little redder, as Numi Tan stepped forward. She was shivering, the wires and metal adornments around her body rattling against each other in a tinny music. Her face flared up with a fierceness that filled her visor completely. She took another step, faltering. Then she collapsed. Yanish was there before she could hit the ground, gathering her weight in his arms.

Cady said, "Let's get out of here." She led the way to the end of the alley. Numi murmured as she was helped along, supporting herself on Yanish's shoulder. They skirted the village square, where the main body of the mob still worshipped. The cacophonous chanting had settled into a long complex chain of syllables. *Gog Gogma Gogmagog Mamagog Gogmama Gog Gogmamagog Mamamamagoggog Gog! Gog! Gog! GOGMAGOG!* And so it went on, loud and vibrant enough to make the air shake, and for the giant clay and metal icon to shimmer in the smoke and the flames. Cady felt sure she saw something rising up from the statue's form, a second body, this one made of black mist and ashes – the shadow of the dragon stirring into life. A trick of the light and the flames and the smoke, surely?

Numi had recovered from her shock a little, and was now able to lead them by a hidden route, back towards the riverside. When they reached the first of the raised platforms over the river, Cady saw that a crowd had gathered there, a fierce looking bunch, twenty or so of the younger Nebulim; they were looking up at the tiny figure who stood atop the platform. It was Brin. Brin Halsegger, her face lit by the converging glow of two nearby lanterns. She looked older and fiercer, somehow. More than a child, more than flesh itself. Flashes of blue and violet light fluttered around her head. Cady could not look at her directly, and had to shield her eyes.

The Nebulim were also affected by this apparition; they stood in silence, all holding the same posture, their face-flames displaying the exact same colour: scarlet. They were all of one mind, but what that *mind* might be, Cady could not conceive. Perhaps they would once again turn to their true faith, seeing how Faynr laid her loving colours over the girl. But instead, an angry guttural cry went up, made of many different tones and sounds, all blurring together. *Gogmagog Mamagog Gogmama Gogmamagog Gogmagog!* The crowd pushed against the base of the platform and a few began to climb up the netting. It was slow-going, and Cady took some little solace from that. But they would make their way to the upper level soon enough.

Yanish spoke quickly: "We have to do something."

Cady turned to Numi Tan for advice, only to see that her friend had also been taken over by Brin's magical presence.

She stared up at the young girl, her face of flames painted that same scarlet colour. Yanish nudged at Cady and pointed upwards. Thrawl Lek was now standing beside Brin. He looked down at the Nebulim crowd and raised his fist at them, only to receive jeers and shouted threats in return. He tried to make Brin step away from the platform's edge, to get her back to the boat. But the girl would not be moved. She stood defiant.

The first of the Nebulim had now reached the top of the netting.

Brin raised her hands.

Storm clouds settled, a dark weight that pressed down upon the village. Only darkness ruled here, a darkness from which there was no escape. And yet, within this darkness, flickers of violet light were seen, dancing at the tips of Brin's fingers. Sparkles of light gave her a halo. She was alive with this energy. Behind her, along the length of the visible Nysis, the Xilliths shimmered over the water, their bodies made of the same energy that flashed at Brin's command. Their colours and their light joined with hers and she glowed like a living crystal transmitter, something not of this world, or something new upon the world.

And seeing this, the crowd fell silent. The Nebulim were fearful of this ten year-old child. Many of the climbers had fallen back, in fear, but one Nebulim persisted in his attempts to scramble onto the ledge. Brin's hands joined together, acting as a point of focus. A bolt of fire was released from where the hands lightly touched at the palms, pure Xillithic energy brought to bear as a weapon, or a warning. It formed itself into a spear of incandescence.

The lone Nebulim staggered on the edge of the platform as the bolt hit him, and he fell back, back down towards the startled faces and the catching hands of his fellows. He landed among them, and was soon swallowed up into the tribe's protection.

Now Brin reigned supreme, her body aglow, her face barely recognisable.

Cady could not move, captured as she was by the sight.

And then the storm broke. It fell from the heavy clouds of Faynr's body, in raindrops as black and mucilaginous as blood-ink dripped from the dragon's veins. It fell sharply, cascading off the wooden platforms onto the bank, instantly soaking all there attendant, and turning the ground into a thick greasy mud. The river was pockmarked, where each drop made its impact.

Brin stood upon the platform's edge, her body fizzing under the downpour, the sparks at her hands and head flashing brighter and then trailing off into smoke. One last bolt of energy zipped from her joined hands, hitting the ground below with some force, sending the crowd back, away from the bankside. Many ran for cover in the nearest buildings, others stayed where they were, but empty of all strength now.

Cady pushed Yanish and Numi forward, and they scrambled up the netting. Lek was waiting for them. Once Numi was at the top, Yanish reached down his hand for Cady, to help her.

But Cady had stopped climbing. For she had heard something, a tiny noise.

Yanish called to her. "Come up, old chiv, quickly now."

The rain fell on her upturned face. "No, you go on, Yan, get them in the boat. Go on!"

She stumbled away from the ladder, ducking under the platform, onto the muddy ground at the river's edge. The rain's force was lessened here, but could still be felt against her face, driven sideways as it was by the rushing wind. All around was noise and chaos, and flashes of light and fire, and the river's cold pull waiting for her if she made one false step. But she could not stop now. Not now. She cupped her hand to her best ear. Surely a useless gesture in this tumult, in this storm. Yet she listened, and heard the same sound as before.

Yes! There it was! At last!

The sound of a bell ringing, ringing.

She lumbered out from under the platform's meagre protection and slogged along the river's bank, boots sinking into the clutching wet earth. Gritting her teeth, she stumbled on, entering a bed of tall reeds. Here, she disturbed the myriid cocoons in their multitudes. The air was clogged with strands of fine silk, clammy against her face like a mask.

Cady wiped at her eyes frantically.

Her clothes were heavy and damp and her feet sank further down.

Each step was a puzzle to be solved.

She peered through the curtains of the rain. Her optic gland had been fully activated, and the slope of skin between her eyes glowed with an emerald light. Yes, there was something about this particular stretch of bank: the reed beds, the long line of weeping willows and the half-submerged rusted cannon… it all reminded her of days past, long past.

The bell was louder now.

A high sound, a silvery ringing. And then a low clang. She heard it clearly.

The *Juniper* was making its way around the platforms, following Cady's slow progress along the bank. Brin had climbed onto the cabin's roof, where she waved frantically. But Cady trudged on, seeking the source of the bell's sound.

Bell, gravestone, bomb. Bomb, gravestone, bell.

Yes, it had to be close.

She slipped and fell head-first into the soft ground. It was a struggle to escape, and her hands and feet scrabbled about frantically. And then she felt herself rising up, grabbed from behind. It was Yanish, her friend. He was helping her. "What are you looking for, Cady?"

"The bell. Can't you hear it?"

Yanish listened. It was obvious from his face that he could hear nothing, nothing at all. But Cady broke away from his grasp and she set off once more, finding a new path. Yanish followed closely behind. Here, the river's muddy bank popped and bubbled with some gaseous substance, which rose in small puffs of purplish-grey vapour, mixing with the rain. Cady felt giddy, as these noxious fumes entered her nostrils and set her eyes stinging. She pushed all thoughts of the plague pits from her mind. And she kept going, there was no other option.

Now the *Juniper*'s spotlight swept the bank, illuminating the pair as they moved on, past a stunted elm, past the skeleton of a rowing boat. The bell called Cady forward, the bell ringing, high, then low, high, then low. Louder, louder!

Here! Yes!

She dropped to her knees and started to dig blindly but with purpose, her hands clawing back the dense mud, quickly making a hole deep enough for her arms to sink into, her body leaning over, her head bowed, lowered into the ground until only her sailor's pigtail was visible. The spotlight rested upon her and upon the bubbling earth all around. Yanish knelt beside her, urging her to hurry up, whatever it was she might be doing.

But Cady was alone now: all other thoughts – of the boat, her crewmates, the village and the Nebulim, and the rain, the endless rain – all had left her. Instead, a single memory had taken her over. All she had to do was find the treasure, the wooden box she had buried here all those centuries ago, under Dr John Dee's precise instructions. Contents unknown. But it had to be here, it had to be! Her fingernails were cracked and filthy, and her face was streaked with mud, and her clothes were wet through, as the rain came down harder. But she kept on digging, digging, until at last her hands clattered against wood, and she pulled the box free from the earth and held it to her, drawing a much-needed breath into her lungs. She put her ear against the box.

The bell sounded from within. Cady's heart was gladdened. The never-nevers had spoken to her in a dream, and she had followed their riddle to this one point in time, this place.

The *Juniper* bumped against the rotted timbers of a jetty, and made fast. Lek was at the helm, while Numi Tan stood in the bow, shouting down at Cady, urging her to climb aboard.

Yanish added his own voice: "Come on, let's go now."

But over his shoulder Cady could see a group of villagers had gathered on the high ridge of the bank; they stood and stared, and were silent. Above them in the cold and pitiless sky, the eyes of Gogmagog glared down, made of sparks that had travelled here from the bonfire in the village square, gathered together, and formed into these fierce yellow orbs. Likewise, the creature's body of smoke and dust and grime and ashes writhed like a giant born of the flames of the villager's ardent worship. Invoked by the archmage, the passions of Ponperreth had brought forth a visible form for the Night Serpent, to give him this nebulous unreal body. The rain streaked through the creature of smoke and was taken in as a kind of blood, or ichor. The monster was ingesting what he could, to give himself more substance.

Seeing this apparition in the sky, Cady felt a fear she had never before known. She reached for Yanish, allowing him to help her to her feet. His aphelon glowed brightly, showing his concern, and his love for her. They made their way to the jetty, hand in hand. Yanish was still holding onto his father's new shroud. Cady dared to look back.

Gogmagog's brumous body writhed around the posts and wrecks on the mudbanks. He was suckling at the sludge pits, at the bubbles of gas as they popped up from beneath, from underground chambers; he was taking in the rancid puffs of vapour as food or fuel. Sustained and nourished, he took on a slightly more solid form. Here and there, his smoke coagulated into lumps of thick dust. His yellow eyes kindled to a radiant life. From the rotten materials of this world he was adding to himself, devouring anything he could find that was dank, damp or putrid. He nuzzled amid a pile of dead fish. At the water's edge he drank of engine oil and effluent. He looked a little like the statue erected in his honour, but had very quickly outstripped the villagers' imaginative powers. His true shape was not yet seen, only glimpsed, as he rose up, hovering in a monstrous hulking form above the cocoon beds. Where the *Juniper*'s spotlight passed over him, the patches of oil on his now forming skin glistened in rainbow colours. The myridi flies swarmed in their countless numbers, becoming his cape, his mantle, his pelt.

And he screamed!

Lud alone knew where it came from, this noise: it sounded like the entire population of the village shrieking at once, giving collective voice to a set of nightmarish desires. Or had some other sound emerged, from deeper yet in the river's history of plague and warfare and public drownings? No matter its origin, the monster's call was loud enough to freeze the heart. Cady could feel him at her brow and temples, seeking her weakest points, a way inside the skull. The smoke engulfed her and Yanish in a cloud of grey sooty air. They both started coughing, and Yanish stumbled a little. Cady held him tight, urging him on. But Gogmagog had found his opening, his tiny brightly lit doorway, and he reached out with a single elongated tendril of oily malodorous vapour, tapping against Yanish's forehead, seeking admittance at the aphelion.

The smoke wormed its way inside, slithering.

Cady tried to call out: she was afraid, dreadfully afraid. "Yanish!" Her friend collapsed into her arms, and from there to the boards of the jetty. The silvery grey of his aphelon lingered for a moment longer, and then turned to black, jet black. His head lolled backwards and his eyes rolled up into the lids, leaving only the whites exposed.

Cady held him tightly to her.

He shuddered, once, twice, and then fell back again, breathing heavily.

And no matter how many times she called his name, he would not respond to her.

Yanish, Yanish, Yanish!

His hands fell open weakly and the silk shroud was stolen by the wind and the rain. Cady tried desperately to catch it, but it tumbled from the jetty down into the mud at the river's edge and was quickly taken away by the current.

Oh Lud! Great Lud in heaven, why are you doing this to us!

She was vaguely aware of approaching footsteps as Lek and Brin came to her side. Lek bent down to examine Yanish, the beams of his eyes passing quickly over the shivering body. He spoke urgently: "We have to get him back to the boat." He lifted Yanish up, carrying the heavy form in his two strong arms. Cady and Brin followed, the girl leading the old lady along. But at the very point of boarding, Cady stopped and looked back. The Nebulim stood in ragged assembly along the bank, their faces showing only the scarlet fires of their master, the Night Serpent, who hovered above them all, his dark mass resplendent in fog and rainclouds.

The wooden box still sat upon the jetty. Cady hesitated, but then took a step towards it, only to see Brin run past her, to scoop up the object herself. And now they climbed aboard. Lek went to the helm as Brin and Cady knelt beside Yanish, trying to calm him. It did little good. But at least the *Juniper* was moving now, into the midstream.

Only one thing mattered: sailing free of the Myhr, and Gogmagog's command. Cady had to believe that the demon could not move beyond the village's reach, that the villagers' worship was a prime source of his vital energies.

Numi stood at the prow as a pilot, shouting out her orders. Lek acted immediately on every call as the rain smashed down upon the suddenly flimsy vessel. The air was jet black, and the boat's spotlight spluttered helplessly. And yet the *Juniper* made her way, working as she could.

The border of the next region lay a mile beyond Ponperreth's boundary: a vast wall of ghostly flesh that yearned for the crew, reaching out with fingers of mist, with flowers of pink light, with speckles of gold and silver, with faces human and otherwise, so many of them, each one a gaping mouth and a set of eyes, all calling, all quivering, all seeing, a mass of life at its wildest expression. It was a vortex. A horrible slurping song was heard, the sound of many tongues slathering. Only madness lay ahead, the strangeness of realms beyond any they had yet encountered.

The boat's engine spun on and on with a violent motion, the pistons almost breaking free from their cylinders, oil spraying everywhere, the funnel belching smoke, the water churned into white foam under the propeller's gyre.

Cady stood up. Her face was a green mask, as she made her way forward. She pushed Numi aside and took up her true role, her natural role in life: to set the course, to chart the darkness, to surge ahead wherever it would take her, away from the old, the painful, the lost companions. No more. No more of that! And if she screamed then, no one heard it: Not Brin, and not Numi Tan, although the flames of her face wavered in blue and red; and not even Lek, who worked the wheel with a resolute expertise. And not even Cady herself, even though she occupied the exact centre of the scream, where it was loudest, and most silent. And where that silence gripped her, the scream went on, unheard. It was made of the fibres of Cady's being, of her roots in the soil as a Haegra, of the particles that emanated from her lungs, from the twigs and leaves of her hair and the rich loam on her breath, and the buds that grew larger on her arms, laden with ovules, getting ready to flower. And because it was made of her own body, this scream would never leave her, not ever.

She glanced back and saw the two yellow eyes of Gogmagog blinking, high above the village, each orb dripping with a red-tinged ichor. The howling of the Night Serpent could still be heard, muffled now: a sound born in the mists, in magic, in those terrible moments when King Lud had run Haakenur through. There was blood on the long-lost blade of Ibraxus – and this howl was enough to break the sword in two.

The dragon breathed, sending forth a great cloud of smoke which enveloped the boat, stern to bow. He was at the very limits of his power, Cady could feel that. But still, she was as good as blinded, her optic gland pinched, her vision fogged. Because of this, she had to direct the boat by feel, trusting to her instincts.

She was the pilot. The steersman. The watchwoman!

Her mind was focussed only on the Winding Way, all the knowledge stored within of currents, crosscurrents, countercurrents – anything at all to stop from thinking about Yanish. Keep going, that was all, just keep going, don't stop. Never stop!

And she shouted out her instructions in a voice that broke on every word: *Ahead, steady, to starboard, steady, half ahead, ease to port, full ahead!*

Finally, they were leaving Gogmagog's darkness. The rain fell in shards, splintering the deck. Lightning hit the foremast in a crackle of fire. And through it all, Cady could still hear that noise, the silvered bell ringing in her skull, deep inside.

The borderline closed around them. Brin was laughing, screaming, crying.

And the *Juniper* battered on.

PART TWO
The Tithe Gate

To speak of the Haegra is to speak of mystery. For centuries their true genesis was hidden from the common people, their patterns and process held in volumes belonging only to the Priesthood. From these books now unbound I have taken sure knowledge, that the Haegra have worked among us in secret, long protecting our Realm and our Kindred. Many declare them dead, or dying. While others claim they work at their tasks still, their faces masked in shadow.

Mistress Pynne – A Chronicle of the Kethran Isles, Their Varied Peoples, and Their Rulers.

A Beautiful Day
in Kethra

It truly *was*. Quite the loveliest day Cady had experienced in many a while. She walked along the pathway, feeling the sun on her face and hands, a gentle breeze at her neck. The land shimmered in a haze of yellow and green light. Climbing over a stile she entered a field of grass, the stalks reaching her waist. Bees buzzed and a hidden grasshopper burred. A suitable distance from the path Cady lowered her bell-bottoms and bloomers and squatted down to have a wee. Her fingers rubbed at the squidgy bump on her thigh: a new arrival. It was a pleasant feeling. She had a fair collection of buds by now: on both forearms, right thigh, the back of her left hand, her belly, and high on her left shoulder. Seven all told, all them arriving in just the last few hours. It was funny, because she'd never been a *flowery* person before, not as such, more herby, really, *herbaceous*, even. Yes, that was the word. Probably because her mixture was more human than plant.

Bodily functions completed, she walked on a little further and then lay down in the grass. The sun dazzled and when she closed her eyes, colours danced in the dark. She could sleep here, for an hour or two; yes, why not? Just doze off and leave it all behind, all the problems onboard the boat: Lek's whining, Brin's skipping and scampering, and most of all Yanish's troubled soul. Instead, she listened to the song of a lark, high in the sky, and enjoyed the feel of an insect crawling on her skin. The sensation made her sit up. It was a butterfly, tickling the bud on the back of her hand with its antennae. Perhaps it was interested in pollination? But then it flew away.

Cady sighed. She wanted to be filled to the full, but instead she was unfulfilled. And that, my dearest dears, was a goddamn problem!

In the undergrowth she spied the lilac petals of a fipple flute. She recalled showing Oswyn – her sister Nabs's boy – how to pluck two of the petals, hold them together, and blow through them. She did this now, just to please herself. The sound was high and pure. There was a tale that went with the flower: how the fipple flute, blown just so, might summon up the ghosts of the past. They had fluted well and long, her and Oswyn! And indeed a shadow had passed along a brick wall, that day, a shadow that belonged to neither nephew or aunt. How Oswyn had laughed, but with a nervous tinge to it. He had been, what, seven or eight at the time?

Now she stopped her whistling and listened carefully. Was there someone moving through the grass, close by? She was sitting cross-legged, cut off from view, and for a moment was glad of it.

But the noise had faded.

She blew on the two leaves again, and waited. Yes, there it was again, the sound of a person or an animal walking, the stalks bending over, and back again, rubbing against themselves.

Cady stood up suddenly. She looked around in a full circle.

The meadow was empty, herself the only occupant.

One more time, she blew on the fipple.

The grasses stirred a few yards away from her, forward and back, disturbed by some invisible presence. Cady held herself still and quiet, following the progress of the ghost, if such it was. "Who are you? Show yourself." The grasses bent steeper and stayed where they were, creating a depression. The air whispered and a dark shape appeared, at first fuzzy and indistinct, and then taking on a little more form, enough for her to recognize the figure who now occupied the meadow. He wore the black skullcap and the white neck-ruffle she remembered from their previous meetings, always the same outfit, no matter the time or the season. His beard was silvered and groomed into a point. His long black robes shushed against the grasses.

Cady was staring at Dr John Dee, Astronomer in Chief, Designer of Marvels, Professor of the Magical Arts to her Royal Highness Queen Hilde.

Three hundred and thirty-eight years dead to this world.

"Dr Dee? Can you hear me? John?"

Dee's eyes passed over her as they would over a tree in blossom or a mural on a wall, taking a momentary interest, nothing more.

Cady grunted. Trust the old bugger to turn up, and then ignore her!

"Here's a problem for you, Clever Clogs. Yesterday I stepped inside my effigy, all ready to be made young again, and guess what? Well, take a look at me. Look!" She displayed herself, arms wide, legs akimbo. "Take a ganders, Johnny Boy, go on!"

Dee walked around his circle in the grass. Cady saw that he carried a sheaf of papers with him, she hadn't noticed them before. They slipped from his fingers one by one, to be caught by the breeze. One fluttered nearby and Cady grabbed it and gazed at the words and diagrams: a map of Faynr from her tail in the Tangle Wood to the west of Ludwich city, down to her head at Woodwane Spar, and marked with her different regions and her various bodily organs: brain, heart, womb, spleen, liver, and so on. Dr Dee had been the first to truly explore the true meaning of the dragon's ghost. A second page showed an ink drawing of the womb of Haakenur with young Queen Luda wrapped within, various tubes and veins interconnecting them. The flow of blood and maternal fluids was clearly demonstrated. Another page was a diagram of a Mechanical Man, a *Thrawl*, as Dee named it, an idea that would take centuries to come to fruition, once Jane Polter took up the basic concept and made it a reality.

The paper crumbled to dust in Cady's hand; this page and all the others. She looked up and was surprised to see Dr Dee standing close to her. Very close. His eyes were as black as his skullcap and they stood out fiercely against the silver beard and the waxed moustache. His face creased with lines of worry: yes, he had something of import to say, that was evident. His lips parted. Would he speak to her? *Come on, you quivering phantom, let's hear the news. What's in store for me?*

Out of the blue cloudless sky, a fighter plane flew across the meadow, diving low, its wind-rush pushing the grasses back and almost blowing Cady off her feet. There was an airfield at Little St Jessop: the pilots must be missing the days of action, a feeling she knew well enough. The Hellblaster passed over the land, tipping its wings aslant the meadow's edge before flying off into the distance. And when the quiet returned, and the stalks had resumed their height… the phantom of Dr Dee had vanished.

Cady was alone. After a moment of heartache, she turned and made her way back to the path that ran alongside the River Moule. The shallows of the waterway were alive with fish, the blue filament of a haakenfly hovered amid the reeds. After a short walk the smaller tributary joined with the River Nysis. The land was flat for miles around and the great length of Faynr was visible on both sides, to west and east, making a vast shimmering wall. At this region its outer skin was mirrored, brightly so: the sky was reflected in the curvature, the gleam of the sun, and the V shape of a flock of birds. And lower down, herself. Arcadia Meade.

Her hand touched the streaks of mud on her face: they were caked on. Her hands were bruised and cut, her clothes torn in places, and the lobe of her left ear was mangled, giving her the look of an aged wrestler. Great Lud Almighty! On top of which, her right eye was having trouble staying open; it twitched madly like a warning light on a ship's dashboard.

She pushed at the soft skin of Faynr and made her way inside. The mirror closed around her. The sun and haze of the Kethran countryside was cut off instantly, to be replaced with a tropical atmosphere. Known as the Freyh, this chamber of Faynr's body was dank and hot and swarming with midges. Bullfrogs croaked. Spiders made their webs. But it was safe here, or safe enough. A curtain of fronds hung down from the trees. And there, sitting on a bed of blood-red mud in a drained lagoon, leaning against a jetty, was the *Juniper*.

Cady stood and stared, taking in the damage done, the scars on the upper hull. One of the tyre fenders had been lost and a second was in a sorry state of deflation. Thrawl Lek was scraping some kind of purple gunk off the keel with the blade of a shovel. His features held two expressions at the same time, one happy, one sad, which gave his face a blurred unreadable effect. He nodded at Cady. There was nothing to say. She climbed aboard. Numi Tan was at work with a broom and a pail of water. Her face-flames fluttered weakly. She was losing fuel. Cady entered the cabin, where Brin was trying to coax some life into her sprite toy. But the poor little thing was dead. A little over an hour had passed since they had escaped the madness of Gogmagog at Ponperreth, yet the girl looked different: the trials and tribulations of Faynr had stripped some of the innocence from her. Her temples were raw at the hesting points. She was ready for the next stage of her life. They had been travelling since eight o'clock that morning, when the *Juniper* had left Anglestume. Cady stared at the cabin clock, hardly believing it was twenty past five. Faynr played tricks with time. Ludwich city was seventeen miles away according to Maguire & Hill, along the river that wound its way around the old sailor's heart, and pulled tight enough to make her fear she was drowning.

A gulp of gin helped to quell the jitters.

The hessian shroud lay in a crumpled heap on the opposite seat. Cady picked it up and folded it carefully. She placed it inside the left-side bench locker and then walked out onto the afterdeck. Yanish was sitting on the transom, his back against the flagpole. His eyes were closed. He had fashioned an oily bandana to wrap around his head, concealing his aphelon. Cady had never seen it hidden away before, and she realised just how much she relied on its subtle gradations of grey to help in understanding her friend's moods. She said, "As soon as the blood tide comes in, we'll have to set off. How are we doing?"

He opened his eyes. A curiously wide smile took over his lips. "Matchless, old chiv. Sparky as all hell." He stood up and bopped about, spinning on his feet like one of those lizardy specimens on the dance floor of the Lido Ballroom on a Saturday night. "Stoked. Just swell."

She didn't even know what he was talking about any more, and he made her nervous with his sudden movements. Ever since Gogmagog's attack at the Nebulim village he'd been like this: skittish, madcap, irritable at times, and more jittery than a toad on a bed of thorns. She would have liked to enquire after his health: how did he feel, was he ill, was he scared? But every question was met with a slurry of street slang and neologisms. His true feelings were out of reach, but Cady would not give up on him.

"How's the engine? It looks okay to me?"

"Like a whistle. Squeaky."

"Good. That's erm… yes, good." She kept her eyes on his. "I had a nice conversation, just now. John Dee came to see me, in a field. Dr Dee, himself. You learned about him at school, didn't you? He had travelled through the centuries, and was very tired. But he showed me some pages from his notebooks." She coughed. "Of course he was only a ghost. Or a trace memory, recorded in the landscape. Or a vision in my head. Who knows? Still, he was real enough to me, and isn't that all that matters, eh, what do you say, Yan? Um?"

In answer, the young man unwrapped the strip of cloth from around his head, to reveal his aphelion – coal black, a blind triangular eye. Cady felt she was gazing into the grave's mouth, and she trembled with it. She thought of the terrible moment when that tendril of Gogmagog had bored its way into Yanish's brow. What terrible thoughts must stir there...

"How do you like it, chiv?" His hand traced at the spot. "Bright as a king's crown, I'll bet."

Cady realised that he hadn't looked in a mirror since the attack, and was perhaps living in a dream world. But she let it pass, instead saying brightly, "Righty-ho then. Let's get the old girl shipshape."

Quarter of an hour later the blood tide came in, seeping from a set of glands in one of Faynr's inner walls. People called it blood, they called it a tide, but really nobody knew what it was: some phantom chemical flowing from death to life, back and forth on a secret pulse. Now it lapped at the *Juniper*'s keel. Soon they would be lifted clear of the mud.

They waited in the cabin, all five of them. Their attention was focussed on the wooden box sitting on the table, the box Cady had dug up at Ponperreth. It was a foot high cube, all its sides engraved with an intricate abstract pattern. There was a brass keyhole. Lek leaned forward. The sliver of metal emerged from the knuckle of his index finger. This was inserted into the keyhole. It didn't take long: there was a soft click from the tumblers. Cady lifted the lid. The handbell, now revealed, was a thing of silvered metal, with a black handle. How it made such a loud noise, to call to her through that storm, from the soil, no one could imagine. It was remarkably well-preserved. Cady examined the lines of prayer around the rim, the same as those glimpsed in her never-never vision. First seen in a dream, solid, massive, larger than she was; now held easily in her hand, a refined object.

"It's an old Wodwo tradition," she explained. "A witch's

bell designed to prevent evil forces from entering a village or household. My friend Fable Duncliffe has a tinplate one above the door of her shop, to keep the nasties away."

Brin was reaching into the box. She had found something else, a second object.

"What have you got there, Miss Brin?" Lek asked.

"It's a coin." She showed it to everyone; a silver coin with a head on each side, one male, the other female.

"I've never seen anything like it," Cady told them.

"This is King Lud," Brin explained. "And this side is Queen Luda."

"How do you know that?"

"Who else could it be? It's a Ludluda coin."

Lek asked, "But why is it in the box, alongside the bell?"

Nobody could answer that one.

Numi fluttered her flames. "Cady, pray tell us what you know."

Everyone craned forward as Cady told the story. "In the Year of the Blight, Dr Dee designed and created a series of these boxes. He appointed his agents to distribute them along the length of the Nysis, from Woodwane to the outskirts of the maze at Tangle Wood. In other words, along the length of Faynr's body."

Lek said, "I've read nothing of the like in any of the books in my library."

"I was alive then." Cady looked at each person in turn. "I worked with the doctor. I buried the box at Ponperreth."

There was nothing to be held back now, not after all they had been through together. And so she added calmly, "I am a watchwoman, a Haegra."

They all looked at her. Lek was the first to speak. "I had such a notion."

"Well I *knew* all along," Brin announced proudly. "Mrs Meade told me. But I was sworn to secrecy."

The Thrawl found his best surviving frown and displayed it.

Yanish laughed out loud. He clapped his hand together in mock applause. "Very good. Well done, Madam. Oh, Cady's full of secrets. She spits in the eyes of her best friends."

"Yanish…"

He turned away from her gaze, saying to the table at large, "Five years together on river and land, and not a word, not a seed, not a leaf, not a root, only stories."

She looked at him, hoping for understanding. But when he looked back at her, his face was set in stone. Only his shadow moved to show a tremble of emotion.

Numi Tan asked, "What purpose did the boxes serve?"

Cady was glad of the change of subject. She answered truthfully. "I don't know. The box was sealed when presented to me, so I had no idea of its contents. Memories came to her in dribs and drabs, activated by the dust released from the box's interior. "I know that Dr Dee was very worried about a new invader, someone or something that would take over Haakenur's ghost. He linked it in some way to the Blight, the plague that infected the city in that year."

"Perhaps he meant Gogmagog?" Numi said.

Cady looked to Brin's face when this word was said, hoping to see any sign of knowledge, a recollection perhaps of her time at Blinnings Hall, and of Olan Pettifer. But the girl's face showed only intense interest, especially when Numi went on to recite Una Goodperson's legend of the two ghosts, the twin spirits of Haakenur, one made from the heart's blood, and the other from the venom stored in the dragon's tail. Inspired by this, the crew pondered over the bell and the box, putting together a story. It was, Cady thought, the first time they had all spoken together properly that day, since the escape from Ponperreth; and more importantly the first time they had spoken of their true and slowly revealed purpose in this voyage.

The assembled idea went like this: the Blight weakened Faynr, allowing Gogmagog a possible entry point, a doorway. Fearing this, Dee took precautions, burying a number of boxes at key points along Faynr's body, at points of weakness or trauma or damage where Gogmagog might find a way through. Cady didn't know how many boxes had been buried, nor the location of any of the others; in fact, until this day, she had forgotten all about the Ponperreth site.

Numi Tan offered her own thoughts. "Something happened a few years ago that made Faynr ill. As Faynr weakens further, we might see Gogmagog making further appearances along the river, as he finds the weak spots."

Cady agreed with Numi's assessment. But she suspected that other forces were at play in this game, not least Lord Pettifer.

"What of the Ludluda coin?" Brin asked. She was still playing with it.

"Perhaps Dee meant it as a talisman of some kind," Cady said. "He was full of magic."

Everyone was silent for a few moments, until Numi spoke of their common fear.

"Faynr is dying, and Gogmagog is gaining power."

Lek placed his hand on Brin's shoulder. Cady noted this. The Thrawl had invested so much in the power of Faynr to cleanse and heal her, only to learn that Faynr herself was in grave danger.

Numi asked, "What use is the little bell, against such an entity? I mean to say, what was Dee thinking of?"

Cady could not answer this. She looked across the table at Yanish. He was staring back at her, cold of eye and cold of aphelon. It made her shiver. Lek must have felt the same, for now his anger burst into life. He said harshly, "There's one here, who could help us." He turned to Yanish. "He has the *monster* inside him."

"Lek, don't…" This from Brin, but her voice quickly trailed off.

The Thrawl's eyes shone with a piercing blue light. "I will scan him, to see what he's made of." The twin beams emerged from their sockets and started to roam across Yanish's skull. They focused on the damaged aphelon. Only to be reflected back, straight into Lek's face, half-blinding him. The Thrawl staggered back. Brin reached up to help him, but he pushed her hands away. He was still fixed on the Azeel. "He is contaminated!" Yanish made a scuttler's cry and bounced on his heels; he pushed hard at Lek's shoulders, knocking him back against the table. Brin jumped up from her seat, and Numi Tan did the same.

Lek quickly regained his stance. He swung at Yanish, first with one fist, then the other. Yanish ducked both blows easily. This only made the Thrawl wilder. His face clicked from one display of anger to another, each more vehement than the last. His mouth spewed forth a rapid stream of clicks and clacks.

Brin had hold of Lek now, trying to pull him back, as Numi Tan did the same with Yanish. It was easy for both men to shake off all such constraints. And now they faced each other, their faces less than an inch apart, Lek shouting abuse, Yanish silent and blank-eyed.

Cady picked up the witch's bell by its handle and swung it up and down in a wide arc. It rang out with a slow steady rhythm. Once, twice, three times, four times. Each ring seemed to change the atmosphere of the cabin, making it colder. The air was visible in blurred waves of sound. And by the fifth ring, time itself drained away: Yanish, Lek, Numi and Brin, all were frozen in their places, as fixed and as breathless as stone statues. Cady, from her position behind the bell, was unaffected; she rang on, her hand growing tired, but the peals still travelled, still having their effect. She saw everything in exquisite detail.

Brin cowering, her eyes wide in shock.

The flames of Numi's face flickering to one side, away from the fight.

Lek, his hand raised at the start of a punch.

Yanish, his face fixed, shining with a crystal actor's vehemence.

Only one other thing in the cabin moved, and that was Yanish's shadow. The dark shape had slipped almost clear of the body, and was suffering dreadfully as each ring of the bell sounded: the shadow's length vibrated as though struck. Its face was stricken with fear, and malformed, so that it no longer matched Yanish's features completely; but had features of its own which intersected with his. Two yellow eyes blinked slowly, the eyes of the Night Serpent, of Gogmagog, but smaller in scale. They wept not tears, but streams of red smoke.

The bell slipped from Cady's grasp.

She was horrified.

The creature looked at her for one more moment and then slipped back inside Yanish's body, as quickly as an eel darting under a rock.

The Needles

They sailed along the river at a pace until they reached Wayland Point. By then, Numi's face was represented by a single valiant flicker of blue flame. She could hardly speak. Cady helped her down onto the narrow spit of land and they walked along it together, Cady holding her friend by the arm to keep her from stumbling. On both sides the ground was soft and marshy, held together by webs of snaggleweed. A low-lying mist clung to the earth. One wrong move and a body could disappear beneath the ooze in a matter of minutes.

The slop bucket banged against Cady's leg, its stench rising. She was glad when they reached the replenishing post; here she tipped the bucket's contents into the murk pit that bubbled close by. The little creatures of the pool thrashed about, fighting each other for tasty morsels of shit, mushy leftover food, and blood-soaked rags.

"That will keep them happy for a while."

Numi could not respond.

Cady went on. "They must be starved, with so few boats coming through."

She watched as Numi pushed a few coins in the machine's

slot. The Nebulim held her face away from Cady's gaze, perhaps ashamed of her present state.

"How's it looking? Let me see." Cady checked the gauge on the post. "A little bit remaining. Hopefully enough."

Numi took the rubber pipe from its hook and attached it to the nozzle in her chest: it slotted neatly into the clay skin.

Cady nodded. "Good, good."

So many things had gone to rack and ruin, thanks to Faynr's illness. In the last hour or so, the *Juniper* had passed boatyards, petrol stations, waterside inns, chandlers, bungalows and fishing huts, all of them abandoned. And this was the third replenishing post they'd visited, and the first to still have some vapour in its tank. There was the soft hiss of gas escaping around the faulty nozzle; Numi pressed at it tightly, to make a seal.

Numi's voice was returning. She made a soft gurgling sound.

The needle on the gauge dipped into the red zone. Empty. Numi pulled the pipe free of her chest and turned to Cady, to show off the flames of her face, all bright and fiery, fully formed.

"Ooh, look at you! Miss Glamourpuss."

Numi laughed. And they walked back towards the boat. But on the way her mood changed a little. "What did you see, Cady?"

"What's that?"

"When you rang the bell?"

"I saw Yanish's shadow, that's all. Just your regular common or garden Azeelian shadow, trying to make its way in the world, to leave the flesh behind."

"But they never can, can they? Not until the final moments of life."

"This is true."

"When they cling to the shroud as their new home, and paint themselves into it."

Cady spat in the marsh, a nasty black gob of it.

But Numi had not finished with her. "You didn't see any sign of Gogmagog, then? He wasn't lurking there?"

"No. Nothing of the sort."

Numi's face flickered into bright yellow. "Cady, I don't even think you're lying. You're just hiding the truth from yourself."

"Oh, go and gutter yourself, flamebrain."

Numi laughed heartily and the jingle-jangle of her wires and her ornaments sounded merrily, like a collection of lucky charms on a bracelet.

They reached a rock-strewn curve of the river. Here, not too far the bank, the Nysis and Faynr mixed together in a very small but very powerful whirlpool called the Withy. The place was known as a drowning spot for doomed lovers. Numi stopped as her feet crunched on the pebbles. She said, "I've never told you this, Cady dear, but once I was in love, in my first life. I was a young Wodwo, he was an Azeel. I was seventeen, he was a year older. Our families were against the match and would not allow us to marry. We took the step that many have taken here, at the Withy."

"What?" Cady was genuinely shocked. "You drowned yourselves?"

"Oh yes." Numi didn't sound at all concerned. "We tied stones to our wrists and around our necks, and walked into the water, hand in hand." Now her flames formed a smile, which flickered away almost instantly.

"Where is he now, your friend? Was he ever retrieved? Did he become a Nebulim?"

But there was no time to answer. They had reached the *Juniper*, and Brin jumped into sudden view, full of lively spirits. She helped them clamber aboard.

They set off. Lek took a place at the prow. He was looking ahead keenly, one hand resting on Queen Hilde's shoulder. An abandoned factory was visible in the distance, a squat angular shape swirled with fog. An engineering company used to manufacture Thrawl there, so many hundred every week. There were houses and cottages along the bank, where a number of the workers used to live. In the fields beyond, a housing estate had been built, and was still occupied; but here, within Faynr's grasp, the bankside houses stood empty, windows smashed, walls covered with creepers of scarlet hue. Loneliness crept into Cady's heart. It was bad enough in the unoccupied areas of the river, but now, as they drew ever nearer to the city, the effect of the sickness on the human population became more evident. Strangely, the windows of the houses were not blank, but covered in some whitish material from the inside, which puffed outwards, pressing against the empty frames. Cady thought it might be a fungus of some kind, an especially prolific variety. But the species was a mystery; there were new species springing up around every bend in the river, as the riverside plants mutated in different ways to fit in with the changing environment.

Lek came to her. "I think we should leave Yanish behind at some point."

She was all set for an argument, in fact, desired one greatly; but she controlled herself and answered, "I'd take action myself, if I were certain."

"So then, you're not *certain*?"

"That's what I said."

"Which means that some doubt exists?"

"Of course it bloody does. I mean to say, Gogmagog climbed inside Yan's head. But I need proof that he's been taken over."

Lek looked at her intently, but she kept her profile to him, not giving in.

"And if I find you proof?"

Cady hesitated, for in a way she already had proof, in Yanish's malformed shadow. But she wasn't going to let the Thrawl have his way so easily. "Then we tie him up and stow him in the bilge till we reach Ludwich, and we find him a doctor. Or a priest. For an exorcism. Whatever it takes—"

Clink.

The sound stopped Cady in mid-sentence. What the hell was that?

Clink, clink, ping!

Cady felt something hitting the crown of her bowler. The clinking sounds continued, as many tiny objects bounced off the Thrawl's metal body. He was wiping them away. Cady plucked one of them from the thickness of her hair: it was a needle, or more accurately a thorn, a couple of inches long, with a barbed tip.

"What are they?" Lek asked.

Cady didn't know. She looked aftwards, to see Yanish at the helm. His hand went up to his neck and he pressed it there for a few seconds. Then he keeled over and hit the deck with a heavy thump.

Ping, ping, click, ping, click.

"We're under attack!" Cady was already on the move.

"Get the girl!"

Lek responded instantly, running to the cabin, where Brin was working on her mathematics assignment at the table.

Cady hurried after him, calling out for Numi as she did. The Nebulim had been sitting on the sun deck, but was now entering the cabin through the aft door. Cady bent down to Yanish, where he lay flat-out beneath the boat's wheel. She heard Lek calling out to Brin that she take cover: all this in a haze of noise as the needles clattered all around. She got hold of Yanish and tried to yank him across the deck, but his dead-weight was too much for her. "Lek! Help me!" Together, Cady and the Thrawl managed to drag Yanish into the curve of the starboard bulwark. This offered them some protection, but the rain of needles continued apace, without let-up.

Cady made a quick examination of Yanish's exposed flesh: his neck, head and hands had all received their share of the stings. She pulled one out, feeling the barb of the hook resisting; when it came free it oozed out a droplet of white sap.

"It's poisonous. It must be."

Lek squatted down next to her. "You don't know what it is?"

"No, never seen it before."

Lek used his beams to scan for a pulse. "He's alive."

"Thank Lud for that." She pulled out all of the thorns she could find. "Lek, where are they coming from? Can you see?"

He stood up and braved the needles for a full minute. The noise was dreadful. He bent down next to Cady again and said, "From the windows of the houses. All along the bank."

"Aye, I saw something strange at the windows, pressing outwards. It's some sort of fungus. They see us as a predator."

"They're shooting at us."

"They're not taking aim, Lek."

"Are you sure?"

"They're firing willy-nilly. At least, I hope they are!"

"Cady, there are a lot of houses here. What do we do?"

The Thrawl was genuinely alarmed.

"First of all, take charge of the boat. She's drifting towards the bank."

"Right, right." He stood up.

But Numi Tan beat him to it: she had emerged from the cabin and was now standing at the helm, working the wheel. Cady saw that Numi's clay shell was peppered with the needle thorns, hundreds of them. But she seemed to be unaffected by the poison, at least for now.

Lek went to her. "How is Brin?"

"She's safe. Under the table."

Cady called out, "Numi, take her to mid-channel, and keep her there, full ahead!"

The rain of needles lessened a little as they moved to port, but many of them still reached the Juniper, and were still capable of hitting and piercing bare flesh.

Numi cried out suddenly. "Cady, there's something in the water! We're going to—"

Her words were cut off by the screeching of the hull against a fixed obstruction.

"What the hell was that?"

"I don't know, I don't know!"

Lek was running to the port bow. "It's a wreck," he called out. "Just under the surface. We're stuck on it."

Cady cursed herself. It was HMS Progress, a minesweeper that was bombed in the war, and was now stuck on a rock shelf. She knew about it, she knew all about it! And now this! "Oh bollocks! My wits are like scrambled eggs."

The Juniper was not going anywhere: the pistons whined

and the crankshaft thrashed and the propeller sang its crazy maddening song. Instinctively, Cady stood up and took a step to the wheel, hoping to reverse the engines. But Lek came to her in a hurry, and pushed her back down, next to Yanish's prone body. "I'll do it," he said. "We can't lose you." He was pulling needles out of the rubber of his skull mask.

"Aye go on!" Cady ordered. "Full reverse."

Numi moved aside to allow Lek to take the controls. The engine protested and the keel crackled and flexed, and the hull groaned in all its planks. *Come on, Junie. Come on, you can do it!* And then the engine died, choked off. A final rumble. A smell of burnt oil.

They were dead in the water.

And still the needles were flying over, hitting the deck, the sides, the cabin walls, the roof, the awning, Numi's clay shell, Lek's tinplate body, and the head and torso of Queen Hilde at the prow. If anything, they seemed to be coming over with even more force now, in greater numbers. Careful to keep her fingers hidden, Cady held her bowler above the rim of the gunwale and then brought it back down: the thing looked like a pin cushion! She looked over to the port bow where Lek had taken up the boathook and was now trying to push the *Juniper* away from its obstruction. It wasn't working. Cady felt the weight of the boat in her body, every screw and nail and rivet, and every line and knot in every plank of wood stretching her muscles tight, close to breaking.

Numi squatted down next to Yanish. Her glass visage was webbed in little scratches where the needles had made contact, and within it the flames were fluttering crazily this way and that, causing the Nebulim's face to almost fly apart in six different directions.

"Cady, we're stuck."

"I know that. What can you see? The needle blowers. What are they doing?"

Numi stared at Cady with wild fiery eyes. "I'll have a look, shall I?"

"You do that. Go on!"

Numi stood up. All Cady could hear was the sound of the needles embedding themselves in the clay body, and the ornaments tinkling in a constant sing-song.

"Well then?" She dragged Numi back down.

"They've left the... they've vacated the houses... they're floating on the water, bobbing along... great fluffy white puffballs, with the needles shooting out of little spouts. They're coming towards the boat... so many of them... as big across, as... as... Haakenur's eyeball!"

Cady didn't say a word. But she was thinking to herself: *Plants should not be fighting plants! Don't they know who I am? I am a Haegral! Boss of the fuckin' plants!*

Numi grabbed her friend in panic. "What can we do? What can we do!"

Cady closed her eyes tightly. She still had a hand on Yanish's shoulder and she kept it there. Sweet Lud in heaven, hadn't she survived nineteen wars, two revolutions, the Great Conflagration, several plagues, the Blight, the pox, cabin fever, four duels at dawn, a dozen battles at sea, three miscarriages, the doldrums, jail (thrice), the hangman's noose (twice), scurvy, gout, smut, canker, glanders, basal rot, black mist, the runs, measles, dandruff, aphids, four husbands, countless cads and scoundrels, untold near drownings, and not to mention a nasty case of the spives, on top of which, twenty-five or more regrowths inside the effigy! For fuck's sake! She was not going to let some sodding needle thorns get the better of her, or her own boat! No, sir!

Yanish's shoulder spasmed under her hand. She opened her eyes to see that he was writhing on the deck, foam spewing from between his lips. Numi tried to hold him down, to little avail. Cady felt icy despair come over her. And then she looked up and saw to her horror that Brin was peeping out of the half-open cabin door.

The needles pinged and clattered and fell as hail, oozing with sap.

Lek was already running towards the cabin. He slammed into the door, forcing it shut, almost trapping the girl's fingers.

Cady knew what she had to do. It came to her in the blink of a cataracted eye.

I am Haegra. I am the Deep Root.

She picked up one of the needles from the deck and pushed it without hesitation into the flesh of her wrist, seeking a vein.

I am the Deep Root, I am the Deep Root.

The poison made its way quickly through her body.

I am the Deep Root. I sink down in the earth, I travel the vines and tubers of the green world, I am the seeds in the eyes of Luda, when she first woke up within the womb of the dragon, the dark soil welcomes me, the weeds encroach, the worms feed off me, the beetles scurry and the blind mole nuzzles at me, I taste the Nysis river in the damp earth, the hidden tributaries underground which freshen the deepest roots with their waters. I am the deepest root, where all plants mingle as one, where the five Great Trees of Ludwich meet and merge into the One Tree, where the Never-Never spirits gather knowledge of what might happen and what must never happen, where the dreaming seeds drift by on the four winds and the pollen

I am the Deep Root.

Cady groped forward in the darkness of the earth, seeking a path, the one lighted by the very poison that had oozed from the needle thorn. The toxins moved in her flesh, guiding her.

It had been many, many years since she had dug down so deep within the living body of unreal earth. All around her the veins of the land were set out, the tangled system that connected all to everything, and everything to all. Pulses of sap moved through the roots and fibres at speed, taking their messages to the furthest corners of Kethra, wherever a plant grew or a flower opened its petals or a leaf was beaded with raindrops. Cady could sense every pulsation in her body.

She came to an open area, a chamber with walls of packed dirt. It was lit by luminous plant bulbs that hung down on fibres from above. Before her stood the giant mass of soft white flesh that made up the rooted spirit of the puffball fungus. The Queen of Needles. Her body filled the space entirely, and was made of many tinier versions of herself all clinging together, moving constantly, bubbling, frothing, seeping with ichor, opening and closing their many spouts, from whose black mouths the tips of the thorns protruded. Cady felt strong. The new buds on her neck, arms, thighs, stomach and shoulder pushed against the stretched skin that covered them, as though ready to burst open in a cascade of bright petals. But no, she stayed them with a single thought. Not yet. Not yet, my little ones, we have a fight on our hands! The Deep Root merged with her by some unseen root, feeding her with sap. A spirit came upon her, something very new. Cady cried out with a mighty voice, "Know me by my real name, for I am Lady Haegra!"

The giant puffball slithered and whistled and hissed in response.

grains stick to the crown and thorns of the Lord and Lady of All Flowers, to the Woman of the Woods, to the Mistress of the Knotted Vine.

Its needles slipped inside the flesh and then re-emerged, this time tipped with the poison.

Cady stood her ground. "Begone, Queen Puff! Prick yourself, stab yourself in the heart with your own needles. Let the stippled beetles nibble at you, let the farmer pluck you from the soil in the dawn light, let the dogs snuffle for you in the dank mould at the base of the dead tree, let the black mould crumble your belly, and the canker gnaw at your guts."

The puffball throbbed and pulsed within the confines of the chamber and its great wobbling flesh shook with anger. Scatters of earth dropped down onto Cady's head from above, dislodged by the tremulous movements.

She raised her face and let the earth fall onto her tongue.

She devoured the earth.

Her voice rose in up volume, invigorated. "Do your worst!"

The puffball inhaled – there was no other way to describe the dribbling sucking motion of its entire form. And then it made the opposite movement, in quick succession, and its many thousands of spouts opened at once, this time to shoot the needle thorns on their flight. They rushed towards Cady like a fusillade of arrows on a battlefield; but these missiles were longer than arrows, sharper at the tips, and loaded with Lud knows what concoction.

Lady Haegra raised a single hand. From her palm, from the outer fields, the roots unclenched and the stalks popped up and the leaves opened and the tendrils spread and grew in length at great speed. Cady's own thorns sprouted along the length of every branch and twig. A great cloud of dirt and dust rose up, filling the chamber.

Many of Queen Puff's needles were stopped in mid-flight, caught in a vine's grip. Many more were knocked aside. But some got through the defences, only to embed themselves in the earth walls of the deep chamber. And one, one alone, found the side of Cady's neck and struck there, deep.

And the poison entered her veins.

But Lady Haegra had already taken on that poison, and made it her own. She was inoculated.

The outer fields drew back into her hand in a whip-like fashion. The dust cloud parted and the Queen of Needles was revealed, her soft damp flesh punctured all over by the sharpened tips of branches, by Cady's thorns and prickles. The sap seeped from the queen's wounds in rivulets, curving down to the soil on which she rested. Her body was dimpled and hollowed out and she gasped for air, she belched and bubbled.

Cady watched her, face half-hidden under a green mask of leaves. Her thorns emerged once more, but this time only one specimen from each palm, each a long, curved sword ready to strike the death blow.

Yet Cady backed away, and the thorn branches returned to her body.

Let it be, let it live, as it may. Each creature and each plant in their rightful places.

And then Cady felt faint, as the pain of her wound made itself known, and she staggered back a little, before falling to the ground, to the soil, to the soil that opened up for her...

"Cady, Cady! Cady, wake up!"

It was Numi Tan, shaking her. A few seconds had passed, that's all. Cady came to, wondering for a moment where she was. And then seeing Yanish lying at her side, his body calmer now. And Numi kneeling close by, all three of them nestled in the safety of the bulwark.

"You fainted, Cady. Just for a moment. Out cold."

"Right, yes."

"Your... your neck! Cady, you're bleeding."

"So I am."

Lek was standing by the closed door of the cabin, keeping

Brin safe within. The needles still fell, but with lesser impact, and fewer of them. They gave up on the deck, hitting the outer hull instead, and then the water, making little popping sounds as they sank beneath the surface. Cady got to her feet. Numi had to help her up, for the old lady was tired suddenly. But she was gladdened to see the puffballs drifting back to the bank, some of them deflated, others painted with mould and mildew. Some of them actually exploded, their skin and inner flesh cascading over the waters. The battle was won. Put that in the history books, Cady thought. Write it up in the crystalpaedias. Let them watch it on the news reels and goggle their eyes out.

Working steadily, each in their task, the crew eased the *Juniper* free of the submerged wreck. Numi swept the needles from the deck, while Brin sat in the after-deck, pulling thorns from the dragon ensign. Yanish was alone in the cabin, dabbing his wounds with a special herbal preparation that Cady made up for the purpose, fresh from her outer fields. He was groggy, but strong. And she had to wonder just what part Gogmagog had played in the young man's survival. For herself, she stood at the helm and caressed the precious bud on her neck, glad to see that the thorn attack had not damaged it.

The *Juniper* set off once more. Without anything being said or any decision being made, Cady Meade was now in charge of the ship, the true captain, returned to her rightful post. But there was no celebration, not even in secret; too much had been lost to bring it about. They sailed past the houses where the puffball fungi lived, until they reached the first waters of the Luhm region. The River Nysis changed its appearance here, the water becoming glassy. The bank of mist that hung above the river was a dull silver in colour, with streaks of orange running through it in chaotic patterns. Xilliths flashed their puckish blue and violet transmissions in the gossamer fog, and sang a keening song, adding to the sense of phantasmagoria. Brin was gazing at a group of seven or eight of them that hovered over the boat, their bodies intermingling and sparking together. Their electric song rang out loudly.

Cady asked, "Do you know what's happening up there?"

"Of course I do. Mr and Mrs and Mr and Mrs and Mr and Mrs and Mr and Mrs Xillith have gotten married. And this is their honeymoon! And soon, in a few weeks' time, they'll have lots of little baby Xilliths."

Cady couldn't help smiling, especially when Brin went on, "You know that Mr Lek has a small portion of Faynr inside his head? The crystal interacts with it, and bonds with it. It's how the Thrawls get to think, and to talk and to see pictures in their heads."

"Aye. Foggy of brain, foggy of thought." Cady scraped sap from deep within her nose.

"Only here," Brin went on, "in the *mating grounds*..." She was slightly embarrassed by the word. "Only here does that special kind of Faynr exist. It's why they built the factory close by, for ease of delivery."

The Xilliths, their conjugal orgy complete, flew away. The factory was close now, its dark structure looming out of the mist. Giant steel pipes led from the river to the building, evidence of the river's connection to Thrawl manufacture. But the place was desolate now, a skeletal edifice. There were massive growths of purple lichen climbing the walls and roof. Ugly mutated skirls nested on the chimneys and cranes. They screeched at the *Juniper*.

Lek stepped into the wheelhouse. His face settled into a

serious expression, slightly pained. Cady asked him what the matter was, and he answered, "I'm picking up a signal. It's faint, but steady, a series of pulses in the crystal wave."

"A wireless signal? But we're the only boat on the river."

"It's the kind of signal that one Thrawl sends out to another." He looked to the building as they passed a loading dock. "And it's coming from the factory."

"We can't stop, Lek. Not now."

"It's a distress signal, Cady. Like a mayday call. I am duty-bound, and that is that."

The decision was made.

A Glorious Future for All

Some of the machinery was still in place, but in ruins, broken, or in pieces scattered about. Many devices and engines and tools had been taken away for scrap or repurpose, and only the cast-offs remained. But the closure of the river had put paid to the salvage work. And so the factory slowly settled into its present existence, where weeds and rust and damp took charge.

Brin climbed up onto an assembly belt and ran along it, leaping the gaps with a wild shout of abandon. Cady had to marvel. All evidence of the shakes had left the girl, and thankfully there had been no more convulsive fits: so maybe Lek was to be believed: the ghost of the dragon held a cure. Maybe the blood of Queen Luda truly ran in Sabrina Halsegger's veins.

As they came upon a huge regulator engine, Cady asked of Lek, "You weren't built here, were you?"

"No. I was put together in Middleminster, in the Year of Spark Fire. It was a smaller factory, making only the domestic and service models. Here, they produced the worker Thrawls, for mining, construction, weaving. They placed the specific instructions within the skulls."

Some of these skulls were piled in a heap in a corner, empty now, forgotten. Other metal and plastic body parts lay in a tumble. The factory's active life had come to an end in consequence of the Frenzy, and the Government Act to shut down Thrawl production. There had been plans in place to change it into a munitions plant, but then the dragon's ghost had fallen ill, and the air had soured, and many workers had taken sick. You could see thickened strands of Faynr floating about in the great hall, their usual orange colour now dimmed to a dull ochre.

Brin jumped down from a platform. "Mr Lek. Can you still hear the signal?"

He nodded. "Just about. It's very quiet now." His expression was carefully chosen to hide any discomfort he might be feeling.

"I'll find it first!"

And she ran off with a whoop and disappeared through an open doorway. Cady went after her, stepping into an atrium. A huge side wall was covered in a mural depicting a troop of male and female Thrawls, all bright and sparkling, straight off the production line, marching towards some future paradise carrying spanners, drills, and bolts of cloth. In the middle distance, painted people danced and picnicked in a park whose grass was greener than any green had ever been green. All was good, all was fine. *The Thrawls will lead us out of servitude, freeing us from sweat and grime and endless hours of drudgery.* A life-size statue of an Ephreme woman stood in front of the mural. She was dressed in the billowy clothing popular in the last century, her hair set in chignon buns, one each side of her head. Each feather of her half-grown wings was finely rendered.

Lek bowed at the waist before the statue. Cady asked him what he was doing.

"Paying homage to Miss Jane Polter. Our mistress and creator, the first of the thrawlsmiths." A serious expression settled on his face. "A Thrawl's final act before leaving a factory was to stand before her likeness, and take the Oath of Fealty." He recited in his Sunday-best voice: "*I promise on my faith that I will always be helpful to creatures of flesh and blood, never cause them harm, and will observe my homage with grace and without deceit.*" His head was bowed.

"Oh stop it," Cady said. "There's no need for all that palaver, not these days."

He came up slowly, his face showing a new and very twisted emotion. His entire body tensed up, like a longbow at the point of the arrow's release. He made a quiet but painful noise. Cady wondered which edge the Thrawl was heading for this time; he was always on the teeter.

"The signal is piercing me." His mask screwed up. "Like a dagger in my brain."

Brin grimaced. "Ugh, that sounds… it sounds horrible!"

Lek's hands made a series of angular chopping movements. His voice took on an icy tone: "I was born in a place such as this, eighty-seven years ago."

"Well there you go," Cady said, trying to calm him. "All those years, all that time, speaking, thinking, feeling."

"Not *feeling*, not enough *feeling*. Never enough!"

Cady laughed. "Tinpot, I hate to tell you, but you're the meanest, nastiest, angriest, craziest, most volatile person on the boat!"

Brin giggled nervously.

Cady went on, "Come on, Lek, old trooper. Let's keep searching."

The Thrawl spoke plainly. "No."

"No?" Cady was puzzled by this.

"No. No more."

"Right then, so let's go back to the *Juniper*, eh, continue on our journey?"

"No. I would rather not."

Brin went up to him, held him by the hand. "What's wrong? Won't you come with us?"

"No."

The word was stuck on repeat.

"Mr Lek, you're scaring me. Please, you have to—"

"No."

Cady watched the Thrawl carefully. He had returned to the place of his birth, or at least to a location very like it, and was now stuck in one mode of thought, one pattern.

"No. No. No. No. No."

The volume and the tone of his voice was the same for each utterance; it was quite unnerving. Brin was especially upset by it.

"But Mr Lek... I can't go on alone... not without you... I just can't!"

Lek looked to the statue. "I need Miss Polter to speak with me. I need her to help me, to tell me the truth."

"The truth, Lek." Cady couldn't work out what he meant by this. "The truth about what?"

"About the day of the malfunction."

"You mean the Frenzy? It's not happening again, is it?"

Lek started to shiver and shake. The screeching sound came again, this time modulating to a higher key.

"Sweet Lud in heaven! My ears are gonna pop, if he keeps that up."

The Thrawl stood before the marble statue of his maker.

He kept his face hidden by one hand. The other hand opened and closed in a spasmodic manner. Cady had the impression that he was struggling for control of his essential being, whatever that might be, wherever it might be hidden in the depths of his nurtured soul. He spoke with a great effort.

"I am not... *frenzied.*"

Cady stood her ground. "That's good to know. So what the hell is going on, then?"

"Such an ugly, ugly word."

"What is?"

"Frenzy! Frenzy!" He stood up ramrod straight. "Don't call it that, I beg of you, madam. Such an ugly word." His voice had clicked into Exaggerated Butler Mode.

"But your behaviour was ugly at the time!" Cady reminded him.

"I know, I know."

His eyes shone: red light, blue light. He lurched forward crookedly. Touching the bullet in his skull, he screeched again. Seeing Lek like this, Cady couldn't help looking up at the giant mural on the wall, with its proud marching Thrawls and its sweeping slogan: *A GLORIOUS FUTURE FOR ALL.* The reality of that dream stood below the image, mewling and bleeping, staggering from one foot to the other.

With an effort he found a quieter voice: "You all went mad at the same moment, all the Ludwich Thrawls, every last one."

Cady grunted. She reminded him of the truth: "It was a collective malfunction, that's all."

"Yes, but for twenty-two seconds only."

"People died—"

Lek smashed his fist into the mural, raising a shower of

fragments, punching a hole in the painted grass. The statue of the Maker rocked on its pedestal. Cady and Brin backed away, holding onto each other. Lek's mask furrowed in doubt. "I don't know," he said. "I don't know what went wrong." His eyes were on Brin now, to speak to her alone. "I woke up the night before, in the early hours, with the strangest... *sensation* I have ever felt."

"What was it?" the girl asked, finding some strength. "You've never told me this before."

"I dreamed." He uttered the word as though it were a precious object in his mouth.

"But Thrawls don't dream, Mr Lek. It's just not possible."

"I know, Miss Brin." The butler's voice took over once more. "But it happened. Only that once, never before or since, I promise."

Cady asked him, "And what did you dream about?"

He turned to the statue, gently caressing the cold face. "Miss Jane Polter came to see me. My queen, my mother. The one who set us on our journey."

He gazed longingly into those blank grey unseeing eyes. His hands settled on her, at shoulder and waist. His feet bounced lightly on the spot, like a dancer's. Cady actually thought he was going to uproot the statue by force and set off waltzing with her around the floor of the atrium. But no. He lifted his hands from her body and stepped back a little way. He turned to Cady and then to Brin and spoke of his dream in a gentle voice.

"Miss Polter appeared to me. She was wearing a lovely well-tailored dress, and her hair was beautifully coiffed, as befits a lady. She stared at me across the vastness of a withdrawing room. There must have been a mile or more from one wall to the next. Yet I could see her plainly, and I heard her voice as though she were standing in front of me. She said, 'Dear 247LE54K...'"

"That's his real name," Brin whispered. "Dear 247LE54K, the time is at hand. Tomorrow, at noon, you will join with your brothers and sisters of Ludwich, a miracle to perform'. In such manner, Miss Polter spoke to us."

Brin asked, "You're saying that all the Thrawls dreamt the same dream?"

"The same dream at the same time of the night. Exactly so."

Cady needed to know more: "And when the appointed time came, on the morrow?"

Another bout of madness took Lek over. His face lost all expression and his voice chanted tonelessly, "The same dream... the same dream..."

Brin was stern with him. "Mr Lek, stop this. Now!"

Lek looked upon the girl with loving kindness. "As you desire, Miss Halsegger. Shall I serve tea and plum duff on the lawn?"

"Not just now, thank you. You were telling us about the malfunction. About what happened at noon, the next day. Carry on please."

"Of course, my lady." His eyes closed. "I felt a terrible pain in my skull. The blue light of my crystal went out. There was darkness. And then... and then... I seemed to wake up." His eyes now looked like twin fireflies lost in the daylight. "I had a silver service steak knife in my hand. The kitchen was in a shambles, with broken plates and cups everywhere, and the cook and the kitchen maid were cowering away from me. I approached them, knife in hand, as though to... as though I wanted to... to hurt them..."

Cady whistled. "Not much of a miracle, then?"

"No, no… it went wrong… the dream did not turn out… as desired. Instead…" He hesitated. "Instead, we became little more than wild beasts."

Brin was upset by this idea. "Lek! That's not it. That can't be it."

"There's no other explanation, Miss—"

"You're not a beast! You're a *human*, a human machine."

"I am not human. I am mechanical, crystal-driven, and Faynr-powered."

"You're my friend."

This brought Lek up short. He looked at the girl, an edge of understanding flickering on his mask. He made to answer her, but then stopped before a single word could be said.

The high-pitched sound came back to his lips.

"There! Can you hear her? She calls to me."

"Who does?" Cady demanded. "You mean the distress signal?"

"She's in danger."

The fingers of one hand pinched tightly at his temples. Cady looked on, worried that he was going to go into another seizure. Inner turmoil showed in his heterochromic eyes and the shudder of his limbs. And then, finally, his poor bullet-addled brain clicked onto a new pathway. He made one last bow to Miss Jane Polter and set off, hurrying back onto the factory floor. Cady and Brin tried to keep up, but he moved quickly, pushing aside bulky machinery as though they were made of papier-mâché. Nothing would stop him. And yet his head jerked about and his eyes darted here and there as he tried to locate the exact source of the mayday call. It could not be pinpointed.

He wailed, tilting his head to let the sound bounce off the ceiling.

"Where are you? Where are you, my Thrawl sister!"

And then he stopped and listened intently, holding a finger up to silence his two companions. He stayed immobile for a few moments and then set off once more, heading towards a side door. This led to a stairwell, down into the cellars of the building. His feet clattered on the metal steps, and his voice echoed along the stone chambers.

"Keep calling! I will save you." Cady and Brin ran after him along an underground corridor, past chambers where giant vats sat empty, and rooms where ducts and pipes fed into strange apparatus, all broken now, all discarded. Cady saw scatters of crystals across the floors. Their usual blue light had faded to a dull white, emptied of all thoughts, all feelings, all plans, instructions, promises, yes, and of all dreams.

They came to a branching corridor, a long expanse that must have stretched the length of the factory. Here Lek came to a halt. There was a closed door at the far end, only just visible through the gloomy air.

"She's in there," he said. "I'm certain of it."

Cady responded, "Are you sure? I don't like the look of this place." The atmosphere forced her voice into a whisper.

The walls were damp, covered in moss and patches of oil. Water dripped from the low ceiling. Everything smelled of decay and corrosion and general nastiness. Great long strands of Faynr's mist had reached here, into the depths, dark orange in colour, with floating pink motes suspended within. Cady had to suppress the urge to cough. She felt Brin grab her hand for comfort. Something stirred at the end of the corridor, low down, close to the door, something shadowy and angular and bulky. Cady held her breath in fear. Her hand closed around Brin's. She could feel the sparks of a Xillith, warm and ticklish, flickering from the girl's fingers.

A sudden blast of orchestral music startled them all. It was loud, both strident and romantic at the same time, a lush melody laid over a martial beat.

"I know that tune," Cady hushed. "What a racket."

"It's Fleikmann's Ninth Symphony. The final movement." Lek held them both back with a raised hand. "An Enakor favourite."

The music came to a sudden halt, replaced by a metallic scraping noise. Cady strained her eyes. A shiver ran through her as the gloom of the corridor's end closed over the shape, joining with it. Nothing could be seen. Lek walked on. His eyes sent out a shifting double arc of yellow light, like the headlamps of a motorcar: the beams passed over some person or creature, squatting down. Cady heard it grunting, and then making weird hissing noises, like steam escaping from a set of valves. But Lek was more confident now, having seen the figure's defensive stance. Cady and Brin kept pace, a few steps behind.

A voice spoke to them, rising from the gloom. It sounded like a blunt knife carving language into words: *Mik eklebar, mik Kelbar zo enti ravispek, Molokoi.*

"My Enakor's rusty," Cady admitted.

Lek listened for a moment, translating. "A name, *Kelbar,* and a rank. Nothing more. The same standard phrase repeated."

"What the hell is it, a soldier?"

"Yes."

"Is this the distress signal you heard before?"

"No, something different."

"He's a guardian at the door," Brin imagined. "Like the knight Sir Allemayne standing guard the chamber of Princess Mia, you know, in the faery story."

"Yes, something like that," Lek said. "Perhaps..."

He had no time to speak further, for now the figure emerged fully into the light-beams. It was still crouched down, only its elongated head held proudly aloft.

Sweet Lud Almighty. Cady remembered a news reel about the enemy's wartime plan to build their own version of the Thrawl, a 'mazinenmenker', which they named the Molokoi. But there had been no sign of any such thing during the latter years of the war, so the story had fallen into the realm of rumours and horror tales. But now, crouched before them, here was such a specimen.

Mik eklebar, mik Kelbar zo enti ravispek, Molokoi.

Cady joined Lek, to get a better view of the robot. It possessed a single crooked metal wing, half-extended. The other wing had broken off at the shoulder blade. Its arms and legs were spindly and jointed, giving it an insectoid look. The head and body were gunmetal grey, marked with numbers and codewords. In shape it was designed for speed, highly streamlined and ornamented with ridges and tiny fins. Scratches and gouges on the skull and chest attested to various cutting tools brought into use. Evidentially, the thing had been dismantled, and then put back together in a slipshod fashion.

Brin spoke excitedly, "It looks like a racing car. Or a glider. Or like a glider and a racing car combined with a tank. And a metal angel, and a spider."

Cady said, "Looks like the engineers here were trying to uncover its workings."

Lek nodded. "Or its secrets."

The Molokoi gazed at them with one green eye. The other eye had been removed, leaving a clean aperture from which bare wires protruded. Its mouth opened to speak, showing metal teeth and a rubber tongue. But instead of words another burst of Fleikmann's final symphony was heard, quieter now, its glorification of the Enakor homeland disturbed by wow and flutter. The robot's music box was in dire need of repair.

Cady muttered a prayer: "Lord and Lady of Flowers, save me from bitterness and hatred towards my enemy."

With a great effort the machine got to its feet, its numerous joints almost buckling under the top-heavy weight of its structure. Cady watched in horrified fascination as a short-barrelled gun poked out of an aperture on the Molokoi's chest. The weapon stuttered into life before anyone could even make a move, but the firing pin landed, again and again and again, on an empty chamber. It was out of ammunition.

Cady dared to open her eyes.

Lek had walked forward to meet the shots head on, in the act of protecting Brin. He spoke to the robot in Enakor. "What are you saying to it?" Cady asked.

Lek didn't answer. Brin translated for Cady, as best she could. "He's saying that he needs to... yes, he needs to get through the door... to rescue the Thrawl who's trapped within."

Lek repeated this demand. But the Molokoi had other ideas. The robot was now stretched out to the limits of its broken condition, straining to get at the Kethran Thrawl, it's sworn enemy. The two of them stood face to face. The Molokoi's green eye blinked, making a sound like a camera's shutter. Lek's scanning beams traversed the long ovoid skull. "No living tissue," he reported. "Classic Enakor technology. 'Mechanised mysticism', as they like to call it. Two tiny blue crystals between a length of magnetic tape. A way of delivering information to the machine: orders, tactics, battle plans. But I'm not sure you could call it actual thinking – uk!"

The Molokoi whipped out an arm at speed, to clamp its fingers around Lek's throat. And it was squeezing! Lek's body jerked in spasms from that anchor point, his arms and legs jiggling helplessly like a puppet's. Cady didn't know what to do. Without quite knowing it, she had taken her penknife from her pocket and was brandishing it about, somewhat pitifully.

Lek tried to make a noise but the sound was cut off instantly.

His feet were now off the ground.

The Molokoi was far more powerful than the Thrawl. A soldier versus a butler. A crunching sound came from the Thrawl's neck.

Cady's little knife thrust forward. Useless, useless.

A light blossomed.

A ghostly light, bright blue tinged with violet.

Cady felt herself running cold, blood and sap freezing in her veins.

The ghost light sizzled and collected itself into a creature of well-known shape.

Haakenur!

The First Ruler of Kethra. Lizard Queen. Arch Denizen of Red Moon Hill.

The dragon gathered every last speck of stray Faynr for its purpose, and so empowered, it shot forward like a missile towards the Molokoi, coming to a halt a bare inch away from the robot's head, focussed entirely on the centre of its brow.

The machine's single working eye widened in shock.

Cady looked back to see Brin standing there, eyes half-closed, hands raised, her body glowing with Xillithic fire that she sent forward from the centre of her chest, her sternum, as a weapon, a means of shaping the mists that swirled around the factory's cellar, forming them into an expert semblance of the once-living dragon. Cady had witnessed this act of magic once before, through Thrawl Lek's eyes; but this was happening now, and she was right in the middle of it. Haakenur breathed and pulsed in a slow noiseless rhythm. The body of light filled the corridor end to end. A burst of illusionary flame shot out from between her jaws. It was real enough to make Cady cower against the wall.

A ferric scream filled the space as the Molokoi cried out in pain, or in shock; perhaps both.

The machine's hand opened.

Lek gasped as he was set free, and staggered back, dizzy.

The corridor darkened in an instant, as the fake Haakenur disappeared in a shower of sparks and dots of Faynr mist.

Cady took in the scene before her. The Molokoi was crumpled up, its thin legs folded under the hulking body like a set of spindles. The machine's face was caught in a state of bemusement. Seeing the legendary dragon Haakenur rise up before you will do that, for how can such a thing be written in any set of taped instructions?

Brin came to Cady's side. The girl's body flickered with the last remnants of the Xilliths. Lek gazed in wonder at his charge, one expression slowly changing to another. Cady felt herself in the same state of confusion, torn between relief, and utter dread at what had taken place: for one terrible moment she had actually been inside the dragon's body!

Now the three of them stood together, looking down at the Molokoi.

Lek bent down and said, "Kelbar? That is your name?"

The machine stared back at him.

Lek persisted: "Can you speak? Do you know the Kethran language?"

The machine nodded, its lumbersome head creaking.

"The war is over, do you understand that? Eighteen months have passed since the liberation of Salicana, and the signing of the peace treaty."

The Molokoi settled back a little. Its perfectly round green eye was now on Brin, the shutter open to its fullest extent, perhaps with the hope of seeing once more the famous creature. And indeed, Kelbar spoke then, saying the dragon's name in three long syllables:

"Haaaaaaaakenuuuuuuuuuuuur."

It was a chant of submission before a mightier opponent.

Cady asked, "You're immobilised, is that right?"

The Molokoi spoke a few sentences in Enakor, which Lek translated: "The engineers here at the factory disengaged the motor control, the cogs and pulleys that work the lower limbs." He asked another question, this time in Enakor, and translated the Molokoi's answer: "Kelbar has a few days to live, no more. His fuel cells are almost drained."

Cady felt a mix of anger and compassion. She said to Lek, "We could mend the poor bastard, fetch Yanish from the boat, together, the two of you could work on . . ."

But her words trailed off when she saw Lek's frown, and when she saw the Molokoi's one good eye slowly weep with oil.

Brin asked, "How long have you been here, Kelbar?"

The Molokoi took a moment before answering, this time in faltering Kethran. "Two years... three months... in factory. No talking... never talking. Before which... four years nine months... Ludwich... prison cell."

Cady did a quick calculation and said to Lek: "So he came here before the war?"

"It seems that way. Probably dropped out of an aeroplane. You see the wings? It could glide down to the target zone."

"Target? Before the war had even begun?" Her old anger was winning out.

Lek asked the Molokoi, "What was your mission?"

The robot spat out a rapid string of sentences, all in Enakor.

"What did he say?" Cady asked.

"It was a rambling stream of fragments. I'm not quite sure. It doesn't make much sense. But something about the Tangle Wood, I think."

Brin offered, "Maybe Kelbar's instructions have become mangled."

The Molokoi nodded to the girl, as if in answer. Its single eye closed and the big metal body came to rest in a tremble of the folded, half-broken legs.

Cady saw the look on Lek's face, and knew that a job had to be done. She drew Brin away, a little way down along the corridor.

"What's happening? What is Mr Lek doing?"

"Nothing, kid." She blocked the view of the doorway, and said, in distraction, "Say, that was quite the trick you pulled back there, girlie."

Brin just looked at her, anger filling her eyes.

"You did the same on the Night of the Dragon, didn't

you? Eh? Oh yes, Lek showed me. Lud in hell! You near shaved my hair off with that dragon's fire!"

A shrug in answer from the girl. It was simple: "I had to save Lek."

The Molokoi screamed. And then whimpered. And then hissed. And then fell silent.

Brin skipped around Cady and ran to Lek. "What did you do? What did you do?"

"I put Kelbar out of his misery."

"You switched him off? Why?"

"Brin... Brin... He wanted it to happen."

The girl stared down at the Enakor robot, which lay in a broken heap now, to one side of the door. He looked like a pile of discarded machine parts, nothing more.

Cady traced the shape of a Wodwo rune in the air, and said quietly, "The final battle."

Lek returned to his task. He placed the side of his head against the door, and listened closely. His mask displayed so many furrows it looked like a roadmap, something Maguire & Hill might concoct after smoking too much crone's poppy. "The Thrawl is in here. She's trapped." He tried the handle. He banged on the door with his fist. And then tried again at the handle. "She's in pain." He threw himself against the door with his full body weight behind his shoulder, again and again.

Brin called to him. "Lek, you'll hurt yourself!"

He stood back and raised his leg to kick forward as straight and as powerfully as he could. Once, twice! The door crashed open, almost flying off its hinges. Lek rushed forward. Cady and Brin came after. But the room was empty. Damp walls. Some empty filing cabinets. A crack in the ceiling. A heap of junk in one corner. That purple lichen creeping everywhere it could. That was all. But Lek attacked the tumble of metal parts and rusty tools. He threw them aside in a fit of anger, or need, or whatever Ludforsaken hope might be going through his brain-pot. The floor was soon littered with debris. Cady and Brin looked on, wondering when the Thrawl was going to stop, when he would realise that the search was futile, that no Thrawl could possibly be hiding there. But he didn't stop. There were white crystals everywhere, rolling along the floor like marbles. A spanner hit the wall with a loud crack. The air was grey with dirt and brick powder. A rat scurried away.

Lek reduced the pile to a mess of scattered objects, with nothing to show for his efforts. But he continued to search, to actually dig into the floor, fingernails cracking the concrete into powder. Brin took a step forward, but Cady held her back with a look that said: *Let him do this.* And he did it well, with commitment, getting up from his hands and knees, holding a small object in his palm for all to see. "Here she is!" It was a crystal. A blue crystal. Cracked, yes, discoloured, yes, covered in dust and fur, yes, but still blue, still shining, still alive. Lek's eyes shone brightly the exact same shade as the treasure in his hands. His beams explored every line, surface and inner facet with eager tenderness. He held it to his ear, to better listen to the wavelengths.

His face lit up with joy.

The trio made their way back through the factory, to the riverside dock where Yanish and Numi waited for them aboard the *Juniper*. They cast off. Lek stood at the prow, next to Queen Hilde, his eyes eagerly scanning the fog banks ahead. He was searching for something, out there in the Luhm. It only took ten minutes of travel to find it: another Xillith orgy in action. Lek directed the boat towards the bank. He wrenched the head of Queen Hilde from her shoulders and leapt down into the shallows. Queen Hilde's head glittered and gleamed as he moved along; Lek had fixed the newly discovered blue crystal into the Thrawl's empty skull. Now he reached up high, the open skull held aloft. The crystal pulsed more brightly, attracting the mating Xilliths. The air around them was foggy in texture, kindled with orange flecks, charged with life – and it seemed to choose the crystal willingly as its new home. It bonded itself to the crystal, forming a small cloud around that shining centre. Lek quickly closed the skull, trapping the small portion of Faynr within. Cady couldn't imagine such an effort would have any good purpose. Yet once he was back onboard, Lek refitted the skull onto the shoulders of the figurehead.

As they sailed on, Cady and Brin watched the Thrawl with interest. He was standing next to Queen Hilde, bending down now and then, lowering his head to hers.

"What's he doing?" Brin asked. "Is he talking to her?"

"Bugger me, I think he is."

"What's he saying to her?"

"Lud knows. Probably billing and cooing."

"Oh look at him now… oh no… is he?… Mrs Meade… he's kissing her!"

"Avert your eyes, kid."

"Ugh! It's horrible! Horrible!" But then she stopped her howling and instead started to dance and to sing. "Mr Lek's in love! Mr Lek's in love!"

The Xilliths must have approved, for they frolicked and cavorted with fresh abandon.

The Path of Aphelon

"West to starboard five degrees nought seven south by north east recurring pok my stout fellows and a bottle of rum pok pok sing hearty and roll me down deep where the dead men drift and turn to bone pok where the fishes peck at their eyes aye aye six fathoms deep thy mother sleeps her metal body rusting creeps along the riverbed pok pok full ahead in reverse port to starboard swing eleven degrees west of north of five fathoms by sixty knots for seven leagues pok until we reach the haven harbour, row, row me boys, handsomely does it, handsomely, we are Ludwich bound!"

Cady spat and cursed and stamped the deck and thumped the figurehead hard on the shoulder to make her shut up, which worked, at least for a little while, knocking the tin skull askew.

Lek rushed up, admonishing Cady for her behaviour. "I beseech you, do not treat Pok Pok in such a manner."

"I'll remind you, that I'm the captain of the vessel, and what I say goes, especially concerning the directions and speed thereof! Now *beseech* that!" And she shot him her very best evil eye.

The figurehead spoke up in her own defence: "My name

is Pok. Pok Pok." Her eyes flashed green and red, green and red. "I live inside the body of Queen Hilde. Therefore I am Queen Pok Pok. All should bow to me!"

"I'm going to tear her head from her shoulders!"

But Lek restrained Cady. "Please, Captain. Pok Pok is adjusting to her new life. You have to understand, she was built and programmed to run as a weaver in a cotton mill. Instead, she ended up with her body torn to pieces and sold for scrap, and her crystal... well, it must have rolled away into the dirt and rubbish on the floor."

"It's very sad, I'll admit that, yes," Cady said, nodding.

He took heart from this. "But she's got a new job now. Figurehead. And Ship's Lookout. Isn't it true that Rule 5 of the Shipping and Boating Regulations clearly states... 'At all times of day and night, maritime and inland water vessels shall maintain a proper look-out by sight and hearing–'"

"Don't you quote rules and regs at me!"

The boat sailed on into air and water that had a decidedly chalky taste and appearance. The river was the colour of sour milk, and granules of white dust settled on Cady's clothes and hair. Her fine downy moustache was whiter than usual. Numi Tan's flames burned a soft purple. Lek stood with one arm around Pok Pok's shoulder, soothing her. Brin danced on the cabin roof, practising the Way of the Willow moves Cady had taught her, grunting and gruffing with each sway and kick and punch. *Ewwwf! Yaaaah! Ahhhh Yak!* She held in one hand a sharp-clawed tin opener, which she wielded like a dagger. Her fingertips wove blue Xillith trails in the air.

Yanish steered the *Juniper* forward at a steady pace. The chalk hills of the Clodium rose on the south bank, when Pok Pok suddenly cried out at full volume.

"Ship ahoy, ship ahoy, ship ahoy!"

Cady felt her eardrums crackle and ping. But she took out her eyeglass and scanned the waters ahead. "Nothing," she muttered. "There's nothing there, you nuisance. Not a speck."

The cliffs of white chalk rose higher and higher on each side of the river. A vast cloud of dust billowed softly across the water, obscuring all sight of what might lie ahead. Cady's eyeglass was blinded. She could no longer pilot the boat. But then she heard the figurehead whispering.

"One degree port, two starboard, steady, slow head, to port..."

Cady had no choice but to believe Pok Pok, and to call out the directions to Yanish. And so the boat moved on, nudging aside a berg of chalk floating in the water. The stone crunched against the hull and a pall of white powder floated over the deck. The boat had moved into a narrow channel between two high cliff walls. Lek and Numi Tan kept the boat away from the walls on each side, with boathook and broom, respectively.

It was Dr John Dee who first called the Clodium region the "gallbladder of the ghost". People discussed and disputed this statement, hoping to work out what he truly meant. But then, as the first lumps of chalk appeared near the banks, it became evident: not only was Dee correct, but the ghostly gallbladder was forming a series of ghostly gallstones, mostly smaller clods, but a few of them towering white bergs that shadowed the water. And now, with the river's neglect, the usual dredging, cutting and engineering work had been put aside.

This part of the Nysis was silting up.

Cady kept wiping the end of her glass on her sleeve, to keep the lens clear. Beyond the narrow passages between the bergs, layers of thick chalk floated upon the waters, rather like a series of ice floes. The *Juniper* nudged ahead, pushing aside these obstructions. Pok Pok repeated her *Ship Ahoy* warning, but quietly now, her voice muffled by the powdery air. Cady squinted. Was there a slightly darker shape, just ahead? She leaned over the gunwale as far as she could, adjusting the focus on her eyeglass, until at last a boat hove into view out of the cloying air. It was stranded on the floe, unmoving, its bow lodged into yet another chalkberg.

The *Juniper* sailed alongside and everyone gathered to look upon the other vessel.

It was a small cargo boat. The white words on the white nameplate were just about readable, and Cady's heart gave a flutter of pain. The *Speckled Dove*. She knew the captain well enough, from drinking sessions down the Westward Ho. The *Dove* had left Anglestumne a few weeks ago, en-route to Ludwich, carrying a hold full of tea and spices, thinking perhaps that the ghost waters were clearing. They had only made it this far. Bloody fools! The aft section of the *Speckled Dove* was covered entirely in white powder, while the forward half of the boat had fused with the cliff, a victim to the gallstone's relentless growth. The three-man crew were visible on deck, frozen white, calcified, turned into statues. Bluebirds flew around the radio mast, their feathers heavy with dust. The dragon ensign was now a flag of surrender.

No one spoke aboard the *Juniper*. The mood was haunted.

And then Cady called out. "Ahoy there! *Speckled Dove! Ahoy!*" Her voice echoed against the chalk face. But there was no answer.

Brin asked. "What happened to those people, Mrs Meade?"

"They were taken over by Faynr."

"So they're a part of Haakenur's ghost now?"

"That's right."

"How interesting."

Cady looked at the girl, and mused on the magic of youth, that ability to transform the cruelty of fate into a thing of wonder.

The *Juniper* moved on, struggling through the channels. The chalk floes were larger here, and had fused together in many places, forming a jagged expanse covering the river from bank to bank, cracking and grinding against each other. The river flowed on beneath these rocks and floes, but the way ahead for vessels was narrowing, further and further. Until there was no way forward at all: the channel closed up and the steam launch ground to a halt. The engine groaned, and died. A terrible crunching noise was heard from the hull, as the chalk pressed relentlessly against it. And now they too were stranded, perhaps to suffer the same fate as the *Speckled Dove*.

Lek wasted no time. He took up the boat's axe and jumped over the gunwale rail. Numi Tan followed him down onto the chalk floe. She was carrying a spade.

"I should help," Brin said. "Otherwise we'll go all chalky as well."

"Oh yes," Cady said. "And what are you going to do?"

Brin clicked her fingers together, producing the brilliant Xillith light.

Yanish came to them. "The Blue Spark to the rescue."

"That's right!"

And with that the girl jumped down onto the floe, running over to where Lek and Numi were already at work splintering the chalk, to hopefully find a route through to the cleaner water that lay beyond the gallstone's control.

Yanish stayed with Cady at the rail. He looked to have settled down, after the previous attacks of manic behaviour. His eyes were bright with need.

"We should give them a hand, Yan." Gently she wiped chalk dust from his face.

"I have a job to do."

"Oh aye, and what's that?"

In answer he leapt down onto the floe. He set off, not towards Lek and Numi and Brin, but rather towards the left bank of the river. Only now did Cady notice that he was carrying his father's shroud, the piece of hessian rolled up tightly. Where was he going, stepping so firmly forward? She was now doubtful of the lad's self-composure, thinking it a lie made in his own mind, or else a ruse of Gogmagog to hide himself away until the opportune moment, whenever that be and whatever horror it might lead to. So she clambered down and followed her friend across the floe. The thick chalk crunched under her boot heels and rose in powdery clouds around her. Through the white mist she saw Yanish's shape, already ghostlike, almost lost. It took all of her courage to keep up. Her optic gland helped, showing a green pathway ahead. Once she tried calling his name, only to have her tongue coated in chalk.

She reached the river's bank, where the skin of Faynr presented a dark pulsing membrane of gelatinous nature. The shape of Yanish's vanished body was still present in the wall, a slowly closing aperture. Cady stepped through the same opening and found herself on a narrow country lane edged by privets. The outside sky was taken over by the purples and mauves of dusk, and the air was suddenly clean and sharp, and delightful. She cleared her eyes of chalk and looked along the lane. There was no sign of Yanish, but she had by now worked out where he was going. She reached a gate that took her into the field. Lines of trees were arranged in strict formation, equidistant, each of the same species: the meridian pine. It was a very particular tree, brought over from the Azeelian homelands with the second wave of immigrants; a thin straight trunk from which half a dozen or so branches radiated. To Cady's eyes it always looked a little like the transmission aerial of a crystal station. Bright silken shrouds were tied to the branches of these trees, their lower edges secured to the ground with pegs. They moved in the slight breeze like the colourful sails of moored yachts. Here fluttered the goodly deceased of Azeelian society.

Such deathly fellows caused Cady to contemplate her own flesh, the decay thereof, the black whirlpool at the end of the final voyage. Away, away vile void! She pressed at the buds on her body, taking comfort from their ardent pulpiness and the promise they held of a flowering life.

She was glad to see Yanish in the distance. He was moving slowly, and Cady gained ground quickly enough. But she let him stay ahead.

This shroud garden was smaller than the grand parks in the city and the suburban plots to the south of Ludwich, but it was large enough to be the resting place of a few hundred shadows. And it was well tended, despite the nearness of Faynr. But Cady couldn't work out what Yanish was doing here: evidentially he'd given up on any hope of getting his father's spirit transferred to silk. But still, surely a hessian shroud would quickly be taken down by the garden's keepers.

An Azeelian family stood around a central meridian tree. They were dressed in purple gowns, and their aphelons were lit up in silver. A shroud caught the last of the sunlight and a shadow danced upon it. Mother, father, and two children stood in silent prayer. A grandmother to one side, her face scowling. She spotted Yanish and shook her fist at him. Cady could not hear what was said properly, but knew the gist of it: she was telling Yanish to take his father's filthy spirit elsewhere. He did so gratefully, nodding at her, and moving on. He reached a small copse of trees at the garden's edge and entered within its gloom. Cady followed. This was a tangled group of trees of varied species, some of them meridian, others oak and elm and beech, many of them gnarled and bent double and infected with galls and cankers. She felt their green hearts darken and then gladden as she walked among their leaves and stepped over their roots. A cluster of rusty girders and metal struts were propped up against trunks or fixed into lower branches. Winding sheets adorned these branches as well, but none of silk. Rather, here were shrouds of sacking and corduroy and canvas and muslin, of suede and sailcloth and cheap cotton. The occupying shadows were weak and pallid shapes, some of them barely human in outline, others trembling at their edges. Cady entered deeper into the copse.

She found Yanish standing before a crooked aspen tree. He had unrolled his father's shroud and was now holding it draped over his hands. He stared at it, without action or sound. The darkly shadowed shape of Zehmet Khalan lay upon the material, ruffling slightly.

Cady watched for a while, allowing Yanish this moment.

Then she said quietly, "Yan, my love. Are you sure you want to do this?"

He didn't answer her.

She went on, gesturing to the other shrouds, "I don't know what these people here have done, to deserve this resting place. They might be thieves, arsonists, murderers, rapists, traitors, abusers of the young."

"Yes. And deserters." His voice was icy cold. "This is the best place for him."

Cady took a step forward, and then stopped. "Yanish, please. We can get a nice piece of silk in Ludwich. We'll give him a proper send-off, eh, what do you say?"

He answered to himself, muttering under his breath. Then he turned to look at her. Never in all their time together, on land or water, had she seen his face bear such hurt and despair. The youth had gone from him, and Cady felt herself crumble within, knowing she was in part to blame for this: if only she had persuaded him away from this damned voyage along the river!

"Yan, let's help the others find a passage through the chalk. Numi, Lek, and Brin. They need our help. They need *your* help. Your strength, your knowledge."

He rejected this, and gave her an order. "Cady, take up a candle for me, and set it burning. I need a light to focus upon."

There was a box of votive candles on the ground. Cady took one up and lit it with a match. She held this out in front of her. Its tiny flickering light allowed her to see that Yanish's own shadow was dancing fitfully at the edges of his body, blurring his outline, and she worried that Gogmagog would make another appearance. But the monstrous shadow faded quickly, perhaps waiting his moment. Cady would stay alert, she promised herself that.

But Yanish had no other thought in mind but the ritual. He stared at the candle flame intently. Then he moved his hands, stretching the length of hessian so far apart that his upper arms trembled under the pressure.

He spoke to the shroud: "Father. I cannot know what you went through. The day draws in. I'm cold. I'm alone. You left me, after… after mother died. You left me. I had to make my own way in life, I had to scrape and fight, and… and…" His voice broke. "I lived for your return."

The words ran out. The shroud tightened in his grip. Cady sensed he was undergoing a great struggle. But he found his voice again, speaking to her this time. "I don't know if Naphet will allow my father into Odelai."

Odelai was the Azeelian name for the afterworld. But Cady's knowledge of the religion was limited: this was an entirely personal journey for Yanish. She was the witness, nothing more, and that made her helplessness grow. All she could do was watch.

Yanish held up the shroud. His gaze returned to the candle flame. His aphelon, a dull grey until now, flickered into a lighter shade as he spoke.

"Powerful and kind Naphet, who sits in Odelai awaiting the moment of return, when all may bind themselves to your body, the first body… accept this spirit of your servant, Zehmet Khalan, into your palace."

He waited, as though for an answer. If any came, it was told in silence. But his aphelon had lightened further, turning a whitish grey. He stared deeply into the small flame. "My father went to war. He was one of the first to join up. He did not wait for conscription to start. He was a willing volunteer. Surely, this proves his worth, his courage."

It was odd, to Cady, to hear Yanish talking in a such a way. She was used to the elaborate rituals of the Wodwo religion, of sermons and litanies crafted from sentences as long and as tangled as the roots of the five Great Trees of Ludwich. But Yanish was actually having an argument with

Naphet: he was trying to bargain a way into heaven for his father.

"Kind Naphet, hear me out. Do not turn away from your servant. Zehmet went into battle for his adopted country. He was, until the final moment, willing to die for the cause of freedom. Yes, of course, the *final* moment is the point of the spear, where the blade is keenest. But he trembled in that moment, and turned away in fear. Doesn't this make him human? Doesn't this make him worthy, that he entered into the moment, and felt its heat more fully than the men around him, who ran on into the fire and the terrible rain of bullets. He embraced the moment of fear completely."

Yanish's aphelon darkened. Cady saw despair return to her friend's face. He was losing the argument, and his lowered his arms. He clung to the shroud with clawed fingers.

"Naphet!"

His desperate shout was quickly lost in the dense branches and undergrowth of the copse.

"Naphet, listen to me! Do not turn your back on my father, I entreat you!"

The canopy of trees creaked overhead. Cady felt the grubs moving within the bark as a map of itches on her skin. The clearing was charged with strange energies. Yanish's voice mingled with the rustling of the leaves and the breath of the breeze in the twigs.

"I demand an audience. I wish the long pathway of the Aphelon to carry my words, that they be listened to, and fairly considered."

Perhaps this appeal had some effect, for his aphelon brightened again, taking on a silver tinge. Cady wondered if each station along the road towards Odelai bore a different shade of grey. Yanish was concentrating his entire power to this one goal, to travel further along the road, that his father's shadow might walk alongside. Cady found herself frowning, to add her own willpower to his. The candle fluttered as her arm grew weak; but she kept to her given task.

Yanish's stance wavered, his aphelon flickered. He spoke with a yearning tone. "Yes, yes, kind Naphet, that is true. I have another inside me, a demonic power. A monster by the name of Gogmagog, made of smoke and bile and poison and vomit. Be merciful, for my father knows nothing of this. I have my own battles to fight, once he is at rest in the shadowlands. Only then... only then will I be able to take on the holy task."

His aphelon beamed with a pure blue light, a colour Cady had never seen exhibited before. It seemed to reach out to touch the candle flame. He raised the shroud high once more. The wind whipped through the trees, causing the tattered rags of the thieves, killers and defilers to wave and flutter on their branches. The shadows moaned, and danced the limbo jig. Birds cawed from the darkness between the trunks and tiny animals scraped in the weeds and fungi around the tree roots. Beetles ate their way forward in the sodden crumbling bark. She staggered a little, coming to rest against the skeleton of a dead tree. But still, she held the candle out for her friend and companion.

Jubilation rang through Yanish's voice: "Blessings be with you, kind Naphet. You are most merciful!"

He stepped up to the tree, reaching up to fix the shroud to a branch. A series of nails had been hammered into the wood at irregular intervals, old rusty nails all bent and broken. He used two of these to attach the shroud. Cady felt his relief, and she relaxed a little, allowing the candle to go out and to fall to the ground. But she kept her distance.

And then Yanish cried out in a wordless shriek. His shadow flickered. Without any kind of warning he reached up to rip the shroud from the nails, leaving two ragged tears in the cloth. He stumbled backwards, hardly knowing what he was doing. His face was lit by confusion only.

"Yanish… Yanish, what's wrong?"

He shook his head at her. His face was damp and his hair draggled down over his brow, half-obscuring the aphelon, which had returned to its deadened state. He looked at Cady with eyes as yellow and as dismal as any ever seen on humankind. She felt her soul withering under their stare. It was the monster Gogmagog, showing himself at last, at this exact moment when Yanish had reached towards an understanding with the true god of his faith.

Cady came forward. But her friend's expression made her fearful, for it had the cast of a beast upon it. Slobber hung from his lips and his skin sweated black smoke. His shadow ran wild about the clearing, clinging to the trees in a frightful embrace, capering madly, loving this moment, and then returning to the body to do further damage. Now it clung to his back like a hag's cloak, hugging him at each wrist, at the shoulders, the nape of the neck. Yanish's eyes were coins struck from moon glow. A mighty struggle was taking place within, between his own nature, and that of Gogmagog. Yanish's hands clenched at the shroud, trembling, one on each end, and he started to tear it in half, using the rips caused by the nails as a purchase.

"Yanish, no, please don't!"

Cady grabbed at his hands, to force him onto a new course. He threw her aside easily, and he fell to his knees on the mulchy ground, screaming in pain as he battled against his possessor. But the Night Serpent proved more powerful, and the hessian shroud was rent in two. Cady swore she could hear Zehmet's shadow screaming. But the act was not yet finished; Yanish held each of these pieces together as one and tore at them again, and again, and again, with a strength beyond any human ability. Gogmagog cackled as the cloth was ripped into shreds. The pieces lay on the ground, some already caught by the wind, others pressed into the damp moss.

All the strength left Yanish in an instant. His eyes returned to their normal colour, his infected shadow retreated back to its nest, deep inside. He slumped forward. He was sobbing, sobbing like a child. Cady went to him, kneeling down, to offer comfort, hardly knowing what to say or do. She picked up a few pieces of shroud, knowing it was too late, that they were nothing but empty bits of rag.

Dragonista

The lanterns on the upper deck of the paddle steamer were a blur of colour. Music drifted by in slow motion, curling through the tendrils of smoke from the cigarettes of the dinner guests. Everything seemed to be so far away. Cady felt sick, and very tired. The young man on her left was speaking to her in a drawl. She examined his well-bred Alkhym features: clear skin, defined bone structure, the hesti on his temples silver in colour – they looked like insect antennae that had only partway grown. As he leaned in to whisper a blue joke to her, she could hear the two hesti clicking and popping and whirring, like beetles calling to each other. The joke droned on, without a punchline.

Cady checked to see if Brin was alright. The girl was sitting at the other side of the table, enjoying herself, telling riddles, drinking lemonade, singing sea shanties. The two older teenagers to either side were indulging her. The head of the table was a woman in her mid-twenties – Cady had trouble remembering her name. Silla? Sola? Something like that. She sported long wavy hair parted in the middle around a pair of arched spectacles, and wore a fancy dress of purple velvet, ruffled at the shoulders. Her lips were painted black and her hesti decorated with red sparkles. She raised her wine glass in salutation.

Cady scratched at the bud on the back of her hand. It was growing larger, more pulpy. Her stomach cramped. A bit too much to drink, that was all. Not young anymore, no. Ever more never more. She pushed her chair from the table and stood up, her legs almost buckling under her. She managed to reach the guard rail just in time, to throw up over the side. A man shouted in disgust from below. There was laughter from the table. The music floated upwards; people were dancing on the lower deck to the strains of a five-piece band.

She looked out over the waters of the Fusilaire region.

Black water, grey air. Another of Faynr's moons shining down on the river.

The chalk hills were faintly visible downriver, as a smudge of white. They had been trapped there for some time before the *Glad Rag*'s landing party had come for them in a life boat, breaking a passage through the chalk and steering the *Juniper* safely through the subsequent tar pits. The *Juniper* was now moored to the paddle steamer's stern, near a ladder set into the hull. Cady looked down at her boat, seeing Lek and an Alkhym man working on the engine. It had taken a bit of a bashing as the chalk floes had closed in, tilting the crankshaft out of true. Yanish and Numi were in the afterdeck, Numi sitting upright, Yanish bent over with his head in his hands. He looked lost, a lost soul. Oh Lud. That her favourite should have to go through so much.

Cady held onto the rail for balance, as her stomach settled. The water lapped greedily against the ship, a thick sludgy treacly black bile, emitted from Faynr's submerged spleen. The *Glad Rag* was an old paddle steamer, long out of service, which had served as a floating private club for the upper classes in the years between the wars. In Cady's final voyages along the river, the boat had been dark and silent, gently rocking on its mooring ropes. But now the vessel was back in business as a venue, enjoyed by the young of the best Alkhym families. The crystalcasters called them the *Dragonista*, these pleasure seekers who had caroused and made merry as the world prepared for conflict. With the end of the war, some semblance of normality was returning, or at least being press-ganged into service.

Cheering broke out on the lower deck. Cady leaned over to see a young man being pulled from the water on the end of a rope. He was drenched head to foot in the black bile. His friends patted him on the back and showered him with praise.

The woman with the catlike glasses came to Cady's side. She held a long cigarette-holder in one delicate hand. A trail of dark smoke floated from her lips.

Cady gestured to the man covered in bile, and asked. "Another of your rituals?"

The woman gave an elegant tilt of her head. "We like to prove ourselves, often, and often pointlessly. The Alkhym way." She spoke with perfected vowels, every consonant in place. "How are you feeling, Cady? I saw you throwing up."

"I'm itching to move on, that's all."

"Of course. Your boat will be ready soon. Our engineer is helping with repairs."

Cady nodded. Without the Alkhyms' help, they might well be statues by now, frozen amongst the Clodium Hills. But she wasn't going to give more thanks than was necessary.

The woman gestured to the waters. "My mother's family has owned this section of the river since the reign of Hilde.

The Queen gave it to the Dahls as a gift for their service in the Seven Season's War." Her voice hardened. "We have matters to discuss, I think. Serious matters."

"The thing is... you see... how it goes... Silla... is that your name? Sorry. I'm three sheets to the wind. Or is it four? Now look... I've lost count of the number of sheets."

Cady stopped speaking, trying to collect her thoughts. The woman smiled. Her face was a perfect oval, unsullied as yet by life's frictions. The hesti at her temples clicked and clacked, sending out their signals.

"My name is Syla. In the Ledger of the Nine Families I am listed as Sylaveer Dahl the Fourth, of the Yohansson-Dahls, by way of Lord and Lady Hennessey of Templeton, out of the Berg-Haugens of the South Jessop Estate. My grandmother was the thirty-third bearer of the Shield of the Plentiful..."

Cady's grunt came from deep in her innards, bubbly with phlegm. It was loud and repulsive enough to halt the spoken lineage in its tracks.

"That's some pedigree. Sounds like something off a bookie's racecard. Or a dog show."

Syla Dahl laughed gently. "Not far off. And you are? By which I mean, your family line?"

"Deadly Nightshade herself, come to sizzle you. Out of the mud, by way of the root."

"How delightful!"

"Born of worms and horse dung. Armed with spikes and poison."

"Splendid."

They both turned to face the table. Brin had swapped seats, and was now sitting next to a youth of some sixteen years, whose languid posture and artfully presented ennui seemed to have hypnotised the girl. He was showing her a trick with a coin and a handkerchief.

Cady asked of Syla, "These *serious* matters you wish to discuss?"

"What of them?"

"Do they involve the girl?"

Syla took a moment's consideration. "We have an interest in her, yes."

"You know who she is, I'm guessing?"

"Sabrina Clementine Far-Sight Abigail…" Syla hesitated in the taxonomy.

"Are you faltering?" Cady asked, with a grin.

"Not at all. Abigail Maid-Of-The-Vale Xiomara Delphine… Poppy-Moth Mina-Moth… don't tell me, don't tell me!"

"I don't give a cobbler's, either way."

"Mina-Moth Marion Hollenbeck… and of course, to finish with… *Halsegger*." She put a special emphasis on this last name. And then added: "The Third."

"How do you know her?"

"We are related by marriage. Brin is my brother-in-law's fourth cousin, twice removed. The Halseggers and the Dahls have often inter-wed. I visited their house at Grandthorpe quite often, before the war, and that terrible vexation they had."

"By vexation, you mean selling their soul to the enemy."

"Precisely."

There was a gasp of delight from the table. Brin had leapt up onto her chair and was pointing over the water excitedly. "Look, look!" Cady turned to see. A jet flame had risen from the river's midstream, shooting into the air for six feet or so, before falling back. Another two jets followed in quick succession. The thick tarry water slushed about, disturbed by hidden volatilities. The *Glad Rag* shook at her moorings, as the wave hit them. The little *Juniper* knocked against the much larger ship's hull.

"The Great Mother Voor is turning in her sleep," Syla announced.

The languid youth who had shown Brin the coin trick joined them at the rail. "Syla, dear, let me have a drag of your tar."

She handed him the cigarette holder and he puffed on it eagerly. The Dragonista loved to smear the tarry secretions of Faynr's bile into their cigarettes, for extra taste. The thick smoke made even Cady's old-timer eyes water.

Syla said to her, "May I introduce my half-brother, Tomas Dahl. Of the Dahl-Lindhursts. A bastard child. Sadly, his mother's bloodline rather lets down the side."

Tomas bristled at his sister's words. Cady saw hatred in his peevish eyes, in the squidge of his boyish face. He brushed a long flop of hair away from his brow. His hesti glowed.

"I believe I will witness the Great Mother Voor one day soon."

Syla explained, "Tomas has a dream, that he will capture the mother of all voors and mount its head on the wall of the billiards room at our house at Yawley. Perhaps, by this act, his father will accept him fully as a family member. A poor surmise, I think."

Tomas corrected her: "I wish merely to take a photograph of the beastie. I will sell it to the *Daily Crystal*." He hiccupped. "That will be fame enough for me."

"I've seen her," Cady told them. "The great *beastie*." They both looked at her in surprise. Tomas's eyes lit up. "You have?"

"Oh, some time ago... years ago... centuries... she... uh... she wasn't the Great Mother Voor back then... she was just the Great Baby Voor... Still pretty big, though, yes, massive, and fuckin' tough... and, and, and nasty... but... uh, gentle with it... Oh..."

Her stomach lurched again, and she quickly hung her head over the rail. But nothing came up. Dry heaves. Lung dust. When she turned back to the Alkhym, they were both looking at her intently, their hesti clicking and whirring and chittering like crazy, loud enough to draw mosquitoes from the bankside reed beds. One of the blighters bit Cady on the neck. She splattered it with a palm and licked the goo off her fingers.

The clicking and popping sounds continued.

Cady asked, "Are you two talking to each other? You're making fun of me, is that it? Behind my back... Behind my lumpy nerve-shot back... while I'm standing here! While I'm fuckin' standing here right in front of you?! Why, I should land you both a bunch of fives."

Indeed, her hand formed into a fist and she raised it.

Tomas affected a bored yawn. He made his way back to the table.

Cady turned to Syla and asked, in a calmer voice, "Can you hear what I'm thinking?"

"Only traces. Family members are the loudest, then my friends, then Alkhym strangers. All Alkhyms. But others, beyond the tribe..."

"The Unhested Masses?"

"Precisely. Their minds are quiet to us. But not silent."

"So what can you hear... inside my head?"

Syla concentrated. The sonar pips bounced off Cady's thoughts, and were reflected back into the Alkhym's skull.

She decoded the sound and said, "Seeds cracking open." Cady had to grin at this. "And Brin? You can hear her thoughts clearly, then?"

Syla looked over to where the girl was entertaining the diners with little Xillith creatures that danced across the tabletop.

"I hear a small voice, asking only to be loved."

"Oh dear… oh dear." Cady in her blue-tinged mood, did not like the sound of that.

"You do know, I suppose," Syla continued, "of the dragon's pedigree, by way of Queen Luda? It is rumoured, among the Nine Families, that Sabrina's veins are rich with Haakenur's blood. And the way she manipulates the Faynr… what else can I believe?"

Cady felt her brows furrow. "You want to take her for yourself, is that it?"

"You think she's happy with you?"

"I'm looking after her."

"The girl sees you as her mother, is that it? Or should that be *grandmother*?"

Cady didn't like the way the talk was going. She refused to answer.

But Syla went on, "Examine your own feelings."

"You keep my *feelings* out of this."

"As you wish. But the girl has needs of her own, perhaps hidden as yet. But one day soon they will emerge into the light." The Alkhym stubbed her cigarette out on the safety rail. "Let me ask you… Do you know of Olan Pettifer, and his work?"

Cady answered warily, "Aye, I've heard of him. A little."

"Lord Pettifer made it known, if ever a boat named the *Juniper* should make its way to the Fusilaire region, that we should delay it. He knew, you see, of our party, our planned entertainment aboard the *Glad Rag*."

Cady shrugged in answer.

"Nothing so untoward was necessary. For you made your own delay." Syla looked at Cady with dark eyes. "Through incompetence. Or stupidity." Every last ounce of goodwill had left her voice.

"You little…" But for once, Cady held back the curses. She needed to learn as much as she could. To this end, she asked, "So you're working for Pettifer, is that it? You're willing to kidnap a little girl. What's he offering you? Money?"

"I am overflowing with riches. As you must know."

"What then? Power. A place at the high table?" Cady gestured to the dinner guests. "This is so like the Alkhym, to throw a fancy party inside the sickened spleen of a dragon! Can't you see what's going on around you?"

"It's important to maintain standards, yes."

"Maintain this!" And she tried to muster her rudest gesture, but her fingers were slippy from engine oil and gravy.

This misshapen rudeness had no effect upon Syla. The Alkhym simply stated, "I don't think you understand what I'm saying, regarding the child."

"Try me."

"It really is quite simple. I want to protect Sabrina. I want to take her into the bosom of the Yohansson-Dahl family. To house her, and feed her, and look after her. And give her the upbringing she deserves. And that way, Lord Pettifer's grubby plans will be set aside, whatever they might be. Surely, you must believe that's a good thing?"

Cady squared up to Syla. She pushed at the younger woman's chest, rocking her back against the guard rail.

Nobody seemed to notice: the party continued, the music grew louder and wilder, Brin's squeals of delight rose in the warm air. A champagne cork shot out from a bottle with a loud *pop*. Everybody was more than rowdy by now.

Cady spoke plainly: "I'm looking after Brin."

"You? And your little band of misfits. And that rickety boat, the *Jupiter*. No, I don't think so."

"*Juniper*. Juniper, you toffee-nosed bedwetter!"

Syla held her stance. "You will sink in the Glimmie, you do know that."

"We've got this far."

"And no further. So come back with us, to Ludwich. Our chauffeurs are waiting. We can accommodate all of you."

It had to be admitted, Cady was tempted. To a degree. To a silent degree. But still, she could not fully trust this woman, no matter what was promised. So she answered with a sailor's prayer: "Mother Nysis will carry and protect us."

Syla burst into sudden anger, all manners dropped. "You dare deny me?"

The two women stared at each other. This close up, the Alkhym's hesti were chirruping madly, clicking and chirring and beeping and crackling. Cady's head began to ache. She felt the noise as a flash of silvery light, like an emergency flare going off in her skull.

Syla said calmly, "I can make it worse, Cady Meade. I can make it louder."

She did so: *chirr, bip, click clack skreee, pop, szzzzzt.*

"I can walk through the forest of your head, and pull up your roots, one by one. You Wodwos have so little power."

Cady staggered back. The pain was intense.

Her hands fluttered hopelessly. People would think her drunk.

The silver light reached her heart, where it burned. And then it stopped, stopped instantly. The pain was gone.

Syla spoke without inflection. "We are civilised people. So then... how about this... We let the Halsegger girl decide for herself. What do you say?"

"She's only ten years old."

"Exactly. The age of transition, for Alkhyms."

Syla didn't wait for a reply. She walked to the table and tapped a spoon against a wine glass, getting everyone's attention. She spoke with clear intention. "We are gathered here aboard the *Glad Rag*, in friendliness and good-fellowship, to decide upon the fate of a child. A young girl about to engage upon the true adventure of her life."

She paused for effect, casting a glance at Cady, before returning her focus to the group.

"I speak of course, of Miss Sabrina Halsegger the Third."

A cheer went up from the collected diners, ten or so people altogether. Some others had joined them from below, curious to see what all the fuss was about. A butler stood to one side: he was holding a covered silver goblet in one hand and a small metal box in the other.

Brin looked up from her seat. The lights gleamed in her lovely green eyes, and her skin shone with youth and vitality.

Cady's heart contracted in pain. "No!" she said. "No, no, this is wrong! Brin, don't listen to her."

But Syla announced simply, "Sabrina, I propose that I take you home with me, to our family house at Yawley Park. We will welcome you into our family. My mother and father were close friends with your parents. They will adopt you, and look after you, and love you as their own." Another pause for maximum effect. "As their own!"

The people cheered again. Tomas tripped over a chair, dropping his glass of champagne to the deck. He apologised in a slurred manner, his face red and sweaty.

Syla continued, "I will be your older sister, Brin. And when... when your parents return from their exile, as they surely must one day... then you will be handed over to them again, safe and sound, and replete with love. What do you say?"

Confusion played over Brin's face. She looked over to where Cady stood at the rail. She made to speak, but could not. Cady tried to help her along, but only the single word came out, repeated helplessly: "Brin... Brin... Brin..."

The girl turned back to Syla. She had made up her mind. "Syla. Syla Dahl. Sylaveer Yohansson-Dahl... Thank you for your very kind offer." She spoke in her poshest accent. "But I'm very much afraid that I must turn you down."

There was a single groan at the table. Others tutted. The music had ceased.

Tomas drawled, "Oh fuck, Syla... I say... that's jolly nasty, all told."

Cady breathed more easily. She was determined to get Brin off the paddle steamer as soon as possible, and back to the *Juniper*. But Syla had not yet finished with her bid. She gestured to the butler, who came to the table, placing the silver goblet down, with the matching box next to it. Cady saw that both items were decorated with Alkhymical symbols. It worried her. "Brin has made her decision," she reminded everyone. "That's an end to it."

Syla kept her eyes on the girl. "I wish to offer the child a gift. Will you allow that, Cady?"

"No. I do not allow it! She's coming back with us. We're sailing on."

But Brin answered for herself. "I'd like to see it. Please."

Syla nodded. The butler opened the metal box and presented it to Brin. The girl peered inside. Her mouth formed into a perfect O of wonder and delight.

"You get to choose," Syla said to her. "Whichever one you like."

"But… But I don't understand, Syla. You mean to say… that I should…"

"It is your time, your proper time. The hesting begins."

Cady came to the table. She saw a pair of myridi cocoons lodged in the box, grey forms of tangled silk, as big as a child's thumb, each one. The wrapping was thin, translucent, a sign that the adult myridi flies were getting ready to emerge.

Cady had had enough. "Stop this. I demand it."

"As we say, let the child choose."

"But… But you don't have a priest. You need a priest, to undertake the ritual."

Syla gave her a sideways glance. "You know so little of our culture. My hesting took place in the hedged garden at Yawley, near our private Faynr pool. My grandfather officiated."

Cady held Brin by the shoulders, forcing the girl to look her in the eyes. "You don't have to do this, do you understand? We can take you to Ludwich, on the *Juniper*. I promise you. You can hest tomorrow, at the proper place, in the proper manner."

Syla interrupted. "You don't think that Lord Pettifer will be in attendance, with his spies and his officers, at such a public event? He will be waiting for Sabrina. He will steal her back. No. This is the only way!" Her tone would accept no further objection. "Now, child. What do you say?"

Brin looked at Cady for one last time.

"Please, Brin. Think carefully. Think of... think of Lek. How will he feel about this? Shall I fetch him now? Would you like that?"

But the Thrawl had already made his appearance. He was standing at the entranceway to the deck, taking it all in. It only took him a moment, Cady could see that from his face, which clicked immediately to fevered concern. "Miss Brin. What are you doing?" But his charge was no longer under his guidance. Brin remained where she was at the table. Her hands went to her temples, left and right, to gently rub at the points of flesh where, in a few minutes time, the hesti would sprout. And then one hand lowered, the index finger moving slowly back and forth across the two cocoons in the box, to stop on the left-side specimen.

"This one?" Syla responded. "Very good. Yes, a very good choice."

And so the ritual began. There was nothing Cady or Lek could do; they were far outnumbered on the boat, and more importantly, Brin herself was determined to undergo the process.

The table was cleared. Everyone stood around it, twenty or more people by now. The butler opened the lid of the silver goblet, revealing a mist of Faynr within. It was a gritty black fog, culled from the tarry realm of Fusilaire, nowhere as pure as the mist used by the priests and archbishops at the hesting pools in the city, but still, it would suffice.

Syla Dahl acted as the officiator. She stood at the head of the table, speaking with a power and authority that belied her age: "Good Faynr, we desire that a child be given unto you, and returned to us, enlivened, with her mind fully opened as a window onto a sunlit dawn. We beseech you, through the workings of your benevolence, through the power of your winged messenger, transport this, your newest subject... Sabrina Halsegger... unto the glory promised us in the First Days."

Syla picked up the chosen cocoon and held it above the silver goblet.

"Take this bound creature, and let it take flight, that it might pass on your knowledge, Good Faynr."

And with that, she dropped the cocoon into the goblet of mist. All eyes were now on the sight of the grey cocoon as it wriggled about, animated by its new environment. Cady saw it curling up and then extending. It only took a moment or two before the first cracks appeared in the silk. It was soon unravelling, splitting open. A moment later, the myridi fly crawled out, pushing its still soft body from the bindings. The thorax and head sparkled with gold and green iridescence. The wings unfurled, and split into pairs, front and rear. The insect's two antennae sprang upwards, quivering.

Cady looked at Brin. The girl's whole attention was on the task. Her eyes never once blinked. The hesting points at her temples glowed, as though already in communication with the insect. And then the myridi fly lifted from the goblet, its wings a sudden blur. It was a small thing, yet the data it held, blood data formed in the Faynr over centuries, held enough power to transform a person into a new kind of being.

Now it hovered in front of Brin's face.

Lek's hand tightened on Cady's shoulder, hard enough to hurt.

Brin's lips parted. The myridi fly flew towards her face.

The boat shuddered. It was sudden and violent, this movement. Cady's hands grabbed at the table edge, but the table itself was now slanted at an angle, and the knives, forks, wine glasses and dinner plates were sliding away. The silver goblet and the myridi box fell to the deck.

People were too shocked to move, or even to make a sound of alarm.

Brin was startled. She leapt onto the table, trying to catch the myridi fly, but it quickly flew away over the water.

The paddle steamer groaned and tipped back in the opposite direction, the deck lurching. Now the Dragonista were crying out, or shouting to each other for help. Cady held onto Lek, who acted as a fixed point in the chaos, perfectly balanced. "Brin. To me!" he commanded. And this time the girl obeyed willingly, leaping off the table.

The *Glad Rag* trembled and then settled into a fragile stillness. The world was leaning over at a severe angle, awaiting the next upset. Cady looked out over the river. Jet flames were shooting up into the air, many of them, more than she had ever seen before. The surface of the water gleamed blackly and then began to surge forward in a giant wave.

Cady braced herself. She held onto Lek and Brin for mutual protection.

The wave hit.

The boat was lifted into the air and then dropped back down, mercilessly.

Cady felt her bones crack and her muscles jolt. She landed on the deck, the breath knocked out of her. In one quick movement, Lek bent down and scooped her up. He had Brin with him as well, clinging to his arm. Together all three of them made their way along the passageway and then down a flight of steps to the lower deck, clinging to whatever cleat or stanchion they could find. They had to reach the *Juniper*! But had the little boat even survived this riverquake?

The *Glad Rag* lurched again. It banged against the jetty with a brutal crunch that shocked its way through Cady's body. She was flipped away easily, losing sight of Lek and Brin. A massive wave of black bile rose over the bulwark and slammed against the forecastle and the funnels. Cady was drenched. She clung onto an open porthole. Night flooded her eyes.

The wave retreated.

People were running this way and that, not knowing where to go. One woman slid along the deck like a rag doll. Now the boat levelled again and Cady dared to look over the side. Yes, there was the *Juniper*, hanging on bravely. Yanish and Numi were on deck, clinging one to the foremast and the other to the figurehead. Lek and the girl had already reached the boat, and were cowered down in the cabin as the waters surged and roared. Cady made her way towards the boarding ladder, but then stopped.

Syla Dahl was standing in front of her, feet firmly planted, unmoving. Only anger controlled her. She screamed, "The girl is mine!"

They met and clattered against each other, struggling to stay upright. The boat shifted again under them. They were pulled apart, but Cady managed to stay on her feet, her hand grabbing by half-chance at a deck support. Syla raised herself up from the deck. She spat out black bile. Her hair was sodden, hanging in raggletails around her shoulders. Her eyes glared. The two hesti glittered, and the cricks and crackles rang out loudly. They attacked the Haegra's skull, causing the old lady to bend over in anguish. The hesti sang louder, ever higher in pitch. Cady's head was made of silver light, her heart the same. At any moment she might split in two down the middle, that's what it felt like. The pain was intense.

The *Glad Rag* tilted back and forth.

Something was roaring over the water, some ravenous beast rising up from the black tar. Cady saw it through a blur of glassy vision – the Great Voor Mother. The massive body soared among the jet flames, weeds clinging to her, vines and tendrils wrapping her. Her face was as white as a moon. But it was a vision of a few seconds only. The creature plunged back down into the water.

Syla was spellbound, incapable of moving. Cady grabbed her. "Quickly, get to safety." But the Alkhym stayed as she was, staring out over the Nysis.

Cady made her way down the ladder and leapt into the *Juniper*. Numi sliced the mooring rope and the steam launch fell into the water, almost capsizing. But she righted herself and floundered and then clung to the top of a wave, and then fell back down. The decks were awash with scum. But Cady gathered focus. She scrabbled her way to the helm and wrestled the wheel away from Yanish's hands. He gave it up easily, for his despondency was still upon him and he would have led the boat to its doom. Now Cady felt every last ounce of the *Juniper's* body entering her own, as one entity, and they moved on, cutting through the waves like the blade of Ibraxus wielded by King Lud. They were thrust this way and that, but the old lady always anticipated the moves, avoiding the worst of the maelstrom.

Numi's flames flickered and flared. Lek's eye-beams

shone out in rays of red and yellow. Pok Pok's arms rose up, pointing to port and starboard, as needed. Brin's hands glowed with sparkles of Xillith light. Cady's optic gland took all this in, every last magical signal given out by her crew, and she took each signal and magnified them all into one pinpointed burst of energy, and sent it freely into the *Juniper*'s soul. From bow to stern, the boat was alive!

Behind them the *Glad Rag* suffered and toiled against the waves of black bile.

Cady imagined the Great Voor Mother, her job done for now, sinking down to the depths of the river. Let her rest there, let her sleep.

Romeo Soul

The pyromancer was sitting on a wooden stool on a little islet close to the bank, a crop of cracked earth no bigger than a bearskin rug. The waters of the Nysis, silvery dark under the shaded moon, lapped gently about the old Ephreme. She leaned forward until her face was illumined by the glow of the fire that flickered from a small pothole filled with natural oil; she was studying the flames intently, ready to notice any slight change of colouration, from orange to blue or green or red to yellow. Cady watched from the bows of the boat as the flame-catcher held an upturned glass bowl over the fire, as though to lower it and thereby trap the flames in the globe. But the flames stayed resolute in orange and blue flickers. Muttering to herself, the woman replaced the glass bowl on the ground. She unrolled a scroll of paper and, in a voice of a cantor, recited the sigils painted there – the name of a drowned person, and the retrieval rune associated and created from the name. Then she cast the paper to the flames where it quickly turned to ash. Cady knew the method well enough: old magic brought to Kethra from distant Phrema, and changed to fit with Faynr's particular nature. However, on this occasion the spell had no effect and the Ephreme leaned back on her stool and took a drink of tea from a mug. Numi called out to her, "No luck tonight?" The pyromancer responded with a shake of the head and a flutter of her tiny wings. Flakes of ash fell from her hair. She eyed the flames and concentrated her mind: watching, waiting, praying.

The *Juniper* moved on, further into the Glimmie. In the distance the lights of the capital could be seen: Ludwich, their destination. So close now.

By the cabin clock, it was a quarter to ten. The last of the moon was taken by cloud, but even now the river shone with a silvery light. Spirits were abroad, the souls of the drowned, gathered here from wherever they had lost their final breaths, upriver, or down. They could neither be seen nor heard, but felt in the chill of the air and the prickle of goose flesh on the arms and neck. Cady felt the shiver. Yanish looked especially upset; he could not keep still and his eyes darted this way and that. Thrawl Lek gathered Brin to him, but the girl made little dancing steps of her own choosing: her hair was wild and frizzy with Xillith light. Numi Tan studied each tiny islet as they passed them. The Nysis hereabouts formed a wider lagoon dotted with the many small outcrops of land like a jigsaw puzzle, an archipelago through which the bigger ships had to steer carefully. But the nimble *Juniper* found an easy course.

The water bubbled blackly. The islets grew in size. By now each outcrop contained a number of Ephreme, two or three or four. These patient men and women waited before the fires that burned continually, fed from below by the oily secretions of Faynr. Numi called a friendly hopeful greeting to each occupant. Her own fiery soul had been retrieved from one of the little pools, nurtured, set in a clay body, and then consecrated and brought to life by the power of an archmage – in Numi's case, by Una Goodperson down at Ponperreth.

More and more of the pools were seen as the boat drew near to the village of Hiskahearn. The pyromancers sang their runic chants. Many were accompanied by Nebulims, whose flames called to Numi's across the river's expanse. Moths and glowbugs flittered in the *Juniper*'s spotlight beam. A cry of delight was heard as a young Ephreme plunged her glass bowl over the suddenly roaring flames of a fire pool. The receptacle captured the flames, helped by the sigils inked on the curved sides. Cady watched as the soul was transferred to a keepsake box. One of the Nebulim took charge of it, carrying it to a handcart parked nearby. It was good to see the practise was still underway. After what they had witnessed at Ponperreth, all hope had been lost of the Nebulim having a proper future in the world. But here in the Glimmie, at least, Faynr was being productive. In some weird response, Cady felt the buds throbbing deliciously on her neck and arms and thighs. In body and mind she was a set of signals close to being deciphered: surely, just a few more turns of the tuning dial would do it!

Yanish nudged the boat against the village pier, allowing Numi to jump down. She chatted to a couple of Nebulim and an older Ephreme standing around a hut selling pies and sandwiches. Steam rose from the hot pastries. Numi seemed to know the villagers well, indeed, to be thrilled by them, or by some news they were giving her. Her face-flames were suddenly bright and powerful within the mask. She was smiling. But the smile died as quickly, as the flames guttered on the wick and turned darker in colour. She came back to the boat with a heavy tread, her visage lowered.

"No word of your friend?" Cady asked, remembering the story Numi had told, of her lover and their shared walking into the river's depths. The Nebulim made no reply. She busied herself with a length of rope, coiling it tightly around her forearm. Cady thought it best to leave her alone, at least for the moment.

They stayed at the pier for a while longer, the five of them sitting in the cabin, eating food purchased from the riverside hut. Cady wrapped her fingers around a mug of tea laced with rum. They had a dangerous passage ahead, before the city truly came in their sights. Brin kept rubbing at her head, pressing hard at the hesting points. The curtailed ritual aboard the *Glad Rag* had affected her deeply, although whether for good or ill, Cady could not say.

After finishing a slice of ginger cake, Brin went out to the afterdeck. Once the door had closed behind her, Lek spoke freely of his fears, and hopes: "Only the dragon's ghost is keeping her well now, I'm certain of it. Only Faynr. But I believe utterly that once Brin has properly hested, all will be good." His face sought out a fierce emotion. "I wish to get to Ludwich, that is my aim. If no one wants to accompany us, I will take Brin on alone from here." But no one was backing down, not having come this far. Satisfied, he went out to give the engine yet another oiling. Yanish took out Maguire & Hill's chart for the Glimmie section of the Nysis. Cady knew full well the river lost all sense of continuity once Hiskahearn was left behind. So many islets, hundreds of them, in so many sizes. The largest of them even had a name: Ludforsakenland. Aye, and it was well-named, for every sailor knew to keep off its crumbling black earth. It was an Isle of the Dead, and was always hungry for new residents: the spirits called loudly from the gloom. Only the highest of the pyromancers dared to walk there.

Numi had not said a single word during the meal. Now she left the cabin and went to stand next to Pok Pok at the prow of the boat. The night was complete, dark in all its parts. The moon stayed hidden. Cady and Yanish worked together at the table, marking a maze-like passage through the archipelago. The Glimmie had always been a difficult section for Yanish to cross, as it was for all Azeels; their shadows were brothers and sisters of the dead, and were easily drawn across the veil. But there was little Cady could say. He had retreated into himself, ever since the incident in the shroud garden. The poor lad. She filled her pipe and went out onto the foredeck. She joined Numi. The two friends stood in silence. The *Juniper* clung to the fenders of the pier for comfort. The little boat and its crew would soon be tested.

A cloud of bats flew across the beam of the spotlight.

Numi spoke first. "It has been a strange season. The dead are reluctant to appear, and when they do, often they go wild. Many in Hiskahearn have been affected by dark and terrible visions. Madness abounds."

Cady nodded. "The times are all upside down, and roundabout, this way and that. Truly."

Pok Pok echoed the sentiment: "Truly. Truly. Truly. Three times truly."

"On top of which," Cady continued, "My verrucas are killing me. It's the damp."

Numi made no response to her friend's attempts at lightening the mood.

Cady made up a new prayer for the occasion.

"Sweet Faynr, what ails thee? By what mortal instrument

can we chart your territories? Upon which vessel can we sail, the better to know your secrets? In your hour of need, Faynr, how can we help you?"

But the ghost of the dragon made no answer.

And then Numi gasped. She cried out. It seemed for no reason, none that could be seen. Her flames lowered themselves almost to a dying ember. She reached out over the gloom-silvered water, as though to grasp something invisible.

"The sirens are calling, can't you hear them?"

Cady couldn't, beyond a soft whistling tone from afar. It might have been a night bird. But Numi persisted: "They make my flames flutter. They are saying your name, Cady."

"What?"

"Your name, your name."

"Oh, I don't like the sound of that, not at all. Bastards."

And then Numi sighed. "Gone now, gone." Only cold air and the drift of ashes. Her hand drew back, to clench on Pok Pok's shoulder, the hard clay fingers almost crunching the metal skin. The figurehead took the pain stoically, allowing it to happen. The moment passed. Numi crumpled. Cady caught her and held her upright and took her to the forward-hatch cover, where they both sat down, their bodies close for warmth and comfort.

Cady let the silence do its work. The *Juniper* settled into one small wave after another, pulling at her hawsers, keen to travel.

Numi spoke. "My first life ended at the Withy."

She paused, gathering her emotions, one flame after another, twisting them into some kind of pattern that she could cling to.

"We both... Romeo and I... we both stepped into the

river, weighted down." She paused and then added, "His name was... uh... his real name was Romi... Romi Omir... But I called him Romeo. It was a little joke between us."

Cady responded quietly: "Of course. I understand."

Pok Pok's torso turned as best it could, the better to hear the story.

Numi went on. "We stepped into the river and the whirlpool clutched at us, pulling us in, the both of us, the stones around my neck and my wrists... his hand in mine... further down into deep currents... but his touch slipped away..." She was trembling. "And then the darkness."

Numi projected the darkness of the river as a series of rippling shadows, holding her hands over her face, over the glass mask and the flames of her face, moving her fingers. Shadow shapes danced in the spotlight beam. Cady remembered when she had first met John Dee, at a shadowbox show. It was an underground affair, six people only, a meeting of rebellious minds in a dank cellar. This was the same effect, but more animated, more detailed: Numi was an expert projectionist. Her fingers danced and fidgeted, conjuring the memory into life. The darkest depths of the Nysis were portrayed and bizarre river creatures swam by in the spotlight, all portrayed by Numi alone.

"My last breaths were taken from me. My final act was to look around for sight of Romi. But I could not see him, and I feared he had drifted away on some stronger tide. And then... and then I felt my memories leave my body. Faynr welcomed me."

Cady watched fascinated as, without any need for words, Numi showed this scene unfolding, her body floating lifeless in the dark water, her memories seen as a sudden cloud of smoke which separated instantly into so many tiny wiggling creatures or filaments: they looked like larvae, and were brightly lit in orange with tints of gold. The sorrowful depths took on a new glow, a most beautiful sight to Cady's mind. And then the Xilliths arrived, a shimmering pair of them, tangled by their blue tendrils. They gathered the larvae into their patterns of energy and set off upstream with them, for the long journey towards the Glimmie. The movements of Numi's hands slowed as they conjured this transportation into view. Never before had Cady been witness to such practices, the true Ephremic way of magic, and the resurrection of the soul. Arriving at their destination, the Xilliths opened their tendrils and the larvae swam free, into the oily bubbling substances that flowed between the islets. They were soon lost in the web-like channels of the archipelago, seen first as flickers of light in the river and then as a strange afterglow that suffused the surface, soon to fade completely from sight.

Numi's hands came away from her face.

Her flames were black fire, as dark as Cady had ever seen them.

After a moment, the Nebulim took up her story once more, this time in words. "I lived in my larval form for many years, in the depths, feeding off tiny scraps of weed and fish droppings." She looked out over the water. "Time passed without my knowledge, until at last I was called upwards towards the flame pools, summoned by an old pyromancer called Emmet Bradhelm. He's dead now, dear Emmet. He gave himself to the waters, to seek his own salvation." Numi paused, and then brought herself fully back to the present world with a tremble of her clay body. "By the calendar of the living, that was fourteen years ago."

Cady asked, "And you never saw Romeo again?"

"For a long while I waited for news that his memories had been found, and made into a flame. Every time I passed through Hiskahearn, or took a weekend trip to Timmusk, I would ask the mages for news, demanding to see the list of the newly retrieved. But always... nothing... no sign... and I despaired mightily." She looked at Cady. "But now..."

"Yes? Numi, what is it?"

"He has been found. Romi's flames were taken to Ludwich, to the village of Timmusk, for consecration by the archmage there, to be housed in clay, to be blessed in the name of Queen Luda, that he might live again."

"But that... that's wonderful, Numi, isn't it?"

The Nebulim drew a breath, to raise her flames a little higher. Her voice broke. "That was two months ago. Two whole months, Cady! And he never came to see me, not so much as a whisper of a flicker of a glow of a flare. Oh, my embers might as well be cold and lifeless."

And she wrung her hands together, causing her metal ornaments to jar in dissonance.

Cady watched her friend carefully, before saying, "Ah, he'll be calling soon enough, believe me. If he knows where his bread is best-buttered."

"Yes, perhaps. As you say." And before Cady could speak in turn, Numi went on, "I will visit Timmusk village." Her face flickered away from any human semblance. "And then... and then Romeo and I will be together again."

She stood up and walked away towards the cabin, leaving Cady alone. Or not quite alone. For Pok Pok said quietly, "My crooked little dot-dashy heart is pained."

"Yes, mine also."

Fifteen minutes later they set sail once more, on their final approach. Lek took Brin into the cabin and wrapped her in his arms. He would hear no word of binding her, even for her own safety. "I shall do my job." Cady nodded. Machines are machines: their souls are made of grit and metal shavings and the semi-random sparks at the heart of a crystal. The sirens would find hard-gatherings there. But Yanish would be the worst affected. Cady remembered one Azeelian, the captain of a sloop, who had given into the siren song; he was currently in Medlock asylum, in a room with no windows. So now they did what they had always done, on earlier voyages through the region: Yanish climbed down into the hold and Cady battened down the hatch, sealing him inside. He would not escape. That done, she took her place at the wheel. Numi lashed Cady's hands to the spokes at the ten-to-two position, pulling the bindings tight and then tighter still, until the old lady cried out with the pain.

Now, they were ready.

Ash floated through the air, greying the boat as it ploughed forward.

This was the first sign.

Cady felt it upon her face as the fluttering of feathers.

All the various pieces of paper, the scrolls of parchment, each one inscribed with the sigils of retrieval and the names of the dead, each one burned over the fire pools, each transformed into ash; and this same spell cast many times over the centuries… and every last flake of ash remained in the Glimmie; they never crumbled nor blew away, but only drifted by on the gentle breeze: not rain nor hail nor fierce sunlight nor war nor flood would destroy them. The air brimmed with grey flakes. Nobody – not even Dr Dee – had ever worked out why the ash was preserved in this way, but it was as much a part of the region as the river and the dragon's ghost, and the solitary boat, and the places where they all met and merged and moved on, further into the dark. The spotlight showed only the skin of the night, nothing more. Pok Pok's arms moved this way and that, gently, slowly, showing direction and degrees.

Starboard three, wheel amidships, straight on, ease to port.

Cady followed these orders precisely, glad of the help.

Now she could smell the rot. The sickening stench of a giant beast long dead, yet taking aeons to decay. Cady felt her stomach cramp. Her throat gulped repeatedly.

Numi's flames were a deep purple in colour, streaked with yellow. She moved from one side of the boat to the other, gazing down into the water, as far as her fiery eyes could delve. Perhaps she remembered her time in the depths, when she wished only for a single word of love in the lonely unwritten night.

The dead waited here, they waited for salvation. They waited on through the endless years for that moment when the life-giving flames would speak to them. Surely, Faynr was most kindly and wise, to allow her subjects this second chance.

The stench grew worse, worse than ever before. Thick black ectoplasmic oil flowed into the potholes on the islets, fuel for the fire pools, which gleamed and fluttered near and far, the only light visible. The boat moved between these signals, seeking a clean channel. But despite Yanish and Cady's careful plotting over the map, and despite Pok Pok's finest piloting efforts, the hull scraped and clanged against rock as the islets grew larger and more misshapen. They passed a few Ephreme pyromancers, isolated from each other, sitting before their chosen fires. They were desperate men and women, this far from the village, for the dead grew restless and angry here. The spotlight stuttered as the deathly forces of the region cloaked the beam. The navigation lights followed suit, glowing one last time in red and green and then fading. Even Numi's flames were dimmed, still flickering but in blackened tones. Her face vanished into the shadows of her shell. With that last human signal fading away, Cady felt she was alone. She knew that Lek and Brin were behind her, bound in each other's protection under the table in the cabin. She knew that Numi and Pok Pok were on the foredeck. She knew that Yanish was curled in the circle of his own limbs on the floor of the hold. She knew that Mr Carmichael shivered in his tank, his crystal spine picking up electric images from the barren lands, images that no living creature could ever view. Aye, and she knew that each living creature or machine mused upon their own end, whether at gunpoint or by sickness, or dismantlement, or from meeting the front end of a double-decker bus on the Thistlehurst Road at five o'clock on a rainy Wednesday, or by blade or poison or neglect, or by their own hand in a moment of despair. The archipelago always drew such thoughts to the surface.

Cady knew all this. But she was alone.

In the achromatic dark. In the wordless silence.

In the wordless silence, the dead whispered words of wordless darkness.

Cady heard them first as sighs, as breaths.

And then very quietly and far away – the wailing of an air-raid siren. It was imagined only, a conjured sound, yet it took her back instantly to the early years of the war, when the bombs fell on the wharves and quays of Witherhithe. And now the screams of the victims were added. But quiet screams, barely heard. And all the worse for that, as though they could never be helped, never pulled from the boiling waters. And then gone, submerged. Whisper, sigh, whisper, sigh. In her ears, directly in her skull. Now a song, a little louder.

Oh the trees they do grow old
and the leaves they do turn brown
And many a time my love and I
did wear the thorny crown.

It was a Wodwo folk ballad, from the Year of the Blight. Cady's heart blossomed and she sang along, for what else could she do? But her words soon drifted away as ashes from her mouth, and the melody died on the river's breath. Her hands tugged at the strands of twine that bound her to the wheel. Blood seeped from the cuts she made, green blood turning red as it flowed.

The voices rose in volume, more and more of them, all calling at once. In one moment, Cady knew them to be illusions; in the next she knew these sirens to be real, that the lost spirits were truly calling to her, luring her into the shadows. Both thoughts battled against each other. Either way, Ludforsakenland wanted her as a resident.

The air greyed further, turning into a thick cloud of smoke. Cady squinted and tried to make out Pok Pok's movements. But nothing could be seen clearly, not until Numi stepped closer to the figurehead. The Nebulim's diminished flames gave out just enough light for Cady to see the directions indicated.

And the wheel turned under her fingers.
And the *Juniper* sailed on.
And the voices whispered incessantly.

They knew Cady by name, and called to her for company.
*Come to me, Cady Meade, come to me in the prison of the depths, in
the darkness of the water, Cady, come to me.* But Cady resisted in
the best way she knew: through ribaldry and bawdy and the
urges that held the true flesh and blood in constant sway.

I am a jolly stoker
I work a pretty ship,
I shagged my way from Calahey
down to the Devil's Dip.
I shagged my way back home again
around the Cape Lorraine,
I shagged the bosun and his mate
in the bed of Captain Caine.

There were eleven more verses of the Jolly Stoker's exploits,
but Cady gave up after two, for her tongue would no longer
sing and her mouth was clogged with ashes.

Her wrists were cut almost to the bone, left and right.

And still the voices of the dead called, tempting her,
beguiling.

*Cady Meade, come to us, join us here, in the cold depths, join
with us.*

On and on they went.

The boat entered a patch of water lilies, whose vast circular
leaves layered the narrow streams between the islets. Their
central flowers were pink and open and wet with sticky
juices to tempt the night-winged moths. Haakenflies buzzed
around the lily pads, electric-blue needles stitching the
gloom. And the stink grew worse, that rancid putrid stench
of decomposition!

The fire pools flared up suddenly on the nearby isles.

And not a pyromancer in sight; for out here life was a delicate substance, easily lost.

Cady heard a violent commotion from the cabin behind her, but could not tell if it were Brin or Lek making the noise. Perhaps both of them, perhaps both were enticed equally.

Pok Pok screamed.

Numi held on to the figurehead, each protecting the other.

The dead called from the afterworld. Louder they sang, enveloping the boat with their hunger, so many of them, the thousands upon thousands drowned in the river throughout its long history, their voices all mingled together, blurred with accents from many lands, from all tribes, adult and child. On top of this Cady heard gunshots, curses, the tightening of nooses, the whistle of falling bombs. The Nysis churned beneath the boat's keel. She saw the glint of blades and swords and spears. She saw blood on the water, the eternal sacrifice Mother Nysis demands of the people. She heard the friends and crewmates and passengers she had lost overboard, from the very first voyage, to the last of the war years. All of them calling to her, wanting her, demanding she leave her post and leap over the side into the deep dark, the welcoming dark. They were louder than she had ever heard them, and more desperate, their voices made sickly as Faynr sickened. The waters glowed silver and orange with the lost souls. The hungry bats flittered about, mapping the night air with their sonic grammar.

Ahead and to port was the ragged shore of Ludforsakenland. Soon they would reach it and sail within its treacherous impulse.

Cady's hands pulled apart violently. The twine sawed the

pulp of her flesh. She wanted nothing more than to break free and to run gleefully across the island, or even to plunge into the water, shivering, to feel herself dancing in the arms of the dead. They would never let her go. All the many voices now formed into one particular voice, a voice she recognised. It belonged to her first ever cabin boy aboard the *Juniper*, young Amos Brightstone, drowned in the river at the age of sixteen, and all at the fault of herself, her own drunken stupidity that time…

Cady, Cady can you hear me? It's Amos. Help me, Cady help me, I'm so cold, it's so lonely here. Please, Cady, you must help me. Join with me.

He called to her from the island, from the black shadows. Cady cried out in pain and despair. She spat out ashes. She sang to herself the loudest rudest song she knew, but it was still too quiet to hide the voice of Amos, handsome Amos, the dandy Ephreme, king of the sailor's knots, the foredeck dancer, the agile leaper from hull to hull across the close-harboured boats, his little wings fluttering, the best-ever map-reader, the maker of tea, the cracker of raw eggs into vinegar every single morning, without fail.

Cady, please help me, come to me, I'm alone, I'm waiting here for you.

Her voice rang out in urgent prayer as she pulled out the throttle. "Let us soon be done with the Glimmie, and let the lights of Ludwich shine on us, brightly!"

But the *Juniper* seemed to be slowing down, not surging forward full tilt, as hoped. The island cursed the boat with a near stagnant tide. Cady ground her teeth together and screwed her eyes tight shut. The voice of Amos was reduced to a whisper, but it was the only thing she could hear.

Please Cady, please. Come to me.

Her wrists were raw and bloody enough to slip from the bindings. One last effort would do it. Yet some other sound had taken over from the cabin boy's voice; not from the river, not from Faynr, not even from Ludforsakenland, but from the boat itself. From down below, from the cargo hold. A banging sound, loud and violent and random and terrifying. It had to be Yanish, poor Yanish down there, going crazy, crazier than Cady herself. The Azeel people suffered so, with their shadows always touching death. And she pictured him in her mind, she saw his fists smashing at the hull, his fingernails scratching at the hatch cover. No, he had gone through enough already, this day. Too much!

Her wrists broke through the twine.

She screamed and she called to Numi and ordered her to take the wheel. "Keep her straight, keep her true."

Numi nodded, her flames alight once more, as she drew on her vapours.

Lek was at the cabin door. "What is it? What's that noise?"

"Stay with Brin, nothing else!"

Her voice was harsh. He backed away instantly, into the cabin.

Cady stumbled along the deck in the near dark, keeping hold of the gunwale rail. From there she made her way to the hatch and pulled back the battens. The banging sound was clearly heard from below, along with Yanish's voice, crying out in pain.

Cady's blood froze.

She opened the hatch. And immediately, the noise stopped.

There were shadows inside, and further shadows upon the shadows.

The voices of the drowned were silent now, as though they knew the truth, that some darker voice was waiting to be heard.

"Yanish? Are you there? Speak to me."

No reply.

Cady peered into the blackness of the hold. She climbed down the ladder a few steps and then bent double, still keeping her feet on the rungs and one hand on an upright. From this vantage, she peered along the length of the boat. All was dark. Except for... yes, emerging into view... at the far end of the hold...

Yanish's aphelon. Shiny white in colour, like a royal diadem.

A good sign, surely. She breathed a little. He must be crouched down there, perhaps scared out of his wits. She called to him again, gently this time.

"Yanish? Are you alright, dear?"

The aphelon flickered in response, once, twice. And then went out.

Yanish growled.

It was a deep and horrible sound, something no living creature could ever make.

There was a sudden movement.

Cady jerked back in fear.

But Yanish had merely pulled away the cloth covering Mr Carmichael's tank. The light was exposed, the flickering display of the electric eel. In this sudden kaleidoscopic effect, the face of Yanish was revealed. It was a ghastly sight, the young man's features twisted into a new shape, devoid of all human pattern. He reached for the slop bucket and drank of it greedily, swilling the ghastly contents against his face and lips. The smell was atrocious. Cady was sickened to the pit of her stomach, for pain of seeing Yanish in this act. *Oh no, no, no no, no.* Her mouth closed on the useless word.

Yanish threw the bucket away and then rushed towards the hatch like a low beast, bent down, his hands and legs scrabbling on the curved planks. His face glittered with sweat. His teeth were bared. His cheeks were stained horribly with his chosen food.

The shiny black aphelon drilled forward.

With a yelp, Cady scurried up the ladder, banging her head in the process. She tripped and fell and rolled along the deck a little way, and then twisted round. Her eyes bulged and her heart beat like a hammer on an anvil.

The *Juniper* was breathing. Steam clouded the deck.

And then the shadow emerged from the hatchway. Yanish rose up. He seemed to have gained a foot in height. His head tilted back on his stretched neck, and he howled. He howled madly at the invisible moon. Then he craned forward again and he stared at Cady with a look that spoke only of madness. He was weeping, and yet his tears were as black as his aphelon; they fell as pitch from his eyes.

His shadow moved independently of his body, not quite attached to his skin.

And within that shadow the true form of Gogmagog was seen.

The face of the monster.

The Night Serpent. The Venomous One.

This ghost of poison seeped out from Yanish's aphelon like smoke from another world. It swirled around his body, yet still clinging to him, still needful of him. Poor Yanish was powerless to act. He was the mere carrier of the monster, the host.

Juniper's spotlight came on, half flood only, but welcome all the same.

Cady could not understand it, not until she looked back at the cabin roof. Lek and Brin were up there, Lek was transferring his power beams to the light, giving it some extra strength. Brin directed the beam of light as a weapon. It had some small effect, causing Gogmagog to tremble back a little.

A bell was rung. *Clang, clang!*

Cady turned to see Numi approaching, the witch's bell in her hand. She was raising it as high as she could and then swinging it low, and back again, back and forth, sending out this great peal of sound. *Clang, clang, clang!* A magical sound, a spell of dismissal. Hearing it, Gogmagog shivered on Yanish's body, his face pinching back into streaks of shadowy muscle and bone. He shrieked in pain. Emboldened, Numi came to him, as close as she could dare. The bell clanged louder than the Old Bell of Bleary in the Tower of Witan, when it had called the nation to arms in the first week of the war. The *Juniper* shook on the water and scraped against rock. The bats of the Glimmie flew away in their swarms, chittering and darting.

Numi raised the bell for another death knell. But Gogmagog was ready for her this time. He cloaked the instrument in his shadow, muffling the sound. Numi cried out as the bell was ripped from her hands. It was thrown aside with a violent motion, landing somewhere far out, on water or on land.

Cady was still sprawled out on the deck. The Night Serpent came for her. He could not move of his own accord, but had to force Yanish to walk forward, like a crooked marionette. The poor lad staggered and lurched, his legs weak from the effort. Gogmagog was feeding on him, on every last speck of disgrace, on the feelings of shame brought on by the death of his father.

Soon, Cady suspected, her friend would die. Or go insane.

The spotlight targeted the shadow creature. His yellow eyes burned, his long teeth were razor points. Drool fell from his lips. He spoke through Yanish's mouth, using the young man's voice but twisting it, mutating it into a harsh grumble.

I seek poison. I am born from poison, I will poison!

Each word caused it sorrow. Such a base *human* activity; speaking! Disgust ravaged its moon-dead face. The shadow had to reform itself on the host's skin constantly, for fear of losing itself.

Cady got to her feet. She saw now a small truth: that this was not the full body of Gogmagog, but only a portion, that which had invaded Yanish's body at Ponperreth.

It was a reflection of the original darkness.

And it was only getting hungrier.

Cady put her hand flat on her friend's chest.

They stared at each other, head to head, Gogmagog and Cady Meade. She searched through the shadows for Yanish's true features. The black aphelion appeared as a hole in his forehead, a tunnel down into the depths of madness. Cady summoned her powers as a Haegra. She called on the old gods, the oldest gods, the ones who vomited soil from their throats to make the planet, who spurted their seeds into the dirt, to grow the first plants, who nurtured in their wombs the first living worms and beetles. Her hand glowed green around the edges and jagged thorns appeared on her palm. She hooked the shadow and pulled at it, lifting it a little way from the body of her friend. She felt she was pulling tar from a road, or ink from the Book of Dark Eden. And she struggled to keep hold. Gogmagog bit and gurgled in turn, and gulped for air and snarled and spat warm excrement in her face.

Yanish fell to his knees under the pressure. The Night Serpent reared up over him, as far as the aphelon's connection would allow. But Cady stood proud, trying still to pull the monster out into the world with her hand of spikes. She trembled. Only passion kept her there, as her flesh weakened. Gogmagog broke away from her hold and snapped back into Yanish's body. The lad yowled in agony.

Cady collapsed to the deck. She was aware only of a blur of movement at her side. It was Brin. The young girl had leapt from the lip of the cabin roof. She landed on Yanish, one hand grabbing hold of him for support, the other raised high... and in this raised hand, the boat's tin-opener gleamed, Ibraxus style. That tiny instrument! And yet in the moment of the girl's power, wreathed with blue sparks, it looked like a talon, or a dragon's fang. She thrust it down with all her strength.

The metal claw gouged into Yanish's forehead. Blood and pus spewed out.

Yanish gibbered and mewled. Gogmagog clung on, his body already breaking apart.

Brin kept to her task. Her fingers crackled with the energy of a hundred Xilliths, as the metal claw dug deep, deeper, until at last the aphelon was pried loose. It fell to the decking, a cold black smouldering triangle. The Night Serpent was no longer connected to flesh. He had no home, no basis in the world of things. He was pure shadow. His voice keened as he fluttered hungrily above the *Juniper*'s foredeck and cabin. His body was a streak of piss from an angry demon, and his lips spewed obscenities.

Cady reached out for Yanish, where he lay close by. They huddled together. His hand probed at the empty place on his forehead. His eyes sought out Cady's, his human eyes, fully restored. She took his hand in hers and squeezed hard enough to show him he was still alive. "You're alright, Yan. We're still travelling." He passed out.

By now the *Juniper* was no longer under anyone's control, and a great shudder ran along the deck as the prow dug into the shoreline of the island. They had run aground. The spotlight fell dark once more. Cady wondered if she could make it to the helm, to push the engine into reverse. But her body seemed empty, used up. Her hand ached and bled where the thorns had erupted, and her wrists were red-ribboned.

Gogmagog screamed over their heads, circling the foremast, writhing madly. He needed a fresh body to inhabit, and, set on revenge, he went for the youngest of them all, for the one who had injured him the most. He went for Brin. Cady was terrified of this happening. She tried to get to her feet, but was still too weak, and dazed. Yet, to her relief, Gogmagog could not touch Brin, no matter how he tried. The two danced around each other, as if they were locked into some weird, ill-starred field of magnetic repulsion. Cady could not understand it, unless to think that there were some elemental truth still waiting to be worked out between Brin, the faery child of the dragon, and the Night Serpent. There was a blood reckoning to come which had been centuries in the making. It would not be ended in a few moments of time.

The Night Serpent retreated, this thin ever-dwindling blackness. His hunger pained him. His tongue flicked out to catch flying insects and flakes of ash. He surged upwards and took hold of a passing bat and clouded it from wing to wing and took some strength from it. The creature fell to the foredeck. And Gogmagog ate further, revelling in the flesh. Two haakenflies took up residence in his eyes, to electrify his senses. He sparkled as they sparkled, and his shadow form pulsed like the black sail of a pirate ship. With his glow back upon him, he attacked again, seeking this time for Numi's flames, for he smelt the scent of her first death. He would put her out! He would smother that flame and take it for his own and thereby enliven the clay anew, himself the occupant.

But Lek was there to meet him. The Thrawl put on his mask of rage as he raised his right hand palm outwards revealing the clicking valve system he had used to gather the information from the shroud. His hand glowed like a huge sapphire illumined by its own inner power. The colour intensified. Cady was sure she could hear a whining sound. Lek stood braced for action, his hand outstretched like a stage magician's during an effect. But this was real! The light shone with a bluer, whiter flare and the valve's parts grated against themselves. Lek began to shudder as a stream of red ichor drooled from the aperture in his palm, some kind of oil, which dripped onto the decking. The sight and the smell of all this roused Gogmagog. He looked now like a slathering dog, or a fly with a bellyful of eggs to inject into meat. He was drawn to both the red juice and the blue light and the aperture, hopelessly, and his shadow soul was sucked up head to tail into the Thrawl's hand in one long whip-lashing movement.

Immediately, Lek clicked the valve back into place. His arm lowered. For a moment there was silence on the boat, dreadful silence.

Lek was standing frozen to the spot.

His face was shut down. Every last emotion was banished.

His body trembled.

His eyelids were lowered and locked.

His metal teeth were clamped together, as he fought to keep the creature inside his body.

His arms hung down at his sides, without purpose.

But his fists were clenched.

Brin called to him. "Lek, Lek, please don't, Lek. Don't go. Don't leave me!"

The girl understood what the Thrawl was about to do, to make his escape and take Gogmagog with him. It took Cady a little longer to work out. Before she could even get to her feet, Lek had already put his plan into action. He rushed towards the gunwale and leapt up onto it, and from there in one smooth motion he plunged down onto the island's shore and kept on running, running, running. He disappeared into the shadows beyond the grounded *Juniper*.

Numi and Brin hurried to the rail, the girl shouting out the Thrawl's name.

There was no answering call, only echoes.

Yanish got to his feet a little unsteadily. Cady helped him up, and they joined the other two at the gunwale. They looked out over the bleak plain of Ludforsakenland, where the grey fog of ashes drifted about the fire pools, and in the distance tall trees stood in attendance, as tall as houses; and enveloping everything was the stench of rotting flesh, strong enough to make Cady gag. The sirens sang out, their voices stripped of all melodiousness. It was a shrill choir.

Pok Pok was making little squeaking noises. Brin was wailing. She wanted to jump down, to go after her friend and guardian. But Numi and Yanish held her back.

"Help him," she cried. "Please, somebody help him!"

The moon came out at last, but had no effect, for the island was too haunted: light would not penetrate the canopy of fog.

Cady said between clenched teeth, "I don't like losing passengers. Not now, not ever!" Yet she knew the Thrawl had good reason for jumping overboard, wanting to protect the girl from Gogmagog's presence. She put her arm around Brin's shoulders and felt her shaking badly, the old affliction coming back.

The girl's voice was weak: "Help him, Mrs Meade, help him, please."

The feelings overwhelmed Cady, the sense of loss in the girl transferred through the fibres and tendrils of her inner being, taking root within her own heart, which uncurled as a green shoot from a seed. "I'll find him, Brin. I promise you." There was no questioning this statement, only the action that followed immediately, as Cady straddled the gunwale and dropped down quickly and heavily into the shallows at the boat's side. *I promise you, I promise!* The water clutched at her ankles with a grip worthy of a river beast. She clambered up onto the flat rocky earth and set off alone, into the darkness.

Ludforsakenland

It happened quickly. A few steps, her feet stumbling over rocks and clods of earth, and then a look back over her shoulder. And she could no longer see the boat. The *Juniper* had vanished clean away. The thought came to her coldly: *I will never see my beloved vessel again.*

Drifts of smog, the woody taste and scent of smoke.

There was no sense here of left or right, forward or back. Any compass bearing would be a lie. Her own living needle – which she had fostered over centuries within the bulb of her optic gland – came up wobbly. No stars to guide her, neither the known constellations, nor the inner stars that sometimes shone in Faynr's outer skin: no, but only black sky and the faint smudge of the lightless moon. It truly was a forsaken place. But Cady had to keep going, to find Lek if she could, or at least a trace of his passing.

Every so often a fire pool came flickering into view, offering a little warmth, a little light. The oil in the pool glistened with its rainbow colours. She had to wonder what kind of drowned souls would be drawn to this island, in lieu of all the other islets. Murderers, perhaps, or the criminally insane. Nasty fuckers of the first degree. The flames danced in her eyes.

The earth cracked underfoot and water squelched around her boots. It made her wonder: was this island not solid ground at all, but merely a crust of rocky soil floating on the river's surface? Or more likely a thin layer of Faynr's skin. The sense of fragility filled her with dread. Fog veiled her eyes. But instead of slowing down and taking care, she ran on madly, her arms waving about in front of her, two useless objects, until she hit a fence of twisted wire and felt the breath knocked out of her. The barbs tore at her clothes. Her feet did an awkward three-step dance and tripped and fell to the damp ground. Ooof! Her face was pressed into the soil, and from this position, through blurry eyes she stared at a gleam of brass. With an effort, she brought it into focus.

It was the witch's bell.

The thing had landed here, all this distance away from the boat, when Gogmagog had flung it away from Numi Tan's hands. Cady struggled to her feet and brought the bell up with her, feeling its good weight. She walked along the line of the barbed fence until she found a gap, housing a wooden stile. Had Lek come this way? She climbed with an effort into the next field. Why had the Ephreme archmages divided this place into separate regions: what were they keeping in, or keeping out?

An animal mooed nearby. Only its mouth was visible in the darkness, hot breath steaming from pink gums. Fog wreathed the short, curved tusks. It looked like an offshoot of a cow and a boar conjured up from one of the darker chapters of Dr Dee's notebooks, those pages the Witan High Council had once banned as being "detrimental to the nation's wellbeing". But the creature only snuffled at the earth for a weed to chew on and then stared at Cady with incurious eyes as she passed by. Wherever life could be formed within Faynr, it would be formed, no matter how inhospitable the land or water might be.

Taking a slower pace, her feet found a pathway. Every so often she called out Lek's name, but her voice was too easily lost in the fog, muffled in soft velvety murk. She walked on until a dark form towered up above her, the first landmark. She had seen these things before, from the deck of boats and ships, through the fog banks, and had always thought them tall trees. They were that, or at least had been, in the past; all the branches had been cut away, leaving only the trunk, which had been formed into the semblance of giant Nebulim. There were no ornaments attached to the bark, no wires or strings, and no glass in the carved head, only a gaping hole where the face of flames should be: the trees were empty, and dead, and this made sap run tightly in Cady's veins of green. More of the tree giants were seen, as she moved on, towards the island's centre. The faceless ones stared out over the landscape, in wait for some sacred flame from the skies to animate them.

Beyond the trees, the land emptied out again. Cady's eyes had adjusted a little to the misty air, and her optic gland glowed warmly in her brow, warning of hidden dangers. Snagged on another stretch of barbed wire fence she found a patch of purple rag, torn from Lek's jacket. Where on earth was the Thrawl going? What did he hope to achieve out here, in the barrenness, other than take Gogmagog as far away from Brin as possible. Would he just stay here until his fuel cells ran down and his mechanisms rusted over, a sealed container for a demon? Cady felt a longing to see Lek's face going through its array of learned and programmed expressions.

Damn him! Damn that no-good broke-down tinplate

piece of cracked-crystal vapour-headed manifesto of all that is opposite to the world of lovely fleshy nastiness!

The island's peculiar nature was taking Cady over, inhabiting her with every breath taken. Her mind felt like the inside of the oil filter on the *Juniper*'s engine, clogged with Haakenur's dragon dung. Her tongue was furry and her teeth tasted of treacle and bluebottles, foodstuffs she had often eaten separately but never in combination. It made her feel bilious and she stumbled, this time landing on her hands and knees. Weak in her bones, with the vital green juices drying up under the influence of this deathly place, all she could do now was crawl, crawl forward like a worm. She kept the handbell with her, held loosely, or sometimes used as a kind of hook to drag herself forward. The voices of the drowned came to her, and she realised that they had been there all along, every step, but only as whispers; now they rose up in unison, all talking at once to call her forth, further into the dark. Their voices were slow and weary and agonised, frothing with spit bubbles, tainted with some disease of the lungs or the throat. She imagined their many mouths dribbling rancid spew upon the stony ground, and the Ludforsaken weeds taking seed in the patches of vomit. The spirits croaked like frogs at the bitter end of the last night of the mating season. There was no song bawdy enough to fight them, nor prayer divine enough. Cady lay on the ground unmoving, her hands clamped over her ears, but the noise was loud inside her head. She screamed. But the scream was quickly lost in the crackles and sparks of the nearest fire pool. Her voice quietened and settled on one word only: *Lek… Lek… Lek…* It was pitiful, and her heart broke with the need, which she did not understand, even now. But at least the dead returned to their low whisperings, perhaps sent back by the simple human sound of one living person asking for another, no matter how that life might be expressed, and in what material.

Cady sat up. She stared ahead to where the drifts of fog parted around a figure, standing some few feet away from her, only half seen in the gloom and the firelight.

"Lek? Lek, is that you, my dear?"

The figure was silent. But Cady's optic gland pinged and fizzed and she saw with more than her fleshy eyes that the figure was no living being, but an effigy.

A Wodwo burial effigy.

How could such a thing be constructed here? It didn't make sense; the Wodwo had no history with this island, nor of the Glimmie in general. The surprise was enough to give her extra strength and she got to her feet with some cricks and pops of her joints. She walked closer, and her surprise grew; for this was no ordinary effigy, to mark a burial place, but a Haegra regrowth device. It was similar to her own, back in Rothermuse Woods, but of older design, and very damaged in places. A wooden frame woven from thin branches and twists of wire around a core support of wire, which had rusted all over to a brown and red patina. The metal crumbled under her touch and stained her fingers. The notches of a calendar were visible, many of them. It must have been here for centuries, left to rot as the elements blasted the flat plains of Ludforsakenland. And yet...

And yet a few tendrils of the haegra plant still grew here, struggling out of damp soil to climb and wind themselves around the supports, the tiny white petals absurdly bright against the hollowed shadows of the effigy's interior. Cady wondered for a moment what would happen if she stepped inside the effigy and pressed the haegra thorns against her wrists, to puncture her veins? A second attempt at regrowing herself. Would she come back to life properly here, made young again, vernal and vibrant and terpsichorean? Why, her feet were already making a little jig, and her hips swayed like those of a young woman at her first Seeding of the Flowers ceremony. But she resisted the urge to enter, instead plucking a single white flower and placing it in her mouth. The juices wetted her tongue with their life-giving spirit. How strange, to feel so lively here, in the land of the dead: the mixture of opposites enhanced the feeling until her whole body flooded with sap and she couldn't help let out a yelp of pleasure.

The witch's bell glowed in her hand.

Cady carried on her search. Maguire & Hill's chart of the archipelago showed the interior of Ludforsakenland as being largely featureless: a few marks representing marshland, another showing an old church, long abandoned. It was large in area, about nine acres altogether. Cady had to admit, for all her expertise in navigation, she was lost. On a whim she rang the handbell, four times, up and down, up and down. And to her surprise she was answered by a light blinking on and off across the field. Cady set off with renewed pace, until she saw a silhouetted figure standing near a building. It looked to be a man. At first, she could hardly distinguish the light-giver from the surrounding landscape, for he seemed to grow out of the ground and to be clothed in fog. His silhouette was irregular. He did not move except for his raised hand, which swung a storm lantern back and forth. The flame within fluttered with each swing. A dimmer light shone from inside his hut, which looked to be the severed cabin and bridge structure of a cargo steamer set down here in the middle of nowhere. With each movement of the lantern, one quarter-moon of the man's face was illuminated, showing a jumble of features. Cady stepped a little closer.

"Who goes there?" he shouted, his voice deep and crackly. She stopped. "Cady. Arcadia Meade."

"Never heard of you."

"I'm well enough known."

"What are you?"

"Wodwo."

He made a loud sniffing noise. "You don't smell like Wodwo."

"What do I smell like?"

"Like Faynr farted."

She was somewhat taken aback, it had to be said. "Anything else?"

"Shit and piss and sweat and snot and engine oil and raw fish and salt air and rum and pipe smoke and seaweed and bird droppings and vinegar and plant sap."

"You know me well."

The man grunted at this: in disgust or delight, she could not tell which. "What brings you here?" he asked.

"A runaway Thrawl," Cady replied. "Did he come this way?"

The man didn't answer, but the lantern waved a little. She took another few steps. "Look. I really need to find..."

Her voice faltered as she saw the man's face and form more clearly. Flowers grew from his skin, from his brow and cheeks and on his hands; they sprouted upwards from the collar of his coat, and they blossomed most of all in his hair, which was abundant and very, very tangled, like the bent branches of an olden tree past its full splendour.

"You're a Haegra?" she said, in some alarm.

"That I am. And so are you." He was sniffing again. "Are you ovulating?"

"Whose business is that?"

"Hmm. Well, you're getting ready for something."

"Bloody cheek."

"What's that? Speak up!" Irritation entered his tone.

"Come closer. Let me see you."

She did as he asked. Now they stood face to face in the lantern's glow. He did not speak. Nor she. Never before had Cady met with such a personage. He was older than her by at least a quarter century, as shown by the lines on the brown bark-like face glimpsed through the leaves and flowers that half-masked him. His eyes were black entirely, except for a red vertical slit in each enlarged pupil, so that together they looked like a pair of black widow spiders sitting on his face. The slits closed and opened a few times and drops of sap sprang forth, to water his eyelash petals. His beard was thorny and twin-twigged, and matted with burrs.

Cady's legs almost gave way under her. Her loneliness was simultaneously brought to mind, and lessened, by the sight of a fellow spirit.

The old man introduced himself. "My first parents called me Aelfred of the Sedeborne. I was planted in the Year of the Myridi, twenty-four years before the fall of King Edgewulf."

Cady worked out the numbers. "But that means…" She could not finish the thought.

"I am the first. The first of the Haegra."

And from the colour of his flowers and the tangle of his branches and vines, from the number of his petals, from the patterns of his leaves, from his croak of a voice, from his thorny fingers and the scent of earth on his breath… Cady knew it was true: here was the prime seeding. The bell fell from her grip and Aelfred caught it deftly in his free hand. Then he laughed and invited her inside his cabin. But Cady stopped on the threshold.

Thrawl Lek lay on a cot bed in the corner, his face turned to the wall. He was very still.

"He was in some disturbance," Aelfred said, "when I found him. Now, he sleeps."

Cady went to the cot and put a hand on Lek's shoulder. He did not respond. She pulled him gently over and saw that his face and body were shut down, completely so, as she had seen before a couple of times. His eyes and mouth were tightly closed. She shook at him with as much violence as she could muster, to no effect.

"He's out cold," Aelfred said.

Cady reached for the bullet lodged in the side of his head and gave it a tug and a twist, hoping it might spark him out of sleep, but all she got for her pains was a blast of electricity which made her hand jerk back in pain.

"Lud damn you, sir! Dragon's blood!" And she licked at her blackened fingers.

Aelfred handed her a cup of tea. "What's wrong with him?"

"A demon is wanking off inside his head."

"Oh, I hate it when that happens."

"Lek's done this on purpose, shut himself down. The fuckin' idiot!"

She took a good gulp and felt the sudden invigoration that only hybrid creatures can give. But the effect only proved how tired she was. She sat down on the edge of the bed. The cabin was small but clean, modified here and there. The ship's wheel and compass binnacle were still in place, long unused. A fire burned in an iron grate. There were no pictures on the walls, no comforts of any kind. A few books sat on a shelf. Cady's eyes were blurring over. The cup fell from her hands, spilling tea on the straw-covered floor. Aelfred came to her. "Arcadia Meade," he said, "I've been waiting for you." But she hardly heard this. Her head was heavy, as was her heart. She wanted only to fall into a dream. A gentle ringing sound roused her.

Aelfred held the witch's bell. His fingers tapped the clanger against the inner rim, making the sound again, as soft as he could manage. He told his story. It came half in words and half in gestures that Cady understood instinctually: tremble of leaves, petals opening, the casting of pollen.

"I settled here shortly after the Blight struck along the river. I had grown weary of life and its attendant vexations, and so retired to the island. Ludforsakenland suits me. The Ephreme employed me to tend the werecows and other animals that live here, and to plant a garden of hardy plants, to fertilise the earth." He smiled in satisfaction. "And I've done the same for these last few centuries as a hermit, living off the land and off the alms the pyromancers bring me. Since then, I have regrown myself four times over."

"I saw your effigy. Out in the fields."

Aelfred nodded. "The roots of the haegra flowers tunnel deep down to reach the river. Faynr feeds us, and gives us strength anew. Often I think of giving up on my tasks, but as watchmen and watchwomen we carry on, do we not? For we have no choice otherwise."

Cady nodded.

Passion entered Aelfred's voice, drawn from a heart grown in dark earth. "We are the Knights of Ibraxus. Romance stirs in us, as worms stir the soil. The ancient Wodwo came down from space in their star chariots, in the Year of First Arrival, to propagate the planet. From their tending, Great Haakenur was sacrificed, that Faynr might be set free. We ride the veins of the ghost of the dragon, unafraid!"

"Is this meant to excite me? Or piss me off?"

"Is it working? Either way?"

"Both ways a little."

"The Deep Root binds us, Cady. We are entwined, your story and mine."

"I just want to save my friend here, that's all." She put a hand on Lek's arm. His jacket sleeve was torn, the metal skin exposed, cold to the touch.

Aelfred knelt by the grate and livened the coals with a poker. He refreshed his tea cup from a kettle that hung over the fire.

"Some years ago," he went on, "the never-nevers seeded. I have a patch of them, not too far from the cabin. The air of Ludforsakenland has a peculiar effect on them, causing the seed people to stay visible for more than a moment, often for days on end, sometimes for a week or more. But this time... this time they stayed in human shape for years. Not even a gale moved them, nor did rain, nor hail. They are still there, not yet dispersed. It is most unusual."

"When did this happen?" Cady asked, suddenly interested in the story.

"A week before the war broke out."

"Six years ago?"

"I stood on the island's shore and looked west to the city, to witness the first bombs falling and the buildings catch afire, and I knew in my deepest soul that my task, as revealed to me by the never-nevers, had to do with the war. I would have some great purpose in the conflict." He hesitated and then turned to his visitor. "But the war came to an end, and here I am, still awaiting my task's completeness." He took in a deep draft of the fire's smoke, which smelled of herbs: seeds cracked in the flames.

"At least you were given notice," Cady said. "When the war started, I felt sure the never-nevers would soon call to me. I could not understand it: surely, we were needed in times of such trouble."

"Perhaps there are greater troubles even than war?"

Cady wanted to agree, but her course was not yet set. Even now, the compass needle wavered. She noticed that Lek's eyelids were fluttering, perhaps in a dream, or from Gogmagog's presence. And she thought of the *Juniper* and its crew, somewhere out there in the dark. Yanish, Numi, Pok Pok, and Mr Carmichael. How were they faring? How was Brin getting on? She must be thinking of Lek; perhaps she was already on the island, searching?

Cady said to Aelfred, "What did the never-nevers show you this last time?"

"Three things, as always, in a riddle. The first was a lighted candle. I waited a year and a day before I saw a shooting star cross the sky. At the very same moment one of the island's cattle fell dead outside my cabin."

"A year and a day? That's a long time to wait."

Aelfred's leaves rustled loudly. "I live to a longer span than a young twig like yourself. You see, when the gardener priests made me, they had not yet perfected the correct mix of haegra sap and blood." He blew out a long breath from his bark-covered lips. "Some one hundred and fifty years might pass, before I need to regrow myself."

"How old are you presently?"

"Young yet. One hundred and one years and thirty-seven days, as told by the notches cut on the effigy."

Cady tried to imagine this, but struggled with it.

Aelfred went on. "I took it as a sign, the werecow falling dead near a fire pool. Its eyes were still bright even as the flesh slowed. In those jelly orbs I saw the flames of the pool reflected. I felt the Deep Root speaking to me. So I took up my knife and cut into the animal's belly and sliced away the lard from around its stomach. This I rendered down into tallow and used it to make the candle. I have it here." He pointed to a shelf, where a rough-hewn candle sat in a brass holder. "The first element of the riddle. I have not yet lighted it, though. For I had two more items to wait for."

"Is that all you do, wait? You don't search?" The idea was ridiculous. "You never leave the island?"

He did not answer directly, instead announcing, "Another three and a half years passed."

"You were waiting now for the second item, as shown to you?"

"That I was."

"And what was this item supposed to be?"

"A book. But the never-nevers did not reveal its pages to me, nor its title."

"Aye, by Lud, they're like that. Taciturn and tongue-tied." Aelfred had stood up from the fire. "Every day I scanned the river for a boat that might land here, or be shipwrecked in a storm. I expected a sailor to be marooned, with his knapsack stuffed full of books, one of which would be a great volume of Wodwodian magic." His eyes lit up within their mask of leaves. "Or that the sky would erupt with fire and noise and a Hellblaster would burst into flames overhead and plummet nose-first into the island. And that in the pilot's map-case I would find my prized tome, a collection of poetry perhaps, or even a diary."

Cady coughed up some phlegm. "No luck, eh?"

"None. The gods of the soil were laughing at me."

"Bastards, one and all."

"I might as well scry in the scum that grows between my toes."

"Sometimes, I'd like to pull the never-nevers up by the roots and feed them to the pigs."

"Be my guest!"

Aelfred had risen to his fullest height, roused by Cady's company. But his shoulders quickly fell and his body slumped. He mooched about, sighing to himself.

"Did the book turn up?" Cady asked.

"It did. It did. I found it in a bag of garbage thrown onto the island by a passing barge. Amid potato peelings and pig bones, bits of gristle and oily rags." He pulled a volume from his bookshelf and handed it to Cady.

"This is it?" she asked. "This is your magic book?"

"No other damned thing has shown up these past years, so what else can it be?"

Cady was holding in her hands a tatty and stained copy of the *Directory of Crystalphone Numbers for Ludwich and Outlying Boroughs*, dated three years previous. She riffled through the pages, releasing a stink of mildew.

Aelfred continued, "I waited a year and a half more before the third object arrived."

"Which was?"

"Yourself, Cady! Yourself! Or rather, and more specifically, the bell in your hand. Ding a ling, ding a ling! Bell, book and candle. Ding a ling!"

Now he was dancing around the cabin, flinging his arms

around, one hand holding the bell so that it made a random carillon sound. And his voice copied each note.

"Ding a ling a ling a ling a ding!"

The bell pealed louder as the Haegra's dance took on a primitive power. In sudden response, a violent shudder took over Lek's body, shaking him head to foot, so that Cady was knocked off the bed. Aelfred dropped the bell and stilled his feet. He came to the bedside, saying, "He's a rum bugger, ain't he? Look at him jitter and jive!"

Cady tried to calm Lek, but he easily shrugged her off. He rolled himself into a ball and lay against the wall, shivering. Cady and Aelfred could only look down at him, helplessly.

"Do you have a name for the demon that possesses him?" the older Haegra asked.

"Aye. Gogmagog. The Night Serpent. Or at least a small part thereof."

Aelfred gasped, hearing this.

"You know the name, do you?" Cady asked.

"I have heard it spoken of, in whispers. But long ago now."

"What did you hear?"

"The gardener priests tried to hide the fact that Haakenur had two ghosts, one of them made from the dragon's venom. They banished him from the people's sight, but he lives on in his place of exile with his yellow eyes open, waiting down the years for his chance to rise again into the light. As he did when the Blight first struck."

Cady looked at him. She understood that her arrival in this isolated cabin on this desolate isle was not entirely by chance, that the never-nevers had their secret maps and routes by which two strangers might meet and come together. But for what goal?

Aelfred came to her. She felt his thorn-tipped fingers tapping at her skin, almost cutting her. But the pressure was light enough only to remind her that she was flesh and blood. His skin, in contrast, was hard and rough. She tingled as he pressed at the bud on the back of her hand, and those on her arms. He told her, "I have seen these before, on one other Haegra woman. Her name was Ingrid Birch."

"So you know what it means?"

"It was a long, long time ago. So many years..."

"Still, I demand that you remember."

He said in a quiet voice, "Cady, you need to be pollinated."

"And how would that happen?"

"Well, you know..." He was suddenly coy.

"That's er... that's not your job, is it?" The very idea both excited her, and worried her.

"No, no of course not. You need to cross-pollinate."

"Now you're making me feel woozy."

"Actually, I do need to share something with you. It's why the never-nevers have brought us together. Just as they did with Ingrid Birch."

"Oh yes."

"Give me your hand."

She did so, hesitantly. Then he kissed her palm, on the opening where the outer fields lay. She felt his tongue licking at her, his saliva on her skin, hot and slathery, watering the flowers and herbs of her fields. His tongue was nipped at by the retracted thorns. Blood flowed. Green blood. She felt the greenness in her soul. One droplet. That was all it took.

"Oh, what are you doing to me, Aelfred?"

"Activating your stigma. Now look, Cady. Look!"

Yes, she could see another world. She was walking an unknown landscape under a clouded sky, an empty plain reaching the horizon all around. A distant city of spires and domes. But close by, a flowerbed watered by an underground spring was tended by a sole gardener whose face was hidden by a monk's cowl. One flower stood out among the varied blooms, a tall flower whose scarlet petals drew her eye. The gardener checked the flower's interior, counting the pollen grains. He paid no attention at all to Cady's presence. Then the clouds parted and twin suns were seen, low in the sky, one gold, the other blue-tinged. Between them, they matched the flower's interior in colour.

Cady opened her eyes; she had not realised they were closed. "What was that?"

Aelfred had removed his lips from her hand. "The home planet," he answered. "Where the first Wodwo people were created, to be sent down to Earth in the star chariots."

Cady was dumbfounded. She could hardly speak. The remains of the vision lent a far-off haze to her sight. Aelfred looked at her intently. "The flower you glimpsed came with the travellers in the first ships as a handful of seeds. I was given knowledge by the early Wodwo priests, that this flower would bloom once and once only, a single blossom every thousand years or so, at times of great disturbance. The Lud flower, they called it."

"I've never heard of such a thing."

"It is extraordinarily rare." He paused. "The Haegra, Ingrid Birch, she was the first carrier of a female flower that would one day receive the Lud pollen. From their union, well, something very new would be created."

"And you think…"

"Yes, Cady. Yes!" His eyes kept on hers, staring deeply. "You will find the Lud flower. And together, you will bring forth the new seeds, I'm sure of it!"

She groaned in despair. "But I've tried for a baby, a good few times. It always fails. Always!"

Aelfred Sedeborne held her hands, feeling them tremble in his grip. "This will be a different kind of child, or perhaps not a *child* at all."

"But what happened last time, with Ingrid?"

He released her hands and looked away, into the fireplace.

Cady was worried. "Aelfred, did something go wrong? Tell me."

"Ingrid died." He was still looking away. "I did what I could for her, helping her at a difficult stage in her progress. I showed her the vision of the home world, of the Lud flower, as I am required to do, by the Deep Root. This connected Ingrid to the Lud bloom, that she might find it easier." He turned to her. "The same will happen for you now."

"And then? Aelfred, cough it up. What happened to her?"

"Then she went on, for she preferred a solitary pathway. There was nothing I could do." He sighed deeply, rustling the leaves of his face. "I heard later that she had passed away. Her body was found in the river, in the Nethering, to the west of the city."

Cady was in desperate need. "That mustn't happen this time."

He nodded. "I have done what I can—"

"No, no you haven't! Not near enough. What about the riddle, the bell, the book, the candle, eh, you old fuck, what about them?"

"I don't know, Cady. I don't know!" He was trembling with his own frustrations.

"Aelfred, guide me in this, please. I'm scared."

He took her hands again, this time squeezing pain into them. "Find the Lud flower. That is your first priority."

She was about to ask for more information on this when Lek set off on an even more violent rolling and rocking, banging against the cabin's wall and almost falling off the bed. Cady rushed over, holding onto the Thrawl with all her strength, thrown this way and that. She cried out. Aelfred backed away. Lek's teeth ground together and then opened to eject the spittle breath of Gogmagog as a mist of dust that stung at Cady's face. "Help me!" she called to Aelfred. "Help me you good-for nothing pile of twigs! Isn't that your job!"

Old Man Haegra bubbled sticky sap at the lips and his spidery eyes blinked their inks. "Yes, yes," he muttered. He managed to bend down to retrieve the telephone directory. His voice stuttered. "They'll be a spell in here, I'm sure of it." Cady cursed him as she clung onto the Thrawl. Aelfred picked a page at random and intoned the first words he saw. "Hecklehyde, Butchers, 11 Chigley Heath. 2796. Hecklehyde, Mrs D, 10 Brigg Str. Bow-in-the-Flood. 4299. Hecklehyde & Sons, Illuminators, Stall 54, The Shrivings. 6676." His voice rose in volume. "Hecklehyde, Lt. Col. No 1 Wickford Rd West. 9455." Then he broke off to ask of Cady, "Is it working?"

"Not a jot. Not a pinch. Not a bleedin' speck." Lek struggled beneath her. "It's just the phone book, you idiot!"

"No, no, it's a list of the… of the…" He was searching for a concept. "A list of the names and addresses, yes, of the sacred practitioners of the Ludwich Society for the Expulsion of Demons."

"Really? Really, Aelfred?"

Ignoring her, he turned to another page in his book of spells and tried again. "Kepple Bros, Builders. 39 Needle Lane, Dunston Hill. 7743. Kepple, Mr and Mrs. 5 Brigden St, Nevernorton. 8756. Kepple, Thomas…"

But Lek only raged louder and with more violence, and

Cady was thrust away once more, landing on the straw with a bump. She cried out in despair. Aelfred felt the same, and he tore out the current page of the phone book and screwed it up and threw it on the fire. It burst into flames, and a pall of smoke billowed out. What a noxious stench it gave off! It hung above the fire in a cloud before setting off to drift around the room. Both Cady and Aelfred were taken by racking coughs, but the smoke had a different effect on Lek. It calmed him immediately, in a tick of a mechanical heartbeat. It held him in its trance, as a snake-charmer might hypnotise a serpent. His eyes opened. Or rather, one eye only: the right. It was a mere slit, but enough for a single beam of orange light to emerge. The smoke writhed around the beam, taking on some of its colour.

Cady looked on, hardly daring to move.

Aelfred came out of his surprised state and said, "My, my, oh my. Didn't I say, Cady, didn't I say the book had a spell to it? Oh my, the names, and the numbers!"

"Let's try it again. More names, this time. And then burn them. Come on!"

"Yes. Yes."

But the old Haegra hesitated. He looked around his cabin, taking in his few possessions. Cady saw that his mind was at work, shown by the flicker of his black eyes, by the rustle of his leaves and the crackle song of his twigs. His flowers blossomed brightly.

First he hung the witch's bell from a hook on the ceiling. Then he reached for the home-made cowcandle as he described the sacred progress of any watchwarrior's task: "The petals of the never-nevers measure disturbances in the air. They transmit those messages down to the Deep Root, where the Lord and Lady of All Flowers stand in the Garden of Dark Earth making their decisions. Those decisions are modelled and sent on by the seed people, to be seen by the eyes of the Haegra, by you and I, Cady. By such means we are given our purpose!" He was shouting now. "I must exorcise the demon. Of course, of course. And then... and then..."

"Yes? And then?" Cady felt his excitement in her own body.

He waved his arms around. "And then you can go on with your voyage."

"One thing's for sure, plantman. I'm not leaving here without the Thrawl."

So they worked together, both knowing what to do as they did it, in the moment unfolding. Aelfred adjusted the bell so it swung freely on the hook. He extinguished the lantern. Cady placed the candle in its dish on the floor, directly below the bell. She took a glowing taper from the grate and sat ready, prepared to light the candle's wick. Aelfred tore a page at random from the telephone directory. He unbent his body and stood tall. Cady lit the candle. Her heart was cold and tight in her chest. She didn't even have time for a single line of prayer before Aelfred started to recite. And she knew, as the first words were spoken, that even in this Ludforsakenland the gods were with them, close by, the gods that lay in the earth wherever a single strand of greenery crept.

"Dee. Arnold. 19 Saltick Ave, Witherhithe. 3432. Dee, Mr and Mrs, 21 Clement Str, Hemple Wick, 4438. Dee, Miss J.S. 12 Jury Court, Daybreak Towers, 1947..."

Dee! Of course. Why not. The occult scientist's power lay behind the page of names. Dee, Dr John. Tenebrae House, Old Hallows. 1609. That crazed thaumaturge was at play!

Calling Dr Dee! Calling Dr Dee! Calling Dr Dee! Hello, can you hear me?

Aelfred went on with his litany of names and addresses, but Cady cried out, "Now, burn it!"

The paper fell onto the flame of the candle, igniting. The smoke cloud bloomed for a second as any cloud might, and then formed into a straight column that rose up towards the bell.

Cady and Aelfred looked on astonished.

Lek lay on his bed, unmoving.

The smoke gathered in the downturned bowl of the bell, every last swirl of it.

The cabin was silent.

The bell rung.

Shring...

Softly at first, and then a second time, a little louder. Nobody touched the instrument. It rang of its own accord, under its own power, or more likely the power of the spell that Cady and Aelfred had conjured up.

Shring... Shring...

Cady turned to look down at Lek where he lay on the bed. The Thrawl's eyes, both of them, were now open. Twin beams of needle-fine light shone outwards, painting two orange dots on the ceiling of the cabin. Gogmagog's smoke appeared at the eye-holes in tiny strands.

"It's working." Cady said, her voice a whisper. "Aelfred, can you see? He's being forced out!"

The older Haegra nodded. But his face showed worry.

Nonetheless, the bell continued to ring in the same quiet way, each peal seeming to disturb the air into slow waves of sounds that Cady could see with her optic gland. And Lek, she felt sure, could hear the bell as well, even in his slowed-down state. His body juddered in accord with each ring, and his hands opened and closed in time to the music, this one-note melody.

Shring… Shring… Shring….

Then he sat up and swung his legs, placing his feet on the floor. He looked perfectly calm, at peace. Cady felt a little hope stir her heart's petals. Now surely the demon would be cast asunder. In evidence of this, Lek started to growl, a shrill rusty note. It made a weirdly dissonant chord with the bell's tone. His eyes flashed red then blue. His hands came up to his face, his head; his fingers twisted the lodged bullet, adjusting the growl one half-tone higher in pitch. Now it matched exactly the pitch of the bell. They rang in unison. The conjoined sound pricked its needle at Cady's head, forming an inner scream. Her eyes watered, snot streamed from her nostrils. Her bowels were loosening. She was aware of Aelfred moving behind her, but could not turn to see him; she only had eyes for Lek. Lek, that messy-headed tinplated fuckwitted out-of-control mechanism! His hands were now tearing at the rubber mask on his face, ripping it to shreds. The translucent plastic skin was revealed fully, with the blue crystal glowing inside his brain-pan and the mist of Faynr around it, and lodged within tightly curled, yes, there was the creature made of venom, Gogmagog, his yellow eyes flashing inside the jewelled interior of Lek's skull. The bell rang on, that one same note drawing the Night Serpent closer to the surface. He would stream out of the Thrawl's body by whatever orifice he could find, Cady was sure of it! The exorcism was almost complete.

But then Lek got to his feet. He stood stock-still except for a slight blur at his edges, giving him a fuzzy silhouette in the enclosed fire-lit gloom of the cabin. His whole body was a tuning fork vibrating at the same frequency as the bell. He spoke, he squeaked, he ranted: "I will not let him out. I will not! He is mine, Gogmagog is mine, he is my captive. I have joined with him, I am Cogmacog! Lord Cogmacog, until the end of days. Metal and venom: one a prison for the other. We shall never be parted, not now, not ever! And after my fuel cells have run out, I will lie here in the mud of the island, slowly being covered over, slowly eroding."

Cady saw the madness in his eyes, as he followed his number one promise of fealty, to protect Brin Halsegger, down to the last possible consequence. He took a single step, heading towards the door. Cady stood in his way. He pushed her aside easily, and then did the same with Aelfred, who collapsed like a cheaply made wicker man.

Lek rushed through the open doorway, out into the fields.

The night was cold and dark except for a faint gloss of silver on the ground. Lek was making erratic progress, shrieking in both pain and exaltation. He ran into a ring of shadows that stood as tall as he did. Cady thought them to be trees or bushes or even standing stones, but they were figures, human figures of dark nature and wavering form, twelve of them, forming a supernatural arena. These were the island's seed people. They had been puffed out from the never-never flowers, but were, in this place, resistant to wind and rain. Their blue-tinged bodies formed and reformed continually, in shape of man and woman. They had remained here for many years, as Aelfred had told, waiting, waiting perhaps for this moment.

Lek came to a halt inside the circle. He seemed fearful of the seed figures.

Cady joined him. They stood facing each other.

"I'm not letting this happen, Lek. I'll cast that demon out and take you back to the boat, if it's the last thing I do."

He stood in silent defiance.

She put up her fists. "I'm warning you. I beat you today at wrestling. And I'm even madder now. I am sorely vexed and three-times wrathful."

Lek spoke at last: "Gogmagog will only seek us out again. He will find us, he will find Brin."

Cady could hear the waters of the Nysis nearby. She could smell the river. It gave her a little strength, something to call upon.

"I swear, I swear by all the gods both good and bad that I won't let that happen. The girl will be safe with us."

Lek made to speak again but Cady had had enough of his claptrap. She let out a howl fit to send a wild wolf dizzy. And then she pounced on the Thrawl, taking him by surprise. He staggered back and fell to the ground. She leapt atop him, her knees either side of his chest as she bashed her fists against his skull until her knuckles were raw and green blood flowed from the cuts, turning red. Lek allowed this beating to happen, he made no protest, made no defensive moves. His skull was bent and battered, so hard did she punch him. But there was no entry point. Electric charges sparked across his head in bright yellow and red arcs, shocking Cady and making her fingers smoke. But she felt none of this, no pain. Every last ounce of her bodily strength was lodged in her fists as they went about their labour.

Only her tongue was busier than her hands. "You crystal-brained, tin-livered monstrosity. You decommissioned piece of scrap. You pickle-pussed hissy. You big lunk of loose screws! Gaggle-flecked chuffer of dust. Petrol-sucker! You're a dreamless bounder. Millyhuffer, glad-haggle, a dung beetle crawling on a pile of Haakenur's shit, a tuppenny pettifogging nitpicker, a click counter, nothing but a piss puddle, nothing but snot wiped from the nose of King Lud!"

On and on it went, this spray of cusses, each accompanied by a blow from her fists.

She changed tack. "Do you think this is what Brin wants of you? It is not, believe me. Is this what Lady Halsegger meant, when you made your promise to her? No, it is not! She wants you to look after Brin, not abandon her."

This statement at least brought a frown to the Thrawl's face. Cady renewed her efforts.

"Lek, you junk-bucket! Listen to me!"

Her hands pummelled at his face, over and over. Spittle filled her mouth, her breath stank of rotten fruit. Her chest heaved. Sap squeezed itself from her pores. Cady's eyes were two plums bruised by starlight and cursed with wickedness. Her hands wearied but never gave up, no matter how bloody they were. Her teardrops were made of rum, ninety percent proof. Her lips were stained black and red by the nasty words she spewed out.

Now she turned her attentions to the beast within Lek. She saw the yellow eyes staring out at her from the depths of the soiled skull.

"Out Night Serpent, out! Begone! Desist! Get stuffed! Drink your own vomit!"

The glowing eyes blinked rapidly. She felt the hatred weeping out of them, directed at her, and she took that hatred and spat it right back at him.

"Poison, poison, poison!"

But none of this had any good effect; all she was doing was making herself ill, weak, tattered, broken at the joints. Her throat was parched, and she had cut her tongue on a crooked tooth. An ugly wheezing sound came from her lungs. She had little left to give.

Lek sent out a shower of electric sparks that sizzled her hands. With one last useless profanity she rolled off him and landed on the ground, lying on her back, staring up at the overarching skin of Faynr, and beyond that transparency, the black empty sky, the cold blue glitter of stars. The moon came out from its veil of clouds to mock her. The People of Never-Never Land swayed to and fro in their circle, their bodies dissipating at the edges and sending out slow drifts of blue seeds, which formed into a cloud above Cady's head, coaxing her into a kind of waking dream. She thought back on her cosy rooms at the sailor's retirement home in Anglestume, and the way she had ground those never-never seeds into a nice little cocktail for herself – a witch's brew, Yanish had called it. Yes, indeed. Oh, that had been a journey, had it not? Under the Nysis, seeing those visions! Was it all to come down to this: a life becalmed, run-aground on this overgrown piece of dried-out dog-turd called Ludforsakenland?

Thrawl Lek lay beside her, unmoving.

The seed people whispered to her, and she to them, using words known only to the plantkind. The Deep Root lay close by, she could sense it. The petals of the Lord were opening.

A prayer came softly to her lips.

"Help me. Now and in my days and nights of need. At the time of planting, and in the Autumn months, when the flowers fade and fall... that a new flower might grow from the earth, renewed. Let pollen gather on the legs of the winged insects..."

Cady felt her two opposing cycles, human and vegetable, coinciding. *One to the other woven about, of flower and flesh both made.* She reached up and placed her hands within the cloud of blue dust. The seeds clung to her fingers, coating them completely like a pair of shiny new gloves. She sat up and, using her hands rather like the conductor of a chamber orchestra, she guided the seed people in their dance. At this point she really didn't have any purpose in mind, only that something could be made from this strange congregation. She remembered the vision of Brin Halsegger that had visited her in her rooms, on the night before the voyage. Yes, the seeds could be manipulated. Her mind concentrated on that task. The bodies of the twelve dancers broke apart and regrouped as one entity, of womanly size and shape, the seeds packed very tightly so that no air was seen between them. There was still the sense that a single gust of a stronger wind might blow them apart; but for now they clung tightly to each other.

Cady directed the shape and the sizing, she made the torso and the limbs, and the head, and the hair, which she patterned into two chignon buns, one of each side. She designed the dress, the petticoats. By now she had worked out the true nature of the figure: Miss Jane Polter. Lek's creator. Cady had seen paintings and etchings of the thrawlsmith in books and at the Museum of Ludwich. She recalled the statue in the riverside factory. She had even met with her once, for a few minutes, back when the world was powered by gas and oil.

Now the radical engineer was complete in all her parts. Cady stood up. She put out her hands to welcome Jane Polter onto her own body. The two women merged together: plant, flesh, memory. A mask of seeds in Polter's countenance settled on Cady's face. The blue of the seeds yellowed slightly, taking on a hint of Cady's greenish shade.

She turned to Lek where he lay on the ground. The voice she chose was old-fashioned in tone, a combination of actual voices she had heard in Polter's era, plus a more artificial accent learned from watching far too many romantic dramas in the flea-ridden crystal theatres of Tolly Hoo.

"Arise, Thrawl."

Lek's eyes came open instantly. He raised himself to look with astonishment at the figure who stood before him. "Mistress." He sounded younger, and his face wore its brightest expression.

"Tell me your name."

He quickly got to his feet and spluttered, "247LE54K, at your service. People call me Lek." In his mechanised madness, he had fallen for the spell that Cady wove for him, and could not stop from bowing before her. She almost expected him to curtsey.

"Oh, do stop that! Stand up straight."

He did so, shoulders back, stomach in, chest out: a butler on parade.

"I have travelled through time to meet with you," Cady said. She was extemporising, nothing more, a poor disguise artist on a music-hall stage.

"How can I please you, Miss Polter?"

Cady didn't know how to answer. Already, she could feel the seeds beginning to drift on her skin, as they lost their hold on this one particular shape. She tried to stay in focus.

"Open your eyes, Thrawl Lek!"

"They are open—"

"Wider, further!" Her words echoed across the fields. "That's it. Let your beams shine forth. Press your buttons, good Lek. That's correct. Let me hear them, clickety-click. Purge your skull of all evil thoughts. Blind those yellow eyes that blink so madly inside you. Retune your crystal, find a new station in the fog. Fire up your sparks. Fuse your circuits. Unplug your mind!"

Cady was losing her grip on the proper language, mixing together two very different eras. Lek was looking at her weirdly, not quite understanding. His body lost all its rigidity.

"Miss Polter, I don't—"

"I can see a stain in your workings, Lek. We need to repair you."

"Yes, yes, I feel it within me. It is ravenous."

"Well then… Will you partake of a cleansing?"

"I will. I will."

But he was uncertain, Cady could sense that. She felt the same, with no obvious way forward. What now? Her face was cold in patches, where a number of seeds had already floated apart. Soon, the mask would be lost. And the necessary words seemed far away. In fact, as she looked at the pitiful figure before her, bowing and scraping, eager to please, she had to feel sorry for him: this wasn't the Lek she had grown used to on the day's voyage, a true adversary, a concocted being like herself, made for one purpose only but filled with dreams of another life, eaten away by rust and disrepair on one side, and by human cruelty on the other. And yet he had carried on and made his way in the world when so many of his kind had been stowed away or dismantled, and he had taken young Brin by the hand and stood by her side through many and varied horrors. Cady could not bear to see him reduced in this way, and herself to blame.

But she had to do this. Binding the mask to herself by sheer willpower, she started to explain her plan, to take Gogmagog into herself and then to… But the words made no sense: Miss Jane Polter would never use such terms. There had to be another way! Racking her brains, she recalled the story Lek had told in the Thrawl factory. Perhaps there was a clue there, a crack in the metal.

Putting on even more of a Polterish voice, she said, "Remember the dream I once sent you, Lek, when the Frenzy took you over?"

He nodded rapidly. "I shall never forget. Truly, it was a wonderful moment."

"Good, excellent. Bring it to mind now, as we dream again, you and I."

"Of what shall we dream, Miss Polter?"

He waited, his eyes aglow with scarlet beams that glittered in the night. And within his naked skull, the eyes of Gogmagog also stared at her. Was that fear she saw in the yellow orbs?

Of what shall we dream?

The answer lay within her grasp, almost, almost. It flickered as a green shoot under the soil, seeking daylight. For some reason she thought of old Granny Meade reading from the Book of Dark Eden before Sunday dinner could begin, every time the same passage, that famous first sentence.

And now the words came simply and cleanly.

"Let us dream of light."

Lek stared at her intently. His eyes were glowing. He was shaking in her grip.

The last of the never-never seeds disengaged from Cady's face and body. She managed to call out one last instruction, as the first Wodwo had called out to the Star Gods.

"I am in darkness. Illuminate me!"

Lek's eyes connected with hers via beams of needle-sharp

intensity. Icy blue, and then yellow, the same colour exactly as the eyes of the Night Serpent. A long curling shadow snake followed the beam of light, attached to it, whipping about frantically: but Gogmagog could not escape the beam's control. Lek raised his aim slightly, to hit the dead centre of Cady's brow. Her optic gland opened up to receive the visitor.

Illuminate me, that my love might know its own shadow.

The seed people scattered to the four winds.

Lek fell to his knees. He was sobbing tears of oily substance.

A night bird scrawked, close by. Either that, or Cady had screamed. Something dragonish had taken residence within. There was one second of absolute clarity, when she viewed the world with her own eyes, and with Lek's eyes, and with Gogmagog's eyes, and with Haakenur's eyes. But that was too much, even for such a very, very, very, very, very old lady.

She blacked out, standing on her feet, swaying.

And then came to, and only just managed to stop herself from falling.

Desperately she called to the Lord of All Flowers, to allow her entry into the Deep Root; but his Lordship was silent in reply, and the soil would not take her.

Her plan was failing. Already she could feel Gogmagog at his tricks, spiking her brain, filling her eyes with smoke. She reeled about in a mad dance, and then set off running across the field towards a shimmer of silver: the river. It was a different shoreline that greeted her, with no sign of the *Juniper*, no boats at all, and no lights, no habitations, only the brittle rocks at the water's edge. She stumbled into the shallows, seeking to escape the pain in her head, but managed only a few steps before she fell forward, hitting the water with a hard gasp. It was freezing cold, and her heart almost shut down. Her body ducked under the surface, pulled by some stronger current. She was being dragged along, farther from the shore, into darkness…

The Deep Root opened up before her, and then around her, containing her. She was crawling forward on her hands and knees along a low dark tunnel whose walls were packed with earth and woven with a multitude of worms and beetles. The ceiling of the tunnel lowered further and now she had to wriggle on her belly. Her optic gland took over, shining with a green light. She followed the bright beam of herself, deeper down. Gogmagog fumed and raged within her head; his eyes burned fiercely and she could picture him, scratching his claws at the inner surfaces of her skull. But she kept on. Scratch all you want, monster, bite me, sting me, strangle me! I care not! I will fuck you over good and nasty. I will dream you dead and scatter your powdered remains on the patch of earth where I was first planted as a tiny seed.

The tunnel closed in entirely, pressing at her body from all sides, squeezing her dry. And even her optic gland went dark.

She lost herself in thoughts of yesteryear. Yearning for love at the Eve of May Dance, around and around the pole they pranced, to the tune of whistle and drum, girls and boys holding hands, young Cady Meade among them but always apart, even as she grew older and it became time for her to leave the village, that first ever journey out into the world on her given tasks, along a map of fantasy that the River Nysis provided her, surely to the place of her future pollination, wherever that might be, if she could only make it that far.

In response to these thoughts she felt the buds expand and pulse on their seven places on her body and she felt giddy from arousal.

Cady opened her eyes.

She was now lying at the centre of a large chamber whose walls and ceiling were made from the trunks and thick roots of mighty trees, buried deep. Strange flowers grew from the soil. Pale translucent moths flitted from one plant to the next, landing on the upturned leaves and taking off again almost immediately.

Cady walked over to the sphere of tightly woven branches that grew at the chamber's centre. Named a puzzle plant in the Wodwo scriptures, it was a yard across at its diameter. Hundreds of curved thorns pointed inwards, towards the hollowed interior. A single orchid adorned the globe, a deep ruby red in colour, except for where its elongated petals were closed in a purple pout. One intrepid moth was trying without success to insert its proboscis into the flower's depths.

Cady walked around the puzzle plant, examining it carefully.

Gogmagog must have seen it too, for he howled inside the prison of her head, and he made every attempt he could to escape.

Cady's eyes were burning from the inside.

Her eardrums spilt.

Her teeth were chittering, threatening to come loose.

Her fingernails stretched away from her flesh.

Her mouth tasted of wet tar.

Her hair crawled with greenflies and boll weevils.

But her mind was set straight and clean and true and made of fresh shoots and green leaves speckled with drops of water where the spectral moths supped.

There was no hesitation. She thrust her left hand into the puzzle plant, finding a way through the conundrum of the knotted branches. Thorns pressed against her skin, digging in. The outer fields blossomed from her palm, or rather seeped out, each herb and flower mixed with oil and sludge and black tears. In this way she cast out Gogmagog. Her palm blistered. The skin puckered as the tiny stalks thrust upwards, one herb after another, a whole field of

He screamed from his new confinement.

Cady tried to pull her hand free of the puzzle. The thorns acted as barbs, they ripped at her flesh, gouging runnels along the length of her forearm. Blood flowed in green and red. Her arm locked in place. She was stuck fast.

Water pooled around her feet. River water, grey and dirty, flecked with spawn. Cady saw that cracks had opened in the trunks and roots that made this place, and water was pouring in at a rate of knots. The Nysis was coming back to claim her, finding little gaps in her consciousness. A surreal and terrible image took control of her, that her skull was filling up with water!

She pulled desperately at her bondage.

Now the water lapped at her waist. But her arm was still clutched by the thorns, which dug in deeper with every struggle she made.

Her body lifted off the ground, buoyed by the rising tide.

Cady took a deep breath and held it as the water came over her head….

Her hands scrabbled at the riverbed, at rocks and pebbles that rolled away from her grasp. The blackness of the river filled her vision. The water's surge rushed in her ears. It was a comforting sound and her body responded, slowing in its struggles, allowing the current to take her where it may. Bubbles popped from her mouth and she wondered at them idly, hardly understanding. A sense of great calm came over her: yes, let it finish here, the endless struggle. The moon gleamed on the river's surface above her. There was another light, smaller, brighter, a flicker of blue that played on the skin of the Nysis. How pretty it looked. She

them, a pasture, until they filled entirely the hollow of the cage of thorns. The smoke-laden body of the Night Serpent lay among the foliage, bewitched by the heavy scent of the red orchid as its petals opened wide to the dank air of the Wooden Chamber.

remembered when Brin had tempted her through the streets of Anglestume, with the little coloured sprite.

She reached out for the light, but it was too far away. And now she panicked.

Holding her breath against the pain in her lungs, she pushed off from the riverbed with her heels and gained as much thrust as she could. The weight of her body and her clothes threatened to hold her in place, even to drag her back down; but fighting against this urge was another impulse, something very different. The buds must open! Now her hands were clawing at the water. The blue light danced and fluttered, a signal calling her on.

Cady broke the surface and gulped down a lovely draught of air, giving thanks to good King Lud for lending her the strength of Ibraxus, and to Haakenur for the dragon's might. She found a purchase on the rock-shelf. The island's shoreline was dark but for that one patch of light where a small figure was already wading through the shallows. The girl's hands were outstretched. Around each fingertip a crackle of sky-blue Xillith sparks shone in a dancing pattern. This was the signal that Cady had seen in the darkness of the river.

Lovely Brin's lovely little light of love, none other.

She moved towards it.

Tonight on Crystal Vision

The *Juniper* passed through a channel formed by a line of moored barges. They had to pay a fee to get through, more of a bribe really, to a gang of scutlers who guarded the Pool during the night hours. Cady was woken up by their shouted instructions. Elongated vowels and burred consonants peppered with choice swearwords: it was a good while since she'd heard a proper Eastside accent. She got up from the bench in the cabin and looked around in a daze, groaning. It was midnight. Just gone. When eight bells toll. Her throat and lungs ached from her ordeal under the water, and she coughed up a slug of scum. She sat on the bench for a moment longer, to get her bearings. There was a bandage around her left hand and she looked at this with some trepidation, remembering the trap of thorns.

Lek had dried her clothes on the engine mounting and left them out for her, neatly folded on the table. She slipped into them now. There was no sign of her bowler; probably rolling away over the fields of Ludforsakenland, or floating downriver by now. Her hair felt like someone had poured lard over it, and let it set.

She went out onto the foredeck. The massive wall of the city loomed ahead, over the land and river. Soon enough they would enter Ludwich, but for now they lay within the Pool of Ludwich, a vast man-made basin that once served as a funnel and crossing place for vessels entering and leaving the city. There wasn't much transit in or out these days, so the place had become more a place of residence, an overflow from the poorer areas of the city. The little boat floated at dead slow, rocking on an uneven current, disturbed by other vessels large and small that puttered about, or steamed into new berths along the quayside. But they didn't seem to be going anywhere, just changing positions. It disturbed Cady greatly: all the bustle of trade and travel reduced to this jam-packed conglomeration. People jumped from boat to boat; a slanging match broke out between two women on the deck of a launch. The smell of the place was bad, mainly coming from the clumps of refuse thrown into the water. It was disgusting: why were people treating the Nysis like this? Cady fumed. Even so, she couldn't help a little smile coming to her lips. She was back! Her Kindred were present, all the different tribes on view. Now her eyes were drawn to the row of terraced houses along the bank, where a courting couple kissed beneath the glow of a gas lamp. A waterside pub was doing a roaring trade: it was way past the legal drinking hour, but this side of the wall, laws were made to be broken. Costermongers walked the quay shouting out their wares of eel pie and mushy peas. A busker sang of Haakenur's fabled love affair with a giant locust. Cady joined in, only remembering half the words.

The city wall was high enough to blot out a good portion of sky. The imposing structure of the Tithe Gate was visible, set within the wall's bomb-damaged patchwork of stones and wooden struts. Lights sparkled along the ramparts, marking the barrier's progress as it curved away into the distance on each side of the river, before fading into darkness. Faynr covered everything in a soft mauve glow, peculiar to the region. The balmy air was filled with half-heard melodies and lovely voices and trillings, very pleasing to the ear: Cady always thought of the ghost serenading visitors to the Pool.

The *Juniper* found a space at a quay between two barges. Cady called the crew together in the cabin. She stood at the aft door, in a commanding stance she had learned from Admiral Crenshaw after the Battle of Five Mile River. Inside, of course, Cady was one leg away from falling in a heap. Her eyes moved from person to person, taking in their scars and bruises, their dirty hair and torn clothing, and the look of tiredness in their eyes and drawn faces. She saw something else as well – a strength in each of them, a measure of how much they had all changed during the long day's voyage. For every two losses there had been a gain. Such is the balance of life. She felt a deep sense of pride.

"Soon we will reach our destination." Cady's throat gulped. "I wanted to thank you all for your service today, aboard the *Juniper*... and to say how very... how very... that is... it's been an honour to, uh, to sail with... Ah sod this for a pile of bollocks! I'm no good at pleasantries, you all know that by now." She could feel the sweat on her hands. "But as my thirteenth granny used to say: Lud's spit ain't worth a penny if you can't clean your arse with it."

She looked at them, waiting for a reaction, receiving only their stares.

"Well... What I'm trying to say... You're not half bad, as a crew, I mean. No, not half bad, but less than... less than three quarters bad... somewhere between half and..."

Her lips clamped shut. Every time her eyes closed, she saw again the depths of the river, and the thorny tangles of the puzzle plant. She took a swill of rum from her bottle, hoping to wash the fear away. If only she could think of the words!

It was Yanish who saved her. His voice rose in song, weaving a tender tune.

My name it is Jackie
I'm a young salt of valour,
I've spent the past year
Aboard the Unknown.

Brin must have learned the old seafaring ballad at school, or from Lek, because she added angelic harmonies to the second stanza.

But now we're a-sailing
West by South Westerly
Steering by starlight
For the sweet lands of home.

Numi accompanied the song by jingling and jangling the many ornaments on her wire frame. Lek took a while to join in, and when he did, his singing voice sounded like a motor humming and backfiring. Nobody cared. Cady looked on, in silence at first, but then singing along merrily as Yanish launched into the chorus.

And it's heave oh, heave oh my lads!
West by South Westerly

Heave away heartily
For the sweet lands of home.

By the third verse, Brin was dancing a merry jig on the tabletop. Everyone was smiling. They were all steering by starlight, aye, each and every one, by constellations both true and mythical, for sweet green idyllic lands. The last two lines of the final chorus carried their own particular magic: by some mysterious shared instinct everybody slowed down in their rendering. Brin's dancing was now balletic in nature. Yanish's tenor returned to prominence, filled with a blue-tinged emotion that Cady could not fathom.

Heave away heartily
For the sweet lands of home.

The song ended. There was a moment of silence.

Then Cady addressed the crew once more, with no trouble this time. "Numi… we'll moor for the night at Witherhithe. You can go on your way from there. Will that do you?" Numi Tan's flames burned a brighter shade in response, a mix of green and red and gold that Cady could read precisely: the flicker of love in the darkness, or rather, the *possibility* of love. Lud speed her, that she might find her Romeo!

Cady turned next to Yanish. He was leaning against the forward door. His hair was combed and teased into its usual style. His eyes were sharply alight, and fresh; and yet Cady felt sure she saw the pain gathered there, beneath the light; she knew him too well. He had been through hell and lived. Lud bless him, and keep him. And she felt she understood the emotion he had shown in the ballad of returning home. The aphelon was a direct line to the shadows of the ancestors; without it, an Azeel was rootless, cut off from the tribe's memory palaces. She desperately wanted to help him, but she had so many kind words to say that they all got clogged up together in her mouth, into a mush. In the end she gave him a smile, and simply said, "Will you stay with the boat overnight?"

"Of course, old chiv."

She turned to Brin and Lek. The girl was sitting cross-legged on the left-side bench, while Lek stood next to her, one hand on the girl's shoulder. Brin was spinning her gold Ludluda coin in the air, catching it repeatedly, and saying the revealed monarch's name each time: "Lud, Luda, Luda, Lud, Lud, Luda…" Lek had the look of a man who had escaped the hangman's noose, but who was not yet accustomed to the life renewed. Cady said to them, "Brin, Lek, you can stay with me at my sister's house in the Hithe. I should warn you though, Nabs is a crotchety muckraker, but pleasant enough when she's not chasing beetles. And then tomorrow, Brin, we'll take you to the hesting pools."

"Aboard the *Juniper*?" the girl asked, her eyes bright.

"Of course. Your royal yacht awaits."

Lek nodded his approval.

Cady took them all in with a gesture. "The city beckons." She walked out onto the foredeck, where she stood beside Pok Pok for while, having a little chat with the figurehead about the weather to come and the state of the world and such like, receiving nods and chuckles in return. Faynr clung to the river, her phantasmal body flowing over the wall, and also squeezing and pinching itself in order to fit through the Tithe Gate. Cady had to wonder what surprises the city held: she imagined the ghost's sickness had its own characteristics as it flowed alongside the grimy riverside tenements and alleyways, factories and warehouses, and onwards to the grand houses and parks of Beltane and Old Hallows. Well, she would find out soon enough.

Yanish came to her. He did not speak, but she knew something was on his mind. His fingers troubled at the blank triangular patch on his brow. She said, to guide him, "We can seek out a new aphelon for you, at the Shrivings. They sell near everything at the market there."

He nodded, lost in thought.

Finally, he spoke: "I'm not sure... maybe I'll go without, for a while. See what happens, you know."

"Why would you do that?"

"To break free." Now he turned to her. His eyes were glinting in the light of the quay. "To break free, old chiv." His shadow quivered at his back like a superhero's cape unfurling, rearing up into the air. "To chase down the night. I fancy myself zigzagging through the alleyways of Tolly Hoo, hounding the villains of Hawkhampton, kicking down doorways. After all, the monster has lived within me. I have dark knowledge." He put on his best crystal show voice for this last sentence. But his face showed the truth of his words.

"That's the way, my lad," Cady said. "The Black Tornado, at his adventures."

"Aye. Or else, you know, just get a job on the docks, and earn a bit of money, and find myself a lover. Who knows, maybe get myself a little boat of my own one day."

"I can see it now. *Juniper's Daughter*, sailing the river." She was choking up. "Yan, my love... do I really have to let you go? I mean, you're the apple of a different tree, but my roots are tangled with yours."

"And they always will be."

This gladdened her a little. "I have something for you," she said, searching the pockets of her coat.

"It's not your old pipe is it? Because…"

"No, no." She tried the pouch of her smock, still with no luck, and went onto the pockets front and back of her bell-bottoms, and at last found what she was looking for.

It was a little square of hessian cloth.

"I… erm… I picked this up, from the shroud garden, you know… when you…"

He looked at her, without speaking.

"I think you should keep a little part of him, of your father… Keep it with you."

"It's just a piece of cloth."

"Well then… use it as a handkerchief or something, I don't know, wipe your boots with it, but go on, take it, take it, before I clout you one."

He did as he was told, carefully folding the cloth and putting it away inside his jacket.

"I'll be gone in the morning."

And with that, Yanish went back to his work at the helm.

Cady closed her eyes tightly, in case her sadness escaped her. She thought of all the sailors she had loved and lost. That was the trouble of living a thousand and a half years: so many bloody partings. *We are carried as seeds on the air, and to air return. So it is, and so it will be.* Then she blew her nose and brought up snot and phlegm mixed together and let the waters of the Nysis partake of it. By such methods are they joined, river and woman.

She went to the hatch and climbed down into the hold. Here, she sat on the stool next to Mr Carmichael's tank and tapped at the glass with the tip of her rum bottle, before taking the last few glugs. *Be strong, me old dear. Be strong.* She fed the crystalback a spoonful of dried shrimp; in thanks he flashed his brilliant colours through the dirty water.

Cady fell into a reverie. She unwrapped the bandage and stared at the sore on the back of her hand. The bud had burst, the calyx torn open by one of the thorns in the puzzle plant. The bunched haegra petals, still half-folded, still small, white as usual but with a pink flush to the edges, were dry and brittle: they crumbled under the slightest touch, and when she pulled at them, they came away from her skin. Cady felt that her heart would break.

Her first proper bloom. Her first *ever* bloom. Dust between her fingers.

She promised to nurture the remaining buds as best she could: three on her arms, the others on her neck, on her stomach and her thigh. Six of them altogether.

She had to find the Lud flower!

Aelfred had no idea where it might be. She had asked him for guidance as they had taken their leave of each other back on the island. But his only suggestion was to search the city, that Ludwich would be its place of blossoming. The thought of this brought to mind the three images given her by the never-nevers in their wisdom: bell, gravestone, and the enemy bomb marked with the name of Gogmagog. She had found the bell, and passed it on, and certainly they had encountered the Night Serpent twice already, in its nascent forms. The grave awaited her. She knew that. If only she could be pollinated before then. She longed to cast her seeds to the wind, or to feel them sticking to the legs and wings of insects.

Her face was warmed on one side, the side facing the tank, and her peripheral vision flickered with colour. She turned to view Mr Carmichael. He was swimming about with renewed vigour, and his long crystal-embedded body glowed brightly. The engine of the boat trembled into life, and the propeller shaft started to spin in its housing. Cady felt the vibration of the *Juniper*'s heart under her heels. They were moving on.

Mr Carmichael writhed about, constantly knotting and unknotting himself. Cady waited until the pictures formed on the screen of the tank, as she knew they must, this close to Ludwich. Open for broadcasting. Tonight, on Crystal Vision: News from the City. Various scenes played before her eyes: busy streets at night, public squares, omnibuses, the dockyards. Many of the places revealed still had signs of the bombing and rocket raids: great gouges in the roads, a car half-drowned in a duck pond, empty spaces in the terraces now taken over by weeds and rubbish, kids playing on the heaps of bricks and timbers. It would take years, maybe decades, before the capital recovered.

And then the pictures slowed and formed into one image alone.

A man's head and shoulders. This was unusual: as a rule, Mr Carmichael didn't home in on individuals. His was a broad vision, more like radar than a telescope. So Cady watched with interest as the man's features came into view. It was an interesting face, with a definite Wodwo cast to it, but also sporting a pair of prominent hesti at the temples. The offspring of a mixed marriage then, or else a willing adopter of the Alkhym way. His hair was hidden behind a blonde wig, a wig worn not to hide baldness, but as outlandish decoration. The hair was spiked above the hesti, brushed back from the brow in a long central wave that landed just above each shoulder in a curl. It was the kind of hairdo sported by a hero in a scientific romance show.

He was dressed in a finely tailored suit and tie, each item adorned with many sequins and buttons of pearly lustre. The outside pocket of his jacket was hidden behind a double row of colourful ribbons. The shoulders were padded almost into wings, and both lapels were decorated with jewelled brooches. Within this flamboyant display the man's face was quite ordinary, nothing to write home about, except for the eyes which were large and very white around the bluest pupils Cady had ever seen.

He stared out of the tank, as though he could actually see the old lady viewing him. But that was absurd, for Mr Carmichael only ever saw in one direction.

And then the man spoke.

"Arcadia Meade. How pleased I am to meet with you at last."

Cady almost fell off her stool in surprise.

The man laughed gently. "I understand your confusion. But please listen… We don't have much time. This connection will not last for long."

He seemed to be sitting outside, in a garden, his face lit by a powerful lamp. "Where are you speaking from? How are you doing this?"

"Your pet creature has a sister. I have access to the pond where she lives. It is a simple enough matter to plug oneself into the crystal spectrum. I have the necessary talents."

Cady took advantage of his explanation to regather some of her poise, mainly by shifting her posterior back into the centre of the stool. "And who the fuck are you then?" she asked. "If you think you're so special?"

He smiled at this. "Miss Halsegger, or Thrawl Lek, might have mentioned me?"

Now she had it. "So… Lord Pettifer."

"Please, call me Olan." He gave her a quick wave, the fingers of his hand heavy with rings. "I've been following your progress upriver, with the help of my various agents, from Anglestume to Maddenholt, and onwards, into the Faynr. I must say, Cady, that was a splendid show your crew put on at the Grand Illumination. I saw that with my own eyes."

"You were there?"

"As much as I can be anywhere, yes. It is difficult for me, these days."

Cady didn't really understand this statement, but she remembered the trembling man she had seen or half seen sitting in the auditorium as they passed under Faynr's cloud-show of death and resurrection.

Lord Olan Pettifer brought a large white handkerchief into view, which he used to dab at the two hesti on his head, wiping some discharge away from them. Cady knew enough about the Alkhym religion to make a guess: he was Wodwo born, but had taken the hesting ritual late in life: such an undertaking always caused problems, mental and physical in nature, and was very rarely performed. He must have brought great pressure upon the archbishop, or else donated a fortune to the church. Whichever it was, he seemed to be unashamed of his dribbling. He wiped vigorously, sniffed at the seepage, and then said with some pride, "Many people hate the stink. I quite like it myself: it is evidence of the pains I have taken in life, to alter and perfect my being."

Despite her best interests, Cady found herself fascinated by the man. Her roots were tingling and her palms ached, where the outer fields longed to emerge.

Pettifer must have read her body's urgings, for he said,

"I am envious of the Haegra, and their ability to live again in each different era. I have made a study of the species, although the written record is slim. But I have in my possession two of Dee's lost notebooks: I'd love to show them to you, Cady, if we should ever meet in person."

"What the hell do you want, creep?"

Pettifer smiled at her. "To discuss the child, of course."

Cady felt her green blood boiling. "You're not getting your hands on her, if that's what you think."

A disturbance to the signal cut off the man's reply. His face and upper torso broke apart as the crystal signal fluctuated. Cady banged on the side of the tank a few times with her fist. The electric sparks crackled red and blue and yellow and the picture reformed, albeit in a more fragile manner. Pettifer's face was cross-cut into a series of disjointed horizontal lines. His eyes peered out at his viewer, and his head leaned forward, almost as though he might emerge living from the tank.

"Cady," he spluttered. "Listen carefully, before we lose contact. There is much you don't know about Brin Halsegger."

She tried to respond but he quickly interrupted her.

"I took willing guardianship of that girl. I was a trusted friend of the family. I nurtured her, and tutored her in her art. Without doubt, she was the most gifted of all my students at Blinnings House. No, no, let me finish!"

Again, his face was harried by interference. But he carried on regardless.

"After a time it became obvious that Brin was a troubled child. The things she created, out of the Xillith and Faynr combined... well, they worried me deeply. Yes, all children have bad dreams, often of a surreal nature. But the images she brought to life were more often suited to an adult's imagination, and a darker imagination at that. I tried my best to steer her onto a clearer pathway, and that worked for a time. Then it came to the Night of the Dragon, as the newspapers called it."

He paused, to gather his face back into some kind of normality. Cady looked to the forward hatch, worried that Brin or one of the others might come down. Perhaps she should close it, but there was no time: Pettifer's fine-tunings worked well enough, and his features were reassembled. Then he wiped at his hesti again, before carrying on with his story.

"The forming of Haakenur's image under Brin's powers was meant only as an exercise in propaganda, a way of filling the people's hearts with the necessary passion and resolve, in order for the war to be brought to a swifter end."

Cady butted in: "Thrawl Lek told me all about it. Actually, he showed it to me."

A sharp anger came to Pettifer's face. "Lek does not know the truth of it; he saw the whole thing through the lens of his own prejudice. He holds the girl in a golden light."

"So what really happened then?"

Cady was keen to know: she found herself wishing that Mr Carmichael might keep the signal open until the tale was done.

Pettifer went on, "Haakenur's image was successfully conjured up. Brin did a very good job. I was overjoyed, I really was. But then I noticed that some other presence accompanied us, in the observatory. Some other creature. I could not comprehend its nature, not at first; in fact, I assumed Brin had made herself a second playmate that night. But no. The creature was real, or as real as a ghost can be. And Brin was delighted to see it there."

"Lek told me that you referred to this as *Gogmagog*?"

"Yes, yes." Pettifer's excitement was mingled with fear. "I had seen the name in one of Dee's notebooks. A whole page headed the 'Gogmagog Equations'. He had spotted an anomaly in Faynr's spectral energy, and he related this missing energy to the old myth of Faynr's vanished twin. The story is long-forgotten, and remains only as a few mentions in some of the illuminated manuscripts from the Years of Conjuring. But this was enough for Dr Dee to posit a re-emergence of Gogmagog; that the demon might use the plague known as the Blight as a means of invading Kethra."

Cady thought about this: she tried to relate it to the three objects of her current task. She knew now that Pettifer was an important part of this quest – but how, and in what way? She asked, "You're saying that the image of Haakenur that Brin created was, in some way, a *temptation* for Gogmagog. One dragon ghost attracted by the presence of another?"

"We might see it like that. I like to think of Gogmagog in his exile, and the sight of the dragon in the Ludwich sky actually entering his dreams, reminding him of former glories." Pettifer sighed. "But it goes beyond that. It's not so much about Gogmagog waking. It's about why, and how, he was woken up."

Cady started to get a funny feeling: she still had no knowledge of Pettifer's true intentions, but a shadow danced in her eyes, and the outer fields had emerged on her palms as two soft thin beds of moss. She peeled at one of these as Pettifer continued.

"Think about it, Cady! When have you witnessed Gogmagog this day? The first time was at Ponperreth, the Nebulim's village."

"Yes. He was conjured there by the local magus."

Lord Pettifer laughed. His face crinkled and came out of alignment as Mr Carmichael sank to the bottom of his tank. The signal would soon be lost. Pettifer knew this, and he spoke rapidly.

"Una Goodperson built a statue, that's all. She goaded her congregation on, into madness. But no, Gogmagog was risen that day by Brin, and Brin alone."

Cady tried to interrupt, but he pushed on.

"Brin did the same at Pomperreth as she did in the observatory on the Night of the Dragon. Both times she opened a doorway, using her powers, and Gogmagog came through, at least in part. His true self, his fullest self, waits in the darkness. And our job, Cady, you and I—"

"No, no, I'm not listening!"

"Our job is to stop Brin before she completes her task."

"No, she's innocent, a little girl, that's all!"

Cady slammed her hand against the tank's screen in her disbelief. Pettifer's face fragmented into a mix of colours and shapes. With one last effort, Mr Carmichael directed the signal.

Pettifer was midway through a sentence: "… but she plays a very clever game."

"It's not a game. Why are you saying this?"

"There's only one more thing necessary, before Brin's power is sufficient to the task—"

"I don't believe you!"

His face, even in its crackled state, was firm and fixed in its intent. "If that girl undergoes the hesting, she will have the power to open the doorway completely. Gogmagog will come through, in all his might and glory, and he will destroy Faynr, he will destroy Ludwich, and all the people who live within—"

The image died.

Mr Carmichael faded back into the gloom of the tank as the water darkened.

Cady felt wrung out. She was hunched up on the stool, bent double, twisted awkwardly. Her ears would not stop ringing. Everything was wrong, everything! That man had lied to her. That so-called stuck-up Lord of Shit! Lord of Fuck! Lord of Cuckoos! Lord of Nothing!

She stood up suddenly, kicking the stool against the bulkhead. Her head banged on a beam. One hand was on the tank, the other touching the curved hull, to keep herself upright. The *Juniper* was picking up speed. The deck trembled with its own passion. A faint light shone down from the hatch, a perfect rectangle. She stepped into it, looking up. Faynr's mauve skin coloured the sky. Bright moonlight. Someone walking on the deck above her, probably Lek, from the rhythm and gait. She knew them all so well, these passengers: a single day's voyage had forced them into intimacy. Brin. That child! Ten years old. No, no she couldn't believe it, she refused to believe it. Gladly, she thought back to the battle on the foredeck, when Gogmagog had been forced out of Yanish's body. Brin had made that happen. But also, Gogmagog had refused to attack the girl. Why? Why? There was no easy answer.

Cady climbed the ladder and stepped onto the foredeck. The Tithe Gate was very near, where the Nysis entered the city through the Eastside wall. For larger ships, the two bascules of the gate's bridge could be raised to allow entry. But the *Juniper* was fine, it would slip beneath easily. A little boat, rocking along. People waved to Cady from the bankside. Perhaps she knew them, perhaps not. She wasn't thinking properly. Her fingers pressed at the first of the buds, on her left forearm, just above the wrist. It was extraordinarily tender. Soon, soon the petals would open.

The city's wall loomed over the puny vessel. The giant uprights, beams, and pillars of the gate and bridge were constructed of animal bones excavated from the fields and hills of Higgston and Harlow and Grenton Sparse and Molbeck and Cludlow in Reverse and Nonsuch Spickle and Dutton Fen. Yes, the great lizards, dragons and serpents of the Primordial Age were long extinct, their bodies reduced now to building materials. Only Haakenur lived on, through her ghost, or rather, her *ghosts*. Two of them. One pitted against the other in some endless battle, only occasionally seen by the eyes of the waking world.

She looked to her crew. Yanish at the wheel, his cleansed shadow playing at his skin's edge. Lek standing next to Pok Pok at the prow. Numi and Brin at the port beam, watching the boat's progress towards the gate. Roving spotlights picked out the *Juniper* from the ramparts. Brin was pointing out the massive femur of a dead monster, her face alight with wonder.

Such a child. A child only.

Numi called Cady over. She said, with a mischievous flutter to her flames, "Cady, Brin here has a question for you."

"Is that so?" Cady kept her worry hidden behind a smile: it took quite an effort.

"Yes, Mrs Meade. I want to know if your sister really chases beetles."

"Oh, she does, she does. A nasty habit." Cady bent down to Brin's level. "You've never heard the phrase *chasing the beetle* then?"

The girl shook her head. The Ludluda coin spun in her hands.

"Well that's good. Because it's the ruination of those who partake of it, it really is. Far worse even than gin and sherbet. Once you start, you just can't stop."

"But *what* is it?"

Cady grimaced. The girl's desire for knowledge was simple and pure. A child only, surely to goodness! But Lord Pettifer's words could not be disregarded. They niggled, like a needle jab. Who could she trust? What could she do? There was no easy answer.

The bonebridge shadowed the deck and cabin. Brin Halsegger laughed with delight, her eyes still on Cady, asking so much of her.

The *Juniper* passed through the Tithe Gate and entered the city of Ludwich.

ACKNOWLEDGEMENTS

Jeff and Steve would like to thank Michelle Kass and everyone at the Kass Agency, especially Russell, Tishna, and Melissa. Lud be with you all.

We also express our gratitude to everyone at Angry Robot Books, including Eleanor, Simon, Caroline, Gemma, Amy, Andrew, and Desola. Thank you for encouraging Cady on her journey.

Thanks also to Katie Smith and Victoria Halford.

This novel grew out of discussions over five years. Most of these meetings took place at Harrisons Cafe in Hove. We thank the staff there for all the cups of coffee, while the streets of Ludwich slowly came to life.

DEEP DIVE — RON WALTERS

THE MOONSTEEL CROWN — STEPHEN DEAS

ANGRY ROBOT

DOORS OF SLEEP — TIM PRATT

THE HOUSE OF CATS & GULLS — STEPHEN DEAS

SPIDERTOUCH — ALEX THOMSON

PRISON OF SLEEP — TIM PRATT

HERALD OF THE BLACK MOON — STEPHEN DEAS

THE SPLENDID CITY — KAREN HEULER

THE INFINITE

ADA HOFFMANN

THE FALLEN

ADA HOFFMANN

THE OUTSIDE

ADA HOFFMANN

Science Fiction, Fantasy and WTF?!

AFTER GLOW

TIM JORDAN

GLOW

TIM JORDAN

THE MALEFICENT SEVEN

CAMERON JOHNSTON

THE PHLEBOTOMIST

CHRIS PANATIER

@angryrobotbooks

MOTHS

Jane Hennigan

THE HOLLOWS

DANIEL CHURCH

A Storm is Coming...

FULL IMMERSION

GEMMA AMOR

HELL SANS EVER DUNDAS

twenty five to life

THE CLEAVING

JULIET E. MCKENNA

FORGING A NIGHTMARE

PATRICIA A. JACKSON

An Accident of Stars

FOZ MEADOWS

MARCH'S END

DANIEL POLANSKY

OBSIDIAN

SARAH J. DALEY

BURROWED

MARY BAADER KALEY

We are Angry Robot

angryrobotbooks.com